Welsh Mythology and Folklore
in Popular Culture

CRITICAL EXPLORATIONS IN SCIENCE FICTION AND FANTASY
(a series edited by Donald E. Palumbo and C.W. Sullivan III)

1 *Worlds Apart? Dualism and Transgression in Contemporary Female Dystopias* (Dunja M. Mohr, 2005)

2 *Tolkien and Shakespeare: Essays on Shared Themes and Language* (ed. Janet Brennan Croft, 2007)

3 *Culture, Identities and Technology in the* Star Wars *Films: Essays on the Two Trilogies* (ed. Carl Silvio, Tony M. Vinci, 2007)

4 *The Influence of* Star Trek *on Television, Film and Culture* (ed. Lincoln Geraghty, 2008)

5 *Hugo Gernsback and the Century of Science Fiction* (Gary Westfahl, 2007)

6 *One Earth, One People: The Mythopoeic Fantasy Series of Ursula K. Le Guin, Lloyd Alexander, Madeleine L'Engle and Orson Scott Card* (Marek Oziewicz, 2008)

7 *The Evolution of Tolkien's Mythology: A Study of the History of Middle-earth* (Elizabeth A. Whittingham, 2008)

8 *H. Beam Piper: A Biography* (John F. Carr, 2008)

9 *Dreams and Nightmares: Science and Technology in Myth and Fiction* (Mordecai Roshwald, 2008)

10 Lilith *in a New Light: Essays on the George MacDonald Fantasy Novel* (ed. Lucas H. Harriman, 2008)

11 *Feminist Narrative and the Supernatural: The Function of Fantastic Devices in Seven Recent Novels* (Katherine J. Weese, 2008)

12 *The Science of Fiction and the Fiction of Science: Collected Essays on SF Storytelling and the Gnostic Imagination* (Frank McConnell, ed. Gary Westfahl, 2009)

13 *Kim Stanley Robinson Maps the Unimaginable: Critical Essays* (ed. William J. Burling, 2009)

14 *The Inter-Galactic Playground: A Critical Study of Children's and Teens' Science Fiction* (Farah Mendlesohn, 2009)

15 *Science Fiction from Québec: A Postcolonial Study* (Amy J. Ransom, 2009)

16 *Science Fiction and the Two Cultures: Essays on Bridging the Gap Between the Sciences and the Humanities* (ed. Gary Westfahl, George Slusser, 2009)

17 *Stephen R. Donaldson and the Modern Epic Vision: A Critical Study of the "Chronicles of Thomas Covenant" Novels* (Christine Barkley, 2009)

18 *Ursula K. Le Guin's Journey to Post-Feminism* (Amy M. Clarke, 2010)

19 *Portals of Power: Magical Agency and Transformation in Literary Fantasy* (Lori M. Campbell, 2010)

20 *The Animal Fable in Science Fiction and Fantasy* (Bruce Shaw, 2010)

21 *Illuminating* Torchwood: *Essays on Narrative, Character and Sexuality in the BBC Series* (ed. Andrew Ireland, 2010)

22 *Comics as a Nexus of Cultures: Essays on the Interplay of Media, Disciplines and International Perspectives* (ed. Mark Berninger, Jochen Ecke, Gideon Haberkorn, 2010)

23 *The Anatomy of Utopia: Narration, Estrangement and Ambiguity in More, Wells, Huxley and Clarke* (Károly Pintér, 2010)

24 *The Anticipation Novelists of 1950s French Science Fiction* (Bradford Lyau, 2010)

25 *The Twilight* Mystique: *Critical Essays on the Novels and Films* (ed. Amy M. Clarke, Marijane Osborn, 2010)

26 *The Mythic Fantasy of Robert Holdstock: Critical Essays on the Fiction* (ed. Donald E. Morse, Kálmán Matolcsy, 2011)

27 *Science Fiction and the Prediction of the Future: Essays on Foresight and Fallacy* (ed. Gary Westfahl, Wong Kin Yuen, Amy Kit-sze Chan, 2011)

28 *Apocalypse in Australian Fiction and Film: A Critical Study* (Roslyn Weaver, 2011)

29 *British Science Fiction Film and Television: Critical Essays* (ed. Tobias Hochscherf, James Leggott, 2011)

30 *Cult Telefantasy Series: A Critical Analysis of* The Prisoner, Twin Peaks, The X-Files, Buffy the Vampire Slayer, Lost, Heroes, Doctor Who *and* Star Trek (Sue Short, 2011)

31 *The Postnational Fantasy: Essays on Postcolonialism, Cosmopolitics and Science Fiction* (ed. Masood Ashraf Raja, Jason W. Ellis and Swaralipi Nandi, 2011)

32 *Heinlein's Juvenile Novels: A Cultural Dictionary* (C.W. Sullivan III, 2011)

33 *Welsh Mythology and Folklore in Popular Culture: Essays on Adaptations in Literature, Film, Television and Digital Media* (ed. Audrey L. Becker and Kristin Noone, 2011)

Welsh Mythology and Folklore in Popular Culture

Essays on Adaptations in Literature, Film, Television and Digital Media

Edited by AUDREY L. BECKER and KRISTIN NOONE

CRITICAL EXPLORATION IN SCIENCE FICTION AND FANTASY, 33
Donald E. Palumbo *and* C.W. Sullivan III, *series editors*

McFarland & Company, Inc., Publishers
Jefferson, North Carolina, and London

LIBRARY OF CONGRESS CATALOGUING-IN-PUBLICATION DATA

Welsh mythology and folklore in popular culture : essays on adaptations in literature, film, television and digital media / edited by Audrey L. Becker and Kristin Noone.
      p.   cm. — (Critical explorations in science fiction and fantasy ; 33)
[Donald E. Palumbo and C.W. Sullivan III, series editors]
Includes bibliographical references and index.

ISBN 978-0-7864-6170-7
softcover : 50# alkaline paper ∞

1. Fantasy fiction, American — History and criticism.
2. Fantasy fiction, English — History and criticism. 3. Fantasy fiction — 20th century — History and criticism. 4. American literature — Celtic influences. 5. English literature — Celtic influences. 6. Influence (Literary, artistic, etc.) 7. Tales — Wales — Adaptations — History and criticism. 8. Mythology, Celtic — Wales. 9. Mythology, Welsh, in literature.
10. Myth in mass media. 11. Wales — In literature.
12. Popular culture — History — 20th century. I. Becker, Audrey L. II. Noone, Kristin.
PS374.F27W46   2011
700'.458429 — dc22   2011015511

BRITISH LIBRARY CATALOGUING DATA ARE AVAILABLE

© 2011 Audrey L. Becker and Kristin Noone. All rights reserved

No part of this book may be reproduced or transmitted in any form or by any means, electronic or mechanical, including photocopying or recording, or by any information storage and retrieval system, without permission in writing from the publisher.

On the cover: "Geraint and Enid Ride Away," illustration by Gustave Doré of Alfred Lord Tennyson's *Idylls of the King,* 1868

Manufactured in the United States of America

McFarland & Company, Inc., Publishers
  Box 611, Jefferson, North Carolina 28640
    www.mcfarlandpub.com

Table of Contents

Acknowledgments   ix

Introduction: Re-Imagining Wales
    AUDREY L. BECKER *and* KRISTIN NOONE   1

Celtic Studies and Modern Fantasy Literature
    C.W. SULLIVAN III   9

"The Rough, Savage Strength of Earth": Evangeline Walton's Human Heroes and Mythic Spaces
    KRISTIN NOONE   18

Branwen's Shame: Voicing the Silent Feminine in Evangeline Walton's *The Children of Llyr*
    NICOLE A. THOMAS   30

Disavowing Maternity in Evangeline Walton's *The Virgin and the Swine:* Fantasy Meets the Social Protest Fiction of the 1930s
    DEBORAH HOOKER   42

"An Age-Old Memory": Arthur Machen's Celtic Redaction of the Welsh Revival in *The Great Return*
    GEOFFREY REITER   61

Magical Goods, "Orphaned" Exchanges, Punishment and Power in the Fourth Branch of the *Mabinogi*
    SUSANA BROWER   81

The Hand at the Window: Twm Siôn Cati, the Welsh Colonial Trickster
    JONATHAN EVANS *and* STEPHEN KNIGHT   91

An Irregular Union: Exploring the Welsh Connection to a Popular African-American Wedding Ritual
    TYLER D. PARRY   108

Constructing Myth in Music: Heather Dale, King Arthur and "Culhwch and Olwen"
  MEGAN MACALYSTRE   130

Torchwood's "Spooky-Do's": A Popular Culture Perspective on Celtic Mythology
  LYNNETTE R. PORTER   140

Everyday Magic: *Howl's Moving Castle* and Fantasy as Sociopolitical Commentary
  CAROLYNN E. WILCOX   160

Loosely Based: The Problems of Adaptation in Disney's *The Black Cauldron*
  JEFF HICKS   171

We're Not in Cymru Anymore: What's Really Happening in the Online *Mabinogi*
  CLAY KINCHEN SMITH   182

Temporality, Teleology and the *Mabinogi* in the Twenty-First Century
  AUDREY L. BECKER   195

Further Reading   213
About the Contributors   219
Index   221

Acknowledgments

The editors gratefully acknowledge and thank Chip Sullivan whose work on Welsh mythology has influenced our scholarship and inspired this project. We earnestly thank our contributors for their efforts and insights. We extend a very special thank you to Don Palumbo for first expressing interest in our project.

Kristin Noone thanks: John Ganim for advice and a copy of his presidential address to the Chaucer Society; Andrea Denny-Brown and Rob Latham for their support and generous feedback; the fellow Riverside graduate students and faculty who lent their ears to various descriptions of the project and asked helpful questions; the organizers of the annual Popular Culture Association Conference, without whom this book would not have happened; Audrey L. Becker, for a truly fantastic collaborative experience; and Jon Poblete, who not only offered tech support but also listened patiently to ongoing musings about cosmopolitanism, enchanted field mice, folk music, and video games, without complaint.

Audrey L. Becker thanks: First and foremost, Kristin Noone for her spirit and devotion to the project; my supportive colleagues in the English department at Marygrove College; the Faculty Development Committee and Dean Judith Heinen. Alyce von Rothkirch tipped me off to Seren Books' New Series on the *Mabinogion* while I was attending the "Theorising Wales" conference in July 2010. Sincere appreciation to Simon Hicks at Seren Books; Noel and Karen Bruton of Arberth Studios; Martin Crampin; and Alex Lumelsky. My husband Adam Druckman warrants immeasurable thanks. I thank my children Ivan and Sadie, who screened *Otherworld* repeatedly. What's more, they never inadvertently deleted any files from my computer, for which I thank them profusely.

Introduction
Re-Imagining Wales

AUDREY L. BECKER *and* KRISTIN NOONE

"Even if we were not holding our Sixteenth Biennial Congress in Wales," John Ganim informed the members of the New Chaucer Society in his 2008 presidential address, "I would have begun with the ending of 'Culhwch and Olwen.'" Ganim then goes on to speak of the lists of heroes who join forces to help Culhwch complete his seemingly insurmountable tasks, a metaphor that allows him to thank his fellow society members while transitioning effortlessly into a call for the alignment of cosmopolitan theory with medieval studies. Culhwch, after all, is not a hero unto himself; he moves in and out of the orbits of human and giant, woman and man, Welsh legend and that quintessentially British symbol of Arthur himself.

It is perhaps not a coincidence that the New Chaucer Society chose Wales for their 2008 gathering, nor that Ganim chose this Welsh tale, invoked before a group of international scholars, to speak to the question of global similarities and differences, of shared languages and legends. Welsh mythology has long been a fertile ground for precisely this kind of transmission, transition, and cross-cultural pollination, but because Welsh motifs frequently materialize in such popular spaces as fantasy fiction, children's films, and video games, their adoption as a shared frame of reference and discourse often goes unnoticed or unobserved. Welsh heroic stories and figures, in fact, inform almost every aspect of contemporary popular culture, a development suggestive on two levels. First, as the essays in this collection will demonstrate, Welsh mythology serves as a case study: in what ways can a particular set of stories, associated with a particular identity, speak to new audiences across space and time? Second, and perhaps more subtle, the very success of these adaptations argues for the possibility of a cosmopolitan identity, grounded in popular culture and a shared enjoyment of the past, that exists as a balancing act, the space between the particular and the universal, the exotic and the recognizable, the fantastic and the familiar.

These adaptations of Welsh stories survive through crossings of genre, media, and temporalities, but they are also always recognizably Welsh, and complicate any universalizing tendencies with an insistence on their unique identities.

In general, Welsh mythology and identity remain understudied, often a side note to discussions that focus on Arthurian romance, or the creation of "Britain," or the so-called "Celtic fringe" (a memorable title of one graduate seminar offered recently at the University of California, Riverside, which focused on the "fringe texts" produced by medieval Wales, Ireland, Scotland, and the Isle of Man). Critical studies that examine Welsh mythology and Welsh identity have for the most part fallen into one of two camps. The first are the historians and medievalists, who frequently study Welsh texts such as the *Mabinogi* in relation to the world of romance, or as part of the "Celtic fringe" in an argument for a postcolonial Middle Ages. Examples of this use of Welsh myth may be found in Patricia Clare Ingham's *Sovereign Fantasies: Arthurian Romance and the Making of Britain* (University of Pennsylvania Press, 2001), which examines the early Welsh references to Arthur in order to comment on the shaping of the British nation in the early Middle Ages; Jeffrey Jerome Cohen's "Hybrids, Monsters, Borderlands: The Bodies of Gerald of Wales," in *The Postcolonial Middle Ages* (Palgrave, 2000), which looks at the writings of Gerald of Wales in terms of postcolonial theory; or Prys Morgan's "From a View to a Kill: The Hunt for Welsh Identity During the Romantic Period," in Eric J. Hobsbawm and Terence Ranger's *The Invention of Tradition* (Cambridge University Press, 1992), which depicts the deliberate production of distinct cultural traditions as a means of creating national identity. These studies, while immensely useful for our understanding of the production of Welsh myth, the construction of a distinctly Welsh identity in an age of conquest and colonization, and the relation of "Welshness" to other identifying groups (such as the English), by their very nature are circumscribed temporally, focusing on the Middle Ages as a time of origins, instead of examining how we interpret that "Welshness" today.

The second group of scholars who in recent years have brought attention to Wales and our inheritance from Welsh legend are those who study modern fantasy fiction, particularly the sources of contemporary fantasy. C.W. Sullivan III's *Welsh Celtic Myth in Modern Fantasy* (Greenwood Press, 1989), Brian Attebery's *Strategies of Fantasy* (Indiana University Press, 1992), and Flo Keyes's *The Literature of Hope in the Middle Ages and Today: Connections in Medieval Romance, Modern Fantasy, and Science Fiction* (McFarland, 2006) all discuss Welsh myth, particularly the stories of the *Mabinogi*, as an important precursor to and influence on the genre of fantasy fiction. However, in an age in which knowledge and conceptions of culture can be transmitted through not only fantasy books but also film, video games, and television shows, very little attention has been paid to the reconceptualization and transmission of Welsh myth and Welsh identity in these new, multimedia ways—ways that dramatically influence a popular-culture vision of "Welshness."

Writing specifically of the fantasy genre, C.W. Sullivan III ends his *Welsh Celtic Mythology in Modern Fantasy* by suggesting that the last two centuries have been "particularly strong" in Celtic influence and reference, and that more scholarly attention should be paid to a theme that resonates so strongly throughout popular literature (151). This is so, he argues, because of the particular character of Welsh mythology and Wales itself. In general, mythology and fantasy share a common goal, as Sullivan points out: "mythology's general function— to enable people to discuss the supernatural—is extremely close to one of the basic characteristics, if not functions, of fantasy: to enable the reader to experience or interact with the preternatural." (79) But Wales itself occupies a special place among mythological, and fantastical, realms. Wales, according to Sullivan, "does have an affective power that only a very few actual geographic locations have had." (89) What causes this affective power? Sullivan offers reasons ranging from the association with medieval romance and especially Arthurian romance, to contemporary tourism and scholarship that "focuses on Druids, stone circles, medieval romance, Celtic languages and literatures, Celtic music, Celtic sources for Arthurian materials, and the like" (89–90), to a form of Welsh nationalism that uses an imagined glorious past as a rallying ideal. In a fascinating conclusion, Sullivan makes the distinction between Wales and mythic Wales, claiming that "the Wales that the reader discovers in these [fantasy] books, then, is not the actual Wales, the Wales of mimesis or what is cognitively possible, or of consensus reality; it is an 'other' Wales than the one to which the reader can travel" (90). In other words, this Wales is not really Wales at all; it is a fantastic space, a space that partakes of the real Wales but is not the same. The "other" Wales exists as an impossible space—and yet, in a very real sense, it does exist. It provides a common space and language for all of those romantics, tourists, scholars, and nationalists, in which they can congregate, speak, and imagine the world to be different; it is a mythic space precisely because it can be shared and appropriated and fantasized about, because it is not particular, but malleable. On the other hand, this vision of Wales, however lovely and idealized it may be, still requires the "real" Wales for its existence: the idea of Wales remains grounded in an earthly setting with a distinct geographical location and history, and traditional elements of Welsh mythology are never replaced or changed (for example, replacing the Welsh dragon with a Chinese dragon would appear inauthentic; even in the realm of fantasy, a sense of essentially appropriate "Welsh" characteristics remains). To speak or write of Wales requires some shared conception of a specific form of Welshness; if Sullivan is correct that the "other" Wales has become a powerful shared fantasy in recent years, we must read the space of Wales as suggesting a means toward a form of cosmopolitanism, arising from the specific, but able to understood universally, without a loss—though perhaps some transformation—of identity. These claims, we suggest, are true not only of fantasy literature, but of other forms of popular expression that partake of Welsh mythology as well.

The study of this popular expression is, we feel, an important one. Louise Aranye Fradenburg has identified pleasure as one of the great undiscussed motivations of medievalists; in "So That We May Speak of Them: Enjoying the Middle Ages," she calls scholars to recognize that too little attention has been paid to our enjoyment of our subject in recent years, and that we tend to create an artificial duality between productivity and pleasure, even though in practice the two are frequently combined. She finds common ground here with popular culture medievalism: "the differences between popular and academic medievalism are of course *made*.... The status of a vast popular knowledge of and desire for the Middle Ages is not so mysterious given the history of medievalism itself" (209). In other words, the discourse of desire for the past operates across both scholarly and popular, non-academic culture, and it is a discourse that informs the creation of communities as a whole. Individuals come together through a mutual enjoyment of a subject — for example, the imagined space of the Middle Ages at a Renaissance Faire — and nations come together by creating and shaping a narrative of their past history, creating an identity out of a "desire for origins," as Allen J. Frantzen has so capably demonstrated in his book of that name. All of these narratives are shaped by desire, by satisfaction, even pleasure, in recreating and re-imagining the past. We hope to demonstrate here that this discourse of enjoyment, bringing together scholarly study and popular expressions of entertainment, is not only operative in the case of Welsh myth, but is also deserving of examination, and should indeed be spoken of as a powerful force for enabling commonality across boundaries of time and space. Shared enjoyment allows for shared engagement, but also appears to counter any overly universalizing tendency — after all, if Welsh myth lost its essential location in the idea of *Wales*, the source of enjoyment would be correspondingly diminished. Thus, reading history and mythology in terms of pleasure and performance may point the way toward a space for a successfully cosmopolitan identity, knowingly constructed, playful, and fluid, as new players may enter into the imagined world at any time, bringing with them new ideas or reinforcing traditional themes.

The essays in this collection demonstrate the power of Welsh mythology to create precisely this imaginative space, ranging from a look at the magical economics inherent in the Fourth Branch of the *Mabinogi* to *Torchwood*'s contemporary narrative of Cardiff itself as a fantastic space, otherworldly and disruptive. Beginning with Welsh mythology in its most familiar context, that of fantasy realms, we start with C.W. Sullivan III's "Celtic Studies and Modern Fantasy Literature." Sullivan offers an overview of the importance of Welsh mythology in the development of the fantasy genre, from the Celtic inspirations of the Romantic period to the feminist retellings of the 1960s and 1970s, which drew on Welsh sources to construct a form of counter-narrative, rejecting a monolithic view of the past for a type of conscientious retelling that gives Welsh Celtic fantasies a distinct power. Three following essays examine one specific case study of Welsh mythology in early twentieth-century fantasy, that of Evangeline Walton's Mabinogion Tetralogy: *The Prince of Annwn* (First Branch), *The Children of Llyr* (Second Branch), *The Song of Rhiannon* (Third Branch), and *The Island of the Mighty,* formerly titled *The Virgin and the Swine* (Fourth Branch). Walton, though neglected for many years, has been the subject of several recent studies, and her thought-provoking rewritings of the *Mabinogi*, begun in the heart of the American Great Depression of the 1930s, provide a space in which Welsh mythology is brought to bear on issues of motherhood, questions of genre, and depictions of heroism. Kristin Noone's "'The Rough, Savage Strength of Earth': Evangeline Walton's Human Heroes and Mythic Spaces" examines the importance of fantasy and the magical world for Walton's heroes, suggesting that magic offers at once a solution and an impossible existence for Walton's humanized characters; Nicole A. Thomas, in "Branwen's Shame: Voicing the Silent Feminine in Evangeline Walton's *The Children of Llyr*," provides a close reading of the figure of Branwen as a character who defies categorization, as she performs multiple roles—a lover, a sister, a mother, a martyr—and by so doing catapults *The Children of Llyr* from romance to tragedy to war story. Finally, Deborah Hooker's "Disavowing Maternity in Evangeline Walton's *The Virgin and the Swine:* Fantasy Meets the Social Protest Fiction of the 1930s" places Walton's first novel in a historical context, reading Arianrhod's rejection of the maternal role as a reflection of the women's movements of the age. For all these authors, Walton's particular rewriting is of special interest, as Welsh mythology provides both a recognizable narrative for Walton to speak to her audience, and a space for her to retell that narrative, to call for cultural alteration, as she engages in precisely that act of altering and rewriting herself.

In "'An Age-Old Memory': Arthur Machen's Celtic Redaction of the Welsh Revival in *The Great Return*," Geoffrey Reiter investigates a neglected novella from the pulp fiction boom that blends echoes of the 1904–05 Welsh Revival with more ancient Welsh hagiology and variants of the Grail legend, and ultimately suggests an imagined space in which all ages of Christian Wales can find commonality. Following the theme of enchanted objects, in Susana Brower's examination of "Magical Goods, 'Orphaned' Exchanges, Punishment and Power in the Fourth Branch of the *Mabinogi*," we find the Mabinogion itself, in the person of Gwydion, appearing as a subversive text, in which magical goods and creations destabilize the gift and exchange economy; for Brower, the world of Welsh mythology is a world, at heart, about cultural exchange and transmission, but also about the difficulties of that transmission, the potential for ruptures and fault lines and misunderstandings to appear. These themes are picked up in Jonathan Evans and Stephen Knight's "The Hand at the Window: Twm Siôn Cati, the Welsh Colonial Trickster," in which Evans and Knight use post-colonial theory to examine the ways in which the "Welsh Robin Hood" was created, performed, and used to examine English-language culture and Welsh self-identification in the early nineteenth century. Tyler D. Parry's "An Irregular Union: Exploring the Welsh Connection to a Popular African-American Wedding Ritual" delves into the connection between Welsh tradition and the marriage ritual of "jumping the broom," common throughout the antebellum American South, exploring the ways in which this particular element of Welsh culture has been translated across time and space until the Welsh aspect all but disappears, subsumed into the history of a very different community.

Questions of mythology and community find a different mode of expression in Megan MacAlystre's "Constructing Myth in Music: Heather Dale, King Arthur and 'Culhwch and Olwen,'" in which MacAlystre examines the folk singer as a descendant of the bardic tradition, in social position and in subject matter, returning to the story of Culhwch and his bride as an example of the mythic space of folk music, in which past and present may productively collide. Past and *future*, on the other hand, come together in the twenty-first-century science-fictional Cardiff of *Torchwood*, as explored in Lynnette R. Porter's "*Torchwood*'s 'Spooky-Do's': A Popular Culture Perspective on Celtic Mythology," where Wales' mythic past erupts into not only contemporary life but also interdimensional cultural conflicts, all located in Cardiff, which thus proves to be a meeting point for the extremely localized and familiar, but also the truly alien and exotic. Carolynn E. Wilcox, in "Everyday Magic: *Howl's Moving Castle* and Fantasy as Sociopolitical Commentary," also examines the intersection of the "real world" of Wales, the homeworld of the wizard Howl, with the fantasy world of Ingary, noting that the most disruptive elements in the fantasy world are actually intrusions from Howl's past life, and comparing Howl's ethical practice in the novel to his actions in the 2004 Miyazaki film version. Similarly, Jeff Hicks examines the problems of adapting Welsh mythology twice over, from legend to book to children's film, in "Loosely Based: The Problems of Adaptation in Disney's *The Black Cauldron*," concluding that while Lloyd Alexander's characters successfully adapt narratives of personal growth and identity formation based in the stories of the *Mabinogi*, Disney's animated version fails to bring these themes to life. In all these cases, successfully or not, Wales and Welsh tales are evoked as an imagined space in which heroes explore the identities of their worlds and themselves, and questions of good, evil, morality, and ethical action can be productively examined.

Finally, turning attention to perhaps the most dramatic reimagings yet, translations of mythic Wales across genre and media, Clay Kinchen Smith and Audrey L. Becker examine iterations of the *Mabinogi* in the most recent pop culture manifestations of Welsh mythology. In "We're Not in Cymru Anymore: What's Really Happening in the Online *Mabinogi*," Smith returns once more to the question of faithfulness, of transmission, of preservation versus transformation, and concludes that the reductive and inaccurate neomedievalism of the game further disconnects audiences from an appreciation of and understanding for the original Welsh tales or the unique aspects of the culture that produced that work — an example of failed cosmopolitanism, as the makers of the game have indeed sacrificed the individuality of the game's Welsh identity in favor of a universalizing and violent capitalism, an essay that can perhaps be read as a warning against this kind of reductive and exploitative rewriting of a particular culture's heritage. In "Temporality, Teleology and the *Mabinogi* in the Twenty-First Century," Becker closes the collection with a look at three twenty-first century adaptations of material from Welsh mythology, analyzing a film, a video game, and a novella which all invest the *Mabinogi* with therapeutic value. Exploring the diachronic modalities of the adaptations, Becker demonstrates that modern Welsh encounters with the Four Branches — as they are depicted in various millennial adaptations — rework the texts in ways that suggest a collective unconscious striving to resolve modern alienation, disconnectedness, or indifference.

We hope that the essays collected here provide a coherent argument for the relevance of popular culture studies, of Welsh mythology, and of cultural fantasy, to borrow a term from Geraldine Heng — the deliberate construction of a fantasized, idealized, and above all desirable romance of history. We also hope that they offer a source of pleasure, setting aside the artificial division between the academic and the enjoyable, inviting the union of popular culture re-enactments and scholarly examination for a more productive investigation of the imagined world of Wales and Welsh mythology.

A Note on Editions and Translations of the Mabinogi / Mabinogion

It has become customary to address nomenclature when translating medieval Welsh narratives. Lady Charlotte Guest's familiar title of her mid nineteenth-century translation — the *Mabinogion* — became the convention until later scholars questioned the accuracy of the title: a now-famous scribal error misunderstood as a plural by Guest. Some translators retain the title *Mabinogion* (Jeffrey Gantz, Gwyn Jones and Thomas Jones) while others prefer to use the corrected form *Mabinogi* (Patrick Ford). Sioned Davies explicitly uses the *Mabinogion* as a title which encompasses a grouping of eleven medieval Welsh tales (including the shorter Arthurian romances such as "Peredur" and the independent tales like "Culhwch and Olwen"), calling the term "an extremely convenient way to describe the corpus" (x). However, she too differentiates between the larger collection of tales and the group referred to as the Four Branches, which, she advises, "are the mabinogi proper" (x).

In *Welsh Mythology in Popular Culture* we have opted to use the title *Mabinogi* when the Four Branches are being referred to generally; *Mabinogion* is retained when a particular edition is referenced or when it appears in a quotation. Additionally, when referring to an author such as Evangeline Walton, who exclusively used the title *Mabinogion*, we have retained that usage. As "a foolish consistency is the hobgoblin of little minds," we have resisted the impulse to require authors to adhere to a particular translation of the text: the variety of translations is a welcome indication of the growing interest in these exceptional Welsh narratives.

Occasionally, spellings of proper names from Welsh mythology differ from translation to translation. Here we have elected to retain all spelling variants — each author's spelling of proper names is consistent with the edition from which he/she was working.

Works Cited

Derrida, Jacques. *On Cosmopolitanism and Forgiveness*. Trans. Mark Dooley and Michael Hughes. Routledge: New York, 2001.

Ganim, John. *Medievalism and Orientalism: Three Essays on Literature, Architecture, and Cultural Identity*. Palgrave Macmillan: New York, 2005.

_____. "Presidential Address: Cosmopolitan Chaucer, or, The Uses of Local Culture." The New Chaucer Society 16th Biennial Congress, University of Wales, Swansea, Wales, UK. July 18–22, 2008.

Fradenburg, Louise. "So That We May Speak of Them: Enjoying the Middle Ages," *New Literary History* 28.2 (1997): 205–230.

Frantzen, Allen J. *Desire for Origins: New Language, Old English, and Teaching the Tradition*. Rutgers UP, 1990.

Heng, Geraldine. *Empire of Magic: Medieval Romance and the Politics of Cultural Fantasy*. Columbia University Press: New York, 2003.

Sullivan, C.W., III. *Welsh Celtic Myth in Modern Fantasy*. Greenwood Press: New York, 1989.

Celtic Studies and Modern Fantasy Literature[1]

C.W. SULLIVAN III

In her 1964 O'Donnell Lecture, "Matthew Arnold and Celtic Literature: A Retrospect, 1865–1965," Rachel Bromwich comments that one of the effects of Arnold's "The Study of Celtic Literature" "was that he inaugurated in this country a dispassionate and scholarly attitude towards Celtic Studies, which made possible their acceptance here as a serious academic discipline" (1). But the field of Celtic Studies has followed only part of Arnold's lead. On one hand, Arnold argued for a dispassionate approach to Celtic Studies, using the principles of linguistics and philology, for example, to remove the discipline from the emotional reactions of both the "Celt Lovers" and the "Celt Haters"— as he termed them. This dimension of Celtic Studies has flourished and cohesive programs have been developed at major universities throughout the western world. But Arnold also argued for a study of the Celtic influence on subsequent literatures. He was not the first to do so, but in spite of his arguments, and the arguments of others, this lead has not been followed in any systematic way. But before I go any further in that direction, a brief retrospect is in order.

The confluence of cultural changes that led to the Romantic movement, with its strong interest in Arthurian and other medieval materials, prompted a number of nineteenth-century scholars to look at the Celtic materials. Among the most prominent commentators were Albert Schulz, Ernest Renan, Matthew Arnold, and William Butler Yeats. In *An Essay on the Influence of Welsh Traditions upon the Literature of Germany, France, and Scandinavia* (1841), Albert Schulz asserts that:

> The beneficent fairies who educated Lancelot du Lac, the giants conquered by Owain, Tristan, and Peredur, the enchanted fountains, the miraculous trees, the dragons and serpents, the magic rings, the sorcerer Merlin, the Fay Morgana sister of Arthur, these ariel spirits which once more resumed their power under Shakespeare do not come from the North nor the East — they are Celtic [65].

Although subsequent analyses would prove Shulz wrong in some particulars—Merlin, for example, first appears in French Arthurian tales (although his ultimate ancestor is probably a Celtic, if not specifically Welsh, druid)—his belief that many of what we would call the fantastic elements of these literatures have a Celtic source is essentially correct.

In "The Poetry of the Celtic Races" (1854), Ernest Renan, following the lead of and in response to the Comte de la Villamarqué's *Brazaz Breiz* (1838), tried to articulate an aesthetic sensibility that would separate the culture of the Celtic peoples from the culture of the Mediterranean peoples.

> Imaginative power is nearly always proportionate to concentration of feeling, and lack of external development of life. The limited nature of the Greek and Italian imagination is due to the easy expansiveness of the peoples of the South, with whom the soul, wholly spread abroad, reflects but little within. Compared with the classical imagination, the Celtic imagination is indeed the infinite compared with the finite [149].

Later in the essay, Renan discusses how the Celtic spirit came to influence all of Western Europe through the vehicle of Arthurian literature (162–74). Although the idea of a distinct or distinctive "Celtic imagination" has been the focus of some debate over the years— see especially Kenneth Jackson's comments in his introduction to *A Celtic Miscellany* (1951) in which he says "the Celtic literatures are about as little given to mysticism and sentimentalism as it is possible to be" (20)— Renan's comments were to set the stage for Arnold's and, to some extent, Yeats's as well.

In "The Study of Celtic Literature," Arnold makes two major points. The first, as I have already mentioned, is his assertion that philology be the method of analyses to assess the Celtic materials. Second, he argues for "a Celtic element in the English nature ... [that] manifests itself in our spirit and our literature" (73). He then goes on to make the second of his two most famous statements from that essay, asserting, with some doubt, that English poetry derives its "turn for style, its turn for melancholy, and its turn for natural magic ... from a Celtic source" (102–103).[2] Arnold's term "natural magic" has drawn as much fire as Renan's "Celtic imagination," but very few scholars have addressed themselves to Arnold's assertion that the Celtic materials have influenced subsequent English writers, among them Shakespeare, Southey, Keats, and Byron.

Yeats acknowledges both Renan and Arnold in his essay, "The Celtic Element in Literature" (1897), and extends their argument for a Celtic influence among all of the ancient literatures of Northern and Western Europe. He argues that:

> Literature dwindles to a mere chronicle of circumstance, or passionless phantastes, and passionless meditations, unless it is constantly flooded with the passions and beliefs of ancient times, and that of all the fountains of the passions and beliefs of ancient times in Europe ... the Celtic alone has been for centuries close to the main river of European literature [290].

But Yeats saw this "Celtic fountain" as not merely a topic of antiquarian interest but as a force that was still a viable source of literary influence:

> ... none can measure of how great importance it may be to coming times, for every new fountain of legends is a new intoxication for the imagination of the world. It comes at a time when the imagination of the world is as ready, as it was at the coming of the tales of Arthur and the Grail, for a new intoxication [293–94].

History has proved Yeats correct only in part; the interest in Celtic Studies that had been growing during the nineteenth century would continue to grow, but the study of the Celtic element in literature, with the exception of the relationship of the Celtic materials to the Arthurian romances, has been limited.

Yeats's prediction that the Celtic materials would be a new literary intoxication for the twentieth century did not, obviously, come true—for several reasons. The first was the Western European cultural preference for the Mediterranean myths and legends that had not waned much in popularity or influence since their whole scale importation into English culture in the sixteenth and seventeenth centuries. The educated populace knew the Greek and Roman myths and legends, which they considered a part of the civilized world and sophisticated worldview of the Renaissance, and those Classical stories and characters were the ones that appeared in literature and that filtered down to the rest of the population. As a result, English and American scholars since have paid little attention to the Celtic myths and legends that they considered, at best, rustic.[3]

The second factor was a tribal and political one. The Welsh, the Scots, and the Irish were of a different tribal stock from the Anglo-Saxon English; that, in addition to the constant political and military friction between the two groups, has caused a great deal of resentment on both sides as well as a feeling on the part of the English that the others, whom they had conquered and annexed (more or less), were inferior. Arnold discovered this attitude in the various responses to his articles and letters, favoring the study of things Celtic, which appeared in the *Times* and in *Cornhill Magazine*. As Arnold himself reports, he was told that his attention to the Celtic materials was a wasted effort and that everyone would be much better off if the Celts became English as quickly as possible.[4]

The third factor had to do with the development of nineteenth- and twentieth-century fiction itself. On one hand, the elite or mainstream novel became relentlessly realistic; that is, the authors of such novels presented a fictionalized version of the society they saw around them, depicting the struggles of real (if slightly exaggerated, perhaps) people in the real (if slightly exaggerated) world. This was serious writing, unlike the popular fiction which had begun to circulate at the same time; and newly-formed university English departments, themselves products of the late nineteenth century, developed curricula in modern literature that not only emphasized realistic fiction as worthy of study and analysis but rejected and shunned popular fiction. Serious study of serious (i.e., realistic) literature was the hallmark of English departments for the first three-quarters of the twentieth century, and there was no place in serious and realistic literature for knights, wizards, fairies, dragons, magic rings, cloaks of invisibility, and the like.

This is not to say that there have not been some attempts to link the Celtic myths and legends to the literatures of other times and cultures. On one hand, much work has been done to show that the Celts influenced and were influenced by their contemporaries. Einar ól Sveinson's "Celtic Elements in Icelandic Tradition" (1957), Nora Chadwick's "The Celtic Background of Early Anglo-Saxon England" (1964), Rachel Bromwich's "The Celtic Inheritance of Medieval Literature" (1965), Patrick Leo Henry's *The Early English and Celtic Lyric* (1967), James Travis's *Early Celtic Versecraft* (1973) and "The Celtic Derivation of 'Somer Is Icumen In'" (1974), Carl Borgstrom's "The Influence of Norse on Scottish Gaelic" (1974), and Martin Puhvel's *"Beowulf" and Celtic Tradition* (1979) are but some of the studies illustrating connections and influences among the cultures of Western and Northern Europe at that time.

In that same vein, a great deal of scholarship has discussed the Celtic influences on and backgrounds of Arthurian literature. Albert Shulz's study has already been mentioned, but such works as Lucy Alan Paton's *Studies in the Fairy Mythology of Arthurian Romance* (1902), John Revel Reinhard's *The Survival of Geis in Medieval Romance* (1933), Helaine Newstead's *Bran the Blessed in Arthurian Romance* (1939), Vernon J. Harward's *The Dwarfs of Arthurian Romance and Celtic Tradition* (1958), and Roger Sherman Loomis's *Celtic Myth and Arthurian Romance* (1926), *Wales and the Arthurian Legend* (1956), and *The Grail from Celtic Myth to Christian Symbol* (1963) were among the earliest twentieth-century examples of the search for Celtic materials in the background of and as an influence on Arthurian literature. These works, like the ones mentioned just previous, are — with the exception of some of Loomis's speculations — rather conservative and use, for the most part, the "philological" approaches suggested by Matthew Arnold.

On the other hand, and somewhat more speculative, are a number of articles only loosely connected by their willingness to explore possible Celtic influences on nineteenth- and twentieth-century authors. The majority of these studies have, as might be expected, focused on Joyce, Yeats, Synge, O'Casey, Stephens, and other such notables. Examples of perhaps less-obvious studies include: Edward D. Snyder's "Thomas Gray's Interest in the Celtic" (1914), Tom Peete Cross's, "Alfred Tennyson as a Celticist" (1921), Robert Hubach's "Walt Whitman and Taliesin" (1947), Peter F. Fischer's, "Blake and the Druids" (1959), Arthur Johnston's "Gray's 'The Triumph of Owen'" (1960) and "William Blake and 'The Ancient Britons'" (1981/82), John Q. Anderson's "Lowell's 'The Washers of the Shroud' and the Celtic Legend of the Washer of the Ford" (1963), Bruce Rosenberg's "Irish Folklore and *The Song of Wandering Aengus*" (1967),

Caitriona Moloney's "The Hags of *Ulysses*" (1996–1997), a journal article developed from her 1995 dissertation, "Hags, Queens, and Harlots: Women from Ancient Irish Myth in Yeats and Joyce," Maria Eleana Doye's "A Spindle for the Battle: Feminism, Myth and the Woman-Nation in Irish Revival Drama" (1999), Thomas Shea's "Patrick McGinley's Appropriation of Cuchulainn" (2001), and Janis Dawson's "Aspects of the Fantastic in Roddy Doyle's *A Star Called Henry*" (2001).

This willingness to consider Celtic influences on specific authors has spilled over from the literary community to the archeological community. In *Celtic Britain* (1979), Lloyd Laing asserts that, while place names are the "most enduring legacy" left by the Celts, "literature is probably the second most important carrier of Celtic heritage." Laing would separate the "pseudo-Celticism of Yeats's Celtic Twilight Movement" from the more genuine Celtic impulses displayed by Dylan Thomas, Samuel Beckett, and D.M. Black (171–77). Barry Cunliffe, in *The Celtic World* (1979), refers disparagingly to "revivalist nonsense" but sees three "separate threads" of Celtic literary influence: satire, saga, and style. These, he suggests, show up especially in the writings of Jonathan Swift, James Joyce, and Dylan Thomas respectively (204–205). And artists and critics from various backgrounds argue for a continuing Celtic influence in Robert O'Driscoll's *The Celtic Consciousness* (1982).

In addition to the rise of modern realistic fiction, however, the late nineteenth century saw the rise of popular literature, and the early twentieth century saw an explosion of what has come to be called pulp fiction — so named for the cheap paper on which it was originally printed. This popular literature was, by design, written for and sold to a lower socio-economic group whom the publishers and the other cultural powers-that-be felt needed both strong plots lines (to keep their attention) and a clearly defined moral structure (for their edification). This was especially true in the United States, which was fast becoming the largest literary market in the world. Such was the American manger-in-Bethlehem into which were born such genres as fantasy, science fiction, detective novels, westerns, romances, and the like.[5] The epitome of this fiction was the series book, and especially the series book as produced by Edward Stratemeyer's stable of writers. The Tom Swift books were not written by Victor Appleton, although that name appears on the cover, nor were the Hardy Boys books written by Franklin W. Dixon; those titles and many, many more appeared from a stable of writers, and any one of several authors might have written a specific title in the series.

Fantasy literature was, of course, the proper place for knights, wizards, fairies, dragons, magic rings, cloaks of invisibility, and the like. As early as 1913 and Kenneth Morris's *The Fates of the Princes of Dyfed*, Celtic materials, and particularly materials from the Four Branches of the *Mabinogi*, began to influence modern fantasy literature directly and have continued to do so — through authors such as Lloyd Alexander, Susan Cooper, Nancy Bond, Alan

Garner, J.R.R. Tolkien, and Evangeline Walton (just to name some of my favorites)—right up to the present. Thus, the Celtic materials become triply damned as a literary influence: First, because they are Celtic and not Mediterranean; Second, because they are Celtic and therefore from a second-rate culture group; and Third, because they are used in a discredited form of literature, damned not for its quality, or lack thereof, but for its fantastic content. And to make matters worse, some of the authors mentioned above write for children, and *everyone* knows that children's literature is not as good (i.e., serious, aesthetically and philosophically sophisticated, important) as realistic literature for adults. And what serious scholar wants to hitch his academic wagon to such a discredited star?

But fantasy literature is the one specific area in which the Welsh Celtic influence is both obvious and integral. The years from 1964 through 1978 saw the publication of fifteen original fantasy novels and the reprints of three others, many of which won major awards, based directly on the Four Branches of the *Mabinogi* or the other materials published with them in volumes entitled *The Mabinogion*; and there were many others during that period and the years that followed that were based on Welsh and Irish myths and legends. Major novels or series by Lloyd Alexander, Nancy Bond, Susan Cooper, Alan Garner, and Evangeline Walton were published during that period; and Kenneth Morris's two Welsh-based novels, *The Fates of the Princes of Dyfed* (1914) and *Book of the Three Dragons* (1930)—and Evangeline Walton's first book, *The Virgin and the Swine* (1936), later retitled *The Island of the Mighty*—were reprinted during that same period. Not only do these authors incorporate Welsh Celtic materials into their plots, but they do so in both aesthetic and thematic ways.[6]

The third and fourth quarters of the twentieth century were also as productive a time for critics interested in the Celtic influence on subsequent literatures as they were for the fantasy writers using those Celtic materials in their fiction. These critics not only looked for the presence of Welsh Celtic materials in modern fantasy, but found that those materials, when used conscientiously in modern fiction, are an integral part of what the author is trying to say as well as the way in which he or she says it. In addition to essays about specific authors, and various articles by Lloyd Alexander in the 1960s and 1970s, various articles and presentations by Alan Garner since 1968, Marion Carr's "Classic Hero in a New Mythology" (1971), Dainis Bisenieks's "'Tales from the Perilous Realm': Good News for the Modern Child" (1974) and "Welsh Myth in Modern American Fantasy" (1974), Susan Cooper's Tir na n-Og Award Acceptance Speech (1978), Barbara Kiefer's "Wales as a Setting for Children's Fantasy" (1982), my own *Welsh Celtic Myth in Modern Fantasy* (1989), Sally Roberts Jones's "News from the Land of Youth: Anglo-Welsh Children's Literature—A Tradition in the Making" (1990), Norma Bagnall's "An American Hero in Welsh Fantasy: *The Mabinogion*, Alan Garner and Lloyd Alexander" (1990), Kath Filmer-Davies's *Fantasy Fiction and Welsh Myth* (1996), and Donna White's *A*

Century of Welsh Myth in Children's Literature (1998) have illustrated the richness of the Welsh Celtic influence on modern fantasy literature. Moreover, these critics have established theoretical paradigms that might be employed by other critics who wish to focus their attention on any aspect of the Celtic influence on subsequent literatures. I would like to say that a survey of the critical literature has shown growth in both the number and scope of such articles and books, and I would like to say that a survey of the Celtic Studies programs at the university level in Western Europe and the Americas reveals not only courses devoted to the Celtic influence on subsequent literatures but major program segments devoted to that study; however, and again the Arthurian materials are an exception here, such is not the case.[7]

But what accounts for the popularity of the Welsh Celtic materials in the latter half of the twentieth century? In an article published in the *New Welsh Review*, to which the editor gave the unfortunate title, "The Lore of the Rings," I suggested several possible reasons for the attraction of the Welsh materials for fantasy authors and readers in the 1960s, 1970s, and 1980s. Among those reasons were the popularity of Tolkien's works which opened the door for other fantasy writers, the realization on the part of editors and publishers that Welsh-based fantasies were something new (and perhaps profitable), that the time was right in American culture (or, perhaps, counter-culture) for a literature that, as Ursula Le Guin said, "isn't factual, but ... is true" (40), and finally that it was "the rhetoric of the Welsh tales that made them so popular" ("Lore of the Rings" 35–39). By that last remark, I meant that the Welsh materials were less polished than the Greek or Roman myths and legends and were, therefore, more vibrant, more energetic narratives that spoke more directly to their modern readers. As I reconsider those remarks, it seems to me that there is something more to add. Like the Arthurian narratives, the medieval Welsh Celtic materials are very "useable." Arthur's basic story, without essential or substantial change, has been used by T.H. White to create in *The Once and Future King* an anti-war novel, by Rosemary Sutcliff to create in *Sword at Sunset* an historical novel, by Lerner and Lowe to create in *Camelot* a tale of personal versus political ideologies, and by Marion Zimmer Bradley to create in *The Mists of Avalon* a novel about the conflict between an older matrifocal culture and a newer patrifocal one — with a little pre–Christian versus Christian conflict as a sub-plot. And those are just the most obvious ones.

The Welsh Celtic materials have similarly provided authors with a solid structure on which they could build their own narratives. Lloyd Alexander tells the story of a young man growing to an awareness of self that does not depend on birthright in the five-book Chronicles of Prydain series. Nancy Bond's *A String in the Harp* is a story about rebuilding a family structure set against the concept of a moral responsibility to the past. Susan Cooper's Dark is Rising series conceptualizes history as an almost eternal struggle between the Light and the Dark, primal forces in almost any ancient myth system. Alan Garner's

The Owl Service is about the ways in which the past, in this case the mythic past of the Fourth Branch of the *Mabinogi*, can affect the present. And Louise Lawrence's *Earthwitch* brings back the fertility goddess and examines the relationship between people and the land that sustains them. In these novels, as in the Arthurian examples mentioned above, it is not just the presence of the old materials that makes these stories so powerful, it is the way in which the authors use that material. In an MLA paper, later published with the other papers from that panel in the ejournal *Celtic Cultural Studies*, I argued that successful writers used materials from the Welsh Celtic myths and legends "conscientiously"; that is, they were faithful to the essential nature of the originals so that when Gwydion appears in Alexander's Prydain series or Garner's *The Owl Service*, he is recognizably and essentially the Gwydion of the Fourth Branch of the *Mabinogi* and not just a borrowed name. What is true of these authors' use of Gwydion is true of their use of scenes and imagery and story lines as well. And I would assert that it is this conscientious use, this faithfulness to the essential nature of the original materials, that makes the good Celtic-based fantasies good, that this conscientious use brings the rhetoric of the Welsh materials which I mentioned above to the fantasy genre and reifies it, and that it is the complimentary character of mythological narratives and fantasy literature[8] that gives modern Welsh Celtic fantasies their power. Finally, it is because these novels are both well-written and powerful that they deserve a more central place in Celtic Studies.

Notes

1. A much shorter version of this essay was presented at the 12th International Congress of Celtic Studies in Aberystwyth, Wales, August 2003. Many of those present asked both interesting and challenging questions; I welcome additional responses from any/all who read this version.

2. Arnold's most famous statement about the Four Branches, of course, is his assertion that they are composed of bits and pieces of older narratives and that the author was "pillaging an antiquity of which he [did] not fully possess the secret" (47–48).

3. For a more complete discussion of the shift to Mediterranean sensibilities in England during the seventeenth century, see my "Cultural Worldview: Marginalizing the Fantastic in the Seventeenth Century." *Para*doxa* 1.3 (1995): 287–300.

4. For a discussion of anti–Celtic prejudice during Arnold's and Yeats's time, see Curtis, L.P., Jr. *Anglo-Saxons and Celts: A Study of Anti-Irish Prejudice in Victorian England*. Berkeley: U of California P, 1968.

5. Forms of most of those genres had certainly existed for some time, but as "popular literature for the masses," these genres evolved less from literary forbears such as Poe and Wells and more from the story papers of nineteenth century America. Especially informative on this topic is Mary Noel's *Villains Galore*, New York: Macmillan, 1954.

6. For a complete discussion of the aesthetic and thematic ways in which Alexander, Bond, Cooper, Garner, Morris, and Walton use materials from the Four Branches in their novels, see chapters 6 and 7 in my *Welsh Celtic Myth in Modern Fantasy*, Westport, CT: Greenwood, 1989.

7. While working on *Welsh Celtic Myth and Modern Fantasy* and again for this essay, I looked at course listings in programs in the U.S., Canada, the UK, Ireland, and other western European countries. I found few courses, Arthurian courses excepted, which focused on a literary influence. There were, indeed, "special topics seminar" slots available, but what might be offered in them was not described.

8. See note 6.

Works Cited

Arnold, Matthew. "The Study of Celtic Literature." 1866. *On the Study of Celtic Literature and On Translating Homer.* New York: Macmillan, 1913. 1–137.

Bromwich, Rachel. *Matthew Arnold and Celtic Literature: A Retrospect, 1865–1965.* Oxford: Oxford University Press, 1965.

Cunliffe, Barry. *The Celtic World.* New York: McGraw-Hill, 1979.

Jackson, Kenneth. *A Celtic Miscellany.* 1951. Baltimore: Penguin, 1971.

Laing, Lloyd. *Celtic Britain.* New York: Scribner's, 1979.

Le Guin, Ursula. "Why Americans Are Afraid of Dragons." 1979. *The Language of the Night.* New York: HarperCollins, 1989. 34–40.

Renan, Ernest. "The Poetry of the Celtic Races." 1854. *Literary and Philosophical Essays.* Harvard Classics, Volume 32. Ed. Charles W. Eliot. New York: Collier, 1910. 143–191.

Schulz, Albert. *An Essay on the Influence of Welsh Tradition upon the Literature of Germany, France, and Scandinavia.* Llandovery: William Rees, 1841.

Sullivan, C.W., III. "Conscientious Use of Welsh Celtic Myth and Legend in Fantastic Fiction." *Celtic Cultural Studies* 4 (2006). www.celtic-cultural-studies.com

_____. "The Lore of the Rings." *New Welsh Review* 56 (2002): 34–40.

Yeats, William Butler. "The Celtic Element in Literature." 1897. *Ideas of Good and Evil.* London: Bullen, 1903. 270–295.

"The Rough, Savage Strength of Earth"
Evangeline Walton's Human Heroes and Mythic Spaces

KRISTIN NOONE

> "The imagination nourishes man and causes him to act."
> — Jacques Le Goff, *The Medieval Imagination*

In a lecture at the 1973 Mythopoeic Society Convention, Evangeline Walton described herself as first and foremost "a storyteller," in love since childhood with the "ethereal heights" of Celtic mythology and folklore (Zahorski & Boyer 116). In her retelling of the great Welsh mythological cycle of the *Mabinogion*, she provides a powerful argument for the continued relevance of myth in determining cultural identity, building self-knowledge through encounters with the past. But, importantly, Walton's retelling also is an adaptation of those myths, notably in the emphasis she places on the humanity of her central figures; placed in magical and otherworldly situations, her characters learn to act with compassion and to deal with inevitable change in their quests for self-identity. Walton's *Mabinogion* tetralogy, drawing on the foundational myths of Welsh identity, expands those myths into a space for exploring human identity as a whole in the twentieth century. Walton's major male characters — Pwyll, Evnissyen, Manawydan, and Gwydion — are rewritten as heroic not by virtue of strength in battle, or use of magic. Instead, these men become heroes only when they learn to act with kindness toward others, even at great personal cost. Walton's work itself, produced during the American Great Depression of the 1930s and rediscovered during the tumultuous 1960s, can thus be read as a heroic act in and of itself: arguing for human commonality and compassion as a means of cultural rescue.

In her introduction to *Empire of Magic*, Geraldine Heng locates the beginnings of romance in Geoffrey of Monmouth's great medieval history of England, calling the *Historia Regnum Britanniae* the moment of "triumphant celebration ... in which the spoor of history and the track of fantasy creation become one, inextricably conjoined" (3). Heng sees the genre of romance as a place of "cultural rescue," a place where historical phenomena and fantasy might collide and permit a response to "crises of communal and collective identity;" she asks whether postmedieval magical narratives can be considered in the same light, and concludes that they can: romances like Tennyson's *Idylls of the King*, for example, "show how a medieval genre can be reanimated to produce a flexible structure of ideological support and literary-theoretical justification," (11) and the descendents of romance can be found even in *Star Trek*, which Heng calls "that most popular concatenation of late-twentieth-century travel romances," noting its concern with the "cultural politics of race, gender, and empire" (11). Doing similar work in his collection *Mass Market Medieval: Essays on the Middle Ages in Popular Culture*, David Marshall asserts that "popular contemporary interest in the medieval can be a barometer for cultural shifts;" that is, by studying the ways in which the medieval is used in contemporary culture, it is possible to read communal desires and concerns (7–8). And J.R.R. Tolkien defended fantasy in his classic essay "On Fairy-Stories," in which he asserts that it is "a higher form of Art, indeed the most nearly pure form, and so (when achieved), the most potent" (69); for Tolkien, the fantastic world is "founded upon the hard recognition that things are so in the world as it appears under the sun" (75), and thus becomes a space inextricably intertwined with the realities of "the world," and of cultural formation. The noted Tolkien scholar Verlyn Flieger agrees, observing that "a modern use of these motifs reaffirms their value as a vital part of literature in an age when only scholars and children (and too few of those) read the story of King Arthur, or of Jack the Giant-Killer, or the adventures of Sigurd dragon-slayer" (124). The work of the modern fantasist, particularly a fantasist focusing upon a mythology of proud cultural celebration at the time of its original formation, is always a space, like Heng's definition of romance, in which questions of collective identity can be worked out in the collision of the historical and the magical.

In 1936, Evangeline Walton's retelling of the Fourth Branch of the *Mabinogi* appeared for the first time, under the rather unusual title *The Virgin and the Swine*. Despite this memorable name, it did not sell. Betty Ballantine notes in her introduction to the reissued *Mabinogion* tetralogy that "an America just climbing out of a worldclass [sic] Depression was notably uninterested in fantastic legend, still the stuff of children's books" (9) and though Walton continued to adapt the Welsh mythological cycle, she simply kept them to herself, assuming that there was no interest in fantasy.[1] However, after the success of *The Lord of the Rings*, Ballantine Books began looking for authors to become part of a new adult fantasy line, and rediscovered *The Virgin and the Swine*. Since no one had heard from or about Evangeline Walton for fourteen years, she was in fact assumed dead; with the books already reprinted, it came as something of a surprise that she was in fact alive and well in Tucson, Arizona, and she happily delivered the rest of the *Mabinogion* manuscripts (*The Prince of Annwn, The Children of Llyr*, and *The Song of Rhiannon*, which accompany the renamed *The Island of the Mighty*) after correspondence with the publisher. Kenneth Zahorski and Robert Boyer note in their bibliography of her work that, although "not nearly enough critical attention has been paid," it has been "consistently enthusiastic;" citing an early review in *Mythprint* (1973), they emphasize her ability to create "heroes and heroines of epic proportions" that are nonetheless "very human" and "real to the reader" (127). This combination, along with her "meticulous treatment of source material," contributes to her status as one of the great twentieth-century fantasists; Lin Carter, developer of Ballantine's Adult Fantasy line, even declared that "only Ursula K. Le Guin is comparable" (quoted in Zahorski and Boyer, 152). For all these commentators, Walton is worthy of the critical attention which she has begun to receive in recent years. As Zahorski and Boyer note, the power of her novels comes from a combination of fidelity to source material, and universal appeal, and therefore it is worth examining the ways in which Walton uses and modifies her myths, and to what ends.

As Zahorski and Boyer have pointed out, the major theme of the novels is that of the Old versus the New, and the ways in which human society changes and responds to change. In this case, the Old is represented by the Old Tribes of Wales, a matriarchal-matrilineal system that emphasizes nature and older rituals such as the symbolic marriage of the king of Dyved with the White Mare, and the New is the encroaching Christian system of patriarchy, legalism, and even technology. "The ultimate effect," they conclude, "of the dramatic juxtaposition of the two cultures is to put each in bold relief so that its particular strengths and weaknesses can be examined and mulled over" (130); Walton's retellings consider the inevitability of change and the ways in which cultural fantasies can provide a space for the working out of self-identity in such a very changeable world. These moments of cultural examination are most evident in Pwyll's encounter with Arawn, in the redemption of Evnissyen,[2] in Manawyddan's contest of will with the Gray Man, and in the wisdom Gwydion learns with the loss of his son. In the best tradition of fantasy, each heroic character encounters the supernatural or *in*human world, and learns to define himself in relation to it: Pwyll and Manawyddan strike bargains with the Otherworld, Evnissyen sacrifices himself to destroy the magical Cauldron, and Gwydion exists in a web of enchantments and transformations.

In the *Mabinogi*, which Walton consistently cites in footnotes and afterwords (she is working from the *Red Book* and references it along with other historical and scholarly texts[3]), Pwyll's initial encounter with Arawn in the First Branch is a brief one, composed of only simple statements. "How can I earn your friendship?" Pwyll asks, having offended Arawn by taking his stag. "By ridding me of [Havgan's] oppression," Arawn replies plainly, and promptly conducts the Lord of Dyved to the palace of the Otherworld where he must dwell in Arawn's place.[4] The mythic power of the scene is undeniable; the journey to the Otherworld parallels other occurrences in Irish myth, and the Otherworld itself, as Grant McCracken has noted, is frequently a testing ground for cultures and their heroes, a place which allows the preservation of cultural ideals while acknowledging that reality can be quite different (109). Evangeline Walton's version of the scene does similar work by providing a space for building and testing values, but here they are made specific, as Walton emphasizes time and again the need for compassion for human life, and for the acceptance of change, as foundational for human identity.

"You are called a bull of battle and a woe to your enemies—the rough, savage strength of earth may do what we cannot," Arawn tells Pwyll, early in Walton's story of their meeting (*Prince of Annwn* 23). "Whatever happens ... strike [Havgan] no second blow. So I, a God, was beguiled ... I yielded my will to his will, and he who does that has no more power against him forever." It is the rough and savage strength of earth, specifically, that is needed for this battle; notably, it is Pwyll who succeeds where, Walton tells us, even the God had failed. But here Pwyll is given his strength in part by his determination to preserve life. Arawn offers him the explanation for the enmity behind the battle, declaring that "Havgan too is Death, and he will slay as I never slew. All the worlds he can reach he will burn and tear and wreck. He will overturn the order that I have maintained throughout the ages...." In this brief statement, Walton gives the encounter great depth. Pwyll goes to defend Arawn's version of Death, defending as well the concept of death in its proper place as something vital to existence; he acts, paradoxically, to preserve life by protecting death, or at least the version of it that does not burn and tear and wreck indiscriminately. His fight is not only on behalf of Arawn, but on behalf of humanity and the world, who will suffer if Havgan is the victor: he responds to Arawn that he will freely undertake the slaying "because my world, as well as yours, is at stake. That much I think I understand" (*Prince of Annwn* 24). Pwyll, in this version of the tale, protects both the lives of his people from indiscriminate slaughter, and the idea of death as something meaningful and purposeful and aligned with human existence. In refusing to deal Havgan a second blow — a moment that seems to be a failure of compassion — Pwyll is in fact defending all of his world from Havgan's viciousness. In this moment, Walton highlights the problems of compassion and empathy and offers readers an examination of those values, with the worlds of life and death at stake.

Pwyll's fight on behalf of Death as a meaningful part of existence also evokes Walton's concern for change and the inevitability of change in the human world. It is a time of change in Wales that Pwyll thinks of as he rides into Annwn: "the High King was failing," he muses silently, "and with him might die the peace that for many winters his strength ... had kept between the Old

Tribes and the New. Bell was of the Old Tribes, so his heirs would be his sister-sons, the Children of Llyr, but in secret his own son Caswallon was already wooing the lords of the New Tribes...."[5] Death and dying are, obviously, much on Pwyll's mind as he rides into the Otherworld, and he is concerned with the potential for change that death allows. Walton's tetralogy is structured around a supposed shift from the matrilineal Old Tribes to the patrilineal New, and this moment powerfully emphasizes the inevitability of change, as Pwyll descends into the realm of the ultimate change, that of Death, wearing the form of Death himself. (The physical appearance-changing of Pwyll and Arawn at this precise moment is another delicate thematic underscoring by Walton.) Pwyll, then, encounters and is forced to deal with the reality of the mutability of the world in all its manifestations. As he sets off to fight on behalf of Death, he works out ways to accept and deal with change, both in the political earthly realm (as he ponders alliances) and in the metaphysical (as he comes to understand that a meaningful death may be something worth defending).

In the Second Branch of the *Mabinogi*, the character of Evnissyen destroys the cauldron of Llasser Llaes Gyngwyd, the cauldron of rebirth, just as he will do in Walton's version. In the *Mabinogi*, the passage reads, "When Evnissyen saw these corpses and no room anywhere in the cauldron for the men of the Island of the Mighty, he thought, 'Alas, God, wretched am I who have brought this about on the men of the Island of the Mighty, and shame on me if I do not seek to deliver them'" (79). The next moment, he creeps in among the Irish dead, is placed in the cauldron, and "broke it into four pieces, and his heart broke also." This final heroic moment takes place only the day after Evnissyen has started the war, and it is followed by the bald statement that "consequently the victory went to the men of the Island of the Mighty" (79). As with Pwyll's Otherworld encounter, Evnissyen's self-sacrifice is a moment of examination of the nature of heroism and the values that prompt his choices. He becomes redeemed as a hero, despite his terrible deeds, by accepting responsibility for his prior deeds and attempting to atone for them. In Walton's retelling, this idea of personal responsibility is brought to the forefront, and — in keeping with her emphasis on the need for accepting change — so is the idea of Evnissyen's personal evolution.

Evnissyen's moment of redemption as presented by Walton is the moment in which — like Pwyll — he acts out of a desire to deliver others from pain. Having just seen his twin tortured and killed in his place, Evnissyen thinks to himself that "he is dead, and he died for me. Not because he thought it his duty, but because he cared what happened to me" (*Children of Llyr* 255). It is this moment of pure unselfish sacrifice that triggers Evnissyen's mental change; the heart of his story, and the act that thus ultimately has the most power, is Nissyen's enactment of the moment of greatest love for his fellow man. With this example before him, and the slaughter of the Welsh-Irish battle in the background, Evnissyen learns first to accept responsibility for his own actions: "over the frozen wastes a voice howled, a voice that he could no longer shut out. *It is your deeds that have brought the men of the Island of the Mighty to this....* He accepted that; and that was the first time in his life that Evnissyen had ever accepted responsibility for anything that went amiss" (*Children of Llyr* 255). But it is not enough for Evnissyen to take responsibility for himself; emulating the lesson of Nissyen, he reaches the heights of heroism by acting to defend others. Like Pwyll and Walton's other heroes, Evnissyen makes his definitive act one of compassion and protection. As in the *Mabinogion* from which the line is taken, Evnissyen whispers to himself, "O God, woe is me that I am the cause of this slaughter of the men of the Island of the Mighty, and shame be upon me if I do not seek their deliverance." And then, Walton relates, "He lay very still, and out of his pain an idea was born, the far white shimmer of mountaintops upon it, as out of pain a child is born" (*Children of Llyr* 256). Here Walton expands the execution of that idea, in her choice of language — linking Evnissyen's choice with something productive and procreative — and for two pages, as she describes Evnissyen's hiding himself among the Irish dead, his fear of the pain of the Cauldron, and his determination to still go through with his sacrifice. Evnissyen, as his pain and strength are eloquently laid bare, becomes identifiably heroic, even as he dies. Walton's Bran, hearing the Cauldron shatter, acknowledges the passion and compassion of Evnissyen's last act thus: "He gave his life for the lives of all of us, and no man can do more than that" (*Children of Llyr* 257).

Like Pwyll's tale, Evnissyen's tale gives Walton a chance to demonstrate the capacity for change, here on a personal and painful level. Evnissyen undergoes an internal movement from a man who would fling a child into the fire to a man who quite literally lets himself be so flung. His representation here suggests that men are capable of redemption, and indeed of heroism, despite previous heinous acts; Evnissyen, in fact, serves as a figure of hope.[6] He also acts as an instrument of change for the world: "He had come and gone, that dark diseased soul whom the druids had foretold. He had shattered a world as he had shattered the Cauldron whose shape symbolized the world..." (*Children of Llyr* 257–8). Evnissyen's acts first create the world of warfare, and then end it, reshaping the realms of Ireland and Wales into war-torn, denuded, and bereft spaces. He thus acts as a symbol of the power of a man to effect cataclysmic change, to act for ill or for good; as in Walton's previous metaphor, he gives birth to a new era. His understanding of this great power, and his choice to use it in his final act on behalf of others, makes him a warning and a lesson for others. Walton's emphasis on Evnissyen's ability to change the world allows her to retell this story as a space in which the impact of human power can be examined.

In the Third Branch of the *Mabinogi*, Dyved has fallen under the enchantment of the Grey Man, Llywd son of Lil Coed, leaving the land desolate and empty. Manawyddan's dealings with Llywd, holding Llywd's transformed and pregnant wife as a hostage against restoration of Dyved, are given a kind of solemn weight by the ritualistic repetition of scenes and phrases: "Between me and God," Manawyddan repeats steadfastly, "I will not release her." (93–95). Manawyddan's capacity for understanding and knowledge — he recognizes the mouse for what she is and successfully bargains using her — are evident in the dialogue, which is presented with little surrounding commentary, and themes of friendship and devotion are hinted at in the Gray Man's motivation for the enchantment — vengeance for a friend — and his capitulation on behalf of his wife. But Walton's version of the scene draws attention to the human capacity for pain and love as something enabling, leading to wisdom, as well as underlining again the potential for change in a mutable world.

Llywd, named by Manawyddan later as "the Grey Man ... that I think is near enough to one of your names," (*Song of Rhiannon* 417), takes many shapes when he comes to demand the release of his wife: a bard, a druid, a lord, a High Druid, and finally himself, an appearance with which he tries to strike fear into the mortal man's heart. He was "burning," Walton relates, "with terrible, unguessable splendor, with all the cold fire in all the eyes of all the snakes that ever lived.... [Manawyddan] could see that shining death as clearly as if his eyes were open and he held it in his hand" (*Song of Rhiannon* 417). In this moment, it is Manawyddan's love for and connection to his companions that preserves him: "Desperately he called up other images to set between himself and it. The face of Rhiannon, young and tender ... that same face, aged but more deeply beautiful, when she lay beside him at Arberth, knowing him now, truly his. Pryderi himself, playing with his dogs...." With the strength of his love for them, he is able to say to Llywd that "I will take no price that you have offered," a determination that leads to Llywd's resigned response of "Name your own price, man of earth. I will pay it." (*Song of Rhiannon* 417). Notably, Llywd's reply to Manawyddan's strength, drawn from love, emphasizes that he is a "man of earth;" love for others, then, appears as the strongest power an earthly man can have. This theme is unequivocally supported later, when Manawyddan addresses the Gray Man after the restoration of Rhiannon, Pryderi, and all of Dyfed: "Do not think that I am gloating over my own cleverness, Lord. Well I know that of the two of us you are by far the mightier. But throughout our struggle I loved and you hated; ask yourself what difference that made" (*Song of Rhiannon* 421). He goes on to show that he can extend his compassion even to his adversary (who, after all, has enchanted Dyfed out of revenge for an insult and injury given to a friend[7]): "Ask yourself too — you who think I cannot understand what you felt when you saw your friend's back — what you would have felt had you seen your own brother writhing in the agony of a poisoned wound. Had you had to cut his head off with your own hand to ease his pain."[8] Here, Manawyddan uses the language of compassion and of pain as a means of communication and identification; he and the Otherworld lord understand each other, as they both have witnessed and tried to respond to the wounding of those for whom they care. And it is a powerful language; they part upon terms of "genuine respect," even with a smile. For Walton, the language of compassion, of caring, of emotion — both pain and love — provides a space for true communication, and thus is the strongest force of all.

But Walton is concerned as well with the force of change and the flow of time, a theme explicitly dealt with in this otherworld encounter. When recalling the face of Rhiannon, Manawyddan draws strength not from one vision of her, but from two, as they have become closer over time; Llywd's captive wife is pregnant, suggesting a season of birth and newness. "I think," Llywd muses to Manawyddan, "that no Lord of the Bright World will invade earth openly again. Mind is growing stronger, even among mortal men, and the walls between the worlds are growing firmer. We may play with your thoughts again, but only your thoughts." (*Song of Rhiannon* 421). Here Walton explores the move from a mythological and magical era to one concerned with the powers of the "mind" and mortal ingenuity, a theme of this Branch (as depicted, notably, in the various professions Manawyddan and company adopt while wandering Dyfed — shoemakers, saddlemakers, farmers, and so on). Change, birth, and alterations are presented as inevitable, and Manawyddan, as Walton's protagonist in this tale, not only understands this fact, but uses it, as with his memories of Rhiannon, to find strength. His final thought of the tale, in fact, is that it is "good to be alive — alive, and with work to do, and those you loved around you. What better lot could there be in any world?" (*Song of Rhiannon* 424). In thinking of the future, and in emphasizing the presence of love, the character of Manawyddan allows Walton to explore the importance of both, depicting comprehension of the power of both forces as essential for life in this, or any, world.

"One can also admire," says Jeffrey Gantz in his introduction to his translation of the *Mabinogion*, "the control with which Gwydyon is rehabilitated," calling him "clever but unscrupulous" (28–9). In the Fourth Branch, that rehabilitation takes place not only in the moments of punishment, when Gwydion and his brother must spend years as wild beasts, but throughout the tale, as he grows from a self-serving magician to a man tempered by grief at the loss of his son; the *Mabinogi* observes that upon hearing of Lleu's death, "Math was grieved and heavy-hearted, and Gwydion was sadder still. 'Lord, I cannot rest until I get news of my nephew,' said he" (114). Gwydion then embarks on a solitary quest, wandering the Island of the Mighty in search of Lleu and leaving behind the court and the site of his previous, more selfish acts; he does not seek death as vengeance for his son, but practices a punishment that Math himself has previously invoked, that of transformation, suggesting that he has grown beyond the earlier Gwydion who casually brought about violent war to suit his own plans and desires. As with the previous Branches, Evangeline Walton's version of this tale builds on this theme, suggesting both the capacity for personal evolution and the understanding of pain, grief, and loss as the most profound of human values.

Walton's rewriting of the Fourth Branch as Gwydion's story has been previously observed by critics; Zahorski and Boyer call it the "most important quest" of the tale, in which the quest for self-identity is explored: "we see him grow from a rather rash young man who tricks Pryderi out of twelve swine, thus catapulting his own country into war, into the wise and compassionate man who helps nurse Llew Llaw Gyffes back to health" (132). Gwydion's early actions, though they may be partly designed to aid others (the war allows his brother Gilvaethwy to indulge his love-sick passions), are also always tinged with selfishness; as Math comments on his nephew's actions, "He has an intention again ... it is not me that he has gone to serve." (*Island of the Mighty* 524–5). It is the moment at which he loses his son—that product of his earlier selfish desire—that Gwydion learns to act purely on behalf of others, with no intentions to benefit himself. Once he has lost Llew, perhaps for the first time encountering despair, he understands the potential he has to cause pain to others; suffering in "greyness, like beaten warriors on a lost field," he nonetheless considers Math's emotions and asks permission before setting out to follow his own desires and seeking Llew: "Not of his own will alone," Walton says of Gwydion's act, "could he undertake this journey: leave alone the King his uncle who was old and sore-stricken, even if not so bitterly pierced as he was—the King who might need him." (*Island of the Mighty* 655). Instead, Gwydion asks leave to go on his quest, and is given permission. This quest is, importantly, not a quest for vengeance; Gwydion's objective is not destruction, but salvation: "Llew must be somewhere in this world, and if he is I shall find him. So have I ceased to think of vengeance." And to this Math responds, "Then have you made yourself pure for the quest. Go." (*Island of the Mighty* 654). Like Evnissyen's, Gwydion's defining act is selfless instead of selfish, intended to rescue and preserve another's life instead of destroy. With Gwydion, Walton provides a look at compassion and love on a very personal level: with the knowledge of loss and grief comes Gwydion's understanding of his own potential to injure or to heal, as he displays in his consideration for Math.

Gwydion's story is also a story of personal change and evolution, allowing Walton to explore the capacity for human redemption and alteration, in a story intimately bound up with magical alterations. Gwydion exists at the heart of change, physically, magically, and mentally. He practices illusion and enchantment almost continuously; he has it practiced upon him by Math as a punishment. Because he comprehends the mutability of the world, like Walton's other protagonists, he has knowledge and power. But what he must learn is the responsibility that comes with his power for change, and he learns it when his own flesh and blood, Llew Llaw Gyffes, has been changed into an eagle, no longer capable of human form of thought: "If he had one thought of us, we should have found him," Gwydion admits to Math. "And he could turn to none but us. It is as if he were not thinking." And then "both were silent, appalled by that thought of an annihilation utterly beyond the bounds of nature" (*Island *of the Mighty* 654). Confronted with this magical transformation, placing Llew outside the human frame of reference, Gwydion finally comprehends the potential risks and pain that keep company with change. Walton draws attention to this lesson, and to Gwydion's personal growth, in the moment he sets out in search of the transformed Llew, wearing the clothing of a bard, as he had once gone disguised to steal pigs: "They parted at evening. Gwydion had again put on the garments of a bard. The disguise that had served the hot ambitions of his youth would now serve the bitter, it might be life-long, quest of his manhood" (*Island of the Mighty* 655–6). Gwydion has grown from youth to man; he uses his understanding of the world as a place of change and alteration not for ambition, but for the rescue of others. He does not seek vengeance or death, but shows his new wisdom in the punishment he chooses for Blodeuwedd, Llew's wife and the cause of his death. He looks upon her with "sad and weary eyes," without taking joy or satisfaction in retribution, and transforms her, as Math had once done to him, into something inhuman: an owl, which will never again show her face in the sun (*Island of the Mighty* 711–2). In his final act of the tale, Gwydion demonstrates that he has learned the appropriate attitude towards power, and thereby also the power of personal change. Zahorski and Boyer note Walton's interest in the "inevitability of change" (131); with Gwydion, Walton comments on the impact that change can have, the power of men to effect it, and the responsibility of that power.

In a review of *The Children of Llyr* in 1971, Lester Del Rey called Walton's work "timeless, in the sense that the very best telling of tales is always beyond the limits of time and place" (quoted in Zahorski and Boyer, 148), and commended her transformation of mythical figures into fully realized human beings. Evangeline Walton's *Mabinogion* tetralogy is thus itself a transformation, or a translation, quite literally across language, time, and space, from mythic Wales to 1930s Arizona. In the four books that retell the four Branches, Walton provides an examination of the value of compassion, and also the ways in which societies and individuals must deal with the inevitable changeability of the world. The men of Walton's Mabinogion Tetralogy, as they learn to reject more overt expressions of power, find hope for themselves and their worlds—in other words, Walton's text offers an answer to the horrors of a modern world, beset by global warfare and economic woes, in a movement away from traditionally masculinist values. Though her characters deal with inhuman challenges and obstacles, they ultimately triumph—and they do so by becoming more adaptable, more compassionate, more aware of their shared humanity. For Walton, this appeal to humanity arises out of the mythic space of the stories of the *Mabinogion*: the rescue of the future requires not a dismissal, nor a simple repetition, of the past, but the embracing of mythic space as an active part of the present, translated, adapted, and alive. She asks us, in the face of modern and postmodern global trauma, to have compassion for the future, for the past, and for each other.

Notes

1. Walton's own personal interest in fantasy, myth, and the *Mabinogion* in particular may be linked to the Welsh revival just before the turn of the century (see Prys Morgan, "From a Death to a View: The Hunt for the Welsh Past in the Romantic Period"). Walton came from a highly educated family and corresponded personally with the Welsh novelist, poet, and essayist John Cowper Powys for many years; she was no doubt familiar with the romanticized mythic Welsh past. A secondary factor in her unusual-for-the-time interest in fantasy may be that because of respiratory health problems, as a child Walton was treated with silver nitrate tincture, which rendered her skin permanently blue-gray; she was therefore home-schooled and relatively solitary, finding escape in literature, especially fantasy and myth (see Zahorski & Boyer, "Critical/Biographical Essay).
2. All name and place spellings, unless otherwise indicated, are Walton's.
3. Though she never gives a complete bibliography with dates, publishers, etc., Walton also refers to St. Adamnan, Roger Loomis, Nora Chadwick, the Fenian Cycle and Cu Chulainn, Robert Briffault's *The Mothers*, John Cowper Powys, Clifton Furness's *The Genteel Female*, Elizabeth Albee Adams's article "The Bards of Britain," Sir William Boyd Dawkins, W.J. Grufydd, geological studies (for the stones of Stonehenge), Heinrich Zimmer's *The Corpse and the King*, *Sir Gawain and the Green Knight*, Skene's *Four Ancient Books of Wales*, Caesar's accounts of Britain, the story of Tristan and Iseult, John Rhys's *The Welsh People* and *Celtic Folklore*, Lady Guest's *Mabinogion*, Nicholas Roerich's *Altai-Himalaya* for connections between Central Asian temples and druidism, Alexandra David-Neel's *Magic and Mystery in Tibet*, and the *Mythology of All Races*; she also spoke Welsh, as she offers some name and place translations/pronunciations in footnotes and mentions getting help with obscure passages from the *Red Book of Hergest* from a Professor Robinson at Harvard University. This is by no means an exhaustive list, as her notes are extensive.
4. Gantz, Jeffrey. *The Mabinogion* (trans.) Penguin Classics: New York, 1976. p.47–8. All references to the text of the *Mabinogion* are taken from this edition.
5. *Prince of Annwn* 27–8. The Children of Llyr, and Caswallon's desire for the throne, of course, reappear in the following Branches; mention of them here not only supports Walton's interest in mutability and change, but also her desire to create a narrative whole out of the Four Branches.
6. The interest in hope may well have been particularly pertinent given the cultural contexts of the American 1930s, when Walton began writing, and the 1960s, when her works were rediscovered and began to receive critical acclaim.
7. Gwawl, also of the Otherworld, and Rhiannon's original betrothed, whom she rejected for Pryderi's father. See the First Branch of the *Mabinogion* for the tale; in Walton's version, Llywd is a close friend of Gwawl's, and therefore seeks revenge on Pryderi's kin and country (418–419). This connection forges another link in Walton's project of coherent narrative; it suggests that an understanding of friendship and emotion may be shared even across worlds.
8. *Song of Rhiannon* 421. The reference is to the beheading of Bran in the Second Branch, pages 263–4 in Walton's *The Children of Llyr*.

Works Cited

Ballantine, Betty. "Introduction." Evangeline Walton, *The Mabinogion Tetralogy*. New York: Overlook Press: New York, 2002. 7–12.
Carter, Lin. *Imaginary Worlds: The Art of Fantasy*. New York: Ballantine Books, 1973.

del Rey, Lester. "Review of *The Children of Llyr.*" *Worlds of If* #21 (September/October 1971), 144–145. Reprinted in *Lloyd Alexander, Evangeline Walton Ensley, Kenneth Morris: A Primary and Secondary Bibliography*, ed. Kenneth J. Zahorski and Robert H. Boyer. Boston: G.K. Hall & Co, 1981. 147–8.
Flieger, Verlyn. "Frodo and Aragorn: The Concept of the Hero." *Understanding the Lord of the Rings: The Best of Tolkien Criticism.* Ed. Rose A. Zimbardo and Neil D. Isaacs. New York: Houghton Mifflin, 2004. 122–143.
Gantz, Jeffrey. *The Mabinogion* (trans. & intro.) New York: Penguin Classics, 1976.
Heng, Geraldine. *Empire of Magic: Medieval Romance and the Politics of Cultural Fantasy.* New York: Columbia University Press, 2003.
Le Goff, Jacques. *The Medieval Imagination.* Trans. Arthur Goldhammer. Chicago: University of Chicago Press, 1988.
Marshall, David W. "Introduction: The Medievalism of Popular Culture," in *Mass Market Medieval: Essays on the Middle Ages in Popular Culture.* Ed. David W. Marshall. Jefferson, NC: McFarland, 2007. 1–12.
McCracken, Grant. *Culture and Consumption.* Bloomington: Indiana University Press, 1988.
Morgan, Prys. "From a Death to a View: The Hunt for the Welsh Past in the Romantic Period," in *The Invention of Tradition,* ed. Terence Ranger and Eric J. Hobsbawm. Cambridge: Cambridge University Press, 1992. 43–100.
Tolkien, J.R.R. "On Fairy-Stories." Reprinted in *The Tolkien Reader.* New York: Ballantine Books, 1966. 33–99.
Walton, Evangeline. *The Mabinogion Tetralogy.* New York: Overlook Press, 2002. Contains reissued collection of Walton's four *Mabinogion* novels: *The Prince of Annwn* (Ballantine, 1974), *The Children of Llyr* (Ballantine, 1971), *The Song of Rhiannon* (Ballantine, 1972), and *The Island of the Mighty* (Ballantine, 1970; formerly titled *The Virgin and the Swine,* originally published by Willett, Clark, & Co, 1936.)
Zahorski, Kenneth J. and Robert H. Boyer. "Evangeline Walton Ensley: Introduction: A Biographical/Critical Essay." *Lloyd Alexander, Evangeline Walton Ensley, Kenneth Morris: A Primary and Secondary Bibliography.* Eds. Kenneth J. Zahorski and Robert H. Boyer. Boston: G.K. Hall & Co, 1981. 113–138.

Branwen's Shame
Voicing the Silent Feminine in Evangeline Walton's The Children of Llyr

Nicole A. Thomas

In "For Pedants and Others," Evangeline Walton's preface to *The Island of the Mighty* (the fourth novel in her Mabinogion Tetralogy), the author writes "My original rule was never to alter anything I found in the Four Branches of the Mabinogi, whatever I might add or subtract ... but we modern authors have to give our characters reasons for their most unreasonable actions. We lack the glorious freedom of the old bards, and perhaps that is just as well" (Walton 425). Giving reason to unreason, making the seemingly irrational rational, can be seen as the most basic action an author undertakes when rewriting folklore or myth. Such works inevitably fall into the fantasy genre: more fictional than fiction. The presence of magic and those "unreasonable actions" makes it seemingly impossible to consider them serious works of literature. Thus the tetralogy remains elusive on bookshelves, eclipsed by the long shadows of Tolkien and J.K. Rowling. They have transcended the boundaries of genre to be considered appropriate texts for study in the academic sphere. Why Walton's work has not been so considered may be explained by the fact that she is herself a little-known American author working from Welsh folklore that is little-known outside of Britain (and, one could argue, little-known inside of Britain as well). What Walton achieves in her Mabinogion Tetralogy is a work of multi-layered, intertextual complexity, which treats its source material as a historic document with significant feminist implications.

Those implications are made explicit in the treatment of Branwen in *The Children of Llyr*. Her character provides the name for the Second Branch of the *Mabinogi*, although she does not speak until the climax of the story. Branwen, the sister of King Bendigeidfran, is married to Matholuch, King of Ireland, shipped off to that island, bears a son, and is confined to a life of slavery in the castle before uttering a single word. The other women of the *Mabinogi*: Rhiannon, Arianrhod and Blodeuwedd, are headstrong, powerful and always outspoken. Yet Branwen, one of the "Three Chief Maidens" of Wales, "the most beautiful girl in the world" (Davies 23), apparently has nothing to say for herself. Or, rather, she has no say in the trajectory of her story. The events of the Branch named after her seem to swirl around her, happen *to* her, as a child puts a doll through the motions of eating, dressing and marrying. When Branwen sails to Ireland, her brothers "looked at her until she shrank to the size of a child, dwindled to the size of a doll" (Walton 190). It is her brother Bendigeidfran — or Bran, as he is referred to most often in the novel — who first thinks to use Branwen as a doll to do his bidding.

It is his idea to marry her off to Matholuch: the first arranged marriage in the history of the Island of the Mighty, according to Walton. Just as the narrator of the novel speaks in the past tense, the tetralogy itself is set in the distant past, prior even to the written record of the *Mabinogi*, when stories from it would have likely been performed to a pre–Christian audience. W.J. Gruffydd describes the redactor's task as a difficult one:

> He had to make the best he could out of unpromising material which had already been distorted during the centuries when it had passed from cyvarwydd to cyvarwydd, and the particular version on which the author based the final account was by no means the least contaminated [by this transmission] [4].[1]

There are nine spoken references to God in the thirteen pages of the Second Branch and all of them occur within the dialogue (Davies 21–34). Whether it is Matholuch's repeated "God knows" or Branwen's keening "Oh Son of God," each use is perfunctory and easily inserted or removed without noticeable alteration of the story.

It is worth mentioning that Walton repeatedly cites John Rhys's *Celtic Folklore*, in which he posits a theory that the family groups in the *Mabinogi* were pre–Christian Picts (Rhys 684). Walton removed all nine of the dialogic references to God when writing *The Children of Llyr*. Her decision to adhere to the origins of the *story* versus the *text* of the *Mabinogi* is one which anticipates Gillian Beer's advice in her article, "Representing Women: Re-presenting the Past." Beer implores her readers not to try to place pre-modern texts in a modern context. Rather, she suggests "re-presenting" them by "engaging with the *difference* of the past in our present" (80). Similarly, in "Women's Rewriting of Myths," Diane Purkiss discusses the problematic approach of feminists who:

> [b]y rewriting the myth — changing the narrative, changing the position of the speaker, changing the spaces available for identification — are held to be at once making a dramatic break with the myths as told by the fathers, and also to be recovering the dark, secret, always unconscious truths which the fathers have struggled to repress [444].

Such a technique, Purkiss argues, does not uncover a lost feminine, because the authors "refer to a femininity which is itself a product of the culture and language which represses it. Femininity is, precisely, that which is excluded from patriarchal representations and can only be glimpsed in their gaps and silences" (448). The character of Branwen exists in her silence. What Walton does, in re-visioning Branwen, is use a third-person omniscient narrator to recover her voice. Thus, the text avoids the erroneous assumptions made when placing a myth in a modern context, by retaining its historic setting and narrative technique.

As Derrick S. Thomson points out in his introduction to the Welsh-language *Branwen Uerch Llyr*, "*Branwen* might well be described as a novel compressed to the dimensions of a short story" (xlii). He goes on to describe the novelistic elements of the Branch:

> It is a story which constantly retains its interest, by means both of plot construction and of character delineation. These main qualities of the tale are never subordinated to the incidental antiquarian tricks and trapping which the average story-teller of this period would probably have found difficult to control. But the redactor is true to his time and to his class in that he does not entirely expunge these trappings from his story [xlii–xliii].

The same could be said of *The Children of Llyr*. Walton does not attempt to modernize the story. She retains the plot, characters and setting while changing the format from "novelistic" to novel. The major change made is the removal of the narrative to a pre–Christian past. One could argue that this is, in fact, not a change at all, but a stripping away of Christian morality which was applied at a later date. Thompson makes note of the "thoroughly Christian 'milieu' of the Branch," which, he adds, "may well have taken its shape in the mind of a clerical redactor" (xliv). Although it is not the purpose of this paper to debate the issue, Walton's critical indebtedness to Rhys—further evidence of which will be given later on—suggests that she adheres to his theory. Although, as mentioned previously, this choice is not textually problematic when adapting the Second Branch, utilization of Rhys's theory allows for greater moral and ethical debate within the story. This enables the text to achieve what Susan Sellers refers to in *Myth and Fairytale in Contemporary Women's Fiction* as a "balancing act" between following and altering established narratives. Sellers argues that using the given material enables the author to open the text from the inside out (27–30).

Opening the Second Branch of the *Mabinogi* is akin to un-wrapping a set of nested Russian Matryoshka dolls. Branwen is at its center, but who is Branwen? In *Branwen Daughter of Llyr*, Proinsias Mac Cana spends most of the book discussing the Branch's Irish connections. His analysis of the character of Branwen is less than thorough:

> Branwen herself is a shadowy wilting figure of whom it might be said with some truth that she never comes to life until she comes to die ... she is but a shadow ... Branwen [is] morally passive throughout to whatever fate and her superiors have in store for her ... this passiveness adds to the sense of inevitability in Branwen's tragedy, so that her lack of character may be to some degree its own compensation [179–80].

It is unclear from this passage whether Mac Cana is referring to Branwen's lack of character delineation, her lack of moral character, or both. If the former, there is little evidence to the contrary. If, however, Mac Cana is equating Branwen's lack of dialogue with moral passivity, I would argue that he has failed to open the last Matryoshka. *The Children of Llyr* uncovers what Mac Cana stops short of by using Branwen's actions in the Second Branch to inform the delineation of her character in the novel.

The novel describes Branwen's arranged marriage to Matholuch as the first of its kind in that country, although there is no mention of the uniqueness of the marriage in the *Mabinogi*. "Never had a woman of the Old Tribes left her kin and her island save as the victim of fraud or force. Such a thing was unheard of, incredible..." (Walton 160). Bran even expresses a note of outrage at Matholuch's request for Branwen's hand, stating: "I am no king of the Eastern World to give my sister away like a cow" (Walton 160). By referring to Bran's people as "the Old Tribes," the novel clearly places them in a past not only for the reader, but in the world of the novel as well. Theirs is a fading society. Matholuch's arrival by fleet of ships can be seen as a cultural invasion. By transforming a standard political marriage into a revolutionary act, the novel highlights the gender stereotypes implicit in such an arrangement.

Although Bran ostensibly requires his sister's consent, stating: "let the girl get a look at him, and we will talk about it" (160), it is clear that both he and Matholuch are motivated by desires which have nothing to do with Branwen's wants or needs. Caradoc, Bran's only issue, is the first acknowledged son of a High King of the Island of the Mighty (Walton 153), and as such, Bran secretly wants Caradoc to rule after him. Yet according to the matrilineal society of the Old Tribes as depicted in the novel, Branwen's sons will inherit after Bran's death. Matholuch is consumed by a similar patriarchal greed. Although aroused by Branwen's physical form, "he never forgot what else that lovely body was: a strategic treasury, the shaping place, the gateway into this world of kings to come. Of the lords of this island that was greater than his own..." (Walton 161–2). Bran wants to change the laws of inheritance, allowing his biological son to inherit the throne after him, and he thinks his course will be smoother with Branwen married to another king in Ireland. Matholuch wants to use the current laws of inheritance in order to gain power over the Island through the son he hopes to have with Branwen: the rightful heir to the throne. Thus each man, while unwittingly divided in purpose, seeks the same solution to their similar desire.

Yet what of Branwen's desire? The text cleverly speaks through her silence: "Her eyes begged [Matholuch] to make her go, yet not to make her. To do the impossible, and take the pain out of sorrow" (Walton 161). She is torn between love for her family and passion for this new man, yet, if she knew with what eyes he looked at her, she might feel differently. "Branwen, perhaps like many other women in the age and circle of Gruffydd ap Cynan,[2] has divided loyalties..." (Thompson xliv). *The Welsh Law of Women*[3] describes the reason for this division: "Her links were dual. They lay both with the kin into which she was born and with the kin with which she was associated through her husband after marriage" (40). However, as the first wife of an arranged marriage, Branwen can not fully understand either the game in which she is participating, or her role in it. How, then, can she be expected to do other than move in the direction towards which she is guided by forces far more powerful than her own?

Their power lies not just in their higher political position, but in the claims each one has on her affections. Branwen is moved by love more than duty, another result of the novel's alteration of the source material, and one which gives the reader greater sympathy for her character. Love for Branwen plays no part in the actions of Bran and Matholuch. She is, for them, what French feminist philosopher Luce Irigaray would call "a use-value ... an exchange value ... in other words, a commodity," ("Another Cause" 368). Irigaray's analysis of the economic nature of male-female interaction is re-enacted for the reader by the triad of Bran, Branwen and Matholuch. In her essay "Another 'Cause'—Castration," Irigaray reverses Freud back on himself, explaining how woman is relegated to a purely biological function. She becomes the prop of the male sexual ego and guarantor against castration: "in her role as 'wife' she will be assigned to maintain coital homeostasis, 'constancy.' [...] She is wholly devoted to giving life ... source and re-source of life" ("Another Cause" 433–4). Irigaray's theory would have been fact for Branwen, according to *The Welsh Law of Women*:

> In a society dominated by kin groups of male agnates ... the position of woman was inevitably one of juridical inferiority and dual ties ... in most legal institutions, she, like the dumb and the mad, was regarded as a non-person recognised by society only as an appendage to some male with whom she was connected by ties of blood or by bonds of marriage [40].

Bran and Matholuch minimize Branwen to the size of her uterus, making it impossible for her to retain her sexual freedom. Ultimately, this loss results in the loss of her physical freedom as well.

If Branwen is a victim of these men's desire for power through paternity, does this confirm Mac Cana's belief in her moral passivity? Surely the novel would have made a stronger feminist argument had it made Branwen stronger: altered her character in addition to altering the plot. A Branwen who refused the role of a bought wife would surely have resonated more with post–First Wave readers. Such radical reinterpretations of folklore and myth are quite popular, and for obvious reasons. Yet to alter the text so dramatically would change the trajectory of the story. Walton's earlier words, to add only, "never alter," anything in the *Mabinogi*, are evident in the novel's adherence to the plot. This is a choice later advocated by Beer, who stresses the eternal present of a text. When written, the Second Branch was set in an ambiguous present.

It is only considered past tense to us; thus it is not an object upon which we can impose our own present ideologies. Beer goes on to point out that:

> Unless we believe in fixed entities—man and woman—we need to be alert to the processes of gender formation and gender change. We cannot construe this in isolation from other elements within a culture, and, moreover, we shall better discover our own fixing assumptions if we value the *unlikeness* of the past [81].

A novel representation (in both senses of the word) of the Second Branch, if set roughly in the time period of its oral origins, cannot ignore the cultural milieu in which it was created. Branwen must marry Matholuch. What the text provides, however, is an emotional impetus for the marriage — love — which is a motivation a reader of any generation can understand. That Branwen loves unwisely, falling blindly into the duplicitous hands of Matholuch, adds a layer of dramatic tension to the narrative.

Her lack of emotional insight — easily explained by her youth and sexual inexperience — coupled with her muteness, makes Branwen doubly crippled. She is a princess, the mother of kings even before her marriage, woman of a society which gives her the right to choose her partner(s). Yet all the rights in the world cannot protect anyone from their own bad choices. The fact that the marriage was at least partially Branwen's choice provides an explanation for the all-consuming shame which drives her to her death towards the end of the Second Branch. The *Mabinogi* records her last words: "'Oh son of God,' she said, 'woe that I was ever born. Two good islands have been laid waste because of me!'" (33). The blame Branwen places on herself seems puzzling to a modern reader of the Second Branch. The war which resulted in the destruction of both islands was not caused by her plea for rescue, but by her half-brother, Evnissyen, who commits murder during the celebratory meal of the two islands' new-made peace. Again, the novel retains these events, but when given insight into Branwen's thoughts, the reader understands the source of her shame.

When Matholuch orders her from his bed and into slavery, Walton's text views him through her eyes:

> All the pride in her, and all the hope that she, the strong and beautiful, might lie with heroes and bear the mighty ones of the earth.... This was the man she had loved, and allowed to father her child. This was her shame, and the shame of the Island of the Mighty! *But most of all your shame, your sorrow, Branwen, you who are alone* [196. Original emphasis].

These lines evoke feelings which are in accordance with the events of both the novel and its source material. Again, the omniscient narrator enables Branwen to speak in her silence. There is more of hurt pride here than betrayed love. The revelation of her husband's true nature has erased any trace of affection she held for him, leaving her with the realization that she willingly gave herself to someone unworthy of a Welsh princess. Although Branwen also identifies herself in procreative terms, as one given to "bear the mighty ones of the earth," the fact that she also describes herself as "strong and beautiful" shows that she holds her entire self in high esteem. Nor does she see herself as the morally passive victim Mac Cana would have her be. Branwen takes full — more than her share of — responsibility for her marriage. The marriage may have been arranged by two men, who cared little for her desires, but she knows the extent of them, and when faced with the reality of *whom* she desired, the image she held of herself shatters.

Ultimately, this exemplifies the importance which Walton places on both Branwen as a character and Branwen's self-image, making the novel a far stronger feminist statement than those which alter the plot to allow for a heroine who adheres to modern conventions of female strength. Rather than bringing Branwen into the twentieth century, the novel draws out the Branch's use of a much older folklore motif: that of the Calumniated Wife. The Calumniated Wife motif can be briefly described as such: a wife's new-born child is taken from her by a jealous party; she is accused of the crime and imprisoned.[4] In her essay, "The Calumniated Wife in Medieval Welsh Literature," Juliette Wood applies the motif to the characters of Branwen and Rhiannon, pointing out that "their persecution stems from the fact that these women are foreigners, intruders, as it were, into a world which will not readily accept them" (62). In the Second Branch, Branwen is in fact an exemplary wife. She gives gifts, gains honor and friends and gives birth to a son (Davies 27).

The Branwen of the novel is no different. There is no act at this point in the narrative to suggest a motive for her punishment. Mac Cana argues that this places Branwen firmly outside the Calumniated Wife motif, pointing out that her "punishment is not appropriate to her alleged crime" (161). The reasoning for it is so obscure that some critics believe it is the result of interference by a later redactor.[5] Evnissyen, after hearing of his sister's marriage, arranged without his participation, takes vengeance on the horses of the Irish, cruelly mutilating them (Davies 24). In the novel, Branwen reacts to the news with disbelieving laughter (Walton 167). Later, when Matholuch prepares to leave without her, "[s]he tried to scream his name, but a sudden growth in her throat choked her.... She had not wept, but her silence had been worse than weeping" (Walton 168). Again, the text does not merely work around Branwen's silence. It becomes a tool to describe the way in which her character reacts to these traumatic events. Branwen is an outwardly passive figure, as Mac Cana has stressed, a characteristic which conforms to the type of Calumniated Wife (Wood 70). And although Branwen is an acknowledged scapegoat, rather than an accused criminal, Wood points out that "the Welsh stories preserve both the structure and the cultural tensions of the Calumniated Wife motif" (69). Branwen is a queen in a foreign land, accused of a crime of which she is innocent and imprisoned for it.

Bran has already offered recompense for the mutilation of the horses with gold, new horses and a Cauldron of Rebirth, which restores life to the dead;

although, interestingly, it does not restore speech (Davies 25 and Walton 177). Matholuch accepts and the marriage goes forward. In the novel, these gifts are referred to as "face-price." The term is historically accurate. *Sarhaed*, or "insult price," derives from the older *wynebwerth*, meaning "face" or "honour price," according to *The Welsh Law of Women* (46). *Wynebwerth* is given in recompense for breaches of socially acceptable conduct, in addition to physical assault. "In the case of a woman it immediately affected any male on whom she was dependant" (Owen 47). The concepts of shame and honor behind *sarhaed* and *wynebwerth* are deeply imbedded in Welsh society (Owen 41). Rhys explains *wynebwerth* in *Celtic Folklore*, so Walton was aware of it (634).[6] The narrator's use of the phrase "face-price" and, more importantly, its treatment of Branwen as a victim of shame culture are yet more examples of the text's adherence not only to its source material, but to the historic milieu from which it came. The mutilation of the horses is used as the reason for forcing Branwen into slavery, in keeping with the Calumniated Wife motif. Wood remarks that, "The accusation of the wife by her husband's people is unique to the Welsh tales" (62), and Branwen's punishment, according to *The Welsh Law of Women*, is "a very obvious example of one kind of *sarhaed*" (59). Bran is now placed, as her brother, in the position of being both morally and legally responsible for effecting her rescue. The tables have turned, and it is now Matholuch who owes Bran *wynebwerth*.

Both Matholuch and Bran are keenly aware of Branwen's value. In Wales at that time, a woman's "role in society was an important and delicately balanced one ... for she was the genetrice in whose person lay the future of her husband's kin, and her own kin was well aware of this role and conscious of the need to preserve her honour" (Owen 40). These lines echo Matholuch's earlier reference to Branwen's body as a "strategic treasury." And although Bran shares this viewpoint, he also understands that her biological importance places him in charge of guarding her honor. Just as he is responsible for arranging her marriage, which resulted in her enslavement, he is responsible for extracting her from it. In a more familiar example, Malory's *Le Morte D'Arthur*,[7] Launcelot reminds Guenever that "the boldness of you and me will bring us to great shame and slander; and that were me loth to see you dishonoured." Were Guenever to be "dishonoured," the shame placed on Launcelot is akin to *wynebwerth*. Launcelot is clearly aware of this: "if that ye fall in any distress through willful folly, then is there none other remedy or help but by me and my blood" (272). Launcelot is responsible for Guenever because of their intimate relationship, just as Bran is responsible for Branwen because of their kinship.

This responsibility is legal as well as moral. Branwen's shame is akin to Guenever's when she is wrongly accused of murder. It is a public act done *to her*, beyond a private emotion, and Branwen fully realizes this. Both honor and shame have been laid on Branwen's shoulders in equal measure. She is the scapegoat for one king and the mother of another. She is, in a sense, a gateway through which all men must pass in their quest for power. Even slavery cannot degrade her intrinsic value. Branwen may not retain her self-worth, but she still knows what she is worth to others. Though her husband and his people no longer want her as their queen, she has still given birth to a king. Her son, Gwern, is the first in line to rule both Ireland and Wales.

In the character of Branwen the novel combines the modern notion of personal guilt and the pre-modern shame culture in which she lived. In the novel, what Branwen describes feeling can be empathized with by a modern reader as guilt. But the word used in the text is "shame." When the extradiegetic narrator, through exegesis on Branwen's thoughts, writes: "This was her shame, and the shame of the Island of the Mighty!" the narrative voice is not merely depicting a woman who takes too much responsibility upon herself. Branwen, as princess of the Island of the Mighty, is a public body. Her treatment by Matholuch reflects not only on her kinsmen, but on every citizen of Wales. Every blow she receives is a slap in the face to her entire country.

When Launcelot returns to Camelot to fight Sir Mador on behalf of Guenever, he states simply, "this battle ought to be mine" (280). And although love can be read into the text as a motivation, nowhere is the word mentioned. This is Launcelot's battle because, as he said earlier, her shame was his shame, and only his blood will spare hers. Bran's blood-ties to Branwen are more direct, heightening the degree of responsibility. Branwen's shame affects Bran as if it were his own. In medieval Wales, "expulsion from the marriage bed is regarded as one of the three shames of a wife" (Owen 59). Before Christianity took hold — as late as the fourteenth century — mutually consented cohabitation between a man and a woman was considered a legal marital union, giving the woman the status of wife (WLW 104). The *Mabinogi* only states, "And that night Matholwch slept with Branwen" (23): all that is necessary to constitute a legally-binding marriage. Therefore, by ejecting her from his bed, Matholuch has relinquished his role as her husband, thus returning her to Bran's protection.

In Walton, the body which coupled with Matholuch, Branwen believes, is "soiled:" that it has "betrayed her" by desiring him. These words emphasize her sense of public and private shame. Although, through the narrator, we learn that she believes it is "not worthwhile to fight, to try to save anything so cheapened, so degraded as herself," we also hear her resolution at the beginning of her slavery. "I will not break. I am a princess of the Isle of the Mighty, and before I am a person, and I will do the duty of both" (198–9). The novel format allows the reader to witness the internal conflict behind her silence, rather than bulking out the narrative with extraneous action. In accordance with the Second Branch, Branwen is consigned to slavery in the castle kitchen, receiving a daily blow on the ear from the butcher. She lives in this state for three years (Davies 27–8). The Second Branch explains that Ireland places an embargo on Wales in order to prevent news of Branwen's punishment from leaking to her brothers, but Walton's narrator, after quoting this section of the *Mabinogi*, points out that "it seems more likely that he sent false messages to her brothers in Branwen's name. So long a silence surely would have waked suspicion..." (Walton 197).

Such explanations of "unreasonable actions," or, in this instance, unreasonable inaction, are common in the text. Yet the phrasing of these explanations is markedly different from the rest of the narration. The narrator not only steps out of the story to comment on the action, he or she refers directly to the original source material. The explanation offered is not woven into the plot, it is a hypothetical aside. In this instance, the tetralogy is doing something very different from other works of fantasy fiction based on folklore or myth. The text does not merely acknowledge its source: it makes repeated reference to its narrative quirks, offering possible reasons as just that: possibilities, rather than direct action inserted into the plot. It could be argued that there are two narrators of the tetralogy: the narrator who tells the story and the narrator who comments on the telling of it.

According to Rimmon-Kenan, in her work *Narrative Fiction: Contemporary Poetics*, commentary is the sixth and highest degree of narrative perceptibility. The fifth degree is "reports of what characters did not think or say" (97–99) or, in other words, an omniscient narrator such as that used by Walton to tell the story. Such a narrator is extradiegetic, as mentioned previously, meaning it is superior to the story it narrates (95). The novel uses ulterior narration: a text written in the past tense. However, it also uses anterior narration, which Rimmon-Kenan defines as predictive (89–90). By applying this terminology to the text, it becomes clear that the novel has two distinct narrators. The extradiegetic narrator is the one who tells the story. This is the narrator who gives voice to Branwen's silence and illuminates the complex motivations behind her arranged marriage. However, there is a second narrator. It is heterodiegetic: outside the narrative. This is the narrator who uses anterior narration to comment on the story. Although an extradiegetic narrator at level six could conceivably be providing such commentary, the fact that these comments reference an exterior text—the *Mabinogi*—as the explicit source of the novel, thus making it clear that the story is not original, places this narrator outside of the narrative, thus making it heterodiegetic. The use of two separate narrative techniques: extradiegetic/ulterior and heterodiegetic/anterior, make it clear that there are two separate narrators.

The former narrator accepts the tetralogy's use of magic without question or explanation. When Branwen rescues a starling from the kitchen cat and teaches it to speak, the realism of the narrative style insures against a suspicious reader. This is fantasy fiction, after all. Readers expect magic. Yet, once again, that second narrator pipes up from the shadows:

> We do not know how she kept it from speaking in the daytime, or how she taught it where it must go. In those days when the subtle senses were not yet lost, when the walls between the worlds were not yet so firm ... understanding may have been easier between men and birds [Walton 201].[8]

The reader is not allowed the escapism which one could argue is the *raison d'être* of fantasy fiction. The heterodiegetic narrator insists on drawing attention to the inexplicable in the *Mabinogi*. Rather than diminishing the literariness of its source material, however, this has the converse effect of raising it to a level of historic importance worthy of such examination. As Rimmon-Kenan points out:

> [T]he need to attribute textual segments to speakers as well as the urge to account for apparently false statements and reconcile seeming contradictions exists only when the text is grasped as in some sense analogous to (mimetic of) reality [114].

The bifurcated narrator wants us to wonder about the hows and whys of the magic without denying its legitimacy. This is not a fantasy, according to the narrator. It is not a more realistic, or surrealistic, version of a well-worn fairy-tale. It is a creative re-visioning of an important historic document written by a real person, in a real time "long long ago," in a real "land," which is only "far, far away" depending on where you are standing.

Notes

1. From *Rhiannon: an Inquiry into the First and Third Branches of the Mabinogi*. Gruffydd also notes that "the author of the Mabinogi has been unusually successful in dissociating himself from the modern world of his own generation" during its composition (3).
2. Gruffydd ap Cynan was a Welsh prince of Irish birth during the 11th century who repeatedly gained and lost power over the course of his adult life. His right to rule was a source of dissension within Wales at that time. See *Gruffudd ap Cynan: A Collaborative Biography*. Ed. K.L. Maund.
3. Referred to hereafter in the in-text citations as "WLW." The essay within the book, "Shame and Reparation: Woman's Place in the Kin," is referenced in-text by the last name of its author: Morfydd E. Owen.
4. See Stith Thompson's English translation of Antti Aarne's *The Types of Folklore*.
5. See Mac Cana.
6. Rhys's spelling is *gwynebwerth*, which is the full form of the word. The "g" is dropped when converting to the feminine.
7. The medieval composition of *Le Morte D'Arthur*, first published in 1485 after Malory's death, but derived from 13th century stories, makes it contemporaneous with the composition of the *Mabinogi* (found in multiple manuscripts dated no later than 1325, according to Gruffydd). Thus the societal norms are analogous.
8. It is important to note that the text uses the word "men" to represent humankind, a technique which was common in the first half of the twentieth century, when Walton was composing the tetralogy. The feminist movement had not yet raised the issue of its gender-specific connotations.

Works Cited

Beer, Gillian. "Representing Women: Re-presenting the Past." *The Feminist Reader*. Ed. Catherine Belsey and Jane Moore. Basingstoke: Palgrave, 1997. 77–90.

Gruffydd, W.J. *Rhiannon: an Inquiry into the First and Third Branches of the Mabinogi.* Cardiff: University of Wales Press, 1953.
Irigaray, Luce. "Another 'Cause'- Castration." *Feminisms.* 2nd ed. Ed. Robyn R. Warhol and Diane Price Herndl. New Brunswick: Rutgers University Press, 2007. 430–437.
_____. "This Sex Which Is Not One." *Feminisms.* 2nd ed. Ed. Robyn R. Warhol and Diane Price Herndl. New Brunswick: Rutgers University Press, 2007. 363–369.
Jenkins, Dafydd and Morfydd E. Owen, eds. *The Welsh Law of Women.* Cardiff: University of Wales Press, 1980.
The Mabinogion. Trans. Sioned Davies. Oxford: Oxford University Press, 2007.
Mac Cana, Proinsias. *Branwen Daughter of Llyr.* Cardiff: University of Wales Press, 1958.
Malory, Thomas. *Le Morte D'Arthur.* Vol. 2. London: J.M. Dent & Sons Ltd, 1956.
Purkiss, Diane. "Women's Rewriting of Myths." *The Feminist Companion to Mythology.* Ed. Carolyne Larrington. London: Pandora Press, 1992. 441–457.
Rhys, John, *Celtic Folklore: Welsh and Manx.* Vol. 2. London: Wildwood House Ltd, 1980.
Rimmon-Kenan, Shlomith. *Narrative Fiction: Contemporary Poetics.* London: Methuen, 1983.
Sellers, Susan. *Myth and Fairy Tale in Contemporary Women's Fiction.* Basingstoke: Palgrave, 2001.
Thomson, Derrick S. *Branwen Uerch Lyr.* Dublin: The Dublin Institute for Advanced Studies, 1961. i–xlvii.
Walton, Evangeline, *The Mabinogion Tetralogy.* New York: The Overlook Press, 2002.
Wood, Juliette. "The Calumniated Wife in Medieval Welsh Literature." *The Mabinogi: A Book of Essays.* Ed. C.W. Sullivan III. London: Garland Publishing, 1996. 61–78.

Disavowing Maternity in Evangeline Walton's *The Virgin and the Swine*
Fantasy Meets the Female Social Protest Fiction of the 1930s

Deborah Hooker

When commentators of whatever ilk analyze a crisis of the magnitude of the Great Depression, their language tends to recast America's previously sustaining ideologies in literary and, thus, "less real" terms; that is, such rhetoric recasts those prior, collective investments in certain cultural scripts as fragile, consensual illusions. For example, both Edmund Wilson and John Dewey saw the decline of the "myths and legends of new Era prosperity" as "the collapse of a [particular] romance." For Wilson, it was the collapse of "the romance of the legend of the poor boy [that] was the romance of democracy,'" an influential story that functioned to "conceal 'the monstrosities of capitalism.'" Dewey understood the collapse as the "breakdown of that particular romance known as business," imploding because the "normal insecurity [of market society]" had mushroomed far beyond the point of concealment (qtd. in Hanley 243).

Indeed, rhetoric of this sort suggests that to confront suffering as monumental as that experienced by many Americans during the thirties—or in other contemporary situations, for that matter—blurs the line between the common-sensical "real" and the fantastic in both experience and literary representation. Certainly the proletarian, "bottom dog" realism and the journalistic exposés of the thirties are replete with episodes that can only be described as the "scarcely believable." And although speaking neither about that decade in particular nor of its literature, China Miéville's reminder of "the relation between fantasy as genre and the fantasy that permeates apparently nonfantastic culture" (330) is apropos in that context.[1] That is, as a genre "construct[ing] an internally coherent but actually impossible totality," fantasy "mimics the absurdity of capitalist modernity" (331), a "monstrosity" that Leftist social realists limned under the aegis of American Communist Party aesthetic directives.

It is in the context of considering fantasy to be as potentially politically subversive as any other genre that I propose to collate Evangeline Walton's 1936 high fantasy novel, *The Virgin and the Swine*, with the social protest fiction of three Leftist or Leftist-associated female-authored texts of the thirties: Tillie Olsen's *Yonnondio*, Agnes Smedley's *Daughter of Earth*, and Meridel Le Sueur's *The Girl*—a relationship that Walton criticism has not previously considered.[2] Clearly there are many ways in which Walton's lush novelization of the *Mabinogi*'s ancient Welsh myths and legends differs from the fiction of these Leftist-affiliated writers, where working-class characters move through a contemporary landscape of failed farms and mining camps in the American West to the slaughterhouses and speakeasies of midwestern American cities. Walton's mythical time/space of Wales is peopled by demigods who routinely employ the "never possible"—at least in terms of our current scientific gestalt—of ancient magic, where the touch of a willow wand or some well-woven words create day-long illusions or transform erring humans into bestial form. Yet that magic, as Walton's masculine protagonist Gwydion wields it, is primarily devoted to destroying an illusion whose demise science would confirm: that reproduction is a divine female ability in which men have no part.

Walton develops what is latent in her source—the demise of matrilineage, whose presence is evinced by the emphasis on the uncle/nephew relationship, and the subsequent rise of patrilineage (Sullivan, "Inheritance" 347, 353). In its wake, marriage, father-right, and the reified virgin as potential reproductive property are instituted. However, she explores the ramifications of that shift from the perspective of Arianrhod, a woman who is scarcely more than a cipher in the original: Arianrhod disappears from the *Mabinogi* after she is tricked into giving birth and into fulfilling certain maternal obligations against her will.[3] Walton's *The Virgin and the Swine* gives Arianrhod a more extensive and complex narrative presence. While Walton's text, to some degree, reflects the spirit of her source, validating Gwydion's triumphant paternity through the "magical" use of his sister's body, *The Virgin and the Swine* shares the political critique of female sexual vulnerability and exploitation that each of these social realist novels depicts in the context of working-class marriage

In the context of the Communist party-supported male bildungsromans of the thirties, the fiction by Olsen, Smedley and Le Sueur also redresses a neglected perspective: they limn the sufferings of the Great Depression from the viewpoint of working-class woman—mothers and daughters alike. And they, too, foreground the emotional and psychological cost of dutiful, if not coerced, maternity within working-class marriages. As Laura Hapke argues, all three texts challenge the era's glorified and dominant earth mother figure: John Steinbeck's Ma Joad. The selfless maternal buttress of family unity portrayed in *The*

Grapes of Wrath or in Mike Gold's *Jews Without Money*, for example, reflects and helped perpetuate revolutionary party priorities in the United States. While not blatantly ignoring gendered or domestic discontents, the political left and the literature it supported largely subordinated "the woman question" to the larger "project of the transition to workers' power": its primary focus was on the public world of labor and solidifying working class consciousness through strikes and union organizing—contexts in which men figured most prominently and which party literature extolled (Foley 165). In their work, Olsen, Le Sueur, and Smedley expose what Party collectivist rhetoric minimized: "the antagonisms between working class men and women" and the "divisive effects of sexism" (Coiner 157). These texts also evince the tensions involved in representing "the repression of female sexuality" within working-class familial relations, which "precedes" and complicates an understanding of class oppression (Rabinowitz 88).

Olsen, for example, shifts the focus from public to domestic labor and portrays the working-class housewife/mother brutalized by poverty and by equally brutalized husbands, revising the masculine fantasy of the selfless, domestic "heroines" who, like Ma Joad, enthusiastically sacrifice for the workers' revolution. In the tortured, semi-autobiographical retrospective of her early life, Smedley's protagonist, Marie Rogers, explicitly disavows maternity, deducing from her mother's experience that it means emotional and intellectual degradation and the denial of meaningful work. Similarly, the often conflated subjectivities of Olsen's working-class wife and mother, Anna Holbrook and her daughter Mazie, dramatize the "reproduction of motherhood," to use Chodorow's familiar phrase, as an imaginative if not literal "dead end" for working-class daughters. In *The Girl*, conversely, Le Sueur mythologizes motherhood as the prime vehicle for eros, the true source of any political collectivity. Coming dangerously close to affirming the masculine fantasy of the all-nurturing mother, Le Sueur avoids that stance by situating her eponymous Girl's experience of maternity within a desperate, revolutionary all-female collective comprised of widows, abandoned wives and mothers, and prostitutes.

While Le Sueur's concluding vision of "manless motherhood," as Hapke calls it (88), realistically depicts and, indeed, valorizes heterosexual relationships before removing her protagonist to the all-female collective, that all-female formation and its implicitly revolutionary potential to nurture and protect women outside the traditional confines of marriage obliquely echo what *The Virgin and the Swine* suggests about the collective agency of women before the recognition of fatherhood and institutionalized matrimony "enslave[d] women" (Walton 203). Through Arianrhod's enhanced narrative presence, Walton, too, explores the meaning of maternity for a daughter situated within a time of profound "class" and gender upheaval, that is, in a potentially or actual "revolutionary" context. Like Smedley's Rogers, Walton's Arianrhod explicitly disavows marriage and maternity as an obstacle to other ends she wishes to pursue; however, like Rogers and Olsen's Mazie, she will find that her disavowal leads to isolation, madness, and in Arianrhod's case, self-destruction.

What information we have about Walton's early life in Indianapolis during the twenties and thirties gives no sense that her experience of the Great Depression bears any resemblance to Smedley's and Olsen's working-class experiences nor to those of the women that the middle-class Le Sueur documented in her journalism and fiction.[4] However, as Brian Attebery reminds us, speaking of that exemplary high fantasist, J.R.R. Tolkien, the *Lord of the Rings*' author lived and wrote "in the very middle of the Modernist generation," and his work was undoubtedly "shaped by war and disillusionment." The trilogy's "troops and trenches, its heroism and despair, its beleaguered home front and its enemy to the East is as much a product of WWI as is *The Sun Also Rises*" (*Strategies* 41). By the same logic, Walton's masterful high fantasy construction can be similarly assumed to refract the sociocultural milieu of the American thirties despite her use of ancient source material: the sparse and fragmented *Math of Mathowny*, the fourth "branch" of the Welsh *Mabinogi*.[5] The world that Walton depicts, working from Lady Charlotte Guest's nineteenth-century translation of the fourteenth-century *White Book of Rhydderch* and the *Red Book of Hergest*, could hardly appear to differ more from the ravaged rural and urban landscapes through which Olsen's, Le Sueur's and Smedley's working-class protagonists toil. Yet, like texts of social realism, it is a world in which a woman's ability to procreate will illuminate her "real" class position, as a gendered subordinate to men of the same "class."

The world of *The Virgin and the Swine* is a recognizably feudal one, albeit populated by the magical personages of Welsh myth. Its primary agonists are the children of the goddess Don — Gwydion and Arianrhod, who preside over what Walton calls the "Old Tribes" in their individual realms in the northern kingdom of Gwynedd — and the heroic Pryderi, ruler of Dyved and the New Tribes in the South, of the lineage of the sea god Llyr. While her guiding principle was to "alter little, but add much"[6] to her source, the lion's share of her additions occur in her depiction of the sibling relationship between Gwydion and Arianrhod as they square off over the question of who directs and controls maternity (Sullivan, *Welsh Myth* 22) in the context of a waning matrilineal system. *The Virgin and the Swine* clearly suggests that matrilineage implies a different, if not higher, status and valuation of women than patrilineage. And certainly, it depicts a dispensation where the sister's role is essential to the lines of inheritance, power, and wealth — where she provides the heir who will succeed an uncle rather than operating as the lynchpin in the more strictly lineal father-to-son transmission. That organization suggests some "wider" or at least different space for female agency and some near-equality with a male sibling who would act as surrogate father to her child. Arianrhod will be taught her altered position in this transition as a procreative body to be manipulated according to her brother's, not her own, desires. In the transition from matrilineality to patrilineality, Walton's novel suggests, the brother's betrayal is necessary.

Walton's oft-remarked ability to personalize this sociocultural conflict is informed by considerable research. As she acknowledges in her foreword to *The Island of the Mighty*, Ballantine's 1970 reprint of re-titled *The Virgin and the Swine*: "Nobody can prove that the two social systems"—matrilineage and patrilineage—"implied in *The Mabinogion* ever met while both were still in full force—just as nobody can really prove that they didn't. But when peoples like the Picts first began to suspect what mid-Victorian would have called the 'facts of life' they must have gossiped and speculated very much as the people in this book do" (xv–xvi).

The first book of her novel, "The Pigs of Pryderi," is full of debates about the uncertainties of human reproduction, which the skeptical remarks from one of the men who accompany Gwydion on his mission to steal the swine illustrate:

> If a woman's sleeping with a man makes a child, why does she not have more of them at a time? How can we be sure how many gettings into bed, or how many men, it takes to make one child? It might have several fathers; you cannot tell what goes on inside of women ... I myself have slept with some who have never had any children at all, and I am a proper man. You cannot be sure that that is what does it. It may be irreverent to the gods to say so [16–17].

Such remarks punctuate Gywdion's errand to Dyved, whose success instigates a bloody battle in which the victim of the theft, Pryderi, is killed; the theft also parallels, necessitates, and colors the sexual plotting in which female bodies will also be seized to demonstrate—as in Arianrhod's case—a secure knowledge of "what goes on inside of women." That is, Gwydion's theft of the novel foodstuff is accomplished by means of his considerable magic, a skill increasing in power as he is being trained by Math, his uncle, in preparation for Gwydion's ascension as ruler of Gwynedd, a line of inheritance that, in fact, represents the imperiled matrilineage: the passage of the kingship through Math's sister, the goddess Don, Gwydion's mother. The theft both foreshadows and sets up Gwydion's reproductive trickery where Arianrhod is concerned inasmuch as he orchestrates the theft as part of a ruse to engage Math in battle with Pryderi. Taking Math away from his castle enables Gwydion's brother, Gilvaethwy, to rape Math's virgin footholder, Goewyn, a crime for which Math later punishes both by transforming them into beasts of the forest for three years. However, that period of atonement also represents another opportunity to acquire knowledge of breeding and reproduction: each man alternates yearly, taking a male and female animal form, and reproducing. And it is after his release from animal form that Gwydion proposes Arianrhod as Goewyn's replacement since she "makes a boast of her virginity" (119).

As his transformation of Gwydion and Gilvaethwy demonstrates, Math presides over all in the Welsh kingdoms, and he is, as in the source, a murky figure. Both a terrestrial and a cosmic ruler, he is able to intervene in the affairs of his subjects, able to hear their thoughts on the wind, and yet subservient himself to some larger cosmic design. "He was the master of evolution, awarding to each the tests that he was ready for, and the lessons that he most needed to learn (122). However, Walton also employs Math also as a kind of prescient, historical chorus, whose vision of time and change is framed within her personal philosophy of evolutionary reincarnation, " the only religious concept," she asserted in an interview with Paul Spencer, that "makes sense" of "so vast and complex a world as ours" (8). Hers is an organically-figured, cyclical metaphysic, whose ultimate end is imagined as "the true marriage" (203), the annulment of sexual difference in a mystical oneness that will dissolve the gendered conflict at the heart of *The Virgin and the Swine*. Math's historical and moral commentary therefore, allows Walton to present the decline of matrilinearity and the rise of patrilinearity as a temporary stage in the evolution of human perfectibility. While Gwydion's desire for an heir and for paternal control over lineage and inheritance are fulfilled, as in the source, Math's commentary about its harmful effects on women and on male/female relationships nevertheless compromises Gwydion's "victory." Math foresees that "the recognition of fatherhood will enslave women, "depriving her of absolute ownership of her own body." Instead, her body will be at the disposal of "one man's pleasure" ... "his to demand rather than hers to give or withhold as her heart bids" (203):

> It will likewise make it a crime for that body of hers to be aware of any but the one man, while his still retains his ancient freedom. And the end of it all will be that there will be no free women left in the world, to love for love alone as women did aforetime. All women will either submit their flesh to the yoke of marriage, or hire it out for gold and silver in base barter; and both alike will be the bondmaids of men [203].

In a very real sense, Math's prediction resonates with the depictions of the contemporary marital relationships depicted in all three social protest novels: male sexual prerogative and thus female sexual vulnerability obtains in marriage, resulting in the inevitable degradation of affection and the repeated and unwanted pregnancies of coerced maternity; the sexual double standard obtains as well — representations I will address more fully momentarily.

Although neither Walton nor the source elaborate on the meaning of the footholder's requisite virginity, it is presented as a necessity for Math; the only time his feet may be out of that virgin lap is when he fulfills the responsibilities of warlord. At the very least, this configuration seems to symbolize a notion of power or kingship "grounded" in a hyper-valuation of virginity, an importation, Walton suggests, from the "New Tribes" of the South. Virginity, its changing significations and how those significations can be politically utilized, is the issue over which Gwydion and Arianrhod initially square off.

Arianrhod, a powerful sorceress, resides with her less powerful, younger sisters Elen, Maelan, and Gwennan in The Castle of the Silver Wheel. One of Walton's frequent narrative comments about the source material tells us that the name Arianrhod meant "Silver Wheel," and that she was "perhaps worshipped by the common folk as incarnation as well as priestess of the moon, the benevolent silver sky-lady herself come down from her pale bright chariot in the heavens to watch more closely over the tides she ruled, and make them gentle to the coasts of men" (124). Although the scant criticism on the earliest of Walton's *Mabinogion* novels and the frontispiece of *The Island of the Mighty* describe Arianrhod as Gwydion's "Terrible Sister" or as a "power-hungry" woman, Walton goes out of her way to paint brother and sister with very similar strokes. Though Arianrhod is admittedly spoiled and vain, she is no less in the right about shaping the direction of her life and desires than is Gwydion. Her desire for power, in the changing sociopolitical context, is no greater or less than his. Both are impetuous, and have "ever sought new things," (129) as Gwydion's theft of the pigs demonstrates, and both selfishly pursue their own desires, using all the guile and magic at their disposal: "The weakness of both" the narrator tells us, "was to think cleverness supreme above the laws, which were only made for it to outwit. And that tameless mental activity was the secret of their endless attraction for each other, and also of their endless skirmishing" (136). Indeed, there are more than a few subtle hints that theirs is or has been an incestuous relationship and both confess numerous times that their chief sexual attraction is to the other. While Walton depicts Gwydion sympathetically, the means by which he achieves his desire, legitimized by the general male dominance accepted in the source, aren't fully endorsed. In fact, as Math later chides Gwydion, "when you set out for Caer Arianrhod to fetch me your sister, you ... set aside the ancient laws and used guile and trickery ... "as is your way is when your wish is strong" (164–165). Later, Math concludes, "And her fame, not yours, has paid the price..." (235).

That is, when Gwydion suggests to Arianrhod that she replace Goewyn, it is clear that he knows, perhaps from personal experience, that she is not what she claims—not according to the new meaning of "virgin," which signifies a woman without knowledge of sex. For Arianrhod, a virgin signifies, as it had of old, simply a woman who has not given birth. Arianrhod believes, however, that she can trade on the new allure associated with virginity simply by avoiding childbirth; she has no intention of foregoing the pleasure of sex. If the New Tribes prize that virgin condition, then she intends to fashion herself as the object of that fascination, to exploit it, one might add anachronistically, like Elizabeth I, Britain's most famous queen. And if she resides at Math's castle, she will also have the time and opportunity to learn his magic. She understands that the people are beginning to view a virgin "as something precious and rare.... It gives a woman a prestige and a glamour—and a value that she never had before. To the people it is a mystery. They think it makes me stronger in magic" (130–131). Gwydion, nonetheless, chides her for her attempt to create herself as "the image of an unattainable desire; this dream of the beauty of a virgin princess surrounded by sorceresses and maidens on an island in the sea, and cold as the waves about her" (131).

At this first sustained meeting between brother and sister, it becomes clear that both view the new concepts concerning marriage and the overvaluation of virginity as so much foolishness, but foolishness that is, nonetheless becoming more influential. Gwydion "could not conceive of chastity except as a market value and a pose — something contrary to natural laws" (59). He also believes that "if there is mystic might in virginity," that might "lies in the fact, not the name" (130). The institution of marriage also strikes them both as a strange and "unnatural" index of morality, especially the idea of a women's "body always at your lord's pleasure whether love burns in you at that hour or not..." (130).

However, Gywdion offers Arianrhod an alternative role to virgin footholder — what he desires, that she bear a child, presumably a boy, a nephew, who would become the next ruler of Gywnedd according to matrilineal succession. Compared to whatever "mystic might" virginity might hold, he touts childbearing as "the miracle that is greater than magic" (130). When Arianrhod demurs, he offers her marriage, if she insists upon "cling[ing] to the customs of Dyved" (131). Despite the fact that the people of the North would not automatically condemn such a brother-sister union, and despite the fact that Gwydion promises to lay no "yoke or constraint on you" if she will "follow old custom and give the realm of Gwynedd an heir," she refuses: "I would keep my value, not lose it" (131). Yet, aware that "no man could sit securely on the throne unless he were born of a woman of the royal house of Gwynedd," she suggests that Gwydion approach one of her sisters.

Arianrhod rejects the old signifiers of value, maternity and childbirth, as "a miracle that has grown stale through over-much happening. It is a thing that almost any woman can do. And I would do new things; I would have magic and power and splendor ..." (131). When Gwydion reminds her that "Don our mother ... was proud to give us birth" (131), Arianrhod flatly points out that she is "different from the daughter of Mathonwy ... my desires are not her desires ... I live in my time, not hers" (131).

Like Gwydion, Arianrhod sees which way the sociocultural wind is blowing and attempts to capitalize on it; she refuses maternity knowing that her role would be to raise a son who could then become ruler after her brother. Her power would be through him and not her own. Given the growing acceptance of knowledge about sex, that is, that women do not have the power to produce heirs alone but require men in the process, she intends to present herself in the image of what is now what valued in a woman, a virgin, but wielding the allure virginity confers for her own purposes. Despite the fact that the new valuing of virginity already indicates a masculine valuation, Arianrhod thinks she can exploit the appearance of that value for her own ends— not to have it serve another, which would be to fashion her as a mother in thrall to someone else or simply to repeat the "old ways," a context in which maternity is increasingly losing its status as divine. "There is nothing else that you could ask of me that I would not give you. I will not have children and be no longer called a virgin.

Let us be friends, Gwydion" (133). While he appears to acquiesce, "one thread of his being was always likely to remain cold and temperate, unforgetful of his purpose ..." (134).

The noncensorious attitudes about female sexuality that Walton explores through her novelization of the *Mabinogi*, her indictment of marriage and motherhood as female sexual bondage, are frequent and explicit refrains in Agnes Smedley's 1929 *Daughter of Earth*. In Smedley's work, Marie Rogers's retrospective narrative recounts her attempts to escape the formative effects on her sense of herself that a destitute working-class childhood has produced. Raised on a failing Missouri farm and in the degraded shanties of a Colorado mining camp, Rogers attempts to flee that degradation through work, first as a frontier teacher in New Mexico and then as student in various schools in the West, and finally as a Socialist journalist and activist in New York City. Throughout her story, she is "haunted by the specters of her mother and aunt — the grim alternatives posed to most women of her class..." (Lauter 424).

On the one hand, Rogers sees her mother brutalized and degraded by her dependence on a man who frequently abandons his family when he can find no work to support them, and she repudiates the maternal role because she has seen its emotional and intellectual degradation played out in her own mother. The frequent refrain about "nagging, whining women who depend upon men for money" (206) summarizes her views of what it means to be a wife. Her mother's example has also taught her that "the respectability of married women seemed to rest in their acceptance of servitude and inferiority.... Women had to depend upon men for a living" (188). Nevertheless, when her mother dies in Marie's late teens, she comes to realize that what unites the two is "a bond of misery that was never broken" (114).

Although Rogers accuses both parents of "pervert[ing] my love and my life," making her believe that she was "an evil creature" (12), her mother is singled out for the most responsibility because, as a prisoner of the home, she takes out her rage and sense of impotence on those who are there with her — her children. The depth of this abuse is conveyed when her mother punishes Marie for her natural childhood acts of imagination: "It was never clear. What was truth and what was fancy, I could not know. To me the wind in the tree tops really carried stories on its back. The red bird that came to our cherry tree really told me things" (11–12). When Marie revealed these observations, her mother would switch her, announcing to the neighbors that "I have but one child who is stubborn and a liar, and that is Marie.... As the years of her unhappy married life increased, as more children arrived, she whipped me more and more" (11).

Marie clearly identifies the paternal position as the space of imagination and possibility if only for the fact that he is not forced to "stay home." Despite his penchant for brutality and abandoning the family to look for work or on the pretext of looking for work, Marie's memories of her father positively endow him with creative possibilities: she recalls hearing "the voice of my father, the deep beautiful voice, as he labored in the hayfields" of a northern Missouri farm (Smedley 9). "He was a man with the soul and imagination of a vagabond. People listened to his stories, filled with color and adventure, but they did not always believe. For he was not one of them; he was almost a foreigner, in fact. His family was unknown to our world" (10). Marie identifies her father with agency, with possibilities beyond the material circumstances of now. When she embellishes the story about a tornado that spared their house, claiming that "fences, men and horses tumbled out of the air around us" she defends that embellishment: "For I was my father's daughter" (15).

The one female figure that Marie lionizes is her Aunt Helene, whose early wage labor does what Rogers's mother cannot — bring in money to support the destitute family, and Rogers sees the equality with men that a paycheck confers: "When Helen began to draw weekly wages she took an equal place with my father in our home. She was as valued and she was as respected as he...." Her mother, conversely, remained silent and apart, as the "two of them talked to each other as equals; they laughed or they quarreled as equals" (49). When Helene moves away, becomes a prostitute, and continues to send the family money, her stature increases in Marie's eyes; she decides that she "would rather be a prostitute than a married woman. I could then protect, feed, and respect myself, and maintain some right over my own body. Prostitutes did not have children, I contemplated; men did not dare beat them; they did not have to obey" (50).

Like Smedley's novel, Tillie Olsen's *Yonnondio*—a novel written in the 1930s—foregrounds the physical and psychological trauma of brutalized wives, mothers, and daughters. While the Holbrook family moves through environments similar to those the Rogers occupy — the failed tenant farms, the degraded shanties and tents in western mining camps, and, for Mazie's family, the slaughterhouses of Kansas City — her work stays primarily focused on the domestic sphere, on the mother/daughter/familial experience, and how "female working-class subjectivity is constructed out of the memory of childhood experience: gender restrictions, poverty, and sexual vulnerability" (Rabinowitz 99).

Even more so than Smedley's work, *Yonnondio* dramatizes the child's impression of the omnipresent sexual vulnerability of the wife/mother in the male-headed, working-class household, the specter of Mazie's future. When we first meet Mazie in the Wyoming mining community, she is, at six years old, a "precocious child, sensitive and unaffected" (Roberts 81), and we follow her for three years, where she learns what it is to become as a woman in the working-class family: that is reflected in her mother, "a backward-looking character whose young maternal years were the 1930s and who cannot distinguish her decision from a child from that imposed on her" (Hapke 6). What Mazie learns about maternity and the female place in marriage is indeed what Walton's Math had foreseen: that a woman loses "the absolute ownership of her own body"

(208). The sexual vulnerability that is a woman's lot within marriage is telegraphed when Mazie overhears the marital rape of her pregnant mother and witnesses the bloody miscarriage that ensues.

As Hapke rightly describes it, "Mazie's characteristic state is fear" (83) because her mother Anna exists in a state of incipient madness, induced by the degradations of poverty, her exhaustion at producing and caring for four children, and her omnipresent sexual vulnerability. And like Marie's mother, Anna Holbrook takes out her frustrations and helplessness on her children. Bitter and brutal, Anna Holbrook frequently beats Mazie until she is "degraded" (32). However, Olsen's understanding of the depth and source of Anna's desperation is also telegraphed by the fact that in one "projected ending" to the novel, "Anna dies of a self-induced abortion" (Hapke 79).

In Le Sueur's double-voiced text, *The Girl,* there is, as in Smedley, no censure of female sexual expression. In fact, in reframing the "classic story of the country girl who comes to Town" (Pratt ix)—in this case, to St. Paul/Minneapolis in the mid-thirties—one voice of the text is a paean to the power and validity of erotic experience. The sweep of the narrative lyrically carries the eponymous Girl along on a single-minded quest to experience heterosexual sex. When she obtains work at a speakeasy run by Belle and her husband Hoinck and befriends another waitress, Clara, who survives by moonlighting as a prostitute, sex is the thing "everyone around her seems to know ... except the Girl" (Pratt xiv). That desire is, in large part, tied up in her desire to have some intimate knowledge of what her own mother's life has meant. When she returns home to the country for her father's funeral, she begs her mother "to tell me something ... mama had something, she had her life, her children, she knows what it is even if she can't say it right out. She knows something. She knows what it's about. She has felt something" (49). Despite what the Girl encounters in the cold and hunger of St. Paul/Minneapolis, despite the wives, who, like her mother, cling to abusive husbands and give birth to children in abject poverty or who are forced, as the girl nearly is, into backroom abortions, despite her own alienated sexual experience with her "boyfriend," Butch, and her rape by two of his "business associates," her mother's words suggest that there is a depth of feeling derived from that relationship that justifies all of the abuse. Her mother tells her: "I hope you'll marry a man like papa and have children.... To know each other, to touch each other, sing, feel it in your breast and throat. You have to live it and die it and then you know it ... then it's in you and you always know it" (52). Motherhood in Le Sueur is mystically anointed as the prime source of social cohesion. That is but one voice in the novel.

Yet, interspersed within these unfailingly lyrical expressions of fealty to erotic life and maternity are the voices of women acknowledging the degradations of life that make working class motherhood quite nearly a crime. Towards the end of the novel, when she is homeless, jobless, and pregnant, the Girl gets picked up for vagrancy and put in a maternity home; there she faces sterilization after she gives birth and the loss of her child to forced adoption. Amelia, an activist for women on relief and the voice of organized labor, frees her from the home and installs her in a "women's warehouse," while she mounts a public protest for food and health care for the sick and pregnant women on relief. One of the women in the warehouse where the Girl takes refuge proclaims: "You eat and sleep.... Sometimes you sweep the floor, but it doesn't matter, and you hate sleeping with your husband because you're scared of having a baby ... it's got so a woman is crazy to have a baby" (153). Belle, who is listening, and who admits to having had 13 abortions, "began to cry" (152). In a long, Swiftian diatribe on the system that oppresses them all, Amelia imagines the final indignity of capitalist exploitation in addition to being worn "out on the belt, in the mill, the factory. They get your blood and bones one way or another.... It's too bad they can't kill our babies and eat them like suckling pigs. What tender meat that would be. Stuffed babies with mushrooms. Why not?" (Le Sueur 166).

In all but Le Sueur, maternity is represented as an untenable trap, and in *The Virgin and the Swine*, Arianrhod's maternity occurs in the context of a literal trap, one that Gwydion sets for her when he proffers the role of Math's virgin footholder. Convinced that her lack of offspring is testament enough of her virginity, when she appears before Math, she thinks to fool him through her ability, like Gwydion's, to hold "her mind blank as a cloudless sky is blank..." (136). Asked if she is a virgin, "she willed herself into a concentrated forgetfulness as utter as though memory had been drowned in the wash of might seas" and answers, "Lord, I know not otherwise than that I am." (137–138). Math then commands Arianrhod to step over his willow wand bent "into a strange shape" (139), and here Walton frankly embellishes the source with language denoting childbirth: Arianrhod writhes as though in "the grip of a sudden convulsion.... It seemed to her that her own body was tearing itself to pieces ... (138). And from that "test," two curious "objects," as the source says, fall from her body: one is "a fat, golden-haired baby boy, sitting on the wand upon which he had fallen with too much force to please him... (139). That child, Dylan, magically swims off during his druidic baptism, his sea-going nature giving credence to Elen's claim that Arianrhod had, in the recent past, consorted with one of the men of Caer Sidi, the kingdom under the sea. Yet Arianrhod "drops" another "object," as she runs from the hall in shame, and before anyone can see, "Gwydion sprang forward and snatching up the object ... wrapped it in a piece of satin ... and made off with it through the door" (139). He secrets it in a chest at the foot of his bed, which functions as a kind of magical incubator: "What charms Gwydion had put upon that chest to make it complete the incomplete and give the sexless and unshapen, shape and sex, remains a mystery to this day" (148), but months later, he is awakened by a cry coming from the chest. Inside is a boy on whose "shapely small head gleamed here and there down bits of fuzz moon-gold as Arianrhod's own oft-sung locks" (147).

Yet, for all that, I don't think we can call these "objects," as Charlotte

Spivak does, Arianrhod's "natural" children or her "natural sons" (85).[7] Even Gwydion admits that Arianrhod "was not already with child." Instead "the charm of the wand" was to expose her if "she who called herself a virgin had ever held within her man's seed and most of us believe that nowadays that there is such a thing as that — it should come forth from her in that state of fruition which it would naturally have reached during the time that it had lain within her; or should so have lain" (143). Arianrhod was not pregnant — not in the conventional physiological sense. Instead, these "objects" that fell from her body were the materialized traces of her past sexual activity, not children already conceived. What the test signifies in that act of materialization is the masculine prerogative to control and direct the reproductive body of the women. Arianrhod's test depicts a final ideological appropriation as much as and perhaps even more than some physiological understanding. And the coercive nature of that appropriation is unmistakable.

Jean-Joseph Goux in *Symbolic Economies: After Marx and Freud* suggests that "with respect to patriarchal society, the matrilineal family is its beginning" (218). That is, the "isolated position of the father," (218) which Gwydion certainly figures here, "is both very ancient and very advanced ... it is not only the historical beginning of the ideology of paternity but its ever recapitulated origin..." (218). The magical elements of the "test" seems to represent, as Goux suggests, that "paternity is not and never has been constituted on the basis of the genetic function of reproduction but rather — from the beginning — as an *ideological* position or better, interposition — that is, as a power in *another* sort of reproduction...." Matrilineality still admits to the ideology that "the father informs and the mother materializes" (220); or, in more Aristotelian terms, the male is associated with and "brings *form, type, notion, idea, pattern* whereas the female furnishes the materials" (220). This gendered dichotomy between "accidental" reproduction and "design" or pattern also surfaces in Walton's language describing the unique nature of Gwydion's paternity: "most men come by a child by chance ... in the pursuit of their desire for woman; and never greatly labored for and not always highly welcome. But Gwydion "had not got a child save by dint of wishing and willing and plotting and laboring. This child was perhaps more intimately his than any other child has ever been any other man's" (148).

The test and the incubating chest bear the coercive connotations of both a rape and a forced birth inasmuch as both deny female agency. The magic that is deployed exposes an absolute certainty about the workings of Arianrhod's generative body, and it is manipulated for Gwydion's ends. In this, the question of Gwydion's and Arianrhod's incestuous relationship, which is never wholly clarified, is important: is the child's likeness to both a function of "magic" or sex? The ambiguity perfectly indexes the double nature of myths of conception, which Walton's source certainly represents. As Goux explains, "Sexual reproduction is simply in the image of a social reproduction that itself, it is true, derives its most persistent imaginary from sexual generation.... Thus the monopolization of ideological reproduction by fathers, their privileged social power, directly results in the mythical negation of the physiological role played by the sperm in conception and in the associated belief in a perfect, ideal, and supernatural transmission of image and likeness"(224).

A similar ideological trap is figured in *Yonnondio*, although the imagery of that trap, which Olsen presents from a masculine perspective, conflates the maternal body and maternal desire with the agents of capitalist exploitation. The most traumatic event of Mazie's life is recounted in "The Iron Throat," the opening section of *Yonnondio*, in an event that metaphorically blames the reproductive "desires" of women for the degraded and deadly working conditions that men endure in the mines.

In this episode, Mazie is returning home after following her father to a bar. She is assaulted by Sheen McEvoy, the half-crazed victim of a mining accident which has left his face "a red mass of jelly ... like a heart torn suddenly out of the breast ..." (16). In his mania, he kisses Mazie and attempts to throw her, as a placating sacrifice, "a little child, pure of heart," into an empty mine shaft, which he calls an "ol' lady" (15). In his delirium, he imagines that "the mine was hungry for a child; she was reaching her thousand arms for it" (15). He thinks "she only takes men 'cause she aint got kids. All women want kids.... Sheen McEvoy will fill you, ol' lady" (15). Although Mazie is rescued by a night watchman, the image of McEvoy's face and the assault surface to disturb her throughout the narrative, especially at times of other trauma or stress.

The imagery of this episode presents us with the complicated tangle of masculine helplessness and victimization translated into an image of male sexual aggression against an "unfilled," metaphorical mother and actual assault upon a child. In "The Iron Throat," which is itself a metaphor for the mine's whistle, McEvoy transfers his hatred and trauma, born of the exploitative mining industry, onto a maternal, earth figure: the suggestive hole in the ground. Mazie, as a child, thus figures, on one hand, his potency—"I'll fill you, ol' lady"—as well as the literal child sacrificed to the mining company—so it will stop claiming the lives of the men who work there. That disturbing collation of a consuming maternity as the answer to and the cause of exploitative labor recurs in representations of Mazie's mother, Anna. The monstrous woman, as seen by the working man, is repeated when Jim Holbrook, Anna's husband, observes "the querulous children, half sick, always hungry—thinning, while Anna grew monstrous fat as if she were feeding on them" (56).

For Smedley's Marie Rogers, love and the pregnancy it potentially brings is the trap. Her early notion of love, she tells us, is:

> a confused, colorful mingling of the fairy tales I had read as a child and novels I had read later on; a very lovely but forbidden thing. Still it was not connected with that other forbidden expression — sex. Sex had no place in love. Sex meant violence, marriage or pros-

titution, and marriage meant children, weeping nagging women and complaining men; it meant unhappiness, and all the things that I feared and dreaded and intended to avoid [360].

Although she thinks "marriage without sex was possible — a sort of a romantic friendship, two people working together and remaining friends" (193), when she attempts that arrangement, even with the accommodating Knut, her first husband, the Platonic nature of their relationship does not last.

Despite Arianrhod's attempt to capitalize on the illusion of virginity, the aftermath of her forced maternity strands her, as it similarly strands the daughters in Smedley and Olsen, in a realm of subjective torment. Yet her shame and anger ultimately escalate into a vengeful madness aimed at the brother who betrayed her and at those he holds dear. When she discovers that the "object" of her failed virginity test is alive and growing, Arianrhod will not prove anymore flexible on acknowledging the child than she has been in producing it. Though she was "intolerably disgraced in her own mind because she had given birth.... The guilt was that of those others who had caused her deeds to come to light..." (158).

The persistence of mother-right nevertheless lingers in Gwydion's attempts to have Arianrhod name the boy and, later, supply him with arms, the materials and symbols of his manhood traditionally supplied by the mother. When the boy is introduced to Arianrhod, Walton describes "the pain of a woman who has been tricked where she most trusted.... You to betray me, my brother, you of all men on earth." (184). She refuses to give the boy a name and to provide him arms. Yet, through the force of his illusions, Gwydion tricks her into giving the child, Llew, both. However, she stymies Llew's final need—for a wife—by a clever curse: "Never shall his side touch a woman's of the race that now dwells upon this earth" (230).

Again, as if a final magical affirmation of their control over the formerly divine female ability to create, Math and Gwydion create a wife for Llew: Blodeuwedd is formed from "great heaps of the blossoms of oak and broom and meadow-sweet, the finest and fairest to be gathered in the woods and fields.... What better material could there be to shape life than blossoms, the frail blooming beginnings of life?" (240). And yet, their beautiful creation, Blodeuwedd, has a mind of her own; after she and Llew are married, she takes a lover, with whom she conspires to kill her husband, and though Llew is not killed outright, he is transformed into a wounded and decaying eagle.[8] In another instance in which Math mitigates the positive perception of Gwydion's triumph, he reminds him that he is "not guiltless of the boy's misfortunes; for you would have him born before the time came for the men of Gwynedd to know fatherhood. And he whose birth violates the established order of things must always pay" (235).

When Arianrhod learns that Gwydion has "gone forth through the land to seek the soul of Llew" (293), her reaction is a mixture of pity and growing madness: "He had been her flesh and of the blood of Don. His death may have seemed to her but a sterile gain, for it could not re-establish her claims to virginity.... Nor could she rejoice in that for its own sake, for she had never hated him for his own sake. She had not even known him" (295). Instead in a kind of twisted symmetry, she orchestrates the death of her other "son," Dylan, who appears on hearing the news of Llew's death. And thereafter, she descends into the final madness, having "no hates left to satisfy. She had no purpose. She had nothing" (307). But she rages against Gwydion in terms that remind us of the violation she has endured and which indict "the whole race of men, that would not be content with the gifts she gave them, but must beguile her into make more, and then seem right." She contemplates "with joy of the snare in which she had trapped Govannon. He had been her arm to strike Dylan ... as her own body had once been the egg for Gwydion to hatch his chick out of. Now tonight a man too knew how it felt to be a dupe and a tool" (309).

To foil Gwydion's plan to find Llew, in whatever form he may be, she unleashes the dark magic that "no wizard has dared to use" since its secrets had been buried deep in Caer Arianrhod (313). Her sisters desert her and the Castle of the Silver Wheel as she invokes the magic, and Arianrhod and all the sorcerers who remain with her perish .At the moment of her death, when the powers she summons overwhelm her, Arianrhod realizes the "cause of her doom. She had broken the first of laws, that ancient law upon which the being of the race depends: that a woman shall guard, not take the lives of the children she has borne." But her last words are not for her "children," but for the brother who betrayed her: "Gwydion, it was for you I did it! Oh Gwydion! Oh My Brother!" (320).

Gwydion ultimately rescues Llew, and in the book's tenderest moment, the moment that Walton says inspired her to attempt the novelization, he coaxes the nearly dying eagle in whose shape the young man lives down from a tree into his arms, where he restores Llew's human form with a touch of his wand. And yet, in her fidelity to the Welsh materials, Walton's novelization ends with the same image as the source — one of a man alone. After he has exacted his revenge on Gorony Pevr, his wife's lover, Llew "turned and went back toward Mur Y Castell, where Gwydion and the men of Gwynedd waited" (365) and where, as Arianrhod's curse still obtains, no woman waits or ever will. In an oblique way, Walton's novelization and its source both suggest in this concluding image some awareness of the costs, in terms of real human intimacy, of institutionalizing sexual inequality.

Walton confessed in a 1972 interview that despite the fact that "most people think of my work as escape fiction, I always felt they embodied universal truth, but as a rule, people seem to want their universal truths in everyday dress.... I sometimes think people will believe anything no matter how illogical, so long as you put it in a gingham apron" (qtd. in Pavillard 11). Her reference to the truth effect attached to the commonsensical "gingham apron" alludes to a particularly American brand of skepticism, a "strong distrust of the fantastic in our nation's make-up ... expressed in [both] lore and letters" (16), the desire not to be fooled, or fooled again, perhaps—something Brian Attebery documents at length in *The Fantasy Tradition in American Literature*. We are the heirs to a history in which "Puritanism, rationalism, [and] transcendentalism—each in its turn acted to circumscribe or suppress the stock of supernatural legend motifs that American inherited from Europe" (Attebery 26). Nevertheless, like the realist texts' often bleak, often lyrical evocations of working-class life in the thirties, Walton, too, depicts the costs—to women and children—of coerced maternity and masculine dominance in marriage, suggesting its long, long and "impossible," history. As Miéville reminds us:

> In a fantastic cultural work, the artist pretends that things known to be impossible are not only possible but real, which creates mental space redefining—or pretending to redefine—the impossible. This is sleight of mind, altering the categories of the not-real. Bearing in mind Marx's point that the real and the not-real are constantly cross-referenced in the productive activities by which humans interact with the world, changing the not-real allows one to think differently about the real, its potentialities and actualities [339].

And, in a similar engagement between the real and the not-real—between 1930s Great Depression literature and the magical world of the *Mabinogi*—Walton's fantasy also intersects with these female-authored, Leftist-oriented works on the terrain of their own materialist philosophies.

Notes

1. In her *Fantasy and Mimesis: Responses to Reality in Western Literature*, Kathryn Hume argues, convincingly to my mind, that rather than attempting to pigeonhole a particular work as a fantasy and another as "realistic" according to some fixed, generic criteria, a more productive way to proceed is to recognize that all fiction represents a "characteristic blend or range of blends of the two impulses... (20). One is "mimesis ... the desire to imitate, to describe events, people, situations, and objects with such verisimilitude that others can share your experience...." The other impulse is "fantasy, the desire to change givens and alter reality," an impulse motivated by the petty and the sublime: "boredom, play, vision, [the] longing for something lacking, or need for metaphoric images that will bypass the audience's verbal defenses... (20).
2. Smedley's *Daughter of Earth* was initially published in 1929; only the first chapter of what became *Yonnondio*, "The Iron Throat," appeared in the thirties, in a 1934 issue of *Partisan Review*. While not published in novel form until 1974, Olsen composed what became *Yonnondio*'s remaining chapters during the thirties. Similarly, six sections of Le Sueur's *The Girl* appeared in issues of *New Anvil* and *New Masses* from 1935 to 1945, but the novel itself did not appear until 1978, when it was published by West End Press. For assessments of Walton's *Mabinogion* tetralogy, see Shinn, Spivak, and Sullivan (*Welsh Celtic Myth in Modern Fantasy*). Kenneth J. Zahorski and Robert H. Boyer also provide an excellent overview of the earliest critical responses to Walton.
3. The source to which this refers is Lady Charlotte Guest's translation. Walton iden-

tifies the Guest translation as her source in an interview by Paul Spencer, which appeared in *Fantasy Review* in March 1983.

4. Interviews subsequent to Ballantine's reprinting of *The Virgin and the Swine* as *The Island of the Mighty* in 1970 outline some of the general contours of Walton's early life in Indianapolis. Zahorski and Boyer tell us that Walton was born in 1908 into the midst of an extended family that, on her mother's side, had produced "a number of scholars and writers." Her maternal grandmother, for example, was a Quaker minister, with "a real gift for words" and her cousin, Clifford C. Furnas, became a prominent university administrator and co-founder of NASA (114). In terms of socioeconomic class background, out of the three—Olsen, Le Sueur, and Smedley—Walton is probably closet to Le Sueur, who was born in 1900 in Murray, Iowa to a family that Constance Coiner describes as "middle-class and educated." Le Sueur's parents, also like Walton's, divorced when she was young. At the end of the Depression and the start of World War II, Walton moved with her mother to Tucson, Arizona, where Walton lived until her death in 1996.

5. In his "Inheritance and Lordship in Math," (*The Mabinogi: a Book of Essays*), C.W. Sullivan III follows W.J. Gruffydd in asserting that *Math* "is not a mythological document nor, for that matter, is it a socio-cultural or historical document. But it does contain all of those elements—and more." He also agrees with Mac Cana that *Math* "is not a mythological document in the primary sense: it is a literary construct which makes use of mythological and other materials. Its author is not a mythographer conscientiously recording the traditions of the gods for their own sake, but a gifted writer shaping the shattered remains of a mythology to his own literary ends"(qtd. in Sullivan 352–53). Andrew Breeze advances the thesis that the "gifted writer" of the Four Branches is a woman: "Gwenllian (about 1098–1136), wife to "a prince of West Wales" and daughter of Gruffudd ap Cynan," who was "a king of Gwynedd." Among the litany of reasons Breeze submits for Gwellian's authorship are her qualifications as a "woman of high rank," who possessed "an intimate knowledge of courts and a royal attitude to life, especially clear in her women characters," along with "a detailed knowledge of Gwynedd...." Breeze also notes the tales' more substantial focus on female experience than would have been common in a male-authored heroic narrative (75–79).

6. Her precise words, from the Foreword to *The Island of the Mighty,* are: "This is the Tale of Math, Son of Mathonwy, King and perhaps originally High-God of Gwynedd in the druidic days of Britain, not quite as it is told in the ancient Red book of Hergest. I have altered little, but added much" (xv).

7. For her admittedly demented orchestration of Dylan's death and her attempt to drive Llew's spirit beyond even Gwydion's reach, Charlotte Spivak characterizes Arianrhod as motherhood's "negative embodiment:; she is "a Terrible Mother ... who turns her own remarkable powers ... against even her own natural sons" (85–86).

8. This spelling of "Blodeuwedd" follows that in the Lady Charlotte Guest translation from which Walton worked.

Works Cited

Attebery. Brian. *The Fantasy Tradition in American Literature: From Irving to Le Guin.* Bloomington: Indiana University Press, 1980.

_____. *Strategies of Fantasy.* Bloomington: Indiana University Press, 1992.

Breeze, Andrew. *Medieval Welsh Literature.* Dublin: Four Courts Press, 1997.

Coiner, Constance. "Literature of Resistance: The Intersection of Feminism and the Communist Left in Meridel Le Sueur and Tillie Olsen." *Radical Revisions: Rereading*

1930s Culture. Eds. Bill Mullen and Sherry Lee Linkon. Urbana: University of Illinois Press, 1996. 144–166.

Foley, Barbara. "Women and the Left in the 1930s. *American Literary History* 2.1 (1990): 150–169.

Goux, Jean-Joseph. Symbolic Economies: After Marx and Freud. Trans. Jennifer Curtiss Gage. Ithaca: Cornell University Press, 1990.

Guest, Charlotte. Trans. *The Mabinogion*. (London: J.M. Dent; NY: E.P. Dutton), 1906.

Hanley, Lawrence F. "Popular Culture and Crisis: King Kong Meets Edmund Wilson." *Radical Revisions: Rereading 1930s Culture*. Eds. Bill Mullen and Sherry Lee Linkon. Urbana: U of Illinois Press, 1996. 242–263.

Hapke, Laura. *Daughters of the Great Depression: Women, Work, and Fiction in the American 1930s*. Athens: University of Georgia Press, 1995.

Hume, Kathryn. *Fantasy and Mimesis: Responses to Reality in Western Literature* (New York: Methuen, 1983).

Lauter, Paul. Afterword. *Daughter of Earth*. 409–427.

Le Sueur, Meridel. *The Girl*. 2nd Revised Ed. Albuquerque, NM: West End Press, 2008.

The Mabinogion. Trans. Lady Charlotte Guest. Everyman Library 97. London: J.W. Dent, 1937.

Miéville, China. "Marxism and Fantasy: An Introduction." *Fantastic Literature: A Critical Reader*. Ed. David Sandner. Westport, CN: Praeger, 2004. 334–344.

Olsen, Tillie. *Yonnondio: From the Thirties*. New York: Delacorte, 1974.

Pavillard, Dan. "Fantastic Author Escapes on the Typewriter." *Tucson Daily Citizen* 2 December, 1972. 11–13.

Pratt, Linda Ray. Introduction. *The Girl*. 2nd Revised Ed. Albuquerque, NM: West End Press, 2008. ix–xxi.

Rabinowitz, Paula. *Labor & Desire*: *Women's Revolutionary Fiction in Depression America*. Gender and Culture Series. Chapel Hill: UNC Press, 1991.

Roberts, Nora Ruth. *Three Radical Women Writers: Class and Gender in Meridel Le Sueur, Tillie Olsen, and Josephine Herbst*. NY: Garland, 1996.

Shinn, Thelma J. *Worlds Within Women: Myth and Mythmaking in Fantastic Literature by Women*. Contributions to the Study of Science Fiction and Fantasy 22. NY: Greenwood Press, 1986.

Smedley, Agnes. *Daughter of Earth*. Old Westbury, NY: Feminist P, 1973.

Spencer, Paul. "Evangeline Walton: An Interview." *Fantasy Review* Mar. 1985: 7–10.

Spivak, Charlotte. *Merlin's Daughters: Contemporary Women Writers of Fantasy*. Contributions to the Study of Science Fiction and Fantasy 23. NY: Greenwood Press, 1987.

Sullivan, C.W., III. "Inheritance and Lordship in *Math*." *The Mabinogi: A Book of Essays*. Ed. C.W. Sullivan, III. New York: Garland, 1996.

_____. *Welsh Celtic Myth in Modern Fantasy*. Contributions to the Study of Science Fiction and Fantasy 35. New York: Greenwood Press, 1994.

Walton, Evangline. *The Island of the Mighty*. Rrpt. *The Virgin and the Swine*. Willet, Clark & Co., 1936. NY: Ballantine Books, 1974.

Zahorski, Kenneth J. and Robert H. Boyer. *Lloyd Alexander, Evangline Walton Ensley, Kenneth Morris: A Primary and Secondary Bibliography*. Boston: G.K. Hall, 1981.

"An Age-Old Memory"
Arthur Machen's Celtic Redaction of the Welsh Revival in The Great Return

Geoffrey Reiter

Today, the literary reputation of Arthur Machen (1863–1947) rests largely on a series of dark supernatural tales he penned in the 1890s. Though Machen himself maintained a discreet distance from the Decadent movement of the period, he is often associated with the movement because of the imagery and thematic content of his work during that decade. Two of his books—*The Great God Pan and the Inmost Light* (1894) and *The Three Impostors* (1895)—were published as part of the "Keynotes" series from John Lane, the firm which published many of the most infamous Decadent novels. Whether they were concertedly Decadent or not, these books drew the ire of critics for some ghastly scenes and veiled implications of sexual depravity. Many of Machen's best-known later publications—*Hieroglyphics* (1902), "The White People" (1904), *The Hill of Dreams* (1907), and *Ornaments in Jade* (1924)—were first written in the last five years of the nineteenth century. After the scandals of his early work had died down, Machen became relatively obscure for a while, though he saw his reputation rise on two occasions during his lifetime. The first occurred during World War I, when Machen was writing for the *Evening News*. On September 29, 1914, shortly after the British military was forced to retreat at the Battle of Mons, Machen published a short story in the newspaper called "The Bowmen," describing visions of ghostly bowmen who come to the aid of the soldiers and hold off the Germans. For some time after the story's publication, reports began to follow of eyewitnesses claiming to have seen these bowmen or, in other cases, a host of angels. The incident brought brief notoriety to the tale of "The Bowmen" and its author, though the furor died down soon. Machen's other flirtation with popularity occurred in the 1920s. In England, it was Machen's idiosyncratic personality as much as his writing that caught on, but in America, where pulp fiction was entering its heyday, his long-neglected horrors saw a revival. While the Machen boom had largely ended by the close of the 1920s, he was remembered by aficionados and, eventually, by scholars and critics as well.

Because of this chain of events, however, much of Arthur Machen's twentieth-century writing — with the exception of "The Bowmen" — has received little attention. One work which has been unjustly neglected is his novella *The Great Return* (1915). Written from the perspective of a curious investigative journalist, *The Great Return* chronicles sightings of the Holy Grail — or the "Sangraal," as Machen calls it — in the tiny Welsh town of Llantrisant. After its serialization in the *Evening News*, the tale was printed by the little-known Faith Press, despite the fact that Machen claims to have "urged Mr. Burgess [the manager] to desist from his plan" (Danielson 45), fearing the book would sell poorly. And he was apparently right, because "a huge and dusty mound of 'Great Returns'" ended up "lying in a cupboard" (45). Under the right conditions, however, the story might have been just as well regarded as "The Bowmen." It was the circumstances of its publication that led to the disastrous sales, not the inherent quality of the work.

Indeed, *The Great Return* is far more complex a work than most modern Grail books piled in publishers' backrooms. In writing this little novella, Machen wove together several layers of Welsh mythology and history to produce a subtle, beautiful work of fiction. One the one hand, he was evoking recent religious history, tying in features of the 1904–05 Welsh Revival. Largely forgotten now, the Welsh Revival was an impassioned religious awakening that spread through the Welsh countryside for several months, and at the time, it was widely reported by journalists throughout Britain. Yet by tying the revival in *The Great Return* back to the ancient and sacramental symbol of the Holy Grail, Machen transforms what historically had been a low-church Protestant phenomenon into an event with ritualized, mystical resonances that transcend the Welsh Revival's very particular theological context. The result is a mediation of Christian polarities. Machen skillfully blends echoes of the 1904–05 Welsh Revival with more ancient Welsh hagiology and variants of the Grail legend in *The Great Return*, creating a setting in which all of Christian Wales can worship together in the presence of a divine mystery.

Today, the Welsh Revival is little known to any but evangelicals and historians. At the time it was occurring, however, it was widely recorded and remarked upon. Modern technologies of transportation and communication transformed the seemingly local, rustic religious happening into a national, and very soon an international, phenomenon. Newspapers covered it, doctors studied it, and religious leaders and theologians investigated it. And after its conclusion, the revival's impact would still be felt around the world. While other factors may have been involved in revivals abroad, J. Edwin Orr notes that "[t]he Welsh Revival was the farthest-reaching of the movement of general Awakening, for it affected the whole of the Evangelical cause in India, Korea and China, renewed revival in Japan and South Africa, and sent a wave of awakening over Africa, touching also strategic countries in Latin America and the Islands of the South Seas" (189). The notoriety of the event did wane over time, but if it was a flash in the pan, it was certainly a brilliant flash.

The question of what exactly the Welsh Revival was—its origins, its methods, its characteristics, its aftermath—is a question that dogged supporters and detractors alike at the time, and it continues to be debated among scholars, historians, and religious leaders. Even defining the term "revival" can be hazardous. Edith L. Blumhofer and Randall Balmer observe that at its root, "[t]he characteristic of revival (and one implied in the term itself) is that it assumes some sort of decline, whether real or imagined, out of which the faithful are called to new heights of spiritual ardor and commitment" (xii). They "often build upon a sense of loss and the need to recover a former plateau of spirituality. There is an evocation of a golden, halcyon past that serves as an implicit rebuke to the spiritual languor of those who stand in need of revival" (xii). In this sense, Wales seemed—at least to many Christian historians—the ideal place for such an occurrence. Contemporaries read Welsh Protestant history as a veritable sine curve of spirituality. According to R. Tudur Jones, many religious leaders prior to 1904 lamented the Welsh people's spiritual and moral apathy, while predicting that a new manifestation of the Holy Spirit was on its way. One such leader was Dean David Howell, a prominent evangelical in the Church of Wales, who died on January 15, 1903. That month, his petition "The Great Need of Wales" was widely circulated; it enjoined the need for "[s]piritual revitalization! ... Not a local disturbance ... but a kind of spiritual saturation, that overflows the country as a whole, that would immerse all classes with the Baptism of the Holy Spirit" (qtd. in R. Jones 284). Howell's plea was merely the best distributed of many such appeals.[1]

The Welsh Revival was a diffuse affair, and so it is likely misleading to label any particular moment as its "beginning." Its origins are often attributed to a series of meetings in New Quay initiated by Joseph Jenkins, an early leader in the movement. These regular meetings commenced in February 1904, and Jenkins believed the revival began at that point (R. Jones 286). But if Jenkins helped initiate the Welsh Revival, he would not prove to be the public face of it. That distinction belonged to Evan Roberts, a coal miner's son who left his ministry training in late 1904 to travel the Welsh countryside during the heart of the revival. The plain-looking but fiery twenty-six-year-old, roaming the land with a retinue of family, friends, and young women, quickly became a media superstar. At the height of his ministry, Roberts visited countless locations in Wales, often making unscheduled appearances, sometimes not even announcing his presence when he arrived. He might prepare a planned sermon and speak for hours or give a brief extemporaneous address; he would even refuse to speak if he felt a spiritual hindrance in the room. Evan Roberts thus became a supremely mysterious figure, even after reporters from the *Western Mail* began following him regularly. Attempting to direct the spotlight away from himself and toward God, Roberts unwittingly made himself complicit in this perception, as Edward J. Gitre observes: "Not wanting to steal God's thunder, [Roberts] insisted: the revival was not my doing but God's.... Rather than deflecting attention this appeal served only to *enhance* the revivalist's personal mystique" (802).

Gitre maintains that the Welsh Revival, unlike past revivals in the region, was distinctly modern in the way it spread. Media such as the *Western Mail* and other journalistic sources carried news of the revival every day throughout England. Roberts's breakneck pace through Wales, meanwhile, was made possible by the expanded use of the railway, a technology that allowed him to move so rapidly about the countryside that he appeared to transcend space and time. Roberts "could not have achieved this level of self-fashioning without British technological modernization" (Gitre 802–03). But the revival transcended even Roberts, particularly in parts of North Wales where the railway system was less developed. Noel Gibbard suggests that "[i]n some areas of the country Revival broke out spontaneously without any outside influences" (64), small pockets appearing concurrently with the larger tide of revival in the south. Even in the south, Roberts's publicity obscures the fact that he was only one of many revivalists preaching and praying across Wales. The well-known pastor and theologian G. Campbell Morgan had a very pointed response to those who sought a clear origin of the movement:

> In the name of God let us all cease to try to find it. At least let us cease to trace it to any one man or convention. You cannot trace it, and yet I will try to trace it tonight. Whence has it come? All over Wales ... a praying remnant have been agonizing before God about the state of their beloved land, and it is through that the answer of fire has come. You tell me the revival originates with Roberts. I tell you that Roberts is a product of the revival [173].

As Morgan indicates, the revival was a team effort, whose members included not only Evan Roberts and Joseph Jenkins but individuals such as Rosina Davies, E. Keri Evans, Florrie Evans, Sidney Evans, R. B. Jones, R. Tudur Jones, W. S. Jones, Seth Joshua, H. Elvet Lewis, W. W. Lewis, Jessie Penn-Lewis, and Evan Roberts's siblings, Dan and Mary Roberts.

The Welsh Revival ended as abruptly as it had begun, though pinpointing any specific moment or event that marked its conclusion is difficult, if not impossible. One significant factor was the seclusion of Evan Roberts. Even with the assistance of the railway system, Roberts could hardly have been expected to maintain the intense schedule of meetings and visits which characterized his ministry at the height of the revival. The number of engagements in which he participated dwindled as 1905 progressed; and in 1906 he began a stay at the home of Jessie Penn-Lewis, a participant in the revival who had grown to believe that "the cross had not been given its rightful place in Welsh preaching" (R. Jones 332). Perhaps under her influence, Roberts began to feel the same way, and during his stay with Penn-Lewis he became reclusive. By this time, outbursts of revival were sporadic, if there were any left.[2] In its immediate aftermath, many theologians and revivalists lamented its lack of staying power across Wales. J. Vyrnwy Morgan, writing in 1909, asserted that ultimately, "the Welsh Revival of 1904–5 was not preceded by any peculiar spiritual apathy, and it has not been followed by any marked progress of either a political or religious character" (244). While some believed the intensity of the revival was simply unsustainable, others believed that the institutional church stifled the Holy Spirit's power. Nantlais Williams, a Presbyterian minister in Ammanford, lamented,

> Words often heard from the mouths of some during the first years of the Revival were, "Oh, the Revival has ended now, everything has gone back to normal here." For such people the Revival was nothing more than a sad misadventure which disturbed the peaceful quietude of church and country, and because they thought there was no good in it, or rather, they did not want to see any good in it, they rejoiced in the slightest sign that it was disappearing. Very often the words, "Oh, the revival is dead," were nothing but the expression of a deep desire in the speaker's heart [qtd. in B. Jones 272].

Indeed, while many Protestant churches—both Anglican and Dissenting—welcomed the Welsh Revival, others criticized it harshly. Though generally characterized by a spirit of cooperation between denominations, conflicts arose over theological matters, such as infant baptism versus believers' baptism, or Calvinism versus Arminianism (Gibbard 152, 155). Evan Roberts often became the focal point of attacks, as in the case of the congregational minister Peter Price, who distinguished between a genuine revival that was occurring and "a sham revival, a mockery, a blasphemous travesty of the real thing," led by Evan Roberts (qtd. in Gibbard 153).

Whether through apathy, hostility, or inevitability, the Welsh Revival was clearly over long before the first decade of the twentieth century had ended. But while it would eventually become little more than a historical asterisk, its influences were wide ranging. Countries in every continent were impacted, directly or indirectly, by the events in Wales those months. England and Ireland were both affected, as were many European countries, particularly Norway. More globally, the Welsh Revival "was certainly the most important source for the revivals in India, Madagascar, Patagonia and France, while its influence on Korea, Australia and New Zealand was not so direct but not unimportant" (Reinhardt 124). Moreover, clear connections can be traced between the Welsh Revival and the Azusa Street Mission, often regarded as the birthplace of the Pentecostal movement.[3] If a century's distance has caused the memory of the Welsh Revival to fade, those who lived through it or even read about it at the time would have been unlikely to forget what they had seen or heard.

The Welsh Revival of 1904–05 was but one of many palimpsests written across the history of Wales since Christianity's first arrival there. The Christian faith had of course arrived with the presence of Rome, and in 304, the Romans Julius and Aaron were martyred in Caerleon under the persecutions of Emperor Diocletian. Soon afterward, however, the empire began to tolerate the Christian religion under Constantine the Great in 313, and under Theodosius I it became the official imperial religion in 380. But Christianity really began to take root in Wales during the fifth century, leading to what has been called the Age of the Saints (ca. 500–700). With the fall of the Roman Empire, the British Isles were largely cut off from the institutional Catholic Church, while the Angles and the Saxons began to occupy large portions of Britain. Though historical sources from the post–Roman era are sparse, it is evident that Christianity survived, even flourished, despite these conditions.

The fifth century saw the advent of the first so-called Welsh saints. These saints, "fifth- and sixth-century men and women whose lives as hermits, clerics, missionaries, or founders of religious centers, caused them to be termed *sant*, that is *sanctus* or saint, were generally local heroes whose cults did not extend far beyond their own immediate territories" (Henken, "Welsh" 26–27). While often referred to as saints, only a few ever achieved this official status with the Roman Catholic Church. Abandoned by the broader matrix of institutional Christianity, the Celtic peoples of Britain and Ireland continued to worship in their own fashion. This did not necessarily mean that they adopted an entire system of ecclesiastical hierarchies that might rival or compete with Rome. The faith was generally located in isolated pockets, and the early Celtic saints were ascetics and monastics. Their independence was threatened when Rome reasserted its presence at the end of the sixth century. In 595, Pope Gregory the Great sent out a mission to convert the peoples of Britain, led by Augustine of Canterbury (not be confused with his more famous namesake, Augustine of Hippo). The Celtic Christians at this time were not nearly so regimented in their church structure as Rome, but they were accustomed to working independently, and, as a result, they resisted the influence of the Gregorian mission. The conflicts were over matters that often seem paltry and superficial now — the use of the tonsure or the date upon which Easter is celebrated. But underlying these conflicts was the Welsh refusal to recognize papal authority, for the sixth century pontificate was just beginning to take on the dominance it would exercise in the medieval period. The Welsh did not concede the Easter date until the mid-eighth century, and even after Catholicism was well established in Britain, the Welsh church preserved more autonomy than many surrounding parishes.

Everything changed following the Norman Conquest of 1066. The Normans were more aggressive about establishing Roman Catholic hierarchy in Wales than the Anglo-Saxon Christians had been, and they sought to eradicate the Welsh system of *clasau*, the independent monastic communities that traced themselves back to the Age of the Saints. One consequence of this Norman activity was the production of a series of *vitae*, lives of the Celtic saints, designed to celebrate the heritage of Welsh Christians but also to establish their legitimacy and position themselves strategically in the new hierarchy that was being imposed. As Elissa R. Henken observes:

> Although traditions about the Welsh saints had long existed, they were not compiled into *vitae* until the end of the eleventh century when necessitated by changing religious and political circumstances and Anglo-Norman influence. During the centuries of contact and conflict with the Anglo-Saxons, the Welsh Church had remained essentially undisturbed, but the Normans threatened great upheaval. The old system of the *clasau*— the Welsh monastic communities and traditional centres of learning such as St Davids and Llanbadarn — was to be redefined and replaced by newly created dioceses and Latin monastic orders, given precise territorial boundaries, standardized into the continental pattern of ecclesiastical government, and the whole brought under Canterbury and Rome. Due to this restructuring in the twelfth century, both Welsh and Anglo-Norman clerics turned to *vitae* to establish their place in the hierarchy ["Welsh" 29–30].

Welsh saints like David, Teilo, Padarn, Beuno, Illtyd, Dyfrig, Cadog, and dozens of others became the subject of fanciful *vitae*, attaching them to miraculous occurrences or supernatural objects. These writings tended to be largely fictitious, though they laid the groundwork for preserving a sense of Welsh national identity in religious life even as the Catholic Normans were requiring conformity to Rome in ecclesiastical matters.

One individual who figures notably in several lives is none other than King Arthur. Henken notes that in the *Vitae*, "Arthur emerges as spoiled, demanding what he fancies, but basically well-meaning" (*Traditions* 301). It is well beyond the scope of this paper to sort through the myriad accounts and assertions about Arthur, who has been variously interpreted as factual, mythical, or archetypal; as Celtic, Roman, or Anglo-Saxon; or as some combination thereof. But whether or not there is a historical basis for the figure of Arthur, Welsh sources provide some of the earliest known written references to him. Eventually, a large body of literature developed that was dedicated exclusively to the figure of King Arthur, but in many early accounts, and several subsequent ones, Arthur is a supporting character, sometimes little more than an allusion or an afterthought. Thus, Arthurian legends were often tied to other mythical story strands, one of which is the Holy Grail.

As in the case of Arthurian literature, there are countless permutations of the Holy Grail myth, though some basic elements remain more or less consistent (at least until the past century or so). The modern image of the Grail is of a cup, a chalice that caught the blood of Jesus Christ, as exemplified in films like *Monty Python and the Holy Grail* (1975) or *Indiana Jones and the Last Crusade* (1989). But while always connected to Christ's death, the Grail had previously appeared as a platter, a basin, or even perhaps an altar brought to England by Joseph of Arimathea. In several accounts, its custodian is a figure known as the Fisher King, a local monarch often maimed or wounded who must be healed if his kingdom is regenerate. Because of the Holy Grail's connection to Jesus Christ, pursuit of it is always a spiritual journey undertaken by the pure, often the Arthurian knights Perceval, Bors, or Galahad, though Arthur himself seldom if ever encounters it. The earliest explicit references to the Holy Grail appear in the works of twelfth- or thirteenth-century medieval writers like Chrétien de Troyes and Roger de Boron, but there is disagreement among scholars as to whether the idea of the Grail originated with these writers or has a more ancient pedigree. The Arthurian scholar Roger Sherman Loomis identified "the three chief solutions for the problem of the Grail.... The Grail as Celtic talisman, as fertility symbol, as Christian relic" (139). According to the first of these three theories—the one which Loomis espouses—Chrétien's use of the Grail in *Perceval* or *Le Conte du Graal* (written in the 1180s) draws heavily on Celtic myths. Loomis suggests, "All manner of sacred vessels of the Irish and Welsh have contributed to the conception of the Grail" (227). An earlier scholar, Alfred Nutt, also believed in the Grail's pagan origins:

> The Grail Quest romances are, in their extant form, inextricably bound up with the Arthur legend as a whole, and the Arthur legend rests for a very large part upon a basis of Celtic folk and hero tales, representatives of which may still be found in the older heroic romances of both branches of the Celtic race, the Irish and the Welsh [54–55].

Contemporary scholarship acknowledges the findings of Nutt and Loomis, "[y]et while Loomis and others pointed out interesting and important analogies between Celtic tales and medieval romances, it is an oversimplification to consider the tale of the Grail as merely a development of earlier Celtic material" (Lupack 213). Though the image of the Holy Grail may have some background in Celtic folklore, including Welsh objects, in its fully developed articulations, it is in the main explicitly Christian.

Arthur Machen was born in Caerleon-on-Usk, a Welsh town and former Roman outpost that had Arthurian resonances of its own.[4] Though he lived most of his later life in London, Machen looked back fondly on his boyhood in Wales, musing wistfully in his 1922 autobiography *Far Off Things*,

> I shall always esteem it as the greatest piece of fortune that has fallen to me, that I was born in that noble, fallen Caerleon-on-Usk, in the heart of Gwent.... For the older I grow the more firmly I am convinced that anything which I may have accomplished in literature is due to the fact that when my eyes were first opened in earliest childhood they had before them the vision of an enchanted land [14].

As this passage suggests, Machen grew increasingly fond of his ancestral land. The early horror and weird fiction for which he is now best known only occasionally touches on aspects of his Welsh heritage.[5] In his twentieth-century work, however, the history, folklore, and literature of Wales often play a significant role. The appearance of increasing Welsh influence in Machen's later writings is unsurprising, and not only because he was becoming nostalgic while living in London. The turn of the century marked his return to his childhood Christian faith, and in general Machen at the time began to set himself concertedly against the positivistic materialism that he saw invading English culture. As Prys Morgan has observed, Romantic scholarship revived interest in

Welsh mythology and culture for a time, "but when an age of progress arrived it was bad.... Welshness was rejected by a large number because it was associated with quaintness and with a rather discredited mythology" (98–99). Yet this quaintness in the face of "progress" was likely among the most attractive features of the Welsh past to the anti-modern Arthur Machen.

One of Machen's most substantially Welsh works is his novella *The Great Return*, the last of several fictional pieces he wrote on the subject of the Holy Grail. The story is narrated by a reporter who reads a cryptic reference in a newspaper:

> LLANTRISANT.— The season promises very favourably: temperature of the sea yesterday at noon, 65 deg. Remarkable occurrences are supposed to have taken place during the recent Revival. The lights have not been observed lately. The Crown. The Fisherman's Rest [Machen, WP 202].

The narrator travels to Llantrisant and begins to investigate, learning more about the "remarkable occurrences." The smell of incense permeates iconoclastic Protestant churches; feuding neighbors reconcile; a mysterious bell is heard; sailors witness a red light over the water; a young woman has a vision and is miraculously cured of tuberculosis; and a congregation experiences a mystical Mass of the Sangraal in a local church. The entire Llantrisant experience lasts nine days.

Opinion of *The Great Return* has varied widely since its publication in 1915. Machen was not altogether pleased with the book and, in fact, warned his publisher not to pursue the project (Danielson 44–45), though he also told Vincent Starrett in a letter that it had "something of the real stuff about it" (Murphy 26). "There were hardly any reviews," Machen would write (Danielson 45). The lone exception was Thomas William Rolleston's piece in *The Times Literary Supplement*, which in Machen's eyes displayed "sumptuous ignorance" of Grail lore. Machen also expressed some amusement at Rolleston's indignation that the Grail of *The Great Return* appeared "to quite common people, such as farmers and grocers" (Danielson 46). Nor was Machen exaggerating, for Rolleston believed "the majesty and solemnity of the poetic traditions" associated with the Grail to be "insuperably incongruous" with *The Great Return*'s low setting (Rolleston 41). The book's reception among subsequent Machen biographers and critics has likewise been mixed. Starrett, who wrote the first book-length work of Machen criticism in 1918, believed *The Great Return* to be "an extraordinary short tale" (30). H. P. Lovecraft, though he primarily valued Machen's horror tales, found it "[o]f utmost delicacy, and passing from mere horror into true mysticism" (65). While acknowledging its mysticism, Wesley Sweetser maintains, "Broadly speaking, the work is not one of Machen's best efforts" (38). Aidan Reynolds and William Charlton concur, asserting that Machen "felt, rightly, that *The Great Return* is not a more successful attempt than its predecessors," though they also admit that "Machen put a great deal into the story, and never ceased to think that what he was trying to say in it was worth saying" (116). Berta Nash acknowledges that "[f]ew people consider it his greatest work" (119), though she herself appreciates it. Mark Valentine follows closer to Lovecraft's assessment, suggesting that even though the elements of the story differ little from his earlier treatments of the Grail, "they are more gently and allusively conveyed, and the later story has a satisfying unity which makes the reader more at home with the theme" (95). Whatever their assessment of *The Great Return*, however, few critics have devoted much space to examining it in any detail. This is unfortunate, because understanding the many layers of cultural meaning behind the story allows for a much greater appreciation of just how complex and well written it actually is.

One key detail, largely ignored by Machen scholars, is the connection between *The Great Return* and the Welsh Revival of 1904–05.[6] Though Machen had already left Wales by the time the revival occurred, it was so widely reported that it would have been difficult for him to have been unaware of it. Indeed, his native southern Wales was the epicenter of the revival, and his birthplace of Caerleon lay just outside Newport, which was visited by revivalists Sidney Evans, Sam Jenkins, and Mary Roberts from December 28, 1904 to January 1, 1905 (Gibbard 50–51). It is hardly a coincidence that *The Great Return* refers to "the recent Revival" (*WP* 202). The Welsh Revival had ended less than a decade prior to the publication of *The Great Return*, and Machen could have expected his readers to make the connection.

Indeed, Machen would later make the connection explicit in a statement which succinctly names several of the strands of influence that are woven together in the story. Discussing the novella with Morchard Bishop, Machen stated,

> Another little matter is that of *The Great Return*. There is, so far as I am aware, no basis for a belief in the existence of the Grail: a subject upon which I "researched" with great ardour for six months at the Museum. I am glad you like the story. I like it; but my opinion is not generally shared. To my interest in the Grail you may add my liking for Tenby and the Pembrokeshire country; and to that Mrs. Oliphant's *Beleaguered City*:[7] with recollections of a violent Methodist revival in South Wales about thirty years ago: so violent, that people began to see lights shining where there were no lights. And there you are [Bishop 31–32].

The "violent Methodist revival in South Wales" is certainly the Welsh Revival, which, while not exclusively Methodist, did occur primarily in Dissenting circles. Despite Machen's general distaste for low-church Protestantism, he clearly imports aspects of the revival into his account of the wondrous events at Llantrisant. Indeed, the miracles of *The Great Return* occur in just such a low-church context. "They're Dissenters," one lady says of those who experience the Grail, "some new sect, I dare say. You know some Dissenters are very queer in their ways" (*WP* 208). By acknowledging the low-church context of the revival, Machen acknowledges his own heritage. The rector of Llantrisant's church tells the narrator,

> You are a railer and a bitter railer; I have read articles that you have written, and I know your contempt and your hatred for those you call Protestants in your derision; though your grandfather, the vicar of Caerleon-on-Usk, called himself Protestant and was proud of it, and your great-grand-uncle Hezekiah, *ffeiriad coch yr Castletown*—the Red Priest of Castletown—was a great man with the Methodists in his day ... [206].

This passage is somewhat self-deprecating, for the heritage described is Machen's own, and he, like the narrator, was at the time a journalist who might "rail" against Protestantism, which he considered "a Black Smoke of Perdition and a Pestiferous and Stinking Vapour" (*SL* 41). Like the Catholic Flannery O'Connor with her fundamentalist characters, Machen in *The Great Return* would use iconoclastic Protestants to convey his own religious perspective.

There are some aspects of the Welsh Revival which directly inform *The Great Return*, beyond simply its Protestant context. One parallel is the use of hymns. At one point in Machen's story, the congregation sings "My God, and Is Thy Table Spread," a hymn by the eighteenth-century Nonconformist minister Philip Doddridge (*WP* 222). Churchgoers at the climactic Mass of the Sangraal sing the fourth verse of Charles Wesley's "Victim Divine, Thy Grace We Claim" (228). Machen's incorporation of hymns at intense moments of worship mirrors the prevalence of hymn-singing during the revival. G. Campbell Morgan considered singing one of the three characteristics of revival meetings (169–70); many revivalists traveled with an entourage of singers, and almost every story or recollection of the revival features hymn singing. In the actual Welsh Revival, many of the hymns sung were either Welsh or Welsh translations of American revival hymns. Machen, on the other hand, gives his parishioners English hymns of the 1700s to sing. Even so, it is significant that Machen chose songs by the Nonconformist Doddridge and the Wesleys—revivalists themselves and the founders of Methodism—rather than hymns with a more ancient or liturgical pedigree, as one might expect. Moreover, the Wesleyan hymn is sung not in English but in Welsh, just as the hymns were often sung in the revival.

The experience of visions is another way in which Machen's Llantristant tracks with the Welsh Revival. In *The Great Return*, the red light seen by the sailors is described as a vision (220), as is the dream of the sixteen-year-old Olwen Phillips (227), and the final Mass of the Sangraal is a profoundly mystical incident. Visions were a widely reported phenomenon in the midst of the Welsh Revival as well. As Machen himself observed, "people began to see lights shining where there were no lights," just like his sailors. H. Elvet Lewis gives the story of one such person, a certain Mrs. Jones from Merioneithshire, who "had seen, almost from the first, each evening a fire or light between her and the hills which rise from the marshy shore" (152). According to Lewis, reports of such marvels were not at all uncommon:

> So vast, so all-absorbing a movement could not be without its mystical elements, unexplained although possibly not inexplicable. Voices in the air, visions, seemingly objective,

of the blessed Saviour, mysterious lights: these, more or less definite, were so intimate a part of it, that the record would be incomplete and inadequate were they to be omitted or avoided [147].

Evan Roberts, the face of the revival, was known for his "ability to produce explicit signs of otherworldly power" (Ellis 203) during his ministry. Moreover, as John Harvey has observed, the imagery of Roberts's visions, while often directly Biblical, also drew on "recurrent themes" of Protestant hymnology, both English and Welsh (82–84).[8]

In many ways, the final Mass of the Sangraal in *The Great Return* could be drawn directly from accounts of the Welsh Revival. The service is a mixture of Welsh and English; they sing a Charles Wesley hymn in Welsh; members of various Nonconformist denominations gather together at the service. In Machen's story,

> There was no attempt to perform the usual service; when the bells had stopped the old deacon raised his cry, and priest and people fell down on their knees as they thought they heard a choir within singing "Alleluya, alleluya, alleluya." And as the bells in the tower ceased ringing, there sounded the thrill of the bell from Syon, and the golden veil of sunlight fell across the door into the altar, and the heavenly voices began their melodies....
>
> There was a voice that cried and sang from within the altar; most of the people had heard some faint echo of it in the chapels; a voice rising and falling and soaring in awful modulations that rang like the trumpet of the Last Angel. The people beat upon their breasts, the tears were like rain of the mountains on their cheeks; those that were able fell down on their faces before the glory of the veil. They said afterwards that men of the hills, twenty miles away, heard that cry and that singing, rushing upon them on the wind, and they fell down on their faces, and cried: "The offering is accomplished," knowing nothing of what they said [*WP* 228–29].

Many details of this description are in agreement with the extant descriptions of the Welsh Revival. According to Machen, "There was no attempt to perform the usual service," and this abandonment of the prescribed order of worship is quite consistent with revival meetings, which often lasted many hours, deep into the night, and which were composed of singing, prayer, and testimonies, sometimes unplanned and sometimes without a sermon preached.[9] Evan Roberts drew criticism at times for "[h]is rejection of the normal order of service" and "his willingness to yield to emotionalism which was wildly excessive at times" (R. Jones 299). And yet, G. Campbell Morgan, a staunchly orthodox preacher himself, found that the lack of routine did not necessarily hinder God's presence in meetings: "It was a meeting characterized by a perpetual series of interruptions. It was a meeting characterized by a great continuity and absolute order. You say, 'How do you reconcile these things?' I do not reconcile them. They are both there" (169). Like the revival service, Machen's service follows the leading of the spirit and not a prescribed format. The response of the congregants, who "beat upon their breasts" and whose "tears were like rain of the mountains on their cheeks," suggests also a conviction of unworthiness or desire for repentance, which was another significant aspect of the revival. Confession of sin was the third of Evan Roberts's four determining rules of engagement, while H. Elvet Lewis observes that "[s]trong men were shaken, and fell to the ground, helpless" (125) in the face of their conviction, even as "those that were able fell down on their faces" in Machen's story.

And yet, for all the similarities between *The Great Return* and the Welsh Revival, Machen's own innovations are equally intriguing and illustrate how he takes what was a distinctly Nonconformist Protestant phenomenon and transfigures it to fit his own personal Celtic Christian theology. He does this by making the Holy Grail the locus of spiritual experience in his tale, rather than simply suggesting the general sense of the Holy Spirit that so pervaded the actual revival. This distinction is no mere trifling detail. Protestantism, emerging as it did as a counterpoint to the Roman Catholic Church, has often been marked by a profound wariness of ceremonies and images, which Protestants fear can lead to spiritual deadness and idolatry, respectively. As John Harvey has observed, even the content of the visions during the Welsh Revival was often either directly Biblical or drawn from hymns, emblem books, or illustrated children's texts which all drew their imagery from the Bible. More particularly, low-church theologians and parishioners had often downplayed the sacramentality of the Lord's Supper or the Eucharist, anxious as they were not to stray into the Roman Catholic dogma of transubstantiation, which maintains that the wafer and the wine are literally transformed into Christ's body and blood.

Machen was fascinated by the subject of the Holy Grail, and while he may have admitted that there was "no basis for a belief in the existence of the Grail" in reality, he was very opinionated about his theories on how the motif developed in Arthurian literature. Like Nutt, Loomis, and others, he insisted on the Celtic—and especially Welsh—origins of the Grail legend, rejecting alternate theories that the Grail was originally derived from pagan fertility cults or served as a medieval political allegory. Unlike such scholars, however, Machen felt that the Grail was not derived from *pre–Christian* Celtic civilization but rather had its genesis in the Celtic church from the Age of the Saints. He wrote in a letter to Colin Summerford that "the Legend of the Grail is, in one of its aspects, the Legend of the Celtic Church" (*SL* 89). Machen believed that the medieval *vitae* of the Welsh saints represented authentic traditions rather than mere politically motivated inventions and that these traditions could explain the development of the Grail legend. Following a common etymological track, he concluded that the term "graal" derived from the Latin "cratella," which connoted "not so much a chalice as a shallow bowl on a stem" (*SS* 24), a bowl which could be conflated with an altar. He observes that the Welsh saints are often associated with particular objects that could easily have transformed into the Grail as the stories were adapted over time. He also posits Welsh saints as the basis for the Fisher King, the hereditary keeper of the Grail, as the fish symbol once represented Christ's sacrifice, and he points to saints like David or Ilar who are associated with the water and with fishing. In short, Machen did "not think it is temerarious to say that in the legends of these Welsh saints, hallowed in the east, endowed with miraculous altars of divine origin and wondrous form, evangelisers of Britain, there is the probable ancestry of the great romances of the Graal" (*SS* 24–25).

Machen reproduces many of these arguments explicitly in *The Great Return*, and the wondrous events that occur in the story make sense only in the context of his theories, though some ambiguity remains as to particulars. The name of the town, Llantrisant, essentially means "church of the three saints," but it is not entirely clear what three saints Machen has in mind, even though they are described in some detail. Olwen Phillips,[10] in the vision that presages her miraculous healing, sees:

> standing before her bed three men in blood-coloured robes with shining faces. And one man held a golden bell in his hand. And the second man held up something shaped like the top of a table. It was like a great jewel, and it was of a blue colour, and there were rivers of silver and of gold running through it and flowing as quick streams flow, and there were pools in it as if violets had been poured out into water, and then it was green as the sea near the shore, and then it was the sky at night with all the stars shining, and then the sun and the moon came down and washed in it. And the third man held up high above this a cup that was like a rose on fire... [*WP* 226].

The first figure is easily identifiable as Saint Teilo, a major Welsh saint who was often identified with a golden bell with healing powers that he received in Jerusalem. While there is also a legend of Teilo's body being tripled, the other two figures are clearly distinct individuals. The second is certainly Saint David (Dewi), arguably the greatest of all the old Welsh Saints, who received from heaven an altar and who, Machen notes, was to be known as "a man of aquatic life" (227). The real Welsh town of Llanddeusant — "church of the two saints — is named after these two, so there is little question of their identities.

The identity of the third saint who holds "a cup that was like a rose on fire" is a little more puzzling. Nash affirms the first figure as Teilo but goes no further (117–18). In his dissertation on Machen, Karl Petersen assumes the first two saints to be Teilo and David respectively but calls the saint with the cup only "the third figure," making no attempt to discern that figure's identity (202). Gwilym Games likewise recognizes Teilo and David as the first two and speculates Cadwaladr as the third, since Machen elsewhere identified him as a possible precursor of Galahad. However, neither Cadwaladr nor Galahad are ever mentioned in *The Great Return*, and Games himself admits the uncertainty of his identification, listing several other contenders.[11]

It is possible the third figure is Saint Padarn, who, according to the *vitae*, made a pilgrimage to Jerusalem with Teilo and David. But in the text Machen never refers to Padarn, who is associated with a staff, never a cup. A more likely candidate would be Iltyd,[12] a Welsh warrior-saint often portrayed as a cousin of King Arthur. In 1904, the writer Ernest Rhys — with whom Machen would later be acquainted[13] — published a piece in *The Nineteenth Century and After* entitled "A Knight of the Sangreal" which specifically identifies Iltyd as "the type and prime of those shining men that grew in mediæval fantasy into the questing knights of the Holy Grail" (90). In Machen's Grail novel *The Secret Glory*, written only three years later, Iltyd is explicitly linked to Teilo and David in connection to "their marvellous chalices and altars of Paradise from which they made the books of the Graal afterwards" (168). But *The Secret Glory* identifies Iltyd more with the altar than the cup (80). Likewise, in Welsh tradition outside the Triads, Iltyd may be linked to an altar, a bell, or a crosier-staff, but not to a wine cup. Moreover, once again, Iltyd's name never occurs in *The Great Return*, and *The Secret Glory*, though written, had not yet been published in 1915. A stronger possibility is Ilar, whom Machen *does* mention explicitly in the story. Ilar's moniker "the Fisherman" (*WP* 227)—like David's association with the sea—may demonstrate a connection to the Rich Fishermen, a variant of the Fisher King motif. In Welsh tradition, Ilar is extremely obscure, and, apart from his name, there appear to be no substantial traditions associated with him. Yet in *The Secret Glory*, Machen built an entire history around the minor saint, even while acknowledging that "people ... have forgotten all about Ilar" (*SG* 83). Machen's Ilar is associated with a bell and an altar, but also with a well, and it is at such a well that Machen's Ambrose Meyrick experiences the power of the Grail. Thus, notwithstanding his apparent insignificance—or perhaps because of it—Ilar may indeed be the "Fisherman" Machen had in mind when writing the Olwen Phillips scene.[14]

Whoever the third saint in the vision may be, the more important matter is that the Rich Fishermen indicate the arrival of the Holy Grail to Llantrisant. It is through the Grail, or other related Welsh saints and their relics, that the people of the town are able to experience the divine mystic ecstasy that culminates in the Mass of the Sangraal. In other words, Machen takes something that, in its Protestant context, was almost entirely mental and spiritual and makes it sacramental, tying the experience to the presence of a physical object. For, as he would write in his novel *A Fragment of Life*, Machen believed that "the whole world is but a great ceremony or sacrament, which teaches under visible forms a hidden and transcendent doctrine" (*WP* 166).

As a result, even though the Mass of the Sangraal may have been suggested by the Welsh Revival, many of the details present a distinctly Machen-esque spin. Despite the diverse religious backgrounds of the participants, they all meet in the old Llantrisant church, which Machen commends as "a typical example of a Welsh parish church, before the evil and horrible period of 'restoration'" (*WP* 221). It is, in other words, ancient, with far more history—specifically Welsh history—than any of the Nonconformist Protestant churches.[15] Machen slyly indicates that a church such as this is where believers truly belong: "There was not a single chapel of the Dissenters open in the town that day. The Methodists with their minister and all their deacons and all the Nonconformists had returned on this Sunday morning to 'the old hive'" (228). The Wesleyan hymn, "Victim Divine, Thy Grace We Claim," actually applies the often Roman Catholic term "Real Presence" in one stanza.[16] While the Wesleys were certainly no "Papists,"[17] the hymn Machen chooses is thoroughly appropriate to an occasion as solemn as the Mass of the Sangraal, despite its Protestant origin. As noted earlier, "[t]here was no attempt to perform the usual service," but the atmosphere is nonetheless far more reminiscent of high church ceremony; it is literally full of smells and bells, with Teilo's bell ringing and "the odour of the rarest spiceries" (228) redolent in the air. Machen suggests that even his Protestant congregants have a deep need for the mystery of liturgy, so that they recite, "as if an age-old memory stirred in them" (228), a Welsh invocation of the Father, Son, and Holy Spirit.[18]

The most obvious departure from the Welsh Revival is, of course, the presence of the Grail itself. Inherent in Machen's idea of a "hidden and transcendent doctrine" is a belief that the sacraments are "mysteries," as in fact they are called in the New Testament, and that the divine presence must be experienced in a context which preserves that mystery while remaining concrete rather than abstract. The nexus of the Llantrisant revival is thus the very physical presence of the Grail which has briefly returned. Nash goes too far in asserting that Machen's version of the Grail "is not spiritual but material" (120). The whole point of *The Great Return* is that it is both, a physical sacrament that is nonetheless inextricably bound up in the spiritual; as Games points out, *The Great Return* is animated by "the concept of *Perichoresis*, the interpenetration of the spiritual and material" (36).

Because the mystical ecstasy of *The Great Return* is centered on a single sacramental object, the revival is consequently briefer and more localized than its historical prototype. Thus, while people of all denominations in Llantrisant attend the final Mass and people in surrounding towns may hear it, the Grail's return is confined to a single region over a period of nine days, unlike the Welsh Revival, which lasted for months and spread across Wales and, ultimately, the world. The democratic assumptions of such a revival, or of the Roman Catholic Mass, which is available to all communicants, are not in accord with Machen's thought that the mystery of the sacrament is part of what permits its ecstasy. Access is limited — even after the final ceremony is concluded, the narrator's sources "can say but very little of what was done beyond the veil" (228). Of course, the access is not awarded on the basis of superficialities such as education or social class — it was Machen's *dramatis personae* of a "journalist interviewing farmers and grocers" that so offended Rolleston (41). Even so, Machen's Mass of the Sangraal cannot be easily attainable to all, or it ceases to become the mystery he believes it to be.

But while only a fortunate few may experience the full weight of mystic revelation, that moment has effects that ripple much farther, just as the original Welsh Revival had. The communicants are changed by what they have experienced:

[f]or they say that all through the nine days, and indeed after the time had ended, there never was a man weary or sick at heart in Llantrisant, or in the country round it. For if a man felt that his work of the body or the mind was going to be too much for his strength, then there would come to him of a sudden a warm glow and a thrilling all over him, and he felt as strong as a giant, and happier than he had ever been in his life before, so that lawyer and hedger each rejoiced in the task that was before him, as if it were sport and play.

And, much more wonderful than this or any other wonders was forgiveness, with love to follow it. There were meetings of old enemies in the market-place and in the street that made the people lift up their hands and declare that it was as if one walked the miraculous streets of Syon [*WP* 231].

Many Christian leaders lamented that the Welsh Revival did not have as much staying power as they had hoped. Machen — who always believed that morality was the effect and not the cause of divine encounter — gives his own little revival a greater permanence, specifically by appealing to the very physical, very sacramental experience of the Grail. People are physically healed and blessed with stamina because they are able to retain the "glow," to keep some of what they have experienced with them. And this not only transforms them physically but also interpersonally. They become moral — they are able to love — because of their past mystical encounter.

Though he spent much of his adult life in London, Arthur Machen would always be drawn to his native Wales, and that meant loving even aspects of it which he might find unappealing, such as his Nonconformist Protestant heritage. In *The Great Return*, he does not deny this aspect of himself but fuses it into the more ancient, more ceremonial forms of the faith that touched his own heart. Though often looked upon as an obscure work by an author better known for tales of terror, *The Great Return* is in fact, as even the materialist H. P. Lovecraft appreciated, "true mysticism" imbued with "utmost delicacy" (65). It gives an account, moreover, of a sacred ground where all Christian Wales — Celtic, Roman Catholic, and Protestant — can meet. In the Llantrisant church, two millennia of orthodoxies can experience a great mystery together.

Notes

1. Noel Gibbard urges caution in painting too dismal a picture of the Welsh church at the turn of the century, observing, "The religious scene in Wales at the end of the nineteenth century was, in many ways, encouraging" (11). Yet Gibbard also notes several reasons why Christian leaders might have deemed Wales ready for such an occurrence (11–23).

2. Gibbard rightly cautions against overstating the connection between Roberts's withdrawal and the ending of the revival (190–91). Even so, the absence of such a visible and impassioned advocate certainly affected the revival's later fortunes.

3. Joseph Smale, the Los Angeles pastor of First New Testament Church, was friends with Evan Roberts and had visited him during the revival. "So many members from First New Testament Church came to Azusa Street," writes Cecil M. Robeck, Jr., that

one member "claimed Joseph Smale had to visit the mission to find his own congregation" (83).

4. Geoffrey of Monmouth, Wace, Layamon, and even Thomas Malory all place Arthur at Caerleon, which some believe to have been the original "Camelot."

5. *The Great God Pan* and *The Three Impostors* are both set primarily in London, though both also feature scenes in Wales. Sage Leslie-McCarthy does note that Machen's fusion of Celtic fairy lore with some peculiar nineteenth-century ethnological theories place him within the Celtic Revival of the late Victorian age, though he "is not a typical member" (77) in that his treatment of the lore is not nationalistic. Still, she writes, "Machen's tales of 'the little people' succeed in making traditional folklore real and current for a modern, skeptical audience, and in doing so he ensured that his beloved Welsh mythology would survive the fin de siècle" (77).

6. The one notable exception is Gwilym Games's well-researched "The Great Return, the Great War, and the Great Revival."

7. Tenby is a coastal resort town in the Welsh county of Pembrokeshire, and it provides the physical and geographic matrix for *The Great Return*'s Llantrisant. The Celtic church in Gumfreston inspired the Llantrisant church. Margaret Oliphant's novel *A Beleaguered City* (1880) is a story of the supernatural told from multiple perspectives.

8. Gwilym Games notes some additional visions and lights that occurred during the Revival and may have been known to Machen (39–41).

9. This last is particularly striking in a Protestant context, in which the sermon is generally the climax of the worship service.

10. The name "Olwen" carries Welsh Arthurian connotations all its own. Anyone familiar with Welsh lore would immediately trace it back to "Culhwch and Olwen," a tale often included with the Branches of the *Mabinogi* in which the young protagonist Culhwch enlists the help of his cousin King Arthur to perform several tasks so that he might win Olwen from her father, the giant Ysbaddaden.

11. Besides Cadwaladr, "it could be another Welsh saint such as Cybi, or Cadoc, or Gwnllyw. The mystery remains, as it should, a mystery" (48).

12. This saint's name is variously spelled Iltyd, Illtyd, Iltud, Illtud, and Eltut. Though Illtud is perhaps the most common spelling found in English, I have opted to follow Machen's own spelling of Iltyd.

13. Valentine calls Rhys "Machen's nearest Welsh contemporary" (137). Though he can only confirm a single meeting between the two, Valentine notes that they corresponded and that Rhys apparently admired Machen (137–38). Rhys also edited *The Haunters and the Haunted* (1921), which printed Machen's brief tale "Dr. Duthoit's Vision."

14. It is important to note that, while the first two figures clearly fit the traditional Welsh iconography attributed to Teilo and David, Machen deliberately allows for some ambiguity in assigning roles. After all, as I have noted, Iltyd can be associated with the image of the altar; and in Machen's own legendarium, Ilar can be associated with any of the three symbols—altar, bell, or cup. In "The Secret of the Sangraal," Machen claims, "[I]t is known, I suppose, even to those who know but very little of Celtic things, that every Saint in Britain and Scotland and Ireland had his holy bell" (SS 15). This ambiguity of identification shifts the emphasis away from the saints as individuals and places it on their collective role as the Fishermen, the Grail guardians.

15. Philip Henry Gosse, writing in 1856 about the original Gumfreston Church, asserts that "it is indubitably as old as the twelfth century," and adds that "its edifice seems to have suffered little change at the Reformation" (203).

16. The hymn's fifth and final stanza, which immediately follows the stanza Machen reprints, ends with the lines "To every faithful Soul appear, / And shew thy Real Presence here" (Baker 29–30).

17. John R. Tyson notes that Charles Wesley "consistently considered the sacraments to be means of grace," though "their virtue was found in the sacramental presence of Christ, not localized specifically in the elements" (210).

18. Machen believed that the Celtic churches during the Age of the Saints had their own distinct liturgy, a liturgy he surmised to have been closer in form to the Eastern Orthodox tradition than the Roman Catholic form. He regretted that "the anti–Celtic fervor of the Roman authorities was so thorough that there is no such thing as a Celtic Liturgy in existence" (SS 32).

Works Cited

Baker, Frank, ed. *The Representative Verse of Charles Wesley*. New York: Abingdon, 1962.
Bishop, Morchard. "A Chapter from The Table Talk of Arthur Machen." *Arthur Machen: Artist and Mystic*. Ed. Mark Valentine and Roger Dobson. Oxford: Caermaen, 1986. 30–35.
Blumhofer, Edith L. and Randall Balmer. Introduction. *Modern Christian Revivals*. Ed. Edith L. Blumhofer and Randall Balmer. Urbana: University of Illinois Press, 1993. xi–xvi.
Danielson, Henry. *Arthur Machen: A Bibliography*. London: Danielson, 1923.
Ellis, Bill. *Lucifer Ascending: The Occult in Folklore and Popular Culture*. Lexington: University Press of Kentucky, 2004.
Games, Gwilym. "*The Great Return*, the Great War, and the Great Revival." *Faunus* 11 (2004): 26–54.
Gibbard, Noel. *Fire on the Altar: A History and Evaluation of the 1904–05 Revival in Wales*. Bridgend: Bryntirion, 2005.
Gitre, Edward J. "The 1904–05 Welsh Revival: Modernization, Technologies, and Techniques of the Self." *Church History* 73.4 (2004): 792–827.
Gosse, Philip Henry. *Tenby: A Sea-Side Holiday*. London: Van Voorst, 1856.
Harvey, John. "Spiritual Emblems: The Visions of the 1904–5 Welsh Revival." *Llafur: A Journal for the Study of Welsh Labour History* 6.2 (1993): 75–93.
Henken, Elissa R. *Traditions of the Welsh Saints*. Cambridge: Brewer, 1987.
_____. "Welsh Hagiography and the Nationalist Impulse." *Celtic Hagiography and Saints' Cults*. Ed. Jane Cartwright. Cardiff: University of Wales Press, 2003. 26–44.
Jones, Brynmor P. *Voices from the Welsh Revival: An Anthology of Testimonies, Reports, and Eyewitness Statements from Wales's Year of Blessing, 1904–05*. Bridgend: Evangelical Press of Wales, 1995.
Jones, R. Tudur. *Faith and the Crisis of a Nation: Wales 1890–1914*. Trans. Sylvia Prys Jones. Ed. Robert Pope. Cardiff: University of Wales Press, 2004.
Leslie-McCarthy, Sage. "Re-Vitalising the Little People: Arthur Machen's Tales of the Remnant Races." *Australasian Victorian Studies Journal* 11 (2005): 65–78.
Lewis, H. Elvet. *With Christ among the Miners*. 1906. *Glory Filled the Land: A Trilogy on the Welsh Revival of 1904–1905*. Ed. Richard Owen Roberts. Wheaton: International Awakening, 1989. 1–177.
Loomis, Roger Sherman. *Celtic Myth and Arthurian Romance*. New York: Columbia University Press, 1927.
Lovecraft, H. P. *The Annotated Supernatural Horror in Literature*. Ed. S. T. Joshi. New York: Hippocampus, 2000.
Lupack, Alan. *The Oxford Guide to Arthurian Literature and Legend*. Oxford: Oxford University Press, 2005.
Machen, Arthur. *Far Off Things*. 1922. New York: Knopf, 1923.

_____. *The Secret Glory.* New York: Knopf, 1922.
_____. *The Secret of the Sangraal: A Collection of Writings by Arthur Machen.* Horam: Tartarus, 1995.
_____. *Selected Letters: The Private Writings of the Master of the Macabre.* Ed. Roger Dobson, Godfrey Brangham, and R. A. Gilbert. Wellingborough: Aquarian, 1988.
_____. *The White People and Other Stories.* The Best Weird Tales of Arthur Machen, vol. 2. Hayward, CA: Chaosium, 2003.
Morgan, G. Campbell. "The Revival: Its Source and Power." 1905 (as "The Revival: Its Power and Source"). *Glory Filled the Land: A Trilogy on the Welsh Revival of 1904–105.* Ed. Richard Owen Roberts. Wheaton: International Awakening, 1989. 167–77.
Morgan, J. Vyrnwy. *The Welsh Religious Revival, 1904–5: A Retrospect and a Criticism.* London: Chapman and Hall, 1909.
Morgan, Prys. "From a Death to a View: The Hunt for the Welsh Past in the Romantic Period." *The Invention of Tradition.* Ed. Eric Hobsbawm and Terence Ranger. Cambridge: Cambridge University Press, 1983. 43–100.
Murphy, Michael, ed. *Starrett vs. Machen: A Record of Discovery and Correspondence.* St. Louis: Autolycus, 1977.
Nash, Berta. "Arthur Machen among the Arthurians." *Minor British Novelists.* Ed. Charles Alva Hoyt. Carbondale: Southern Illinois Univesity Press, 1967. 109–20.
Nutt, Alfred. *The Legends of the Holy Grail.* Popular Studies in Mythology, Romance and Folklore 14. London: Nutt, 1902. Rpt. New York: AMS, 1972.
Orr, J. Edwin. *The Flaming Tongue: The Impact of Twentieth Century Revivals.* Chicago: Moody, 1973.
Petersen, Karl Marius. *Arthur Machen and the Celtic Renaissance in Wales.* Diss. Louisiana State University, 1973. Ann Arbor: UMI, 1973.
Reinhardt, Wolfgang. "'A Year of Rejoicing': The Welsh Revival 1904–05 and Its International Challenges." *Evangelical Review of Theology* 31.2 (2007): 100–26.
Reynolds, Aidan, and William Charlton. *Arthur Machen: A Short Account of His Life and Work.* London: Baker, 1963.
Rhys, Ernest. "A Knight of the Sangreal." *Nineteenth Century and After* 55 (January 1904): 90–96.
Robeck, Cecil M., Jr. *The Azusa Street Mission and Revival: The Birth of the Global Pentecostal Movement.* Nashville: Nelson, 2006.
Rolleston, Thomas William. "A Legend of the Grail." *Times Literary Supplement* 27 January 1916: 41.
Starrett, Vincent. *Arthur Machen: A Novelist of Ecstasy and Sin.* Chicago: Hill, 1918.
Sweetser, Wesley D. *Arthur Machen.* New York: Twayne, 1964.
Tyson, John R. *Charles Wesley on Sanctification.* Grand Rapids, MI: Francis Asbury, 1986.
Valentine, Mark. *Arthur Machen.* Bridgend: Seren, 1995.

Magical Goods, "Orphaned" Exchanges, Punishment and Power in the Fourth Branch of the *Mabinogi*

SUSANA BROWER

Much previous criticism of the *Mabinogi*,[1] first collected in the *White Book of Rhydderch* and the *Red Book of Hergest* in the 14th to 15th centuries (Jones and Jones ix), focuses solely on matters of the text's structure and history. Studies devoted to the influence of myth and of still older Celtic stories on the two extant manuscripts are not rare (as studies of the *Mabinogi* go), nor are considerations of the formal aspects of the connected tales or of their own influence on other literature as divergent as Chaucer's, Tennyson's, and the modern young adult fantasies of Lloyd Alexander.[2] Yet analyses of the stories' details—the characters, the nature of their interactions, and the tales' events—seems a rare choice for critics. Among the elements thus far ignored by them is the economic system of gift-giving or commodity exchange so conspicuously present in these stories. These take on a peculiar form in the Fourth Branch, where we find Gwydion, nephew of the powerful wizard-king Math, acting as the systems' fulcrum, albeit a disruptive one. Just as others identify Gwydion either as an agent that demolishes the distinctions between genders or who neutralizes the human representatives of a matrilineal system of inheritance,[3] so too can the argument be made that Gwydion represents a subversive force that seeks to weaken his society's economies of gift and exchange by upsetting the relationship between exchange partners while simultaneously exploiting them in a play for power.

Sociologist and political theorist Pierre Bourdieu[4] writes in his *Outline of a Theory of Practice* that all forms of exchange have the common goal of "maximizing ... material or symbolic profit" (183). He considers every human "practice" and "material" production a potential source of "symbolic capital," as a form of "asset" that exists as something "transformed and thereby *disguised*" (183), with respect to its economic origin and use. "Symbolic capital" and the "symbolic power" it generates are inherently available to those positioned at the top of the social hierarchy and allow those individuals "to impose the principles of the construction of reality — in particular, social reality" (165). In other words, they perpetuate, through the tacit and usually unconscious consent of "the dominated," the very system that gives the dominant the power to enforce a particular social hierarchy to begin with (183). Those members of the lower classes whose limited access to real capital consequently minimizes their access to the symbolic type as well become aware of and come to question the hierarchy's "arbitrariness" (164) can leverage these assets into "symbolic power" that, by the simple fact of who wields it, necessarily subverts the social order. Michel de Certeau's socio-historical psychoanalysis of consumerism, *The Practice of Everyday Life*, calls this behavior of the disadvantaged a "tactic" (37). This is Gwydion's role in the Fourth Branch. His interactions with the tale's other figures, in particular Pryderi, Aranrhod, and Blodeuedd, consist almost exclusively of the giving or exchanging of magical goods that literally result from the disguising or transforming of one particular thing into another item of greater economic or symbolic value. He enacts on a literal level the "legerdemain" de Certeau describes in his work (37). By initiating economic interactions with these characters, Gwydion begins a disturbing and distinctive pattern of actual violence (and "symbolic violence" when "overt violence is impossible" [196]), that threads its way through the story, entangling the other characters as he struggles against medieval Welsh hierarchy.

He manipulates others in order to gain power and notoriety — in contemporary popular terms, Gwydion would have made an ideal contestant, or perhaps behind-the-scenes man, on reality television. An essay by Keat Murray emphasizes how *Survivor*'s creator and producer, Mark Burnett, uses that show to endorse a form of social Darwinism that "implicitly valorizes the inequities of cultural imperialism and the rise of the corporate elite" (44). Fashioning himself, his show, and the companion books as manuals for business and personal success, "Burnett's model survivor" "'know[s] human psychology,' learns to disengage himself from current economic, political, and social conditions in order to understand 'the human condition,' and follows 'a gut awareness' toward creating 'the next wave of social evolution'" (46). While not at all suggesting that *Survivor* in any iteration constitutes a re-imagining of the *Mabinogi* nor claiming that its creator exhibited awareness of the Welsh tales as he conceptualized the show, we can nonetheless discern a strong resemblance in the ultimate goal of the main players of each and in the means through which they are supposed to achieve that goal. In the argument that follows, I propose that Gwydion, as Burnett suggests about his contestants,[5] wins the game he engages in by "discovering who [he is] and then controlling who [he seems] to be" (Murray 46) during his increasingly capitalistic transactions with the Fourth Branch's other characters.

Perhaps the extent of this parallel, though largely unexploited by pop culture adaptations of these Welsh stories, is one of the elements that continues to make them feel so current and of continued relevance—the struggles for economic equality that lead, in apparent paradox, to a drive for advantage and a new imbalance, continue to consume us still today. Even magic—certainly an element that attracts readers, viewers, and gamers to most contemporary adaptations of Welsh myths—though absent in literal form from *Survivor* and other competitive reality TV, remains a twenty-first century presence in some ways. Today, competitors and some consumers seek maximum results for minimum effort, while experiencing minimal loss (witness everything from get-rich-quick real estate schemes to each new diet craze). Surely, then, participation in these contests and fads verges on a belief in magic and in magical ends.[6] Although these particular manifestations of "magic" seem distinctly nontraditional, the impetus for them is not unique to modern media: much the same acquisitiveness drives today's use of metaphorical magic that drove Gwydion to it in the *Mabinogi*, and much the same awe-filled response makes witnesses vulnerable to manipulation through it in both times as well.

In the Fourth Branch, Gwydion's penchant for magically created goods presents itself in nearly every appearance he makes. In the tale's initial event, Gwydion provokes a war with Pryderi of Dyfed in order to provide his brother Gilfaethwy the opportunity to rape Goewin, Math's foot-holder. Gwydion and eleven companions, all enchanted to look like bards, travel to Pryderi's court to solicit from him the swine of Annwn in exchange for which Gwydion, "the best teller of tales in the world," initially offers his stories (48). By refusing this proposal on the grounds that the swine's future increase represents an economic agreement made with his people, Pryderi proves himself a genuine participant in the very system that Gwydion seeks to undermine. Unwittingly though, by declining to accept the grounds of this exchange, Pryderi hands Gwydion an opportunity to begin the destabilization of the economic system the former shows he values. The trade Gwydion offers next Pryderi finds more promising: presented with twelve gold-adorned black and white greyhounds and stallions, he accepts them, not knowing that Gwydion has conjured these from the air and that to the air they will return as soon as their creator has traveled a safe distance away (49).

The disappearance of these animals not only prompts the war Gwydion wants, but it also turns an instance of true exchange into what I will term an "orphaned" exchange, in which the first half of the transaction is erased after the fact, and the second is predicated on, quite literally, nothing; consequently the transaction becomes divorced from the usually obligatory reciprocity. Essentially, then, this is a twisted form of gift-giving in which the bestower of the gift—though prepared to trade—unwillingly and unknowingly enters into what becomes a one-sided relationship where the violence that normally follows the gift to its receiver (Bourdieu 191) deflects instead back to its giver. Gwydion kills Pryderi in battle, ridding himself not only of a dangerous war-enemy but also of a dangerous social obligation that, though it is an innate consequence of gift-exchange, becomes greatly magnified in this situation because of Gwydion's deception. Clearly, Gwydion does not desire to form the necessary and "lasting relationships of reciprocity" that Bourdieu describes as necessary in such economic transactions (186). But perhaps Gwydion plays a role that Bourdieu figures as a more productive one by revealing the close relationship that exists between gift-exchange and commodity exchange and the violence inherent in both forms, a fact that society commonly "misrecognizes" (172).

Bourdieu's concern with "risk," "unpredictability," and obligation (186) hints at the power struggle that underlies Gwydion's actions. Though the son of the goddess Dôn and a member of the aristocracy as the nephew of a king, Gwydion functions only as a counselor in his uncle's court (Fulton 235). Early in the tale, he directly interacts only with his social superiors (except in the case of Gilfaethwy), a fact which forces him to proceed through de Certeauian "tactics" in order to assert whatever small power he finds himself endowed with. De Certeau's *The Practice of Everyday Life* describes tactical behavior in this way:

> It operates in isolated actions, blow by blow. It takes advantage of "opportunities" and depends on them, being without any base where it could stockpile its winnings, build up its own position, and plan raids. What it wins it cannot keep. This nowhere gives a tactic mobility, but a mobility that must accept the chance offerings of the moment, and seize on the wing the possibilities that offer themselves at any given moment.... It can be where it is least expected. It is a guileful ruse [37].

Gwydion lacks a home and lands of his own, living instead in his uncle Math's castle where violence, whether physical or symbolic, becomes the primary means by which Gwydion "[makes] a space for himself and signs his existence as an author of it" (Bourdieu 31). The pigs he stole from Pryderi he ostensibly took for Math and so into the king's possession they go upon return to Gwynedd; mobility and the "guileful ruse" are certainly parts of Gwydion's modus operandi, as he performs a series of hit-and-run attacks, always with appearance magically transformed of course, always "pulling one over on the adversary on his own turf" (40), first against Pryderi in Dyfed and then against his sister Aranrhod in her castle. Gwydion functions, in many ways then, as a "pure receiver" (31), taking from those around him and giving very little if anything in return.

The use of commodities created without one's own labor figures as a productive and necessary action for the tactic-using "other" in de Certeau's work (32), but in the Fourth Branch of the *Mabinogi*, this behavior and the destabilization of the social structure's economic foundation does not often go unpunished. The act of raping Goewin makes Math and therefore his kingdom vulnerable, for he can survive only if his feet rest in the lap of a virgin (and, it seems, Goewin's qualifications in this regard were superior to those of most other women in the kingdom when Math chose her) (*Mabinogion* 47). Symbolic values take a serious hit as a result of the brothers' transgression: not only does Goewin's usefulness decrease as a result of being violated — we know that Math makes her his queen (52), but it remains unclear what significance lies in this role since she subsequently disappears from the story — but Gwydion and Gilfaethwy also diminish their usefulness by proving, as Helen Fulton suggests, to be untrustworthy counselors, thereby dishonoring and endangering their uncle and lord (235, 239). Math, a good ruler like Pryderi, understands his obligation to his people and designs a punishment that forces Gilfaethwy and Gwydion into literally productive roles: for three subsequent years, the brothers are enchanted into a series of game animals, first a pair of deer, then wild boar, and finally wolves (*Mabinogion* 52–53). Thus, not only do they provide the court with potential game, but because each year they alternate genders and are forced to mate with one another, they also literally add to the bounty of the land and later to that of the court when Math transforms each of their three sons into a presumably honorable and productive subject.[7]

Punishment for magically breaking the rules of production, as with Pryderi, ironically tends not to fall on the fabricator of that "unreal" product but rather on the head of its consumer, or, in the most unusual situation in the Fourth Branch, on the head of the product itself. When Aranrhod declares that her illegitimate son, Lleu, "'shall never have a wife of the race that is now on this earth,'" Math and Gwydion create one for him out of flowers (*Mabinogion* 57–58). Blodeuedd seems the perfect wife: not just "the very fairest and best endowed maiden that mortal ever saw" (58), she fits the other criteria required of a "suitable" bride as well — she is both a virgin and, in every way, unattached (Davies 78). The ultimate commodity, she in fact appears to be a true "first gift," "an inaugural act of generosity, without any past or future, i.e. without *calculation*" (Bourdieu 171). Or is she? Certainly Blodeuedd lacks a past, and Lleu does not receive her in return for a gift already given, but Gwydion and Math certainly expect something from the young man. They created Blodeuedd as a wife for Lleu, a man with no hope of another companion, much in the way that God created Eve for Adam, and just as He wanted them to "Be fruitful, and multiply" (Gen. 1.22),[8] so do Math and Gwydion want Lleu and Blodeuedd to produce heirs, for he is their heir (Gantz 271; Sullivan 347–48) and owes them the continuation of their line.

The important issue in this part of the tale, though, is not this medieval concern with inheritance but rather Blodeuedd's failure as a perfect wife. As one critic says, "her feelings reflect a flower's impermanence" (Gantz 272) — she is unfaithful and plots with her lover to learn from Lleu how he may be killed and then to complete the deed. This inconstancy and the necessitated punishment are traceable to the manner of her creation. She is, as R. Howard Bloch says of Eve, "associated with artifice and decoration" (40) and like Eve, too, Blodeuedd does not take these things on of her own volition. However, she differs from her predecessor in that she is not just a "secondary" creation as Eve was (38, 40, 42)[9] but, by virtue of her fashioning by beings themselves created by another being, she is even farther removed from that originating act. If we take a cue from Bloch, then, and consider her as Ecclesiastical writers of the medieval period might have, we may at last understand why danger surrounds Blodeuedd, and by extension all the magical goods for exchange or gift in the Fourth Branch. Bloch quotes Cyprian, who says "'They are laying hands on God when they strive to remake what He has made, and to transform it, not knowing that everything that comes into existence is the work of God; that whatever is changed, is the work of the devil'" (qtd. on 42). Here in a nutshell is the problem with Gwydion's economic practices. It seems the danger lies not just in the unbalancing of the gift/trade continuum but instead particularly in the use of goods whose origin, in this tale of blended Christianity and traditional Welsh culture, occurs outside the natural mechanism of creation as determined by God. Consequently, punishment falls on those who receive (or are) Gwydion's magical constructs because they seek to benefit from something that, in its very essence, is sacrilegious. Gwydion protects himself from retribution, however, by "programming" the evidence of his acts to self-destruct in one way or another, thereby transforming himself into the receiver of a gift rather than of a commodity exchanged for something that should, by rights, never have existed at all.

Though they fit roughly the same pattern seen in the rest of the Fourth Branch, Gwydion's dealings with his sister Aranrhod differ significantly from those orphaned exchanges discussed previously. The reason for this perhaps rests partially on the fact that her economic function in the story parallels his, as well as on her considerable independence (Valente 336), which is second only to Math's in this tale. As in all situations concerning him, Gwydion sets in motion the events of Aranrhod's tale when he suggests her as a proper replacement for Math's now disqualified foot-holder, Goewin (*Mabinogion* 54). One critic suggests that Gwydion knew perfectly well of Aranrhod's lack of fitness for the role and that he wished to cause her the humiliation of "demonstrating her fertility publicly" (Valente 335); if true, we might discern his acquisitiveness at work here again. Aranrhod steps over Math's magic wand and, failing in dramatic fashion the virginity test, she immediately gives birth to one son and "drop[s] a small something"— her second son — as she flees the castle. Gwydion snatches the latter up and whisks him away to foster as his own (*Mabinogion* 54). Once again, he twists the situation to his advantage and walks away with an heir in trade for Aranrhod's "everlasting shame" (Valente 335).

But Aranrhod's shame is a small price to pay for her continued independence, particularly since this seems the only cost to her for the abandonment of her children. By refusing to perform the work expected of a mother though Gwydion demands her to, Aranrhod uses tactics to resist pigeonholing as a body marked by its productivity and by pure selflessness. Rather than freely granting the name, arms, and wife that her son requires in order for the court to consider him a consequential member (341), Aranrhod refuses to participate in a game of gift-giving from which she would emerge with nothing of any real use to her. She manifests her power over her son through a series of binding restrictions by declaring herself the only possible source of these examples of symbolic capital and then, one-by-one, withholding them, forcing shame on him in compensation for what she experienced as a result of his very public birth. Thus she attempts to maintain her relatively dominant position — being a landowner and ruler in her own right — by manipulating those sources of symbolic power that, as a woman, she can control. Ironically, Gwydion interprets his sister's behavior as evil ("thou art a wicked woman" [*Mabinogion* 55]), although his own scheming hardly ranks as less harmful than Aranrhod's.

Gwydion exploits her preference for trade when he appears in disguise with her son at Caer Aranrhod, her castle (*Mabinogion* 55–56). In the shape first of a shoemaker and his four year old apprentice, Gwydion presents Aranrhod with footwear of the most beautiful gold leather (in truth, transformed seaweed) for which she promises "'he shall have payment'" (56). On the second visit, disguised as two bards, he offers himself and her son as protectors against the approaching armada of ships he has spun out of the air (56–57). When she solicits these luxury goods and this proposed service from him, Gwydion tricks Aranrhod into providing her son with the name, Lleu Llaw Gyffes, and the arms she originally vowed to keep from him. And as always, as soon as Gwydion receives what he seeks, that which he offered in trade vanishes. Aranrhod, who fought to avoid taking part in the gift economy, ends up in fact doing precisely that, though against her will, for she has indeed made her payment without receiving anything but deception and a challenge to her self-determination in return. Still she fares better than Gwydion's other economic partners in that she remains at least physically unscathed after her encounters with him. This may result from what I suggested above — the fact that she, unlike Pryderi, never actually possesses and consequently never benefits from the ill-produced goods proffered her. Alternately, she may owe her escape from harm to a unique position in the social order: unmarried and powerful, independent of her family, and living distantly with castle and lands of her own, Aranrhod is such a social outrider that her practices would have only the most minimal repercussions on the region.

But what are the repercussions of Gwydion's conduct? The pattern of his behavior and the immediate consequences to his "victims" make it clear, I think, that real intent and calculation underlie his actions, but it remains necessary to address precisely how this destabilizes the gift-giving and exchange economies in the Fourth Branch and why Gwydion should wish to upset the existing balance. Historian Wendy Davies states that in tenth and eleventh century Wales, "the ideology of exchange" was gaining recognition in that country (54) but that evidence suggests a lack of any established market at that time and indicates instead the continued importance of the gift (57). Even without knowing the degree to which trade factored in to the earliest versions of the Fourth Branch, Gwydion clearly takes advantage of the newly-developing trade economy's structure to undermine it: by making it possible that, *after* the apparent "trade," one of the parties involved will prove untrustworthy by engaging in a false exchange, he turns this practice into an extremely risky one that may cost the innocent participant far more than he or she gains, if not everything. Thus, he shifts the balance of desirability back toward the gift, but since he is the only figure in the Fourth Branch who freely engages in this particular system, he benefits doubly: first, by creating the rules of the game himself as he plays it and, second, by always coming out the winner who thus avoids obligations to anyone. He is the consummate tactician, who engages in

> ... an entirely different kind of production, consumption ... characterized by its ruses, its fragmentation ..., its poaching, its clandestine nature, its tireless but quiet activity, in short by its quasi-invisibility, since it shows itself not in its own products ... but in an art of using those imposed on it [de Certeau 31].

Here again, we can discern parallels to modern-day advertising techniques and reality TV shows such as *Survivor*. The self-advancing ethic endorsed by Gwydion reoccurs in these mass media creations as advertisements that promise consumers results far beyond the scope of the product or service's real-world capabilities,[10] as evident in the case of diet products that seem not only to make you slimmer but also to dye and cut your hair and put you in the hands of a Hollywood-quality make-up artist; or in situations that "naturalize ... cutthroat competition" and the need to "'battle tooth and claw for a limited supply of capital and success'" (Murray 44)—despite claims by *Survivor*'s Burnett that "everybody starts off equal" on his show (Burnett qtd. in Murray 47). These "inconsistencies and contradictions" (48), far from being liabilities to the constructions or people they characterize, in fact strengthen them precisely because they remain, as de Certeau explains, "quasi-invisible." Their ephemerality, fluidity, and mobility make Gwydion and his present-day counterparts elusive, promoting such a degree of amnesia among their targets that a consensus opinion becomes not only difficult to establish but also to sustain and then disseminate. Consequently, these tacticians find themselves able to play both beneficent economic partner and opportunist with impunity ... again and again.

Notes

1. Gwyn Jones and Thomas Jones, whose 1949 translation I use here, chose to refer to the Welsh tales as the *Mabinogion* despite their recognition that this convention likely originated in an error made by medieval scribes and perpetuated by Lady Charlotte Guest in the 19th Century (ix–x). To reflect the contemporary movement to correct this error, I will refer to the collected tales throughout as the *Mabinogi*, though I risk being guilty of the "sheerest pedantry" (x) the Joneses associated with this push. References to the Jones translation will reflect their spelling of the title.

2. Some of these critical works include: Gruffydd, W. P. *Folklore and Mythology in the* Mabinogion (1961): U of Wales P; Eggers, John Phillip. "The Weeding of the Garden: Tennyson's Gereint Idylls and the *Mabinogion.*" *Victorian Poetry* 4 (1966): 45–51; Beach, Sarah. "Breaking the Pattern: The Owl Service and the *Mabinogion.*" *Mythlore* 20.1 (1994): 10–14.

3. See Sullivan and Valente, respectively.

4. Bourdieu's hats are many, though his sociological and political interests are most relevant here. For an overview of his thinking on other topics, see *The Johns Hopkins Guide to Literary Theory and Criticism* (ed. Michael Groden and Martin Kreiswirth).

5. Murray's critical analysis of *Survivor* and its creator works to reveal the contradictions inherent in Burnett's own interpretation of the show's ideological standpoint and what it valorizes in and exposes about American society and human life in general (as his *Field Guide* puts it, it exposes "'the core essence of humanity'" [43]). He terms Burnett's invocation of social Darwinism "uncritical," showing that he "employs" it "toward effacing discursive contradictions and naturalizing an imperialistic gaze and the commodification of both the self and pleasure" (43–4)—and also to sell his product. While the emphasis on "discursive contradictions" and imperialism are not my focus here, I find the references to "commodification of ... self and pleasure" apt when thinking about Gwydion. As is the case with *Survivor*, however, the question can still be asked of the *Mabinogi*: to what degree is the presence of such commodification and the economic situation it appears to represent an accurate and complete picture of actual cultural circumstances? Though I treat the shift from gift to exchange-based economy as fact here, historians continue to debate the issue.

6. Linda Dégh's *American Folklore and the Mass Media* (1994) makes a similar argument, suggesting that contemporary Americans have a "need for fulfillment by magic where rational behavior is insufficient" (Dégh 54). Although the chapter titled "Magic as a Mail-Order Commodity" focuses primarily on the present day peddling of supposedly "real" magical products and services like miracle drug cures and psychic hotlines, she also finds a metaphorical use of magic in mass media advertisements for more common objects that use disembodied voices and personified inanimate objects (55). This is the form to which I refer here.

7. Each of the sons born to Gwydion and Gilfaethwy are baptized and named by Math in remembrance of their origins: "The three sons of false Gilfaethwy, / Three champions true, / Bleiddwn, Hyddwn, Hychdwn Hir" (53). Despite the promise of these words, the sons make no further appearances in the Fourth Branch, or elsewhere in Welsh literature.

8. References are to the King James Bible.

9. Though in Genesis 1.27, God creates Adam and Eve at the same time, I take my lead here from Yale's R. Howard Bloch. Bloch's study of attitudes toward women during the medieval period indicates that the attitude toward Eve as "secondary, collateral, supplemental" (42) predominated, affecting and infusing in broad terms the treatment of women.

10. Again, Dégh's book is an excellent resource for further discussion of this topic.

Works Cited

Bloch, R. Howard. *Medieval Misogyny and the Invention of Western Romantic Love.* Chicago: University of Chicago Press, 1991.

Bourdieu, Pierre. *Outline of a Theory of Practice.* Cambridge: Cambridge Universtiy Press, 2000.

Davies, Wendy. *Wales in the Early Middle Ages.* Leicester, UK: Leicester University Press, 1982.
de Certeau, Michel. *The Practice of Everyday Life.* Berkeley: University of California Press, 1984.
Fulton, Helen. "The *Mabinogi* and the Education of Princes in Medieval Wales." *Medieval Celtic Literature and Society.* Ed. Helen Fulton. Portland, OR: Four Courts Press, 2005. 230–47.
Gantz, Jeffrey. "Thematic Structure in the Four Branches of the Mabinogi." *The Mabinogi: A Book of Essays.* Ed. C.W. Sullivan III. New York: Garland Publishing, 1996. 265–75.
The Mabinogion. Trans. Gwyn Jones and Thomas Jones. London: J.M. Dent, 1993.
Murray, Keat. "Surviving *Survivor*: Reading Mark Burnett's *Field Guide* and De-naturalizing Social Darwinism as Entertainment." *Journal of American & Comparative Cultures* 24.34 (2008): 43–54.
Sullivan, C. W., III. "Inheritance and Lordship in *Math*." *The Mabinogi: A Book of Essays.* Ed. C.W. Sullivan III. New York: Garland Publishing, 1996. 347–66.
Valente, Roberta L. "Gwydion and Aranrhod: Crossing the Borders of Gender in *Math*." *The Mabinogi: A Book of Essays.* Ed. C.W. Sullivan III. New York: Garland Publishing, 1996. 331–45.

The Hand at the Window
Twm Siôn Cati, the Welsh Colonial Trickster

JONATHAN EVANS *and*
STEPHEN KNIGHT

They have long been in love, since Twm rescued Lady Joan from the Cardiganshire highwayman Deio the Devil. They meet again in London; then after her husband Sir George Devereaux dies she agrees to join Twm in his cave in mountainous mid–Wales, but her father sweeps her away. They meet once more: she says he must outwit her to win her. Now she is back at her mansion in Ystrad Ffin. Twm, dressed as a soldier, comes to the window. He waves his sword, takes her hand, and vows to cut it off if she will not marry him. He has with him a priest and witnesses. After a lively debate Joan agrees: but she had already decided. Twm finds she has already installed in her own house her own marriage party, including his father, Sir John Wynn of Gwydir.

All ends happily, with that mix of boldness (or rashness), dramatic males, and knowing females which is characteristic of the adventures and the myth of Twm Siôn Cati and most Welsh tradition. Married to Joan, Twm — an outlaw who has been called "the Welsh Robin Hood," — will thrive in respectability and become mayor of Brecon, in addition to his triumphs in riding, fighting, scheming and — this is a Welsh hero after all — writing poetry.

This story of a male Cinderella has itself been firmly kept below literary stairs. Never properly edited, never taken seriously as what was in its own time seen as "the first Welsh novel,"[1] and dismissed by the Anglophile critic Belinda Humfrey as "of no literary merit" (35), Thomas Pritchard's 1828 novel *Twm Siôn Cati* responds to contextual reading, especially post-colonial analysis, as a major text, both shaping and predicting what would be a potent force: the English-language culture and self-identity in Wales.

In Pritchard's account, Joan's husband is English, but he likes Twm well. Twm's early mentor is also the English Squire Graspacre, and though his eponymous land-taking is colonial enough, he also admires local practices and qualities and has the boy educated and act as his secretary — until Twm's mischief emerges too clearly. If the English can be friends of a kind, so the Welsh can be complicit with colonialism, whether pompously servile like the Reverend Inco Evans or meanly submissive like the hill-farmer Morris Grug. Twm's world is that of the colonized hybrid, energized both by his native tradition and by what he has adapted of the incomer's vigor. Both his career and the text he dominates are the first formations of a new identity and social culture, to be called in the colonizer's tongue Anglo-Welsh, and known to the natives as Cym-

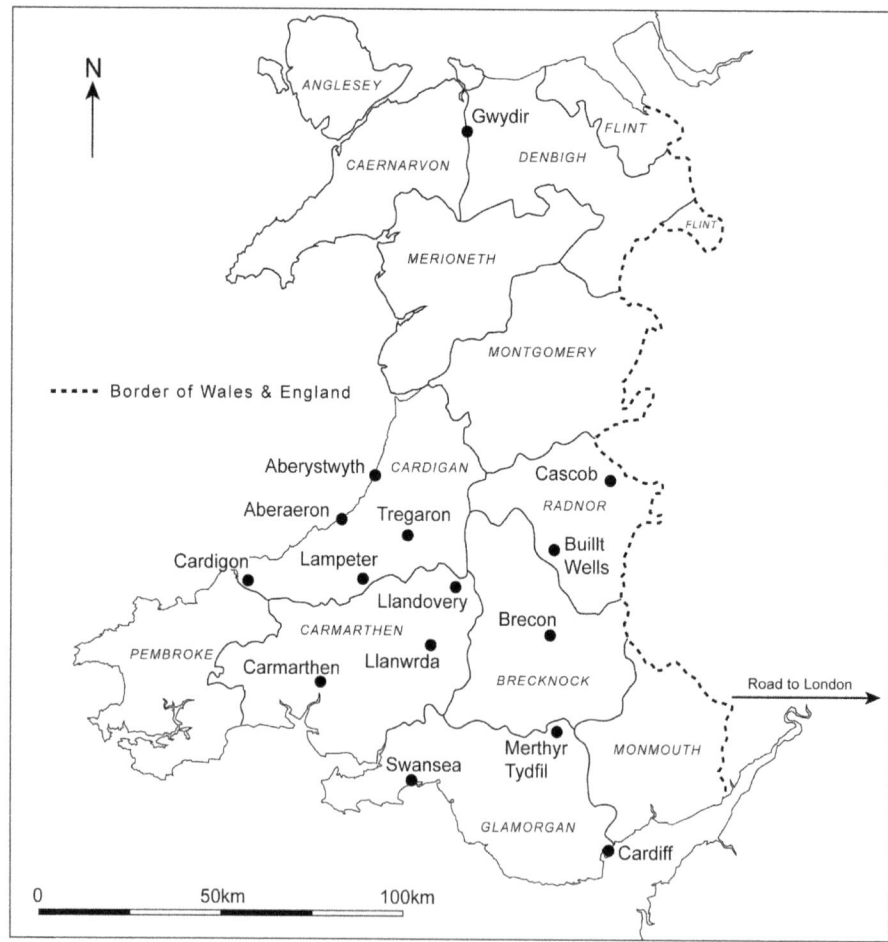

Map of Twm Siôn Cati's Wales

reig, a word, different from Cymraeg, "Welsh"; meaning "from Wales but not Welsh-speaking."

Scholarship tells us Thomas Prichard was born in 1789 in Builth Wells, a market town on the River Wye, where mountainous Wales to the west meets the prosperous farming land running down towards the Severn and England (Adams 51–2). In this dialectical domain Llywelyn the last true prince of Wales was murdered in 1282[2]; from here later came the between-wars novelist of Welsh social and gender tension, Hilda Vaughan, headed for London, New York, and now at last her proper evaluation. Prichard himself looked for success both to England and its language. With an ineffective lawyer as father, he turned actor, and was always a wordsmith — at first on the stage, including in London, and then as an author: unusually for an actor, he wrote poetry and fiction, not plays. Though he never rejected Welshness and returned there in the 1820s to make a living with his pen, he seems to have had little Cymraeg — his letters seek help at times with source material and he often spells names with an English ear.[3] He added "Jeffery Llewelyn" to his apparent baptismal name: Sam Adams suggests that, with a trickster's touch, Pritchard borrowed the name from a Welsh reverend he sought to interest in his career — unsuccessfully (Adams 53–4). With the full glory of three forenames, Prichard ventured into print, first in London.

After the Napoleonic wars, varied political forces were at work in Britain, from English chauvinism and conservative repression to radical, even physical, resistance, and culture was responsively active. Three cultural forces interested and energized Prichard. One of these was encapsulated in the "Waverley" novels, the powerful realization of the past in a fiction that considered national difference within Britain; another strand, more overtly resistant, which Scott himself both realized and displaced in Loxley in *Ivanhoe*, was the crescent interest in the English outlaw tradition: Keats, Reynolds, Peacock, Leigh Hunt, Nottinghamshire radicals, and even Charlotte Brontë were to find value in the tradition of Robin Hood, a figure who, without noble blood, figures native nobility in his resistance to oppressive authority.[4] Prichard had contact with this group: the radical Hunt brothers lent their names as the London publisher of his *Welsh Minstrelsy* in 1824.

Historicity and resistance to authority were no doubt attractive enough to Prichard: more directly appealing would have been a third force, the growth of English-language mediation of Welsh tradition. Much of this was in the form of the novel: Andrew Davies and Jane Aaron have charted the substantial development in Wales-oriented fiction,[5] which meshed with the contemporary growth in tourism — Napoleon was for a while keeping at bay the English who had formerly infested France. A busy London Welsh presence was exemplified in the Honourable Society of Cymmrodorion, founded seventy years before, with support from both fine scholars and grandees like Sir Watkin Williams Wynn, friend to the Prince Regent and lord of the mighty family that had, in myth at least, produced Twm. There were also journals like the society's *Cymmrodor* and the *Cambro-Briton*, and Prichard joined in this exile self-realization with his anthology of English-language poems (some of them his, others translated from Welsh, but not by him), *Welsh Minstrelsy* and the fuller *The Cambrian Wreath* of 1828.

Some poets of the period had an interest in Welsh myth and history, as in Southey's epic *Madog*—in which the Welsh discover America—and Thelwall's verse play *The Fairy of the Lake*—Arthur defeats the Germans, including by implication the Hanoverians. But prose was to be Prichard's major step. Here he surely followed Thomas Love Peacock, whose wife was from north Wales and who published his own Robin Hood story *Maid Marian* in 1822 and would produce a richly learned and comic reworking of an ancient Welsh story *The Misfortunes of Elphin* in 1829 (its source had been included in *Welsh Minstrelsy*). Prichard surely read in *The Cambro-Briton* and elsewhere the work of W. F. Deacon, an English litterateur who was for a while a schoolteacher at Llanwrda in Twm's Carmarthenshire. Deacon mixes Welsh topography and quaint customs—the long standing diet of first-contact colonial literature—with some awareness of tradition, but he shows both his limited respect for that and his determination to try for the mainstream in the novella *Twm Shon Catty* that he published in his own anthology, *The Inn-Keeper's Album*, in 1823—a third of its items have a Welsh focus.

As indicated by Deacon's subtitle—*The Welch Rob Roy*—it was Scott's footsteps he wanted to dog, but at some distance: the plot bears no resemblance to *Rob Roy*, nor any relation to the earlier Twm tradition. Here he is active in the very early fifteenth century rising against King Henry IV, through which those who put him on the throne indicated their discontent at their limited rewards. Twm has become a brave warrior for Glendower (to the Welsh, Glyn Dŵr), leading bowmen in a mode more like English victories at Crécy and Poitiers than the Robin Hood forest-marksman tradition. Though the Welshmen's courage is grand and the Welsh scenery even grander, they are, with an appeal to English attitudes, eventually defeated by the king. Twm has met and married a beautiful lady, here given the English name Elinor (in fact, French), though she is, as usual, from Ystrad Ffin. After his gallant death in battle protecting the Welsh rearguard (surely a memory of Roland, also much discussed in the period), she herself goes mad for love in full Gothic fashion.

Deservedly little-known as it is today for its fatuity, Deacon's story nevertheless made a mark. It appeared in contemporary magazines, which may look like syndication, but the variations in the versions suggest piracy. The version in *The Portfolio* in 1827 is entitled *The Cambrian Freebooter* and Twm has become a Welsh war-leader who withdraws into the forest after the failure of his rebellion against Henry IV, less heroic than in Deacon, but a little more realistic. *The Cornish Magazine* of April 1828 has a short story called "Spiceilegia no 2: A Tale of the Olden Times,"[6] in which Thomas Jones of Tregaron, the authentic sixteenth-century person, has reverted to an ancient Welsh chieftain. Then in 1830 a London publisher released Deacon's story as *The Life, Exploits and Death of Twm John Catty, the Celebrated Welch Rob Roy, and his beautiful bride Elinor, Lady of Llandisent*: she has moved to a very small Carmarthenshire location.

No doubt Prichard felt he could do better than Deacon, and that his nation deserved it. By the late 1820s he was back in Wales in Aberystwyth, living through theatre and writing. John Cox, a local printer, produced at Prichard's own expense in 1828 what was certainly the first coherent gathering and processing of the Twm Siôn Cati story, in either Welsh or English. The 1820s were turbulent times in Wales. The recession of the last two quarters of 1825 was the trigger for the start of serious working-class resistance across the industrial south, to peak in the proclamation in Merthyr in 1831 of a worker-led republic, with the first unfurling in British history of a red flag: the army moved in, not without resistance. There was also a growing awareness of Welsh vulnerability to international forces. Not all responses were admirable — riots against incoming Irish workers occurred across south Wales in 1826, but more in keeping with labor tradition were recurrent strikes against owners of iron foundries and coal mines, many of them English and not a few transferring their capital from running slave-ships out of Bristol and Liverpool. Meanwhile rural resistance to exploitative landowners, again many from outside Wales, began to simmer in the west and led to the spectacular Rebecca Riots of 1839–44. Crews of men with blackened faces, with a cross-dressed leader on a white horse, would by night destroy toll-gates and sometimes toll-houses to make travel free for local people: eventually they attacked Carmarthen jail and liberated their colleagues. They called themselves, with Old Testament reference, Rebecca and her Daughters.[7]

Prichard has no direct relation with this contemporary turbulence, but it shadows his text. Much of his action and reference deals with the interface of Wales and England, rural and urban, peasant production and commercial profit, localizing these tensions in an earlier period of conflict, much as the London liberals, from Ritson to Leigh Hunt, used "the old days of Robin Hood" to displace their democratic anger. Prichard's focus was a native hero of the sixteenth century, famous equally for memorable tricksterism and resistance to the social authority that Tudor England was imposing on Wales. It did not escape Prichard's notice that native complicity played a large part in such a process: the Tudors and many of their agents, both in England and Wales, were themselves Welsh.

Twm had long been heard of, but not in the form which Prichard passed on, and the Welsh still enjoy — the Twm website announces Twm Siôn Cati Day at Tregaron and makes available suitable Welsh outlaw merchandise. To comprehend the development and meaning of Twm the colonial trickster, it will be useful to start with Thomas, the sixteenth-century person.

According to the most recent authority, Daniel Huws, Thomas Jones was born in August 1532, illegitimate son to the grandly named Siôn ap Dafydd ap Madog ap Hywel Moethe from Porth-y-Ffynnon, Tregaron (Huws 635–6). Or, in the English that the Tudor dynasty and its officers preferred, John Davies Maddocks Powell the Luxurious, of Fountain-Gate, Tregaron. So Thomas was, as Dafydd H. Evans puts it, the son of an *uchelwr*,[8] a "high man": this includes gentry, but Hwyel Moethe was a very high man, native aristocracy. Thomas's mother was Catrin (abbreviated to Cati), illegitimate daughter of Maredudd ab Ieuan ap Robert, himself connected to the Wynns of Gwydir. Almost all Welsh surnames are familial and as an illegitimate boy living with his mother, Twm took both his parents' first names, Siôn and Cati. At various times he used the name Moethe as a surname, both for its grandeur and to refer to the mighty Hywel.

Thomas Jones, Porth-y-Ffynnon, was known to the law in 1559, when, called a "gentleman," he was granted a pardon for crimes unspecified. Two years later he was arraigned for felony — Huws expects more records like this to emerge as more early records are catalogued. Early seventeenth-century records link him with Brecon, a busy town and forward English military base on the London-Ireland road; he also bought land near his birthplace Tregaron. As early as 1564 comes the first of several references to him as an *arwyddfardd*, "a poet of portents" or genealogist: one of the pedigrees he wrote in 1580 was for Joan Price's brother 27 years before he married her in 1607 when he was 75, just after her husband, Tomas Williams of Ystrad Ffin, died. Jones himself died in 1609 leaving everything to Joan, and she (already elderly) married again within a year, this time to Sir George Devereaux. By an earlier wife Thomas had three sons and what he calls his "base son" John Moethe, also a genealogist (Evans 14). Jones the poet is recorded too: there are two poems that seem certain to be by him, as well as a number of witty stanzas called *englynion*. One of the major poems purports to be a *marwnad*, an elegy to a drover, Lewys Ddu ("Lewis the Black," aka Lewys Cig Eidion, "Lewis the Beef"), said in the poem to have been killed in a Cheapside inn after chatting up the landlord's wife. But however credible this may sound of the evidently under-nuanced Lewys, it is not true: the ironic elegy was a common form of jest among early modern Welsh poets (and still thrives today). Huws says of Thomas, "satire and bawdry may have been his forte" as a poet (Huws 636). He is also known in poems by others: one splendidly calls him "tarw ag eryr Tregaron" — "the bull and the eagle of Tregaron" (Evans 15): note the elegant consonant-rhyme of *cynghanedd*, the height of Welsh poetic style.[9] Thomas was in his genealogical work a substantial scholar and cousin to the Elizabethan mage and visionary John Dee, himself from north Wales: they met on a number of occasions as Dee's diary records (Huws 636).

This is the life-story of a man basically, if uncertainly, of the gentry, who followed a wild youth with a somewhat, if also uncertainly, dignified career. He may not have reformed that much: records indicate a long conflict with the

Rev. Morgan Dafydd, of Pantsiryf (a farm near Tregaron, with an interesting name-link to legal officialdom — it means "sheriff's (small) valley"). This climaxed in 1601 when the Reverend was accused of trying to stab Thomas with a concealed dagger. The church party were well tooled-up: the court record speaks of "swords, short swords, spears, daggers, javelins, axes, rakes and pitchforks" (Evans 16). Then after marrying Joan, Thomas was accused of forging her dead husband's will (Huws 636).

Seeming like euphemizing approval of this lively life against the law, there is a strong popular tradition of tricksterish mischief developed about Twm. Such a louche career is not unknown for figures who were basically at odds with authority. John Skelton, tutor to Henry VIII and a very learned satirical poet, soon became widely famous as a jokester, and Merlin, lord of socially critical knowledge, had by the eighteenth century developed in popular culture a comic reputation. That process enabled Prichard to combine resistance to authority and native wit and vigor with the ethnically self-conscious interests of the London Welsh, but he also followed Scott's lead in bringing the story to bear on the political relations between his country and England.

While the pamphlets, Welsh or English, had been joke-books (much like those about Skelton), Prichard was clearly aware of the account of Twm found in Samuel Meyrick's *History and Antiquities of Cardiganshire* of 1808: it gave his father as Sir John Wynn and provided several anecdotes, including the hand at the window.[10] He also knew an 8-page pamphlet *Y Digrifwr, Casgliad o Gampiau a Dichellion Thomas Jones o Dregaron*, ("The Jokester: A Collection of the Deeds and Tricks of Thomas Jones of Tregaron"), which he sent to his reliable and generous friend the Rev. William Jenkins Rees of Cascob in Powys, eastern Wales, seeking a translation: he clearly did not know its apparent source, the English-language *The Joker or Merry Companion* of 1763.[11] Prichard evidently shaped the anecdotes in this material through another model, Henry Fielding's novel *Tom Jones*. Though English critics have had no interest in a Wales-based story and the Welsh Twm commentators appear unfamiliar with the English classic, it seems obvious that Prichard found a framework for structuring Twm's life as a novel in Fielding's mock epic. There is no clear sign of the more famous Tom Jones being Welsh — though the name suggests it, he comes from the far west and the squire who patronizes him and is involved in his birth is called Western — but he follows the same road to London as Twm will do, and many of Twm's adventures, with the beauteous lady of his choice and the peasant girl of his youth, as well as on the road, seem structurally parallel to Tom Jones's escapades.

It will be helpful to sketch Prichard's story. The basis is the 1839 second edition, which at times elaborates and sophisticates the 1828 edition:

> Twm's mother Cati, living near Tregaron, had a son by the visiting Sir John Wynn of Gwydir, friend of local Squire Graspacre, who had bought her father's lands. While the squire's Welsh wife despised the locals, the Squire rather admired them. Twm went to his mother's simple school, then one in the village run by Rev Inco Evans, whom he mocked.

Graspacre then employed Rev John David Rhys, a Welsh-language poet, to teach Twm (his wife wanted the boy educated: she too was a Wynn of Gwydir).

When the squire's wife died he sent Twm away to work for "Morris Greeg" on a hill-farm, with the poor Jewish boy Moses. Life was very hard there, and they played tricks on Morris and others (some quite cruel). After Moses runs away smallpox strikes and all four of Morris's children die: Twm is ill alone in the barn and has a vision of a beautiful woman in widow's weeds. Back in Tregaron the squire takes him on as a servant and he likes Gwenni Cadwgan. The squire sends Twm to bring her to him on his horse: he asks for Cadwgan's "lass" but Twm ties an "ass" on his horse and puts it into the squire's bed. Twm beats up Marmaduke Graspacre, steals and sells Parson Evans's horse, and goes on the run disguised as a woman. He is robbed by a highwayman, sees the sea for the first time at Aberaeron and sings ballads at Cardigan Fair (still as a woman), and arranges for the Rev. Evans to be tossed in a blanket. He meets the Rev. Rhys then rescues from a highwayman Lady Joan Devereux of Ystrad Ffin. Her husband Sir George is grateful and Twm stays with them for two years: he wins bets at riding, and plays many tricks—the climax is when he steals a bull by putting it in boots to cover its tracks.

Twm, now knowing Joan is the widow in the vision, goes to London to pay bills for her husband. On the way he defeats two highwaymen, meets Wat the mole-catcher from Tregaron and hears of Gwenni, then rescues the Bishop of St Asaph from a highwayman. In London he becomes a gentleman, meeting socially his father, and Lady Joan, and then hears Sir George is dead.

Back in Wales he and Joan meet, but her family (Prices from Brecon) make her separate from him. He meets Moses again, they play many tricks, especially on the Rev. Evans. He writes to Joan "Cywydd y Gofid" ("Poem of Affliction") and he lives in a cave where Cardigan and Brecon and Carmarthen meet. Joan accepts him (while he is dressed as a woman) but her father stops her meeting him at Llandovery fair, where, alone, he plays tricks, enters court dressed as a puritan minister, hears himself accused and fights his way out with two pistols. At Brecon Twm wins the gold cup for horseracing and Joan wins the eisteddfod for reciting his poem to her. She says he must outwit her to win her. He grabs her money but she grabs it back.

At Joan's house at Ystrad Ffin, Twm appears dressed as a redcoat. He seizes Joan's hand at the window and says he will cut it off if she refuses him. With him he has his friends and a minister to marry them. She agrees, but invites them all in: in the house are her friends and a minister, and Twm's father, all ready for the wedding. They live happily in Brecon, where Twm becomes mayor, and he also builds a mansion on the site of his mother's house in Tregaron.

From the start, Prichard's narrative maneuvers in more complex ways than does Deacon's. W. F. Deacon's use of the Twm story is straightforward colonial appropriation: native scenery and native vitality are admired, but native alterity has no place to stand. The armies of the king of England are as triumphant as the sentimentality of the English audience, and that version of Twm fits into the pattern of first-contact romance, well-known around the world from the native American Pocahontas to the Australian indigenous detective Boney—and Rob Roy, to whom the Welsh outlaw is connected in Deacon's subtitle.

In Pritchard's re-working, Graspacre is a colonizing name and he behaves like it in the opening paragraphs as he seizes Cati's father's land and, after his wife's death, summons girls in sexually feudal fashion. But even then he in part eludes the negative model: Twm's grandfather is actually destroyed by his Welsh lawyer, and the squire's lust is reduced to kissing an ass. On the positive side, Graspacre admires the communal practices of the locals, and has the sense to see they are right to reprobate his Don Juanism — though the family he then protectively gathers round him is much more unregenerately colonial than he is by himself.

If the colonizer can have some merit, the native is not necessarily admirable as either noble or savage. Cati's school is genial, but decidedly backward: Inco Evans's school has neither quality. The Rev. John David Rhys is the only entirely positive character in the whole text, and his wisdom and poetry bring out the best in Twm — but the text wryly reports Rhys at the end as estranged from his *gwerin* origins,[12] having become in turn continental Catholic priest, rich doctor, and eventually a resident of part-English Breconshire. In ordinary life the Welsh of the story waver between the struggles of Cadwgan and his pretty daughter, the sour tragedy of hill-farmer Morris Grug and his family, the opportunistic and sometimes malicious scramblings of the really poor like Wat and Moses, and the bungling approach to life shared cross-ethnically by spear-carrying natives like Jack of Sir Gâr and Ready Rosser and English gentry residents like Sir George Devereaux and Marmaduke Graspacre, as well as the ill-fated criminals, Welsh like Deio the Devil or English like Tom Dorbell.

They are all prisoners at the bar of mischance or misdeeds, and most of them suddenly suffer disasters, many of them fatal. The story of these characters is not simply one of colonial malice and colonized innocence. Wat can be an exploiter; Devereaux can be generous. The overarching colonial situation where English landowners take profits and Welsh producers must plod into England with their pigs and cattle is merely the context against which the multiplicity of human motive and energy constructs its complex dialectical interactions.

Twm himself represents the gathering, overlapping, and mutual contradictions of the social, locational, and national multiplicities of the text. In sequence he is an unruly peasant bastard, an aspirant scholar-bard, a scamp of the heather, an avenging trickster, a courageous rescuer, a champion gamester, a courtly lover, a metropolitan lounger, a poet, harpist, man of decisive action and humor and, finally, like the real early modern Thomas Jones, a man of some standing.

Later writers will create flexible Welsh heroes — Lewis Jones's sickly leftist visionary Len Roberts, Gwyn Thomas's unforgettable quartet of unemployed folk-philosophers, Emyr Humphreys's polyvalent yet pathetic Reverend J. T. Miles — and heroines too, like "Allen Raine" with Gwenifer, her *Queen of the Rushes* and Rachel Trezise's modernly angst-ridden, but also atavistic, Rebecca. But none of them will condense so much of both native Welsh and colonized Welsh variety and tension into one figure as Prichard managed to do with the intensely hybrid figure of Twm, embracing as he does what the Welsh could imagine as difference and response, as first English tourism and then English industry changed the face, and language, of their country for ever.

From the distance of the present it might seem that Prichard, by presenting in English novel form an outlaw who has been called "the Welsh Robin Hood," was, however complex, merely joining the flow of colonial contact fictions that invited English readers, through English publishers, to experience at a comfortable distance the interesting difference of a strange country. But whereas that was primarily the role of the first-contact romances that flourished around 1800 and continued into the twentieth century,[13] it is not true in this case. Prichard's first two editions of 1828 and 1839 were both published in Wales, and the major response was in that country. The sub-title *The Welsh Robin Hood* was not employed until the London versions of the Wales-generated third edition. The first appearance of the novel was as *The Adventures and Vagaries of Twm Sion Cati: Descriptions of Life in Wales, Enterspersed with Poems*. The 1839 replaced the documentary sub-title with the firmly local *A Wild Wag of Wales*: neither invokes a quaint variant of an English outlaw. Twm may be in English and so not Cymraeg, but he is still unregenerately Cymreig.

It is clear from the evidence of newspapers and publications that in the south and the east there were substantial numbers of people who liked to read in English — which does not mean they did not speak Welsh. It is still a common phenomenon for people who use Welsh as their everyday oral language at home and work to prefer to fill in forms in the colonially-imposed English: they have little confidence in their formal written Welsh because in the past it was rarely taught at school. The maritime coastal towns had long been dominantly mercantile and English — that was principally how people and goods traveled around the country before railways — and by 1800 the southern coast had a substantial English incomer presence of varied origins: deliberate settlements in southern Pembrokeshire, from cross-estuary interchanges with Somerset and Devon right along the coast, and in the Swansea and Cardiff areas the growing need for industrial labor; in eastern Wales good and fairly level farming land made penetration of English speakers common by this period — right up to Prichard's Builth Wells, or Buellt.[14] The fact that Carmarthen, today still a substantially Welsh-speaking area, sustained English-language newspapers and publishers makes it clear that in non-mountainous Wales there was both an English settlement and a culturally hybrid community. Prichard, himself just an easterner, came from London to live in the far and very Welsh (but still maritime) west, at Aberystwyth, but wrote for income first a poetic guide to the town and region in 1824, then in 1828 both a real guide to the town and *Twm Sion Cati*, offering in various ways Welsh traditions for dissemination in what was already the second language of the country.

Hybridity is marked in the events and attitude of the text. As the synopsis shows, Squire Graspacre is simultaneously an exploitative incoming landlord, a classical colonizer, and also someone who to a considerable degree sympathizes with the local culture, however little he can genuinely share it. At the very start the text somewhat reassesses his surname by saying he did not enclose the natives' land, but paid for it—not well, but in cash. The story offers a lengthy discussion of his interest in Welsh habits and attitudes, and provides a powerful and even rueful symbol of this partially incorporated figure: at the elaborate folkloric wedding of Cati and Jack Sir Gâr, a large rough figure sits silently, smoking and drinking. Only at the end is it revealed that it is the squire, silent because he is a monoglot, but evidently enjoying the event. He also generously patronizes Twm, at least until he sends him off to the hill-farm, and this, the text implies, is caused by the removal of his wife's influence through her death, not his malice: she is herself Welsh, a Wynn of Gwydir, who adopts English pretensions but feels for her blood. Though their son Marmaduke is therefore part–Welsh and of *uchelwr* connection, he, like many a mestizo, replicates his mother's position of self-distancing and is represented as a typical foolish English-visitor type, essentially liable to be gulled by Twm. The squire's sister and nieces are more unregenerately English, with a frosty gentry manner and hostile to all things native. They come from Exeter: at first sight this is a surprise, as Gloucester or Bristol might seem more likely sources of colonial unpleasantness, but there were in fact large numbers of Devonians in south Wales, through the maritime connection before the floods of industrial workers arrived, and the text appears to be tapping into specific hostility against that region's center of respectability and self-esteem.

The threatening role played by the Graspacre ladies is to a degree paralleled by the Scottish peddler whose plans to exploit Welsh purchases are brusquely frustrated by Twm's pranks (first in the 1839 edition), but the novel does not deal to any real extent with the problem of the mercantile English in Wales— the colonists are rural possessioners, though like Graspacre, Sir George Devereaux is well-disposed to Twm apparently disregarding his devotion of Lady Devereaux, and it is her Welsh father, with Sir George's English family, who is the main agent of their separation after Sir George's death.

A number of the Welsh who are to some degree hostile to Twm ape English attitudes like Mrs Graspacre: the servile numbskull, Ready Rosser, Magistrate Powell from Brecon is unfriendly at first, and firmly opposed to Twm are Joan's Anglophile Price family also from that English forward military base (notably malicious are her aunts Miss Felina Tomtabby Price and Miss Euphemia Polparrot Price). Most complicit of the natives is the regularly hostile and recurrently humiliated the Rev. Evans: the 1839 edition makes him not banal Evan Evans but Inco Evans, a very rare name surely referring to the seventeenth-century Welsh-originated, London-based architect, stage designer, and royal lackey, Inigo Jones.[15]

When Prichard revised his text for the 1839 edition, he appears to have realized at least some of the changes he had in mind when, in the new preface, he spoke of his "deep regret that he could not afford, in a pecuniary sense, to sacrifice the whole edition, at the shrine of his more matured judgment."[16] Presumably he meant that as he wrote for a living he could not afford the time for a complete rewrite. But his changes were substantial, both in terms of detailed writing and structural amplification, and this is certainly the master edition, not the third edition, produced by 1871 in Wales: This is merely a stiff literary rewrite of the 1839 edition, with no structural changes or additions other than English-favoring references. It claims to be based on Prichard's own surviving manuscripts and commentators have accepted this without enduring the labor of textual collation. Even less authoritative is its descendant, the London pirated 1877 edition that has often been reprinted, even in Wales. This is notable for using for the first time "the Welsh Robin Hood" as a sub-title, and many reprints appropriate the story so much as to make "The Welsh Robin Hood" the main title, with Twm relegated to the sub-title.

Of the 1839 revisions, Adams mysteriously says the additions "are almost without exception derivative as well as coarsened" (45), but in fact they are very effective and strengthen both the structure and the development of Twm as a hybrid figure of resistance. Prichard turned the hill-farm episode from a short vignette of Twm's pain into a lengthy and powerful sequence showing the misery and personal deformation experienced by hill-farmers through their acceptance of a servile state, and also linked the sequence into the novel by bringing in the vision of Joan as Twm lies ill, and also the figure of Moses, the near derelict Jewish boy, who will recur as a fellow-trickster in Llandovery (unnamed in the 1828 edition). Adams has linked Moses in particular to the influence of Dickens's *Oliver Twist* (Adams 44), but if he is a condensation of Fagin and the Artful Dodger it is a much displaced and redeployed one. The vision of Joan looks back to Gothic romance as an emotive armature of the story which may be, as Adams says, "derivative," but is hardly "coarsened." The 1839 edition also provides the diverting "bull in boots" episode as a structural climax to the lengthy sequence of Twm's tricks, and shows him being valued by the cheerful, if also self-indulgent, Welsh gentry typified by Prothero and, after their misunderstandings, Magistrate Prosser — in whom the real-life Thomas Jones seems remembered, in his profession, his pursuit of Joan and his connections with Brecon.

Apart from the substantial additions and stronger structuring of the revised 1839 text, it is at times a little more attentive to Welsh matters: the name Peter Penddwl ("Dull-head") is provided (44), a reference is added to the mythic figure Bran (68), the place-name Cwm Ddu (black valley) becomes Cwm y Gwern Ddu ("Black Marsh Valley"); as well as hill-farmer Grump becoming Grug throughout and later in the text Ready Roger becomes Ready Rosser. Very occasionally and without clear reason, 1839 is a little less Welsh than 1828: for example, Joan's home becomes Ystrad Feen, not Ffin and the note on the poetic metrical features Pennill and Triban is omitted (167).

These minor variations, whether authorial or editorial, do not obscure the strong sense offered by the 1828 version and developed in 1839 that this story presents a colonial interface that is far from simple. The figure of Graspacre is the focus for the clearest comment of this kind. Both the first and second editions say:

> He was a plain, bold, sensible man, and although entertaining a most exalted opinion of English superiority generally, in particular instances he had the liberality to confess that he found many things in this nation of mountaineers highly worthy of imitation among his more civilized countrymen.

But they go on more darkly:

> Unlike any of the half-bred English gentlemen who literally infest Wales, and become nuisances and living grievances to the people — building their pretensions to superiority and fashion, on a sneering self-sufficiency, and scorn of customs and peculiarities merely because they are Welsh — he gave them all credit for what was really estimable [1828, 44].

In the third edition of 1871 this extension is calmer, and a little more apologetic:

> There are many exceptions like the squire, but we are sorry to add that in Wales we have more illiberal Englishmen, who sneer at all Welsh customs, because they are Welsh, than people would dream of. They forget that our usages are as dear to us, as theirs are to them, and that however peculiar they may be in the eyes of an Englishman, the Welshman considers them a *sine qua non* of his own nationality.

And finally the rewriter abandons the earlier critical position:

> But these instances are fast dying out. Railroads, free and continued intercourse, and a liberal spirit of toleration enable the Englishman to see our custom and our usages in a different light [1871, 43–4].

The third edition clearly has its eyes on the English market. The return of the colonial repressed to the imperial centre is never easy or unmodified.

These details all show that Prichard was aware of the Wales-focused nature of his text, and that it debated the nature of modern Welshness in the context of both English power and English attitudes. This is also a pattern realized in the structure of the text itself and its journeying, topographical, sociopolitical and ethnic. From his originary deep Welshness, illegitimate son of a pretty peasant woman by an *uchelwr*, then educated half by the Anglophile the Rev. Inco Evans and half by the deeply Welsh the Rev. David John Rhys. Twm moves out through the hill farm, to the shock of seeing the sea at Aberaeron — a journey of some twenty miles to maritime Wales which the highly localized young man had never made. Then he travels through the various market-towns that link him increasingly into the commerce that is sourced from England, then to the English squire with a Welsh wife who acts as a matching frame to his beginning with Squire Graspacre. The early life and adventures of Fielding's *Tom Jones* have been substantially expanded and given a recurrent focus of ethnic complexity. The journey to London, also from Fielding, directs Twm's cunning, courage and probity to an apotheosis as a kind of gentleman like the Welsh gentry of his own kin — a feature expanded in the 1839 edition. But Twm avoids absorption by the colonial power and returns as a more confident and socially forceful Welshman, having appropriated the elements of authority that suit him. There is a possible social, even political, position for the Welsh being descried throughout this narrative: they both confront and reject the possibility of becoming English, but can learn the skill and discourses of the colonizer and deploy them on behalf of the colonized. The text asserts that the hybrid need not, as Fanon thought inevitable, be alienated from self or people. The hybrid has special, and redemptive, strength. Twm is a Bhabha-ist substantially *avant la lettre*.[17]

The final scene sums up and deepens this inscribed narrative of a triumphant hybrid self-consciousness. Twm at the window is dressed as an English soldier, with all that means for a colonized country. But when he gains the hand of lovely Joan, and her freight of property regained from English hands, the text calls up one of the strongest and most pervasive myths of Welsh and Celtic culture. *Sofraniaeth*, sovereignty, in Irish and Welsh myth is consistently represented as a woman. The king is the man who marries the queen: the mythic image carries with it the traces of a matrilinear (and originally matriarchal) culture and the idea was long remembered: the medieval story of Peredur, the Welsh original for Perceval the grail-achiever, is, as Goetinck has shown, dependent on the power of the sovereign woman, and Knight argues the text deploys the idea in post-colonial mode[18]: this mythic motif remains behind national matriarchs like Britannia or Marianne. The name of Joan's property is equally imbricated in Welsh myths of power. *Ystrad* means a wide prosperous valley (from Latin *stratus*, "broad," not a narrow infertile *cwm*, *nant* or *pant*). *Ffin* here is ambiguous: it originally must link to Latin *finis*, "border," because the place is located where the southern counties of Brecon, Cardigan and Carmarthen meet: it is the heart of *Deheubarth*, south Wales. But the word *ffin* also means, in Welsh from the middle ages, the same as English (or rather French) "fine," so Joan's land, now become Twm's, really means "Beautiful Broad Valley in the South Welsh Heartland" — a native Eden of Welsh landed prosperity. Twm's cave was in the same area too, before his translation into a grandeur at once pre- and post-colonial.

Twm may masquerade as a male possessor and an English soldier, but Joan has already, if secretly, accepted him. He never avoided the power of a female disguise, just like the Rebecca Rioters who were in busy action as Prichard revised his book in 1839; it is through the power, and love, of a woman that he attains full heroic status. It is Joan's house and her friends, and within that matrilinear affinity his own father, who welcome him into his inheritance as husband, *uchelwr*, mayor of Brecon (another symbolic land-taking, this time from the English military), and unregenerately Welsh hero, husband of the bearer of *sofraniaeth*. He offers the image of a Welshness that will survive in

English, with its identity varied but still intact, even enhanced, having absorbed the instrumentally useful elements of the colonizer's repertoire of powers and values, but still Welsh, and still wild, and always a wag.[19]

Notes

1. The phrase "the first Welsh novel" was used by Archdeacon Thomas Beynon of Cardigan in response to the first edition, see Adams, p. 85.

2. Llywelyn ap Gruffydd died in war against the English near Cilmeri, three miles west of Buellt (Builth). By tradition, and apparently fact, Edward I promised the Welsh princes in return for their allegiance an overall lord who spoke no English — and gave them his baby son. This political mendacity has provided many unsatisfactory Princes of Wales, up to the present, and is still deeply resented by many of the Welsh.

3. For example, his highwayman is spelled Dio the Devil: this must in fact be Deio, pronounced "Die-o," short for Dafydd. Prichard seems to have thought the phonemically accurate Sheer was the spelling of Sir, the Welsh for county (or shire); for him Ffîn can be Feen, and when in the 1839 edition he varies the simple stage-joke name of the hill-farmer from Morris Grump, he spells Grug (meaning "heather"), as its homonym Greeg.

4. For this context see Stephen Knight, "Romantic Yeoman," in *Robin Hood: A Mythic Biography* (Ithaca: Cornell University Press, 2003), 98–118.

5. See Andrew Davies, "'The Reputed Nation of Inspiration': Representations of Wales in Fiction from the Romantic Period," PhD, Cardiff University, 2001; Jane Aaron, Nineteenth-Century Women's Writing in Wales: Nation, Gender and Identity (Cardiff: University of Wales Press, 2007).

6. "Spiceilegia" is a Greek scientific term for "gleanings."

7. Like much in Welsh culture of the period, this had biblical roots, and not in the cheek-turning New Testament: the reference was to Genesis 24.60: "And they blessed Rebekah and said to her, 'Thou art our sister, be thou the mother of thousands of millions, and let they seed possess the gate of those which hate them.'" The rioters focused on destroying the means by which landowners, often absentees, taxed the movements of ordinary people. There are recorded instances of carnival, as "Rebecca" demanded of her "daughters" why she could not pass a gate and ordered its destruction. The laws were changed in 1844 and the riots ended.

8. Dafydd H. Evans, "Twm Siôn Cati" in *Coleg Dewi a'r Fro* (St David's College and its Area), ed. D. P. Davies (Llanbedr Pont Steffan: Coleg Prifysgol Dewi Sant, 1984), pp. 8–22, see pp. 13–14. Translations from this essay written in Welsh are by the authors of this article.

9. In full cynghanedd, as here, the consonants of the first half-line repeat in the second, except the final consonant: t, r, g, r all repeat — but not the final r in eryr.

10. Samuel Rush Meyrick, *The History and Antiquities of The County of Cardigan* (London: Longman, Hurst, Rees and Orme, 1801). On pp. 247–51 Meyrick outlines the Twm tradition, identifying Tregaron as his origin and Sir John Wynn as his father, and mentioning several tricks that Prichard relates: stealing a pot from a shopkeeper, stealing cloth from a woman at the market, tricking a highwayman with a purse full of shells, and the hand at the window.

11. See Adams pp. 77–8 for a discussion. The Twm-focused version of Y Digrifwr (no place or publisher: 1803) had new editions in 1811— the one Prichard knew, published by Harris of Carmarthen — and 1844. Other pamphlets with this title (.e.g. one in 1820 from Caernarfon) are just general joke-books with only passing reference to Twm.

12. The concept of the gwerin is important in Welsh self-consciousness (and also false consciousness): it translates roughly as "folk" but implies more widely a regionally-identified people without clear social divisions, equally interested in farming, culture and religion. Among the gwerin a prize-winning poet may well be employed as a stone-breaker on the roads.

13. For a discussion of first-contact romance about Wales, see Stephen Knight, *A Hundred Years of Fiction, Writing Wales in English Series* (Cardiff: University of Wales Press, 2004), section 1; for a discussion of texts see Davies and Aaron, cited in note 6.

14. For a discussion of English in Wales see Colin H. Williams, "The Anglicisation of Wales," in *English in Wales: Diversity, Conflict and Change*, ed. Nikolas Coupland (Clevedon, PA: Multilingual Matters, 1990, 19–47) and Alan R. Thomas, "English in Wales" in *English in Britain and Overseas: Origins and Development*, vol. 5 of *The Cambridge History of the English Language*, ed. Robert Burchfield (Cambridge: Cambridge University Press, 1994), 94–147.

15. Inigo is a Spanish name, thought to be of Basque origin; it was used presumably because Inigo Jones's father was Catholic. The name "Inco" has no relation to any known Celtic forms.

16. *Twm Siôn Cati*, 1839 edition, p. iii.

17. Frantz Fanon's final and strongest statement of the inescapability of physical resistance to colonisation is *The Wretched of the Earth*, trans. Constance Farrington (New York: Grove Weidenfeld, 1963); Homi Bhabha's more nuanced argument that the colonized person can attain forms of resistance through hybridized appropriation of the colonizer's vigor is stated in his "Introduction" to the essay-collection *Nation and Narration* (London: Routledge, 1990) and recurrently through his essays in *The Location of Culture* (London: Routledge, 1994).

18. See Glenys Goetinck, "Sovereignty Themes in Peredur, Owein and Gereint," Chap. 3 of *Peredur: A Study of Welsh Tradition in the Grail Legends* (Cardiff: University of Wales Press, 1975); Stephen Knight "Resemblance and Menace: A Post-Colonial Reading of Peredur," in *Canhwyll y Marchogion: cyd-destunoli Peredur*, ed. Sioned Davies and Peter Wynn Thomas (Caerdydd: Gwasg Prifysgol Cymru, 2000), 128–47.

19. The authors acknowledge gratefully the expert advice offered in the development of this paper by Tomos Owen.

Works Cited

Aaron, Jane. *Nineteenth-Century Women's Writing in Wales: Nation, Gender and Identity*. Cardiff: University of Wales Press, 2007.

Adams, Sam. *Thomas Jeffrey Llewelyn Prichard, Writers of Wales Series*. Cardiff: University of Wales Press, 2000.

Bhaba, Homi. *The Location of Culture*. London: Routledge, 1994.

———. *Nation and Narration*. London: Routledge, 1990.

Davies, Andrew. *"The Reputed Nation of Inspiration": Representations of Wales in Fiction from the Romantic Period*. Doctoral dissertation, Cardiff University, 2001.

Evans, Dafydd H. "Twm Siôn Cati" in *Coleg Dewi a'r Fro* (St David's College and its Area), ed. D. P. Davies. Llanbedr Pont Steffan: Coleg Prifysgfol Dewi Sant, 1984. 8–22.

Fanon, Frantz. *The Wretched of the Earth*, trans. Constance Farrington. New York: Grove Weidenfeld, 1963.

Goetinck, Glenys. *Peredur: A Study of Welsh Tradition in the Grail Legends*. Cardiff: University of Wales Press, 1975.

Humfrey, Belinda."Prelude to the Twentieth Century" in *Welsh Writing in English*, ed., M. Wynn Thomas. *A Guide to Welsh Literature*, vol. 7. Cardiff: University of Wales Press, 2003. 7–46.

Huws, Daniel. "Thomas Jones," in *Oxford Dictionary of National Biography*, ed. H. C. G. Mathew and Brian Harrison. Oxford: Oxford University Press, 2000, vol. 30. 635–6.

Knight, Stephen. *A Hundred Years of Fiction, Writing Wales in English Series*. Cardiff: University of Wales Press, 2004.

_____. "Resemblance and Menace: A Post-Colonial Reading of *Peredur*." *Canhwyll y Marchogion: cyd-destunoli* Peredur. Eds. Sioned Davies and Peter Wynn Thomas. Caerdydd: Gwasg Prifysgol Cymru, 2000. 128–47.

_____. *Robin Hood: A Mythic Biography*. Ithaca: Cornell University Press, 2003.

Meyrick, Samuel Rush. *The History and Antiquities of The County of Cardigan*. London: Longman, Hurst, Rees and Orme, 1801.

Thomas, Alan R. "English in Wales," in *English in Britain and Overseas: Origins and Development*, vol. 5 of *The Cambridge History of the English Language*, ed. Robert Burchfield. Cambridge: Cambridge University Press, 1994. 94–147.

Williams, Colin H. "The Anglicisation of Wales," in *English in Wales: Diversity, Conflict and Change*, ed. Nikolas Coupland. Clevedon, PA: Multilingual Matters, 1990. 19–47.

An Irregular Union
Exploring the Welsh Connection to a Popular African-American Wedding Ritual

TYLER D. PARRY

In 1928, folklorist W. Rhys Jones undertook fieldwork among the rural Welsh inhabitants of the Ceiriog Valley in North Wales. Jones's research revealed a rather interesting marital practice occurring among this relatively isolated segment of Welsh people. Neglecting any ecclesiastical ceremony, Jones found that traditional marriage among the previous generation consisted of simply laying a broom in the doorway of the cabin in which the couple was designated to live. After the broom was placed appropriately, "the young man jumped over it first into the house, and afterwards the young woman in the same way ... by jumping over backwards over the besom [broom] the marriage was broken" (Jones 154–155). Jones's respondents explained that this ritual remained a popular form of marriage clear into the year 1840, but lost popularity in the twentieth century due to its association with primitive and pagan origins.

Ten years later, on the opposite side of the Atlantic, Cora Armstrong, an ex-slave in her mid-seventies, was interviewed by an employee of the Federal Writers' Project who sought to document the enslaved experience in the United States. After mentioning basic necessities such as food rations, clothing, and tactics of punishment employed upon southern plantations, Cora then described a simplistic method of slave marriage that was common throughout the antebellum South. The custom mirrors the aforementioned Welsh ritual closely: "The way slaves married in slavery time they jumped over the broom and when they separated they jumped backward over the broom" (Armstrong qtd. in Rawick 361). Unfortunately, Cora left no further explanation as to the practice's origins, as former slaves usually associated the ritual with memories of slavery and subjugation, becoming an embarrassing reminder of past lives many ex-slaves preferred to forget.

The action of "jumping the broom" remains a mysterious and understudied component of the transatlantic exchange in which Europe, Africa, and the Americas became forever connected through the slave trade. Indeed, the similarities between the two aforementioned testimonies, one by a Welsh folklorist in an isolated region in Wales, and the other a former American slave in the United States, warrant serious consideration as to how jumping the broom traveled from small and rural regions of Wales into becoming "nearly universal in the slave south as a wedding ritual" (Joyner 52). Recent studies analyzing the concept of the Atlantic World provide a paradigm in which folk customs and practices can be analyzed as products of this transatlantic exchange. Historians viewing the Atlantic World argue that cultural transactions such as culinary techniques, religious expression, dance, and music made a significant impact on the various nations, ethnicities, and cultures involved in the transatlantic trade, and that it is a fallacy to isolate Atlantic colonies from one another between 1441 and 1888.[1] Folk rituals such as jumping the broom, however, typically receive little analysis beyond a few pages of text, and many analyses rarely venture beyond description of the ritual as anything more than a slave custom birthed in the American South.

Using methods employed by historians of the Atlantic World, and analyzing how the interplay between history and memory impacts the descendent communities, the following investigation responds to this neglect in four sections. The first portion reviews the complex and conflicting historiography that addresses the marriage ritual, while simultaneously demonstrating that the ritual is yet to receive a detailed treatment concerning its origins and subsequent cultural transfer to North America via the Atlantic Ocean. Second, it analyzes Welsh folklore and myth, tracking the Welsh presence throughout the Atlantic World in order to explain possible avenues that allowed the ritual to pass from a geographically small and isolated territory in southwest England, into becoming a well-known practice among slaves of African descent in the American South. The third section addresses the ubiquity and characterization of the practice among all parties involved, hoping to address exactly how prevalent it became throughout the slave South, and why it should be discussed beyond its description as just a "slave marriage." The final segment discusses the relationship between history and memory, and how historians and folklorists can apply the methodology of historical memory to uncover new findings concerning broom jumping's contemporary global appeal.

The broom jumping ceremony gained popularity in the United States during the last quarter of the twentieth century among African Americans, due to the publication and subsequent television miniseries of Alex Haley's seminal novel *Roots: The Saga of an American Family*. Haley claimed his work was historical fiction that traced his family's history beginning in West Africa and ending with Haley himself. Within the novel, the main character Kunta Kinte and his wife Bell "jumped high over the broomstick" on a Virginia plantation when they decided to marry (Haley 418). The huge success of *Roots* as both a novel and a television miniseries prompted a renewed interest in African-American history among black Americans.[2] Additionally, Haley's novel was released at a point in American history where Afrocentric discourses and Pan-African identification were gaining global recognition among many peoples of African descent, primarily due to the effort to decolonize Africa and the continued struggle for civil rights in the United States.

Shortly after *Roots*' release, many African-American couples incorporated jumping the broom as an auxiliary ritual to be done after the "official" wedding ceremony as a method to symbolically pay homage to their enslaved ancestors. One problem this notion led to, however, is that novelists, columnists, and Afrocentric scholars falsely associated the practice with African origins. Harriet Cole, Danita Roundtree Green, and Tolagbe Ogunleye are the main proponents of this school. Cole's argument rests upon a discovery that among the Kgatla people of Southern Africa, the bride and other women in the family sweep the courtyard clean on the day after the wedding (18). Cole's logic crumbles, however, since the Kgatla people reside in the southern portion of Africa, an area where relatively few Africans were taken in the slave trade. Cole's counterpart, Danita Green, finds West Africans in Ghana that incorporated brooms within the wedding ceremony. Within this ritual the brooms are waved above the head of the couple, symbolically "sweeping away the evil spirits from the couple's path" (Green 3). Once again, however, no ritual resembling broom jumping is found. While Green adamantly maintains that broom jumping is African in origin, she is forced to admit: "there is no recognized documentation ... proving this theory" (3).

Tolagbe Ogunleye provides the most recent scholarship considering the African origins of broom jumping ceremonies, and her work is arguably the most detailed addition to the debate of broom jumping's African origins. Ogunleye's argument loses focus, however, in her claim that a significant percentage of Britain's early settlers were black Africans who continued their cultural traditions throughout their many centuries of settlement (18–40). Ogunleye makes painstaking attempts to associate every aspect of Celtic culture with West Africa, ranging from similarities in language to a mutual respect for sacred trees, as she maintains that both Africans and Celts made their brooms from certain branches. Much of her argument holds little historical clout, as she only relies on a few secondary sources written by extreme Afrocentric scholars who attempted to trace Africanisms into every aspect of Irish, Scottish, and Welsh culture. Perhaps the most damaging critique one could level toward Ogunleye's argument is that none of the British "Africans" in Ogunleye's book actually jump the broom, until they arrive in the antebellum South. Additionally, it is interesting that no such practice is found in any other region of the Atlantic World. If it was truly "African," as Ogunleye claims, one might expect to find this type of matrimony practiced in locations like Brazil or Cuba, two countries that imported far more West African slaves than the United States, and for a much longer period of time.³ Ogunleye claims her contribution to this historiography is to dispel the "gypsy myth" supposedly attached to broomstick weddings, which argues that nomadic British gypsies spread the broom jumping ritual throughout the British Isles, and it then transferred to slaves in North America via European immigration (13–17). The main fallacy in this aspect of Ogunleye's logic is that scholars of the opposing school are not necessarily arguing for gypsy origins. Evidence attests that British gypsies did jump brooms to symbolize their marriages, but scholars of the European school are more interested in exploring another culture that utilized matrimonial broom jumping, those being Europeans of Welsh descent.⁴

Great debt is owed to two pioneering authors, Alan Dundes and C.W. Sullivan, in furthering the argument for Welsh origins of jumping the broom. Dundes initiated the first challenge to Afrocentric writers who claimed "African origins for African American folklore that clearly did not come from Africa" (Dundes 324). Through a series of quotes and citations, Dundes argues that the origins of the broom ritual actually derive from Wales, and it was practiced by nomadic British Gypsies throughout the Middle Ages. After cogently arguing the European origins of the practice, Dundes bluntly concludes: "There seems to be no evidence that the ritual per se is practiced anywhere in Africa" and is "an undeniable borrowing from European folklore" (327, 328). Sullivan thereafter followed up on Dundes's analysis. In a brief note in *The Journal of American Folklore*, Sullivan expands upon the Welsh origins of jumping the broom, arguing that they were "more thoroughly documented than Dundes suggests" ("Jumping the Broom: A Further Consideration" 203). Drawing upon three important texts from early twentieth century folklorists T. Gwynn Jones, W. Rhys Jones, and T.W. Thompson, Sullivan illustrates the close connections in performance between the Welsh and African American customs. One year later, Sullivan expanded on his thesis in the journal *Southern Folklore* by detailing elements of Welsh mythology that more thoroughly place the origins of the custom in Wales, while also hypothesizing that Welsh immigration to the United States during the eighteenth and nineteenth centuries was substantial enough to initiate broom jumping's ubiquity as a southern marriage practice.

Dundes and Sullivan make strong cases for the Welsh origins of the practice, but the historiography of the custom's roots remains continually divided, with opposing authors claiming either African origins, or Celtic origins.⁵ The best remedy to this rather confusing debate is to utilize the methods of historical memory and Atlantic history to further understand how this ritual was transported across the Atlantic, spread throughout the southern states, and has recently been revived among the descendent communities. Thus, it is necessary to first begin in Wales and explore Welsh people's mythological and folkloric associations with the broomstick wedding, chart possible paths in which the wedding ritual arrived, and then demonstrate how the cultural dynamics of North American history provided for this transferal.

Communities within Wales had a locational advantage in being able to continue marital practices that ecclesiastical and government officials dubbed "irregular marriages" or "irregular unions." John Davies explains that "pre-industrial Wales was not one integrated society, but rather a network of small local communities ... [E]ntire districts could be isolated for long periods ... [It] is likely therefore that most people lived and died in their native parish" (*A History* 262). David Ross explains that clear into 1750, due to the lack of roads connecting Wales to England: "Coming to Wales was still something of an adventure for the English traveler" (164). Isolation provides a distinct advantage for the retention of culture, since isolated communities tend to stay clear of governmental supervision. Historian Lawrence Stone claims: "In remote areas, especially the Scottish border country, Wales and the extreme south-west, the betrothal ceremony itself, the 'handfast,' continued to be treated by many of the poor as sufficient for a binding union without the blessing of the Church" (30). Given the fact that Welsh and English enmity continued from Edward I's conquest of Gwynedd in 1283 and throughout the early modern period, Welsh people recognized themselves as a distinct category of people within the British Isles.

The long history of English and Welsh enmity was depicted by Shakespeare in his play *Henry IV part 1* when the ethnocentric Englishman Hotspur mocks a Welsh woman's singing by saying "I perceive the Devil understands Welsh; / and 'tis no marvel he is so humorous / ... I had rather hear Lady, my brach ... howl in Irish" (3.1.227–233). In 1622, Puritan minister John Brinsley listed Wales as one example of a region of inferior intelligence, alongside colonies like Ireland and Virginia, due to the population's inability to speak intelligible English (Blank 134). In the eighteenth century, Welsh abolitionist Morgan John Rhys wondered if the Welsh people were condemned to be "hewers of wood and drawers of water" (Rhys qtd. in Williams 71). Historians Peter Linebaugh and Marcus Rediker explain that the phrase "hewers of wood and drawers of water" was used in descriptions of people fit for slavery, signifying that the mid-eighteenth century Welsh identity was still largely associated with subjugation and oppression (36–70). Thus, the relative isolation of many Welsh communities, alongside England's cultural alienation of Wales likely allowed Welsh people to retain many folk customs. While few details of the broomstick wedding exist beyond Jones's fieldwork, Welsh mythology and the unique literature produced by the country's oral history provide clues toward the importance of the ritual for cultural identity and sustainability.

Scholars like Sullivan and T. Gwynn Jones suggest that the ancient roots of jumping the broom might be displayed in the Fourth Branch of the *Mabinogi*. In a test of virginity, a maiden named Aranrhod is put to a test by Gwydion, the nephew of the Lord of Gwynedd, in determination of her status as a maiden. After first asking her if she is a "maiden" (some translators say "virgin"), and she answers in the affirmative, he "took the magic wand and bent it. 'Step over this,' said he, 'and if thou art a maiden, I shall know.' Then she stepped over the magic wand, and as she stepped she dropped a large, sturdy, yellow-haired boy.... After the boy's cry she made for the door" (Gwynn Jones and Thomas Jones 54). Jones claims this process is a chastity test, but Sullivan believes it more likely a test of female fertility power, and her reluctance to step over the rod negates her ability to take a position as an integral part of the ruling elite (Sullivan 21). In either interpretation, the most important aspect to consider is that her reluctance to jump over the rod nullifies Aranrhod's desired outcome, just as not fully clearing the broom in the broomstick wedding prevented the marriage's completion.

Welsh broomstick weddings also placed a particular emphasis on the type of wood used to craft the designated instrument. The brooms were typically referred to as "birch besoms." Besom brooms are typically constructed using bundles of twigs tied to a wooden pole, and are traditionally associated with witches. The birch tree held many mythical qualities related to love, marriage, and new life, and was often referred to as the "Lady of the Woods" (Neasham 157). James MacKillop explains that Welsh courting activities typically revolved around the association of birchwood with love, as "a lover's bower usually stands beneath a birch tree or in a birch bush" (37). Pieces of birch were used quite often in Welsh courting activities, as "wreaths of birch were given as a love token. A birch twig given by a boy to a girl as a love token meant constancy" (Mac Coitir 20). One legend states that a woman's acceptance of the proposal was signified by a return gift of a wreath made of birch, but if rejected the wreath was made of hazel (Pughe 153). The importance of birchwood was continually reinforced in both men and women's expressions of love, courtship, and romance in medieval and early modern Wales. It is important to note that the brooms in Rhys Jones's twentieth century analysis were still referred to as "birch besoms." Broomsticks made of birch held significant value in Welsh folk culture. Though the broomstick wedding's transfer to North America led practitioners to deemphasize specific types of wood in its formation, the broom's centrality in the marriage ceremony was already secure, and retained its position as an important component of the marriage ceremony. Given that this marriage was not only a cultural trait, but an expression of identity for many Welsh people, it is necessary to explore how and when it was likely transferred to the United States.

Tracking Welsh immigration to America remains an elusive and difficult task. Sullivan claims that the Welsh presence was substantial enough in the United States to initiate the cultural transfer, but looking closely at the demographics, much of the evidence seems to speak against this suggestion. John Davies claims a rather striking statistic that "for every person from Wales emigrating to the United States in the second half of the nineteenth century, there were at least twenty-five persons from Ireland" (Davies "Wales and America" 13). The Welsh who did migrate to America predominantly settled in the Northeast, particularly New York and Pennsylvania. Ronald Lewis proposed that fewer than five hundred out of the forty five thousand Welsh immigrants lived below the Mason-Dixon line (18). While these statistics do not appear to support the claim for a considerable Welsh presence, it should be noted that tracking Welsh immigrants is a bedeviling task, since "Port officials did not systematically distinguish Welsh immigrants from Scottish or English passengers until 1908, and immigrants who embarked from small ports along the Welsh coast often went uncounted" (Knowles 247). The Welsh presence could have been larger than the records suggest, and scholars have found that important Welsh settlements existed in Maryland, Virginia, North Carolina, and South Carolina throughout the eighteenth century, though their actual numbers are more difficult to calculate.

Many of the Welsh immigrants embarking to America came from economically depressed conditions, and were typically seen in America as being of lower-working class. Their problems were also compounded by the fact that many Welsh immigrants only spoke their native Welsh, and did not know English upon their arrival. E. Wyn James relates that "the vast majority of poetry (and other forms of literature) produced in Wales from the sixth to the twentieth century was [still] in the Welsh language" (59). Such circumstances forced the Welsh, as with many immigrants, to become clannish and communal, a situation Welsh people experienced numerous times throughout the history of Britain. Within colonial and antebellum America, the Welsh were distinguishable from their Anglo-Saxon counterparts, as attested by numerous commentators in the eighteenth and nineteenth centuries.

In the nineteenth century, John Spencer Bassett commented upon the mélange of ethnicities in the early Republic: "Among those [immigrants] who came one can easily distinguish Scotch-Irish, Germans, Moravians, Welsh, and many Englishmen" (Basset 145). Culturally autonomous communities were found in many locations in early America. As late as 1908, folklorist William Bek found a German community in West Missouri "bound together by like tradition, like speech, and in many instances by blood relationships" who still practiced traditional German marriage customs (60). Records attest that a group of Scotch Highlanders in early North Carolina spoke only Gaelic. While many of the leaders of the community spoke and wrote English, Duane Meyer reveals many of the common people "in North Carolina, as in North Britain, continued to use Gaelic" (118). One female Highlander immigrant actually mentioned that Gaelic speech was so prevalent among the common people of this community, that the slaves actually began speaking near perfect Gaelic, causing the young woman to initially believe that Scottish people became black in America (Meyer119). Frederick Law Olmsted wrote in the mid-nineteenth century that he saw numerous signs posted for the indentured Irish, Scottish and Welsh runaways (226). The indentured Welshman holds importance in studies regarding cultural affinities between lower class Euro-Americans and Africans, as this was the most intimate setting in which the two cultures might come in contact.

As early as 1699, Francis Nicholson wrote to Henderson Walker that "one Thomas Roberts a Welchman ... ran away from the Revd Mr John Bernard a Clerk" (Saunders 515). What is especially poignant about this letter is the fact that it advertised another runaway, David Ross, who was designated only as a carpenter, while Thomas Roberts was categorized ethnically as a Welshman. This signifies that the Welsh were perceived as ethnic and cultural foreigners, and not characterized by the understood Englishness of their Anglo-Saxon counterparts. Indentured servants and slaves held a special relationship in colonial America, as some accounts reveal that both groups saw themselves opposed to the master class. Venture Smith, a slave in the colonial Northeast, recounted the associations he had with an Irish indentured servant Heddy, who convinced Venture to run away with him and two other servants (Smith 16–17). A. Leon Higginbotham documented accounts in Virginia's legal records revealing attempted escapes of groups comprising both black slaves and white servants, signifying that the two likely had more close-knit associations when laboring in this capacity (Higginbotham 27).

Olmsted related that in his travels through Virginia he viewed a group of miners, and took notice that "The white hands are mostly English or Welchmen" (47–48). Olmsted followed up this statement by explaining that he witnessed some of the white hands being chastised for fraternizing with the slaves. The master class attempted to keep the two groups separated, but it was not a particularly easy task when they worked side by side. While it is not likely that the Welsh outnumbered any particular nationality within the servant community, these citations do allow the assumption that the Welsh were perceived as a distinct community of individuals, and that their occupations in the New World typically placed them around both whites of lower economic status and black slaves. Besides settlement, however, one other Welsh occupation deserves some attention in this discussion of cultural impact, as it compensates for the lack of high numbers of Welsh settlers in America.

One comment by former slave-turned-abolitionist Olaudah Equiano reveals an additional possibility for cultural transfer. Equiano mentions that one of his ship's captains was a "Welchman," and that this captain treated him particularly well (56; vol. 1). Equiano's distinction of his captain's nationality introduces two important points. One is the fact that Equiano understood the innate difference between an Englishman and a Welshman. Equiano's familiarity with English culture likely educated him concerning the tension between the two nations, and that they comprised two different cultures and traditions. The second is the importance of the associations between sailor and slave. Becoming a crewman was an attractive option for enslaved and free people of color, as it provided a more egalitarian role than plantation labor. A black seaman could earn a wage comparable, if not equal, to the white seaman. If a black man advanced in rank, he sometimes earned more than a white man employed in a subordinate position. Sailors were well known for fraternizing with slaves and free blacks at the ports they docked. This practice became so prodigious that one authority complained that seaman spent their time in "cabarets, in dark gambling houses, or among the slaves" (Desch Obi 201). In 1751, the governor of Cape Coast Castle complained that many sailors would desert their crew and go to live among the slaves (Desch Obi 201).

These close associations suggest that many white sailors were obliged to accept people of African descent as equals and companions. The bond that developed between the crewmen was likely closely knit, and as they relied on each other for companionship, stories of their homelands and their associated traditions were likely spoken of frequently. One noteworthy example of cultural transfer occurred in the story of a West Indian slave named Alexander transported from St. Vincent Island in the Caribbean to Liverpool. The captain of this ship was a Welshman. Due to his associations with the captain, Alexander became acquainted with the Welsh language rather quickly, and in one conversation, explained his mastery of the Welsh language: "I came to England in a Welsh ship, and now I can speak, I can write, I can read, and I can sing in Welsh" (*Liverpool and Slavery* 51). In addition to their language, Welsh sailors in particular were known to carry one intriguing item that would have aroused the curiosity of their shipmates. Between the seventeenth and nineteenth centuries, "it was a widespread custom in Wales for young men to carve love tokens ... in the form of wooden spoons" (*Folklore, Myths and Legends* 405). Welsh sailors were particularly drawn to this custom, as they typically carved their spoons at sea, and returned home with a trinket to give to a young woman they wished to marry (Tangerman 1–8). This peculiar custom was likely to initiate a few conversations among crewmen of all ethnic and national identities. Additionally, sailors were the most mobile individuals throughout the Atlantic. Sailors were sources of news, rumors, and sometimes rebellions, making their cultural impact that much more pronounced. In the case of Welshmen employed on these ships, their unique marital practice was likely a topic of conversation, and provides one way of how some white and black people may have become acquainted with the concept of how jumping a broom sealed a marriage commitment.

The question of transfer remains a difficult question, since there are no records of the first time a slave jumped the broom in North America. Oscar Weiss claims that when slaves married in colonial America they jumped the broom, but there are no examples of slaves performing the custom prior to the antebellum period (Reiss 53). Betty Wood suggests that this may be due to the fact that during the colonial period "white commentators did not record the precise details of the marriage ritual" undertaken by slaves (43). People documenting common-law marriages were typically not interested in chronicling the specific festivities included in the ceremony, if there were any at all. Most of the descriptions of the broomstick wedding come from the WPA narratives, and the narratives of slaves who escaped to the Northern states in the antebellum period. Few of these narratives describe any motivation for slaves' use of the ritual beyond practicality, leading some scholars to assume that slaves were either "forced" to perform the ritual by their masters, or that the master developed the ritual as a joke.[6] Such statements, however, overextend their reach. True, masters did hold a significant amount of power among the enslaved community, but denying slaves any agency in the planter-laborer exchange does a great injustice to not only African-American history, but Southern history as a whole.

There are numerous cases where slaves either violently or passively refused their master's impositions, especially in cases of marriage and family establishment. Historian Rebecca Fraser argues that enslaved men often eluded slave patrols, or even disobeyed a master's refusal to marry in order to offer romantic gestures to the woman he desired most (32–87). Kevin Dawson found that slaves with adept swimming skills used rivers and creeks to visit their spouses secretly, and were sometimes able to evade repercussions from slave patrollers who usually could not swim (46). Historian Marie Schwartz argues that when slaveholders refused to grant slaves their permission to marry, "slaves took it upon themselves to ensure that couples pledged their love publicly and according to their own understanding of God's command" (204). James Curry, an antebellum North Carolina slave, recalled that his master forbade him to marry a free woman of color, and even threatened to slit Curry's throat if he tried. Curry disobeyed, however, and recounted that he was never afraid of his master's empty threats: "I knew he would not kill me, because I was money to him, I knew I could run away if he punished me" (Blassingame 139–140). In most cases of marriage, it is likely that slave owners were ambivalent as to how their slaves solemnized their vows. Schwartz states that masters typically "left details of the ceremony to the slaves" (204). Despite the wishes of masters for complete obedience among their slaves, the theory of the forced imposition of a marriage custom largely loses clout when viewed from the perspective of the enslaved.

While it appears that broom jumping was not a forced imposition among the enslaved, it is possible that masters introduced the ritual into the slave community. Offering an alternative analysis to the Welsh origins, Brenda Stevenson rejects the African origins thesis and contends that southern planters saw jumping the broom as a pre–Christian ritual hailing from rural Anglo-Saxon villages "probably passed down to later generations as an amusing, perhaps quaint, relic of their 'pagan' past" (229). Folklorist W. Crooke found that one practice called "jumping over the petting-stick" was practiced in Ford, Northumberland, in which a pole was laid across the principal exit of a churchyard. Another tradition called "lifting the bride" consisted of having "a stool taken to the churchyard by the villagers, and the bride is 'jumped' over, a man taking hold of each arm to help her over" (228). Apparently this ritual was pervasive throughout the village "among the working folk," but the woman who Crooke interviews cautions that "just above the common folk the custom is considered vulgar" (229).

While these customs may provide some links to southern antebellum broomstick weddings, the Welsh ritual mirrors its southern counterpart most closely. Forms of irregular unions involving jumping were known throughout parts of England during the early modern period, but Stevenson's assertion that rural folk did not take the ritual seriously is overstated. The Welsh community Rhys Jones interviewed took the practice very seriously continuing into the 1840s. The English began importing enslaved Africans to Virginia as early as 1619, and Peter Wood argues that planters in colonial South Carolina in 1690 began to favor enslaved African labor for rice cultivation, and quickly established a "black majority" throughout coastal South Carolina (37). If the American version has specifically English roots, one might imagine that colonial records would at least mention the practice occurring earlier than the antebellum period, even if the colonial marriage records are not as detailed. It seems more likely that Welsh immigration and influence throughout the eighteenth and nineteenth centuries contributed to the broomstick wedding's rising popularity in the antebellum South. Considering that many of the aforementioned Welsh communities were established throughout the eighteenth century, it seems that their associations with their neighbors and slaves may have been another catalyst for introducing the concept of the cheap and affordable broomstick wedding as an alternative to formal church sanctioned celebrations.

Some Welsh came to the South as slave owners, and there is some evidence that points to the fact that their slaves became acculturated within the community. In 1797, the Welsh Neck Church in Society Hill, South Carolina had an even ratio of 63 whites and 64 blacks, and Carter G. Woodson wrote that by the mid-nineteenth century it "had 477 Negroes and only 83 whites" (112). Welsh Neck became known for its outspoken abolitionist ministers who typically allotted slaves greater amounts of ecclesiastical participation. As with the case of the aforementioned Gaelic speaking Scotch Highlanders in North Carolina, communities in which white and black interacted more intimately led to a greater degree of cultural mixture. In one striking example of acculturation, an advertisement for a runaway slave in Maryland stated that a 26 year old slave named Peggy, who sometimes called herself Nancy, ran away from her owner. Peggy apparently had a "yellowish complexion," spoke with a "Welsh accent," and was believed to have run away with a Portuguese indentured servant ("Eighteenth Century Slaves" 215). This example reveals three important points. First, the Welsh accent was still distinguishable to American colonists in the late eighteenth century, revealing that a Welsh cultural identity in the Post-Revolutionary period was still a distinguishing feature. Second, it provides another example of white and black cooperation that defied the master class.

The third point is that accents signify surroundings. It is unknown if Peggy came from a Welsh community or not, but her noticeable Welsh accent speaks to the fact that she attained a significant level of acculturation by the time she absconded. The cultural intermixture between white and black formed a southern culture that crossed racial lines, even if southern culture is popularly believed to be one of segregation and racial oppression. Jumping the broom provides one aspect of this cultural sharing.

The broomstick wedding's emergence in the records coincides with a period of southern history when many of the American slaves were of a "creole" generation. These creole slaves held more cultural similarities to the master class than the previous generations who came directly from West Africa. Wedding ceremonies comprising Christian elements as well as the broomstick tradition give further evidences of acculturation that altered enslaved Africans' cosmologies. Enslaved Africans did, however, retain memories and stories of Africa, and blended elements of the New World with the Old. Slaves married in a variety of ways, and it seems that while broomstick weddings became quite popular in the antebellum period, it was not the only method. Slaves like Charity Bower of North Carolina received a formal marriage ceremony in the presence of witnesses: "I had a wedding when I was married; for mistress didn't like to have *her* people take up with another, without any minister to marry them" (qtd. in Blassingame *Slave Testimony* 262). Others claimed that no wedding customs existed at all, but that slaves just began living together. Jumping the broom, however, provided a median between those slaves not favored enough to receive an elaborate ceremony from their master, and those who were not content with beginning a marriage without any ceremonial expression. One testament to this lies in the prevalence jumping the broom gained as a marriage ritual throughout the U.S. South during the antebellum period.

The transatlantic slave trade was closed to North American ports in 1808. For a variety of reasons, American politicians decided to ban the importation of slaves from foreign soil (Ford 112–130). Slavery could still exist in the South, but the slave population was now to sustain its numbers through natural increase. The difficulty in this decision, however, was that planters moving into newly annexed western territories, such as Louisiana, now needed enslaved labor to drive their economy. While some slaves from West Africa and the Caribbean would continue to be imported illegally throughout the United States, the closing of the transatlantic slave trade initiated an event that historian Walter Johnson calls a story "of human beings broken down into parts and recompensed as commodities, as futures promised, purchased, and resisted" (3). The new slave trade would mirror its transatlantic predecessor in many ways, but now the slaves would travel in caravans from firmly established slave states such as Virginia and South Carolina, to newly annexed slaving regions like Louisiana and Alabama.

Johnson argues that amidst all of the inhumanity, the domestic slave trade was responsible for one important function, being that by the time of the Civil War in 1865 "slaves had a common culture that stretched from Maryland to Texas" (215). These "acculturated creole slaves" as historian Steven Deyle calls them, were responsible for spreading a common culture of food, music, religion, and dance throughout the antebellum South (Deyle 35). While scholars in the past mentioned this phenomenon, the cultural developments were overshadowed by quantitative and demographic analyses. While the Old South was certainly not a homogenous culture, many black and white communities throughout the southern states held similarities ranging from folklore to food, and jumping the broom is one expression that holds pertinence for this discussion.

According to Michael Tadman's 1989 analysis of the domestic slave trade, the New Orleans slave market in Louisiana was consistently the largest importer of slaves from the Upper South, with Alabama coming in second (12). The largest exporters of slaves were Virginia, South Carolina, Maryland, and North Carolina. Interestingly, these four states all possessed distinguishable Welsh communities in the eighteenth century. Due to the trade in human chattel, slaves' families were frequently destroyed, forcing enslaved men and women to either break from psychological pressure, or attempt to recreate a semblance of their old life. Jumping the broom provided one avenue where slaves could quickly restructure familial livelihood. Emanuel Elmore describes his father's first marriage in South Carolina to a woman named Jenny. When his father was sold to Alabama, his wife was left behind, and he eventually remarried Emanuel's mother Dorcas. In a description of his father's double marriage, Emanuel stated: "Pa married twice ... of course, pa just jumped the broom for both of them" (qtd. in *Slave Narratives* Vol. XIV Part 2 8–9). Slaves seemed to repeat the ritual as they were taken west, and jumping the broom quickly became associated with southern slavery, as revealed in a poem entitled "slave marriage ceremony" that circulated widely in the oral history of the south after emancipation:

> Dark an' stormy may come de wedder;
> I jines dis he-male an' dis she-male togedder
> Let none, but Him dat makes de thunder,
> Put dis he-male an' dis she-male asunder.
> I darfore 'nounce you bofe de same.
> Be good, go 'long, an' keep up yo' name.
> De broomstick's jumped, de worl's not wide.
> She's now yo' own. Salute yo' bride [Foster 90].

The poem reveals some particularly important details. The portrayal of the likely exaggerated form of speech suggests that many southerners associated this ceremony with an uneducated class of individuals. Additionally, it reveals the central use of the broom to seal the ceremony. For after the broomstick was jumped, enslaved couples were eligible to begin their lives together.

While jumping the broom is popularly associated with antebellum slave marriages, slaves were not the only group to use the ritual. As stated before, common whites and enslaved blacks engaged in an unofficial system of economic and cultural exchange. While the elite planter class would prefer that the two groups not associate with one another, as they were both opposed the elite class in economic circumstances, the reality of enforcing such regulations was much more difficult. As mentioned, the Welsh settlements in the slave exporting states were likely a crucial element in introducing and popularizing broomstick weddings prior to the substantial exportation of slaves to the newly annexed southern territories. Louisiana, the largest importer of this creole generation, is important for discovering the dynamics of white and black cultural exchange in the antebellum period.

It seems more than coincidental that written records reveal groups of antebellum whites in Louisiana conducting broomstick weddings coinciding with the period of the domestic slave trade. While it is possible that whites moving throughout the South may have assisted in introducing the ritual, the evidence is difficult to find. One predicament is that it remains unknown if any people of Welsh descent continued to use the ritual in North America. It is likely that they did, but once again, the lack of documented references to the formalities of wedding rituals, especially those of the working-class, elude the researcher. In Pennsylvania "jumping over the broomstick" was a popular children's game, which may be traced back to the significant Welsh presence in the colony (Bausman and Duss 402). Wayland D. Hand found that potential brides in Kentucky would jump over brooms placed on chair seats to determine if they would marry within a year (72). The only whites found, as of yet, that actually jumped the broom in matrimony, are the white French-Creoles of Louisiana who received increased contact with the enslaved during the antebellum domestic slave trade.

Sullivan, however, finds the possibility of whites borrowing the custom from blacks unlikely: "It seems to me that ... Whites in the American South would not have borrowed a marriage ritual from the Blacks" ("'Jumping the Broom': Possible Welsh Origins" 18). While it initially appears strange to assert that Europeans introduced the ritual into the south, Africans utilized it, and then the custom was transferred back to communities of European descent, the evidence in the Louisiana case suggests that this was likely the way it occurred. Scholars of southern cultural history have firmly established that slaves of African descent had the most substantial cultural impact of any other group in the South, and that southern whites of various classes were able to look past racial boundaries during activities of entertainment and leisure. Mechal Sobel's seminal study of eighteenth century Virginia provides important evidence that white and black southerners frequently interacted "in ordinary times and at times of celebration" (166). Enslaved cooks, musicians, entertainers, and healers all made a profound impact on southern culture and society, and their skills frequently transcended racial and ethnic boundaries.[7] For Louisiana specifically,

Gwendolyn Midlo-Hall cogently argues that the impact of black people on many poor white Louisianans remains "engraved on the language they still speak today" (236). These are but a few examples in an expanding literature of acculturation in the U.S. South. While racism did exist, cultural borrowing was a reality, even if the descendants of these antebellum whites would later deny the possibility. Jumping the broom was no different.

In other rural areas, there is testimony to white fascination with broomstick weddings. One account related by a white woman relates how some whites were fascinated in how slaves internalized the ritual:

> My mother lived in the South when a little girl during the Civil War. I have often heard her tell when the colored folks got married the man would lay the broom down on the floor with the bushy end to the north, then he would take the girl by the hand, then they step over the broom, then backward again. Then the girl picked up the broom, laying it down again with the bushy end to the south, then the girl took the man by the hand and they step over it and backward again, to keep evil away and bad spirits through their life. Mother said many a night she would steal down and watch when she heard some of the colored folks were going to get married [Hyatt 465].

The passage reveals two important aspects of how jumping the broom was conceptualized by both parties. The first is that some whites were fascinated by the broomstick ceremony, and studied how slaves incorporated the broom into their wedding nuptials. In this particular case, the slaves were methodical in their approach and mindful of the supernatural. The fact that this woman's mother spent "many a night" viewing the nuptials reveals its complexities beyond a simple ceremony. For the couple involved in this particular case, elements of African spirituality appear to be present, or at least an amalgam of supernatural understandings brought on by cultural contact between enslaved Africans, American Indians, and Euro-Americans. Additionally, the slaves in this particular case appeared to initiate the ritual independently of any master imposition, further crumbling the argument that this was a custom impressed upon enslaved people by the planter class.

The most likely scenario for this cultural fusion in Louisiana is that rural whites had few possibilities for formal marriage ceremonies. Preachers and church establishments were rare in parts of the rural south, encouraging rural whites to develop methods in which they could solemnize their vows while they waited for a minister to solemnize the marriage. The massive annexation of creole slaves into Louisiana slave markets makes a strong case that Louisiana was influenced by the cultures brought from slaves in the upper South. Louisiana always held a strongly Africanized slave culture, and the French creoles were, to some degree, more willing than Anglo-Americans to openly fuse their culture with slaves of African descent. One narrative from a white Louisiana family reveals striking similarities to the broomstick ritual employed by slaves:

> The major next asked for a broom which he held down before the couple saying, "Jump over."

"Hold it lower," said Nelly, and they stepped over in a business-like manner.

"Now," said Major Bee, "I solemnly pronounce you husband and wife, and I hope and trust that you will dwell together lovingly and peacefully until you die. I have at your request tied this matrimonial knot as tight as I possibly could, under the circumstances" [Merrick 95–96].

Apparently the broom ritual was used under the condition that the couple sought a minister at the first opportunity. Eager couples likely used the ritual to enable themselves to enter into marital activities, such as procreation and cohabitation, without the stigma of immorality attached to them. Thus, this simple ritual, hailing from the rural regions of a demonstrably small region of southwest England produced a surprising impact on antebellum southerners. Jumping the broom became a central feature in many southern marriage ceremonies, and even had the ability to cross cultural and racial barriers.

Given the near universal nature of broomstick weddings among the enslaved, one might imagine that it continued after slavery's demise. The evidence suggests the contrary, however, even to the point of complete denial by some former slaves. When ex-slave couple Laney and John Hook were asked about slave marriages, Laney quickly interjected and described her understanding of slave weddings: "My mother said they used to make up a new broom and when the couple jumped over it, they was married." It is at this point John vividly reveals how the concept of "forgetting" is utilized in these narratives, he responds: "Laney, that was never confirmed. It was just hearsay, as far as you know, and I wouldn't tell things like that" (qtd. In *Slave Narratives Vol. IV Part 4* 84). Other narratives reveal similar sentiments. While many usually admitted that the practice occurred under slavery, they quickly mention that as soon as freedom came the slaves had a "real" wedding. Ex-slave Rena Raines recalled that during slavery her mother and father married by jumping the broom, but asserted that her "mother an' father come ter Raleigh atter de surrender an wus married right" (qtd. in *Slave Narratives Vol. XI Part 2* 195). Raines's assertion suggests that the further African Americans drifted from the antebellum period, jumping the broom became a less valid marriage ceremony.

As the twentieth century continued, African Americans continued integrating into "American" cultural norms, a process usually synonymous with distancing themselves from an enslaved heritage. As mentioned, a shift in mentality emerged in the mid-twentieth century as African Americans challenged the indignities of the segregated Jim Crow South, while also identifying with the African countries revolting against colonial subjugation.[8] Jumping the broom became integrated into modern African American heritage weddings in the 1980s, and the way African Americans "remembered" the practice shifted. Instead of being identified as the demoralizing practice associated with slavery, many African American authors portrayed the practice as something inherently African; a belief that, as demonstrated, remains well into the twenty-first century. In contrast to the denial by the aforementioned John who corrected his wife Laney's presumption, or the assertion by Rena Raines that jumping the broom was not a valid marriage, African Americans in the 1980s and 1990s jumped the broom in memory of their enslaved ancestors *and* to commemorate an African heritage.

Understanding historical memory is crucial in understanding why this particular practice ceased and why it was revived. For former slaves in the early twentieth century it symbolized oppression and subjugation, but for African Americans in the late twentieth century it symbolized heritage and survival. Memory was recreated by the descendant community to dignify the practice, which explains why some authors still propose possible African origins for the ritual. Thus, jumping the broom was resurrected as a "Pan-African American" phenomenon, with evidence of broom jumping continuing to occur throughout every region of the United States.

In a similar vein to their African-American counterparts, pockets of white communities also revived the practice publicly, harking back to a Celtic heritage in opposition to the Christian norm. Internet sites and neo-pagan literature continue to promote the broomstick ceremony as a cultural expression for those who identify with Celtic heritage. When matched against the historical records, it is evident that the revival of this practice has been altered for a Pan-Celtic audience. Neo-pagan religions are not a homogenous entity. "Neo-pagan" is a general term for communities that express a desire to call for a return to Pre–Christian roots, and typically utilize similar cultural expressions to mark their identities. While broomstick weddings are used in their ceremonies, one additional element is included that signifies a shift in how the practice is understood in modern communities, against how it was conceptualized in the past.

Neo-pagan communities blend elements from a variety of Celtic cultures in their ritualistic proceedings. A neo-pagan broomstick wedding typically includes a "handfast" ceremony, which is essentially a "tying together" of the couple's wrists, symbolizing that they are bound together and will never separate. Lexa Rosean writes that after the handfasting rite, "the couple jumps the broom to bless their union" (47). The Welsh records reveal no such practice. Handfasts are typically associated with traditional Scottish weddings, demonstrating that the heirs to this marital rite took a traditional Welsh ritual and combined it with another Celtic practice from Scotland. Pan-Celtic authors claim that this form of common-law marriage was popular among ancient Scottish and Irish people (Dunwich 59–60). Unfortunately, these recent works make similar mistakes that the Afrocentric authors made earlier. The authors write for audiences that already subscribe to their ideology, and their works leave few citations, and no path for curious readers to follow. Is it possible the Scottish and Irish people also practiced the ritual? Perhaps, but the lack of documentation weakens the argument. It does demonstrate, however, the importance broomstick weddings hold in defining cultures that appear to have few historical links to each other.

Amidst these numerous accounts of cultural transfer, jumping the broom becomes difficult to categorize in terms of popular culture. The ritual is certainly Welsh, but popular culture touts it as both an African-American and "Celtic" cultural tradition. Surely one cannot deny a ritual to one culture over the other because they were not the original practitioners. Former slaves and poor whites adapted the ritual to their own economic and societal worldviews, as have African Americans and neo-pagans as the modern heirs to this tradition. The surviving evidence reveals the broomstick wedding's history through the paradigm of Atlantic exchange, where intersecting Welsh and African diasporas shared and transferred cultural characteristics until the borrowed trait became difficult to distinguish from the original. Former U.S. slaves never revealed where the ritual came from, most likely because they did not know; all they were concerned about is that enslaved southerners jumped the broom as a form of marriage for specific purposes. Rural southern whites also used the ritual for their own purposes, not terribly concerned as to whether or not it was of Welsh or African-American extraction. Yet, the Welsh roots are clear, even if they remain unnoticed.

While some modern Wiccan communities emphasize the centrality of the use of birchwood in the ritual, the mythology surrounding the sacred connections to brooms and birchwood are deemphasized among many modern practitioners, both white and black. But regardless of race, modern consumers of this cultural heritage are indebted to a group of people whose culture was isolated by their colonists for centuries, and only emerged within the context of an "Atlantic World" that placed continents isolated from one another for thousands of years into an interconnected web of economic and cultural exchange. What is notable is that there are a few potential solutions to decipher the broomstick wedding's mysterious origins, and even more mysterious transfer to the United States. The analysis, however, is far from over, and "jumping the broom" is in need of continual analysis and revision. It remains certain, however, that this particular aspect of Welsh culture and myth holds incredible staying power, even though in a world filled with technology and advanced methods of transportation it may no longer appear useful or practical. The ritual will continue to reinforce group solidarity among its practitioners, and will (sometimes unknowingly) commemorate the heritage and resilience of a small region of western Britain that likely did not anticipate it would have so large an impact on popular culture throughout the world.[9]

Notes

1. For studies explaining "Atlantic History" see Greene and Morgan (2009); Canizares-Esguerra 215–233; Games "Atlantic History" 741–757; Games Migrations. For a critique of the Atlantic model see Coclanis 725–742.

2. For studies of media impact see Fairchild, Stockard and Bowman 307–318; Tucker and Shah 325–336; Ball-Rokeach Grube and Rokeach 58–68; Protinsky and Wildman 171–181.

3. For statistical analyses and comparisons of slave importations see Curtin; Eltis and Richardson.

4. For literature on gypsy customs see Thompson 336, 337, 341; Jarman and Jarman 19.

5. For recent claims to African origins see Janes 876; Baker 93; Calkhoven 42. For Celtic origins see Griffyn 17; Dunwich Witch's Halloween 155; Dunwich Wicca Craft 59–60.

6. For claim of "forced" marriage see Dundes 325; Beside a few of the slaves themselves, one of the first scholars to propose the belief that this ritual was a joke was John Blassingame, *The Slave Community* 166–167.

7. Southern 42–46; Fett 64–65; Brown 70–76.

8. Anosike 435. An African identity can be traced very early in African diasporic literature, and the notion of Pan-Africanism is relatively early as well. See Manning 3; Sidbury.

9. The author wishes to thank Daniel C. Littlefield, Matt Childs, Kevin Dawson, Shanelle Parry, Michael Woods, David Prior, Allen Driggers, and Evan Kutzler for contributing valuable comments, critiques, and insights that furthered this project's development.

Works Cited

Anosike, Benji J.O. "Africa and Afro-Americans: The Bases for Greater Understanding and Solidarity," *The Journal of Negro Education* 51.4 (1982): 434–448.

Baker, John F. *The Washingtons of Wessyngton Plantation: Stories of my Family's Journey to Freedom*. New York: Atria Publishing, 2009.

Ball-Rokeach, Sandra J. Joel W. Grube and Milton Rokeach. "Roots: The Next Generation — Who Watched and With What Effect?" *The Public Opinion Quarterly* 45.1 (1981): 58–68.

Bassett, John Spencer. *The Regulators of North Carolina (1765–1771)*. Washington: Govt. Off., 1895.

Bausman, Joseph Henderson, and John Samuel Duss. *History of Beaver County, Pennsylvania: and its Centennial Celebration Vol. 1*. New York: The Knickerbocker Press, 1904.

Bek, William. "Survivals of Old Marriage-Customs Among the Low Germans of West Missouri." *Journal of American Folklore.* 21.80 (Jan., 1908): 60–67.

Blank, Paula. *Broken English: Dialects and the Politics of Language in English Renaissance Writings*. New York: Routledge, 1996.

Blassingame, John W., Ed. *Slave Testimony: Two Centuries of Letters, Speeches, Interviews and Autobiographies*. Baton Rouge: Louisiana State University Press, 2005.

_____ *The Slave Community: Plantation Life in the Antebellum South*. New York: Oxford University Press, 1979.

Brown, William Wells. *My Southern Home: or, The South and its People*. Boston: A. G. Brown & Co., 1880.

Calkhoven, Laurie. *Harriet Tubman: Leading the Way To Freedom*. New York: Sterling Publishing Co., 2008.

Canizares-Esguerra, Jorge. *Puritan Conquistadors: Iberianizing the Atlantic, 1550–1700*. Stanford: Stanford University Press, 2006.

Coclanis, Peter A. "Atlantic World or Atlantic/World?" *The William and Mary Quarterly* 63. 4 (Oct., 2006): 725–742.
Cole, Harriet. *Jumping the Broom: The African American Wedding Planner.* New York: Henry Holt and Company, 1993.
Crooke, W. "The Lifting of the Bride." *Folklore.* 13.3 (Sept., 1902): 226–251.
Curtin, Philip. *The Atlantic Slave Trade: A Census.* Madison: The University of Wisconsin Press, 1969.
Davies, John. *A History of Wales.* London: Penguin Books, 2007.
_____."Wales and America-Address." *North American Journal of Welsh Studies.* 1.1 (2001): 11–19.
Dawson, Kevin. *Enslaved Watermen in the Atlantic World, 1444–1888.* Diss. University of South Carolina, 2005. Columbia.
Desch Obi, T.J. *Fighting for Honor: The History of African Martial Arts Traditions in the Atlantic World.* Columbia: University of South Carolina Press, 2008.
Deyle, Steven. *Carry Me Back: The Domestic Slave Trade in American Life.* Oxford: Oxford University Press, 2005.
Dundes, Alan. "'Jumping the Broom': On the Origin and Meaning of An African American Wedding Custom." *The Journal of American Folklore.* 109.433 (1996): 324–329.
Dunwich, Gerina. *Wicca Craft: The Modern Witches Book of Herbs, Magick and Dreams.* New York: Citadel Press, 1991.
_____. *Witch's Halloween: A Complete Guide to the Magick, Incantations, Recipes, Spells, and Lore.* Avon: The Provenance Press, 2007.
"Eighteenth Century Slaves as Advertised by their Masters." *The Journal of Negro History.* 1.2 (Apr., 1916): 163–216.
Eltis, David and David Richardson, *Extending the Frontiers: Essays on the New Transatlantic Slave Trade Database.* New Haven: Yale University Press, 2008.
Equiano, Olaudah. *The Interesting Narrative of the Life of Olaudah Equiano, or Gustavus Vassa, the African. Written by Himself. Vol. I.* London: Published by Author, 1789.
Fairchild, Halford H., Russell Stockard and Philip Bowman. "Impact of Roots: Evidence from the National Survey of Black Americans," *Journal of Black Studies* 16.3 (1986): 307–318.
Federal Writers' Project. *Slave Narratives: A Folk History of Slavery in the United States from the Interviews with Former Slaves 17 Vols.* Washington D.C.: Library of Congress, 1941.
Fett, Sharla. *Working Cures: Healing, Health, and Power on Southern Slave Plantations.* Chapel Hill: University of North Carolina Press, 2002.
Folklore, Myths, and Legends of Britain. London: Reader's Digest Association Ltd., 1973.
Ford, Lacy K. *Deliver Us From Evil: The Slavery Question in the Old South.* Oxford: Oxford University Press, 2009.
Foster, Francis Smith. *'Til Death or Distance Do Us Part: Love and Marriage in African America.* Oxford: Oxford University Press, 2010.
Fraser, Rebecca J. *Courtship and Love Among the Enslaved in North Carolina.* Jackson: University Press of Mississippi, 2009.
Games, Alison. "Atlantic History: Definitions, Challenges, and Opportunities," *American Historical Review* 111.3 (June, 2006): 741–757.
_____. *Migration and the Origins of the English Atlantic World.* Cambridge: Harvard University Press, 1999.
Green, Danita Roundtree. *Broom Jumping: A Celebration of Love. A Complete Guide to Keeping Traditions Alive in your Family.* Richmond: Entertaining Ideas Ltd, 1992.
Greene, Jack P., and Philip Morgan, eds., *Atlantic History: A Critical Appraisal.* Oxford: Oxford University Press, 2009.
Griffyn, Sally. *Wiccan Wisdomkeepers: Modern-day Witches Speak on Environmentalism, Feminism, Motherhood, Wiccan Lore, and More.* Boston: Red Wheel LLC, 2002.

Haley, Alex. *Roots: The Saga of an American Family.* New York: Doubleday, 1976.
Hall, Gwendolyn Midlo. *Africans in Colonial Louisiana: The Development of Afro-Creole Culture in the Eighteenth Century.* Baton Rouge: Louisiana State University Press, 1992.
Hand, Wayland D. "From Idea to Word: Folk Beliefs and Customs Underlying Folk Speech." *American Speech.* 48.½ (Spring–Summer, 1973): 67–76.
Higginbotham, A. Leon. *In the Matter of Color: Race and the American Legal Process: The Colonial Period.* New York: Oxford University Press, 1978.
Hyatt, Harry Middleton. *Folklore from Adams County, Illinois* 2nd ed. New York: Alma Egan Hyatt Foundation, 1965.
James, E. Wyn. "Welsh Ballads and American Slavery." *The Welsh Journal of Religious History.* 2 (2007): 59–86.
Janes, Gerald David, Ed. *Encyclopedia of African American Society, Vol. 2* Newbury Park: Sage Publications Inc., 2005.
Jarman, Eldra, and A.O.H. Jarman. *The Welsh Gypsies: Children of Abram Wood.* Originally pub. 1900; Cardiff: University of Wales Press, 1991.
Johnson, Walter. *Soul By Soul: Life Inside an Antebellum Slave Market.* Cambridge: Harvard University Press, 1999.
Jones, W. Rhys. "'Besom Wedding' in the Ceiriog Valley." *Folklore.* 39. 2 (1928): 149–166.
Joyner, Charles. *Shared Traditions: Southern History and Folk Culture.* University of Illinois Press: Chicago, 1999.
Knowles, Anne Kelly. "Immigrant Trajectories Through the Rural-Industrial Transition in Wales and the United States, 1795–1850." *Annals of the Association of American Geographers.* 85.2 (Jun., 1995): 246–266.
Lewis, Ronald L. *Welsh Americans: A History of Assimilation in the Coalfields.* Chapel Hill: University of North Carolina Press, 2008.
Linebaugh, Peter, and Marcus Rediker. *The Many-Headed Hydra: Sailors, Slaves, Commoners, and the Hidden History of the Revolutionary Atlantic.* Boston: Beacon Press, 2000.
Liverpool and Slavery: An Historical Account of the Liverpool-African Slave Trade. Liverpool: A. Bowker and Son, 1884.
MacKillop, James. *A Dictionary of Celtic Mythology.* Oxford: Oxford University Press, 1998.
Mac Coitir, Niall. *Irish Trees: Myths, Legends and Folklore.* Ireland: Colour Books, Ltd., 2006.
Manning, Patrick. *Slavery and African Life: Occidental, Oriental and African Slave Trades.* Cambridge University Press: Cambridge, 1990.
Merrick, Caroline Elizabeth. *Old Times in Dixie Land: A Southern Matron's Memories.* New York: The Grafton Press, 1901.
Meyer, Duane. *The Highlander Scots of North Carolina 1732–1776.* Chapel Hill: University of North Carolina Press, 1987.
Neasham, Mary. *The Spirit of the Green Man.* Somerset: Green Magic, 2004.
Ogunleye, Tolagbe M. *The African Roots of Jumping the Broom.* Philadelphia: Cowrie Publishing Co., 2004.
Olmsted, Frederick Law. *A Journey in the Seaboard Slave States, With Remarks on Their Economy.* New York: Dix and Edwards, 1856.
Protinsky, Ruth A. and Terry M. Wildman, "Roots: Reflections From the Classroom," *The Journal of Negro Education.* 48.2 (1979): 171–181.
Pughe, William Owen. *A Dictionary of the Welsh Language, Explained in English; with Various Illustrations, From the Literary Remains and From the Living Speech of the Cymmry.* London: Thomas Gee, 1832.

Rawick, George, Ed. *Bearing Witness: Memories of Arkansas Slavery: Narratives from the 1930s WPA Collections.* Little Rock: The University of Arkansas Press, 2003.
Reiss, Oscar. *Blacks in Colonial America.* Jefferson: McFarland & Company, Inc., 1997.
Rosean, Lexa. *The Encyclopedia of Magickal Ingredients: A Wiccan Guide to Spellcasting.* New York: Paraview Pocket Books, 2005.
Ross, David. *Wales: History of a Nation.* New Lanark: Geddes and Grosset, 2005.
Saunders, William, Ed. *Colonial and State Records of North Carolina Vol. 1.* Raleigh: P. M. Hale, 1886.
Schwartz, Marie Jenkins. *Born in Bondage: Growing Up Enslaved in the Antebellum South.* Harvard University Press: Cambridge, 2000.
Shakespeare, William. *Henry IV: Part 1.* Eds. Barbara A. Mowat and Paul Werstine. New York: Washington Square Press, 1994.
Sidbury, James. *Becoming African in America: Race and Nation in the Early Black Atlantic.* Oxford: Oxford University Press, 2007.
Smith, Venture. *A Narrative of the Life and Adventures of Venture, a Native of Africa: But Resident above Sixty Years in the United States of America. Related by Himself.* New-London: C. Holt, 1798.
Sobel, Mechal. *The World They Made Together: Black and White Values in Eighteenth-Century Virginia.* Princeton: Princeton University Press, 1987.
Southern, Eileen. *The Music of Black Americans: A History.* New York: W. W. Norton & Company, Inc., 1997.
Stevenson, Brenda. *Life in Black and White: Family and Community in the Slave South.* Oxford: Oxford University Press, 1996.
Stone, Lawrence. *The Family, Sex, and Marriage in England 1500–1800.* New York: Harper Row Publishers, Inc., 1979.
Sullivan, C.W., III. "'Jumping the Broom': A Further Consideration of the Origins of an African American Wedding Custom." *The Journal of American Folklore.* 110.436 (Spring, 1997): 203–204.
_____. "'Jumping the Broom': Possible Welsh Origins of an African-American Custom," *Southern Folklore* 55.1 (1998): 15–23.
Tadman, Michael. *Speculators and Slaves: Masters, Traders and Slaves in the Old South.* Madison: University of Wisconsin Press, 1989.
Tangerman, E.J. "The History of Welsh Love Spoons." *Carving Spoons: Welsh Love Spoons, Celtic Knots and Contemporary Favorites.* Ed. Shirley Adler. East Petersburg: Fox Chapel Publishing Company, 2003.
The Mabinogion. Trans. Gwyn Jones and Thomas Jones. London: Orion Publishing Group, 2004.
Thompson, T.W. "The Ceremonial Customs of the British Gypsies," *Folklore* 24.3 (Sept., 1913): 314–356.
Tucker, Lauren R. and Hemant Shah. *Race and the Transformation of Culture: The Making of the Television Miniseries* Roots, *Critical Studies in Mass Communication* 9.24 (1992): 325–336.
Williams, Gwyn A. *Search for Beulah Land.* New York: Holmes and Meier, 1980.
Wood, Betty. *Slavery in Colonial America, 1619–1776.* New York: Rowman and Littlefield Publishers, Inc., 2005.
Wood, Peter. *Black Majority: Negroes in Colonial South Carolina from 1670 through the Stono Rebellion.* New York: W. W. Norton and Company, Inc., 1974.
Woodson, Carter G. *The History of the Negro Church.* Washington, D.C.: The Associated Publishers, 1921.

Constructing Myth in Music
Heather Dale, King Arthur and "Culhwch and Olwen"

Megan MacAlystre

When telling others that I was writing on Welsh mythology in popular music, they seemed to have a moment of profound pause. This pause was born not only of the lack of familiarity of most people with what constitutes Welsh mythology or, sadly, even that there *is* Welsh mythology, but of the seeming disconnect between the topics. But this reaction, and indeed the distance between the myths of centuries past and the modern music, is actually revealing and significant to the topic at hand. Popular music as a term seems to connote the modern, the commercial, the trendy, or the fleeting. It narrows the gaze in a way that suggests, or perhaps more accurately *risks*, the exclusion of precisely that genre which is perhaps closest to the original presentation of many traditional, namely medieval, tales: the genre of the folk song. Relying upon the aforementioned connotations of popular music, folk music is a deliberate construction of folk singers as modern storytellers. They position themselves consciously as the direct descendents or even the embodiments of those venerated bards of the past who found their livelihood and purpose in the recounting of tales of the heroic past, a past that for the medieval storyteller was often more immediate but not any less legendary.

This binary between myth and modernity is, at once, the heart of their respective definitions and entirely erroneous. The nostalgia for the past; for a time of chivalric knights and fair maidens, for magic and epic adventures; is part of the human condition, part of our means of understanding and fashioning ourselves. It is that quest for and remembrance of a past that did not exist and yet has formulated millennium after millennium of contemporary identity. The folk singer depends on this, as a method of constructing him or herself within an elevated continuum of the artist that is more than entertainer, but is the timeless transmitter of legendary, and even universal, wisdom to the awaiting listeners. They relate stories which, by their own assertions, will impart understanding of the self and of the surrounding world, in a manner that has its power and value in ancient traditions.

However, despite certain (in)famous claims that the storyteller and, indeed the author himself, has died a rather unflattering death due to the inundation of technology into our lives,[1] it is those very progressive mediums that, I believe, are giving new life to this tradition. The vitality of Welsh mythological influence has not waned and has indeed found its way into a range of media, beyond books and into film and video-games. The digital age carries on and carries out the epic mythos of Wales, her stories, and her storytellers. The internet creates, as many scholars have explored, communities developed around common interests, rather than simply shared geography. And within this virtual world, the myth and myths of Wales have a parallel. Both technologically constructed space and mythological constructed space have one proverbial foot in reality and one beyond it. They are standing in a fantastical Wales, in a place that exists only within cultural memory and therefore predetermined to exist at the equally predetermined intersections of tradition and modernity.

It should be no surprise, then, that the knowledge and importance of these myths and mythmakers also find expression and dissemination within the virtual world, even for a medium more directly associated with traditional tales. The internet, for many musicians, has become the forum of developing identity, a compensation for the expansion of our world and the globalization that would at first appear to have removed the possibility of the continuation of the tradition of the independent bard. But the internet has the advantage of social networking, of at once narrowing and expanding our circles, and offering a space for self-construction and self-advertising that permits, in many ways, the resurgence of the individual storyteller, the independent singer. Through personal websites, social networking sites like Facebook or LiveJournal, the online publication of concert or album reviews, and the online media staple that is YouTube, the solitary artist has the potential to reach millions, without "selling out" to a corporation for exposure. And within these millions, he or she can develop a community of fans that can then either become or provide the modern series of hearths at which their stories are told.

Some of these artists so rely upon the popular conception of the medieval storyteller that they now perform predominately at "house concerts" in which individuals will open their homes for an intimate concert of a particular artist or group, rather than perform at large or established venues. This consciously replicates the journey from entertaining at one fireside then another. As increasing numbers of artists are offering their talent for such performances or indeed preferring them, there are entire websites dedicated to pairing interested hosts with interested musicians. These websites advocate the house concert as a way for performers "to connect with these audiences in a meaningful way" (Snyder). Obviously, this does place the modern, larger venue as an empty place of alienation, symptomatic in many ways of modernity itself. Unsurprisingly then, while these house concerts are an option for any performer, it is the folk singer that seems to be predominant in these environments. And in fact, two of the most accessible websites on the matter, ConcertsInYourHome.com and HouseConcert.org, link directly to the Folk Alliance International, making the dominance of this type of performance venue even clearer.

More importantly on these webpages, though, are the direct assertions of and repeated emphasis on the historical connection; the continuation of the wandering minstrel finding a hearth at which to perform. In turn, to the benefit of the artists in question, this positions the host as the lord or lady of this mythic manor, allowing him/her a place in this glorification of the past and its musicians, despite the clearly modern method of facilitating and organizing it.

One artist who constructs herself in the rich place between the mythic past of the medieval storyteller and the driving force of modernity is Canadian folk singer and songwriter Heather Dale. Since 1997, Dale has released eleven albums, most of which focus on her retellings of Celtic myth and legends, particularly those surrounding King Arthur. However, she also borrows stories from Inuit, Scandinavian, Greek, and Roman traditions in addition to writing songs inspired directly by the *Decameron*, the trial of Joan of Arc, the ruins of Hamburg Cathedral, and the life of Gandhi. According to her website's biography, she identifies this as her "cosmopolitan outlook" in which she "cheerfully disregards the stereotypical limits for both Celtic balladeers and folk singer-songwriters. She excels at finding contemporary themes within old material." The self-awareness of her musical and inspirational appropriation makes for an oeuvre that is essentially pastiche, deliberately emphasizing the piecing together of genres, stories, and musical styles to present a unified and unifying body of work.[2]

Dale speaks directly, as many folk singers have, to the aforementioned contrast between pop and folk music, glorifying the latter as a reactionary return to myth and nostalgia in which existential wisdom can be found:

> Pop music exists in the moment, but folk songs are all about context ... They look at the unusual, strange, beautiful and crazy parts of life, and we all have the opportunity to become a little wiser because of it. Modern audiences are bombarded with two-second blips of information: Billboards flying by along the highway, laugh-a-minute TV shows, (and) pulsating CNN ticker-tape. Folk music gives us a chance to reflect, a chance to figure out where we came from, and where we really want to find ourselves tomorrow [Dale in Mowat HS8].

By aligning herself with the past, in particular a predominately Celtic past, Dale sets herself up as a medium. There is a timelessness in this perception and presentation, a constant link between centuries past and contemporary existence, that if we "all have the opportunity" to find as an escape of the rapid-fire assault of modern inanity. This privileging of the past is as much of a mythological construct as the myths Dale utilizes in her music, but not one that necessarily needs denigration as humankind, on some level, is on a constant quest for themselves and their position within cultural and world history. By emphasizing the context of the folk songs, which according to Dale is their primary significance, Dale has placed even greater weight upon the adaptions of the tales she utilizes, as they have an overarching and all-encompassing goal. This is not without its risks, as we will see particularly in the case of "Culhwch and Olwen."

While Dale focuses in many of her songs on reworking and literally giving voice to the tales of Arthur, her most clearly Welsh song is that of "Culhwch and Olwen" taken from the Welsh prose romance "How Culhwch Won Olwen."[3] Often grouped with the Four Branches of the *Mabinogi* (and considered by some translators as part of the larger grouping of tales called the *Mabinogion*) this tale seems particularly apt for translation into musical verse, as critic Sioned Davies has argued in her work "Performing Culhwch ac Olwen," asserting that the tale is particularly and poetically suited to performance in structure and detail. However, this appropriateness to performance doesn't seem to be enough for it to be approached frequently in music. Only a handful of musical settings of the tale could be found; Heather Dale's song is the most readily available one. Additionally, it is to be the only one of that handful that is not solely instrumental and distinctly separated from the tale by the lack of lyrics or by being sung in Welsh and thereby narratively and linguistically inaccessible to English only listeners. One remaining means of musically approaching "Culhwch and Olwen" is to provide supplemental music to the spoken tale, as in the case harpist Robin Williamson, most famous for his founding of The Incredible String Band during the 1960s (Windling). As singer and songwriter, Heather Dale has united music and lyrics to create a singular song that is readily approachable and comprehensible to its audience, but one that has undergone significant changes in its plot, meaning, and context.

Dale's musical version of "Culhwch and Olwen" is included on an album entitled *The Trial of Lancelot*, which is based upon the wealth of Arthurian legends but with a particularly divergent focus. She presents a range of perspectives circling around Arthur, giving life and voice, often literally, to other figures, from the unnamed young woman of "Lily Maid," who coolly recounts Lancelot's callous treatment of her (an earlier tale of Tennyson's "The Lady of Shalott"); to a cloistered Guinevere quietly speaking to Lancelot after Arthur's death in "Miles to Go"; to a vengeful Morgause in the dark, pulsing "Mordred's Lullaby," though Dale identifies her as Morgan Le Fey in her comments on the work (*Music*). "Hawthorn Tree" details the final days of Merlin; and "The Prydwen Sails Again," as Dale explains, "honours the Knights of the Round Table lost overseas in a doomed expedition to Caer Siddi, the City of the Dead" (*Music*). Lancelot is the focus of two other songs, including "Tarnished Silver" near the end of the album, in which Dale narratively embodies Lancelot as he speaks to the dying Guinevere, urging her to find her much deserved rest. Lancelot's treason provides the basis for the titular song of the album, a song in which the listener hears the testimony of Kay, Gawain, Tristan, and Galahad. Although we actually hear the words they speak before the king and Lancelot's short defense of himself ("I'm tried for love of Guenivere / My crime was love"), Arthur himself is not given an actual voice. He does weep and "call[s] the wrath of Heaven / on the lovers who'd betrayed him" but interestingly Dale does not sing the actual words Arthur speaks at any point in the song, as she does with the other characters. In fact, in the entire collection of songs, this is the most clearly active role that Arthur ever has. He is referenced and invoked frequently, and clearly the tales Dale adapts all circle around Arthur. But, he never speaks directly in any of these songs, and his actions are dramatically limited in scope and effect. In fact, the only song that centers on Arthur himself is "Measure of a Man" which closes the album and is the mournful invocation sung at his funeral. He is quite literally here the dead king who only provides the occasion for the song, just as he symbolically does throughout the album. Dale's Arthur is never a truly active figure, even when the original tale relies entirely upon his power and action, as is the case with "Culhwch and Olwen."

"Culhwch and Olwen" stands apart from the others on the album, both as a story likely unfamiliar to most listeners and for its musical presentation. Amidst the solemn ballads and sweeping melodies, it is a jaunty tune, relying upon only the brisk beat of drums and the trill of a tin whistle to accompany Dale's vocals. The simple instruments and bright rhythm evoke cheerful drinking songs or an energized march, both appropriate to the nature of the tale. The perspective of the song moves the listener farther away from Arthur, until he is nothing more a distant character to be mentioned and invoked, not a focus or a force within the song. Dale transforms this medieval Welsh tale into a very different story in which Culhwch takes the control and the power to fulfill a plot that is more in keeping with a modern view of a traditional fairy tale. This perspective is enhanced by the requirement of the listener to infer and construct numerous elements of a story with which, by and large, they are not familiar.

From the outset, the transformation of the lengthy tale of "How Culhwch Won Olwen" into a five-minute song demands considerable condensing. However, as with any adaptation, particularly one of reduction, the choices of what to keep and what to discard are significant and textually rich for the questing scholar. In Dale's "Culhwch and Olwen," the overall plot is dramatically transformed. Rather than a lengthy series of increasingly daunting, detailed, and interwoven tasks; Culhwch is only set to "bring [Ysbaddaden] Mabon son of Modron / Who was taken from his mother even as his lips first cried" (Dale 2000). The dozens of remaining tasks are unmentioned as is the reason behind the giant's request to have Mabon brought to him. It is presented as one troublesome task, and indeed, one relatively brief one, that must be completed before Culhwch can have Olwen as his bride. Ysbaddaden isn't viewed, in this song, as attempting to set forth the impossible task to maintain his life. There is no meaning given to the singular task beyond the quest itself, and it is only through the subsequent verses that the listener learns that this is anything other than a simple retrieval mission. We are not told that Mabon's whereabouts are unknown, only that he was taken from his mother at the time of his birth. However, as Culhwch and the accompanying knights ask for information about him from talking animals, there is an expectation that the years that have passed are many and that the memory and magic of speaking creatures is needed to find Mabon. The listener must infer that this is some arduous task and a worthy one, to be well-rewarded with a fair wife. Additionally the listener must infer the fierceness of Ysbaddaden himself through his description as a giant, rather than the defensive and spiteful overburdening of Culhwch in order for Ysbaddaden to escape death or even his ability to withstand repeated injuries after attempting to kill Culhwch's companions. Dale's Ysbaddaden is not violent or devious; he is large. Beyond the reference to his size in the song, it is only through the listener's associations with other giants, like ogres in fairy tales traditionally bent on capture and cannibalizing, does Ysbaddaden exist as a threat.

The significant reduction in "Culhwch and Olwen" extends beyond the plot, as King Arthur himself is greatly eliminated from Dale's song. He exists in reference, something to be invoked more so than Culhwch's invoking of his sizable court in the original tale. Arthur has no action, no *direct* influence upon any part of the Dale's story. It is here that I must note that the lyrics for "Culhwch and Olwen" printed within the cd booklet have four extra lines, two of which are performed in place of two others, and two (Culhwch's direct address of Ysbaddaden to literally shout his purpose) that appear only in the written lyrics and not in either the album version nor in available live versions of the song. These variations, however, all have the same effect upon Arthur; they are degrees of disconnection. According to Dale's printed lyrics, Culhwch "[goes] to Arthur, his kinsman and his cousin / To ask for aid in seeking fairest Olwen for his bride." However, this line does not appear on the version performed on the album, though she does sing it in performance, as a replacement for the naming of those knights that journey with Culhwch (Dale 2009). As sung on the album, Arthur is neither sought after nor asked for assistance. He remains only the object and the possessor, as the next line tells us "Arthur's knights they joined him" (Dale). The knights have agency even when they aren't named in live performances; they make the choice and the movement here to aid Culhwch on his journey. They are not directly called for by Arthur as in the original tale. The men go themselves to help and accompany Culhwch, only as men who serve their king. In fact, in no version of Dale's song does Arthur actually answer the request for help. Culhwch seeks him out and his knights respond; Arthur is the passive object upon which and for which others act.

Furthermore, while later the Salmon of Llyn Llyw does address the knights as "his companions," the possessive pronoun does little to bring Arthur into the quest, only referencing their allegiance and potentially close relationship to the king. Again, he is the passive possessor, a descriptor used to enhance the knights, to put them into context within Arthurian legend. Although he technically has grammatical ownership of the knights, Arthur is the absent modifier of unfettered characters who need no permission to act. Despite two further references in the song, Arthur never truly comes any closer to the story, its characters, or its listeners. The Salmon agrees to show the knights to Mabon's location "for Arthur's faith and honor." Arthur here is the possessor once more, this time of abstracts to be lauded; he is a distant ideal, a reputation to be called upon for veneration and motivation, not the man of involved action that he is in the original story. In his final mention, he is once again the object to which other characters gravitate: upon his release "Mabon did pledge his life to Arthur, and homeward all did ride." But he is pledging his life to the idea of the king, not the man himself. At no point are we ever given cause in the song to think that Arthur traveled with them, even to wage war upon Mabon's prison, so again he is only the legendary king to whom one can swear his or her life. The only character who does direct the actions of the knights is Culhwch himself who "call[s] the knights to ride" in search of Mabon. In the prose narrative, Arthur has the power to instruct the knights to "go on this errand on [his] behalf" then later it is he who "summon[s] the warriors of the island" to free Mabon from his prison (164, 166). However, in Dale's song, Culhwch directly replaces Arthur's control and power in this realm. As a result, the success of this quest is given to Culhwch, allowing him the triumph to "win fair Olwen as his bride."

Arthur isn't the only character to be significantly transformed. Dale's musical version of the tale replaces Kilydd's second wife, Culhwch's stepmother, with his first. This may seem like a trivial transformation or perhaps one born of needs for meter, but neither is the case. Dale informs us that Culhwch "was counseled by his mother to seek Olwen as a bride." There is no threat here, no curse laid upon Culhwch for his refusal to marry his stepsister as in the medieval tale. Instead, he is given counsel, advice on who to marry, from his own mother. The mother here, limited though her existence is within the song, connotes all those positive qualities that have placed upon the role: that of loving nurturer, of gentle caretaker, and of loving wisewoman. Subsequently, the listener is presented with the non-threatening imparting of wisdom from maternal concern. This decision was made, I argue, not for reasons of meter. The article "a" preceding "bride" could easily have been left out to allow for the extra syllable in "stepmother." Because the loving mother begins this quest, not an angry or vengeful stepmother, the quest itself becomes elevated as a search for an accurately identified, worthy wife. It encourages the listener to overlook Olwen's own threat to Culhwch as the daughter of a giant, a risk that the original tale countered with the meeting between the nobleman and his future bride.

Interestingly, on her website, Dale includes a brief description of this song as a "rollicking adventure" which is "well-peppered with Welsh names." She calls attention to the use of the names, marking them as the spice, not the main ingredient, of the song. They add interest, they add atmosphere. On one hand this makes those names, those figures, she chooses to incorporate all the more important by virtue of their selection. On the other, it sets itself apart from perhaps the most memorable passage within the original tale: that lengthy list of names and ever-so brief descriptions of those of Arthur's court, described by Jeffery Gantz as "a veritable kitchen sink" of names (134). Instead of the pages of names we are given in the original text, beyond the titular characters and their fathers, Mabon and his father, and Arthur; only Kei, Bedwyr, Gawain, Menw, and Kynddylig are identified by name: "Arthur's knights they joined him: Kei, Bedwyr and Gawain /With Menw the magician and Kynddylig as their guide." But within the song as performed, there is more connection with that original roll-call than initially expected. Just as the storyteller's recitation of so many characters may cause the listener (or the reader of the written text) to lose track of these individuals, the first three knights in Dale's song blur together within the pacing and punctuation of the song. This is especially true for a listener who may not be familiar with the sound or pronunciation of Welsh names. At best the song lets Gawain have slightly more recognition as a name for it being at the end of the trio and thereby proceeded by the identifiable "and." Moreover, the use of "Gawain" instead of "Gwalchmei" furthers this recognition for those who may have more knowledge of Arthurian legends. Grammatically and audibly, the three men become a collective of King Arthur's knights, a single unit to act, rather than the individual identities of Menw and Kynddylig who are graced separate enunciation, phrases, and skills. Even so, these last two skilled figures become one with the others as the song progresses, for they are never again named; they are hereafter the plural pronoun unit of "they" or twice "companions."

Those familiar with the tale of Culhwch and Olwen will have noticed the one missing knight. In the story as recounted in the Arthurian tale, Culhwch is accompanied by six knights when he journeys to confront Ysbaddaden. In Dale's song there are only five; we are missing Gwrhyr, the interpreter of languages, who is, with little argument, the most important of the knights for the task that Dale chooses to relate. In the Arthurian tale, it is Gwrhyr who speaks to the animals on behalf of Culhwch, who presumably cannot understand their language. He is the seeker and the interpreter of their knowledge, as well as the one who speaks first to Mabon, asking the identity of he who "is crying in this stone house?" (166). However, in Dale's song, he simply does not exist. Rather it is Culhwch and the other knights who collectively ask for information from the animals. In all but one case it is "they" who travel about to ask "Know ye Mabon, stolen from his mother's side?" (Dale 2000). The remaining instance Culhwch and his companions are identified as "the party"; again, they are not individualized. They have a unified goal and a unified voice, but it is a voice that apparently needs no translator. This transforms the animals, more than the knights, elevating the former from simple creatures to anthropomorphized creatures imbued with extensive, mythic knowledge and human voice. The animals, not the humans, have magical ability, making the tale more akin to traditional fables, rather the original tale where the mythic power was given to men. The only mention of magic itself in Dale's song is in the identification of Menw as a magician, but this term for a modern audience connotes the entertainer, diversionary slight of hand, not supernatural abilities. Once more, the tale transforms in its adaptation. While Culhwch may be elevated in other ways, he is made to seem even more of the heroic leader here in comparison to his companions who are average men, the most important of whom is either good at entertaining (Menw) or adept at directions (Kynddylig).

Overall, Heather Dale's version of "Culhwch and Olwen" is a distinctly more romanticized tale of a titular hero that fits more within a modern concept of a fairy tale. The hero is a noble but essentially average figure who must overcome manageable, if potentially perilous, obstacles to find his love, a love that was wisely selected by a caring parent. Culhwch relies upon others for assistance but not so heavily as in the prose original, where the majority of the action is carried out by others, including Arthur himself. Arthur and the knights complete (some of) Ysbaddaden's tasks for Culhwch's benefit by virtue of his relation and to avoid the slander he threatens.

In Dale's song, Culhwch takes the role of the leader of a group of "companions" to actively complete the singular task he is sent upon in order to "win" Olwen. This alteration to more directly reflect the modern expectations of myth and legend extend beyond the song, beyond the story, and to the singer herself. Dale's deliberate fashioning of herself and her musical persona as a traveling storyteller who adapts and retells a wide range of tales, illustrates the glorification of a legend: the medieval bard from whom great stories are passed. However, in the end, it is neither the story nor the storyteller in isolation that carries its meaning, nor the assertions they make about their importance. Heather Dale's earlier claim that folk music is all about context was correct, if too narrow in scope. It is the way these elements are understood in context, the way they are put into dialogue with one another, their precedents and their descendents, that truly mark their lasting vitality and their substantial influence.

Notes

1. For discussions of the death of the author, see Walter Benjamin's "The Storyteller" in *Orient und Okzident* (1936), quoted from Walter Benjamin, *Illuminations*, ed. Hannah Arendt, trans. Harry Zorn (Schocken Books, 1969); also Roland Barthes's "The Death of the Author" in David Lodge (ed.) *Modern Criticism and Theory: A Reader*. London: Longman, 1998; and Michel Foucault's "What is an Author?" *Screen* 20: 13–33.

2. For full treatment of pastiche, which does not always carry with it the implication of satire, see Simon Dentith's *Parody*. London: Routledge, 2000.

3. As expected with musical performance, there exist a couple of versions of Dale's song, though unless otherwise specified I shall be discussing the version as sung on her album *The Trial of Lancelot*.

Works Cited

Dale, Heather. "Culhwch and Olwen" *The Trial of Lancelot*. Amphis Music, 2000. CD.
_____."Culhwch and Olwen" 31 July 2009. *YouTube*. Web. 22 September 2010.
_____. *Music*. Web. 22 September 2010. <www.heatherdale.com>
_____. "The Trial of Lancelot" *The Trial of Lancelot*. Amphis Music, 2000. CD.
Davies, Sioned. "Performing Culhwch ac Olwen." *Arthurian Literature XXI*. Ed. Ceridwen Lloyd-Morgan. Boydell and Brewer, 2004. 29–51. *Google Books*. Web. 22 September 2010.
Gantz, Jeffery. "Culhwch and Olwen." *The Mabinogion*. New York: Penguin books, 1976. Print.
Mowat, Bruce Farley. "Freewheelin' in their Support; Canada's Best in Folk Line up for Radio Station." *Toronto Sun*. 27 March 2005: HS8. *LexisNexis*. Web. 22 September 2010.
Snyder, Fran. "About CIYH." Concerts in Your Home. n.d. Web. 21 October 2010.
Windling, Terry. "The Magic of Wales." *The Journal of Mythic Arts*. 2004. Web. 21 October 2010.

Torchwood's "Spooky Do's"
A Popular Culture Perspective on Celtic Mythology

Lynnette R. Porter

"Is that another of your 'spooky do's' then?" Police Constable Andy Davidson asks Torchwood's Gwen Cooper as she arrives on the scene of yet another strange occurrence in Cardiff ("Kiss Kiss, Bang Bang," 2.1). Since Gwen left the police force to join the secret alien-tracking organization, PC Andy has come across more than his share of strange events, what he calls "spooky do's," and most of them seem to have something to do with his former partner's job. On the BBC science fiction series, which premiered in 2006 and, for its first three seasons (through 2009), took place in and around Cardiff, Wales, most strange events—including gruesome murders, Blowfish sightings, random energy spikes, explosions and citywide destruction, and incidents involving a racing black SUV—have something to do with Torchwood.

Designed to be an adult spinoff from perennially-popular *Doctor Who*, *Torchwood* at least somewhat bases its plots in the real world, although the number of guest aliens and their futuristic technology certainly mark the series as science fiction. Captain Jack Harkness, a time traveler from the fifty-first century, finds himself stranded on Earth for more than a century. During that time he first joins and later becomes leader of Torchwood Three, the Cardiff branch of the U.K.'s alien-policing agency. Torchwood conveniently works outside the police and only tangentially with governmental agencies; during the first three seasons, Captain Jack and his team of field operatives mostly work independently and pool their knowledge of science, technology, history, alien anthropology, and local culture to help them protect Wales (and often the rest of the world). Among the team during seasons one through three are computer whiz Toshiko Sato (Naoko Mori), physician Owen Harper (Burn Gorman), former police constable Gwen Cooper (Eve Myles), and archivist/support specialist Ianto Jones (Gareth David-Lloyd).

Although not all spooky do's involve elements from Celtic (specifically Welsh or, at times, Scottish or Irish) mythology, *Torchwood*'s premise and setting, not to mention its immortal lead hero, create an image of Wales as a land of mysterious happenings that take place in plain view of local citizens. In TV Cardiff, the mythic past is very much part of the cosmopolitan present, and even in the real city, *Torchwood* tourism is encouraged. The local economy (and BBC ratings) benefit from fans' expectation that Cardiff is the perfect base for *Torchwood*. Wales' mythic past is alive and well in *Torchwood*'s episodes, novels, comics, and even fanfiction reflecting the first three seasons on BBC.

In 2010, *Torchwood* officially became a BBC (U.K.)-Starz (U.S.) joint venture, and much of the series' setting, it was decided, would move outside Wales. In a 2010 *SFX* magazine interview, series' creator Russell T. Davies noted that, in the post–"Children of Earth" world (after season three, in which the Hub was destroyed, the surviving team members became estranged, and Captain Jack beamed off planet), Torchwood itself would seem like a faded myth. As Davies explained, "Time's passed since *Torchwood* was last on the air [broadcast in summer 2009 but filmed in October 2008].... In episode one, Torchwood is forgotten ... Torchwood is now like a legend" (Berriman 55).

Season four, entitled "The New World," by its very title suggests that the Cardiff-based seasons are the "Old World" in which a mythic Torchwood once protected the Welsh populace. This new premise for *Torchwood* places the first two seasons' episodes, in particular, in a different televisionary context: Torchwood dealt with mythic beings—some alien, some elemental from Earth's past—as befitting the rich Welsh cultural heritage of Celtic mythology and Arthurian legends. During that time, the larger-than-life Captain Jack became a mythic hero within both Torchwood the organization and *Torchwood* the television series. That he and Torchwood become considered the stuff of legend, being hunted by new season four American characters, changes the audience's and the new characters' perception of Torchwood as depicted in seasons one through three.

By season four, Torchwood, the agency dealing with Celtic mythic beings as part of its mission to track aliens and remove threats to humanity, has become a similar type of entity—a mythic organization that once protected humanity from all kinds of unexplainable events and beings. Captain Jack Harkness, once Torchwood's leader, by season four has become more than a man from the future who understands Wales' myths and highly possible scientific explanations for their origins—he has become a modern Welsh myth, with the truth about his exploits in Cardiff around the turn of the twenty-first century taking on legendary proportions. That the Torchwood organization deals both with Celtic cultural myths but also becomes mythic makes *Torchwood* the perfect science fiction TV series to be based in Wales, a land rich in mythic heritage.

Although *Torchwood*'s purpose as science fiction entertainment isn't primarily to reflect Celtic myths or Welsh culture, the selection of Cardiff as the first three seasons' site of all types of spooky do's implies the appropriation of at least some Welsh myths. The *Doctor Who* spinoff revolves around mostly extraterrestrial life that slips through a Rift in space and time that conveniently runs through the heart of the city. Some villains or monsters-of-the-week aren't alien in origin (e.g., the human cannibals in "Countrycide" [1.6]), but *Torchwood* often posits that aliens on Earth are the explanation for mythic creatures or characters. The series' mythology, provided through the first three seasons' episodes, as well as novels and a *Torchwood* comic, reflects a Welsh storytelling tradition that involves tales of the sea or rural countryside. However, three stories in particular — the episode "Small Worlds" (1.5), dealing with fairies; the BBC-sanctioned novel *Something in the Water*, a story about a water hag; and official *Torchwood* magazine's comic "Selkie," offering a different perspective on a Scottish sea creature, specifically reference mythic elements and give them a science fiction twist.

Through *Torchwood*, fans develop an appreciation of Wales, and especially Cardiff, as a hotbed of strange events and a mixing of interdimensional cultures. The series makes the stuff of Welsh mythology seem possible, even today, and the barrier between otherworldly times and beings seems plausibly breachable. As the narrative introduction to each *Torchwood* episode proclaims, "The twenty-first century is when everything changes—and you've got to be ready," and *Torchwood* heavily relies on knowledge or acceptance of Celtic mythic themes for its science fiction plots and ambiance. Celtic mythology, as much as the series' mythology surrounding immortal hero Jack Harkness or even its status as a *Doctor Who* spinoff, makes *Torchwood* memorable among dozens of contemporary science fiction series.

With the fourth season's geographic move from Cardiff's familiar Hub and temporal move a few years past the third season, "The New World" distances itself from Wales and its myth-steeped culture. The shift in the series' time frame, setting, and premise from season three to season four further emphasizes the original mythic quality of *Torchwood*. Like the flashback episodes in which Captain Jack's story reveals glimpses of historic Torchwood's operations from the late 1800s until 2000 (e.g., "From Out of the Rain," 2.10; "Fragments," 2.12), the *Torchwood* episodes with which long-time fans are familiar and which offer plenty of spooky-do's relating to fantastic stories of alien visitors or Earth elementals who became part of Celtic myths have become the within-series "myths" on which *Torchwood*'s fourth season is built. New characters, who try to determine if the old Torchwood was real and, if so, how it might help humanity in 2011, consider Captain Jack Harkness as mythical as many of the aliens or elementals he once tracked in Cardiff. In hindsight, *Torchwood*'s first three seasons, BBC-sanctioned novels based on the characters and Cardiff setting of those seasons, and official *Torchwood* magazine stories involving beloved characters (many of them long dead by the start of season four) underscore the fact that these early episodes have a different "feel" to them. As PC Andy notes, they are truly spooky-do's often based on Celtic myths or in a Welsh setting highly supportive of the belief in strange visitors from other worlds who wreak havoc on ordinary humans.

Torchwood is a reflector of Celtic myths and legends that present a modern (science fiction) interpretation of the origins of those myths and the reasons behind their continuing presence in modern Welsh or Scottish culture. Throughout the first three seasons' story development, Captain Jack Harkness increasingly becomes a mythic figure: immortal, "magical," and entrenched in local culture to the point that stories arise about him. Captain Jack as a mythic figure in Cardiff's fictitious past is yet another way that *Torchwood* illustrates the creation and persistence of myth, even in modern culture. Finally, with the series' change in premise and primary location for season four, *Torchwood* presents Torchwood Three as a mythic entity that, a few years after the end of season three, seems almost impossible to believe ever existed. Nonetheless, new characters seek out that "mythic past" to help them deal with out-of-control current events. That *Torchwood* mythologizes its own past and brings back the mythic Captain Jack for adventures in a new time and place makes this series even more interesting in a study of Celtic myths. Within four seasons of episodes, *Torchwood* illustrates several key aspects of mythology: it first reflects traditional Celtic myths and legends and weaves them into episodes, then creates a mythic character in fiction that mimics the creation of real-world myths, and finally synthesizes real-world myths with science fiction series' mythology.

The latter is well represented in real-world Cardiff Bay, where *Torchwood* episodes from seasons one through three were frequently filmed and where fans still visit the "site" of the Hub. By mid–2010, an impromptu memorial to deceased character Ianto Jones continued to draw enough attention, as well as flowers, poems, photographs, and gifts, that the Mermaid Quay management made the memorial permanent. They placed their own document at the memorial, stating that "Ianto Jones (1983–2009, Torchwood Three), gave his life in defense of the children of this planet. The management of Mermaid Quay salutes you."[1] For the many *Torchwood* fans from around the world (including documented visitors from Finland, Norway, Poland, Spain, Germany, France, Russia, Japan, Canada, the U.S., and all across the U.K.), the "mythic" aspects of a science fiction television story about those who protect the Earth from all supernatural foes — whether elemental from this planet or extraterrestrial — have been incorporated into their vision of modern Cardiff as a site where such spooky do's are likely to happen. *Torchwood* continues to fuse fiction with reality, mythic past to mythic present.

Placing a legendary Rift in time and space in Cardiff provides a setting in which the revitalized urban waterfront starkly contrasts Torchwood's mysterious subterranean Hub, a symbolic well of all that is hidden beneath the society's surface or submerged in the psyche. Although he's a fifty-first century kind of guy, Jack Harkness has a unique perspective on the many folktales woven into the fabric of Welsh culture, simply because of his travels through Earth's history. When Jack fears the arrival of fairies in modern Cardiff, for example, he knows that they are a primeval force far different from Disneyesque sprites. The ancient gargoyle-like fairies can control the elements and create the "glamour" (according to its old meaning of a magical illusion) of an ancient forest now languishing in a neighborhood. Cardiff's glittering modern veneer glosses over a darkly mythic, rural past, just as the episode "Small World"'s ancient fairies are oppositional to the pigtail-haired pixie of a child chosen to join their ranks.

Cardiff's weather — even without elemental interference — often provides a murky backdrop for *Torchwood*'s stories. Even in the city, the "darkness" creeps through the pervasive rain, and citizens are so accustomed to the gloom that they seldom see even darker forces at work around them. The Rift bisecting Cardiff — and what slips through the Rift — largely goes unnoticed by the locals, unless an alien takes hostages or tries to annihilate humanity. Even then, carefully-leaked cover stories or a few doses of memory-eraser Retcon return the population to complacency. The Rift simply is part of Cardiff; it is an invisible force that has been around longer than the city.[2]

The spooky do becoming commonplace is an appropriate theme for a Cardiff-based TV series. Much of Welsh mythology illustrates how the otherworldly live near to or among humans. Myths arise from stories of the times or ways the two worlds intermingle, although one culture is hidden most of the time while the other remains in plain sight. Even in the darker political drama of the third season miniseries "Children of Earth," a few references to mythic creatures manage to surface in the characters' everyday conversations.

As Gwen walks along the Quay to work, she greets a man scanning the sea. "No sea monsters," he tells her. Gwen grins: "ah, it's early yet" ("Children of Earth," 3.1). Later that morning, Gwen interviews a potential Torchwood employee. She asks about his recent relocation to Cardiff. Although the young man is glad for the change of scenery, Cardiff "is kind of weird, though." In fact, he approaches Torchwood because local legend suggests that this supposedly secret organization deals with aliens. Ianto isn't surprised that the young man has found Torchwood so easily: "Ask about Torchwood, and most people point toward the bay." Linking this organization with the bay area and anything "spooky" seems a common assumption for Cardiff locals.

Torchwood is, indeed, well established in the community, for all that it's supposed to be a literally underground organization. Jack Harkness and his team often descend into the Hub via an invisible lift that looks like an ordinary paving stone on busy Roald Dahl Plass, a public plaza near Cardiff Bay. The Hub (at least until its destruction during season three's "Children of Earth" [3.1]) is Torchwood's underground base, a series of levels of labs, offices, cells, morgue, and vaults. The dead remain alongside the living, a frequently-used element not only of science fiction or horror stories, but also mythology.

Life after physical death becomes the basis of several *Torchwood* episodes.

Owen physically dies from a gunshot wound ("Reset," 2.6) but is brought back to life by a mysterious glove dubbed the Risen Mitten. He then continues as Torchwood's physician, although his body is dead and cannot repair itself. The episodes following Owen's death and resurrection illustrate how he copes as the undead, unable to enjoy pleasures of the flesh but still required to go to work every day (e.g., "Dead Man Walking," 2.7; "Exit Wounds," 2.13). He dies permanently only when his body is dissolved by nuclear radiation and nothing is left to house his "spirit." Team member Suzie Costello ("They Keep Killing Suzie," 1.8) cleverly sets up a way for her former employer to resuscitate her long after her death. She returns from the dead for one episode, at the end of which she is permanently killed. Her body, like Owen's, cannot revive itself without the "magic" of alien technology. The use of "magic" or an unexplained force to prolong life or bring the dead back to life, even temporarily, is the stuff of fairy tales or myths of gods having the capability to grant life or death to mortals.

As is common in myths, the dead often are as important to the story as the living. Deceased Torchwood employees are entombed in the vaults, and even Jack "rests" there as he waits for the appropriate time to emerge so that he doesn't cross his own timeline ("Fragments," 2.12). He is able to awaken himself technologically years after he ensures he is entombed in the Hub in order to avoid two Jack Harknesses from different points in his personal timeline walking around Cardiff in the same time frame. Such problems don't exist for ordinary characters. What is below the surface—the Torchwood team, the undead or immortal—interacts with the natural, ordinary world above, and everyday citizens of Cardiff, while increasingly aware of Torchwood's presence, often choose to ignore it. Unless they go looking for spooky do's, as does the potential employee Gwen interviews at the beginning of "Children of Earth," they can live rather complacently alongside the aliens or undead in their midst.

Symbolically, *Torchwood* taps into all that is beneath the surface of Cardiff's "normal" world. The Hub is buried in the dark, monitoring the surface, and its team frequently travels or hunts at night, in the darkness or through storms. Only in "Children of Earth" is Torchwood's cover literally and figuratively blown when another governmental agency wants to eliminate Jack as part of a conspiracy cover-up, a not-too-surprising plot development given Jack's long life and shady past. Up to that point, *Torchwood* was content to deal with long-buried myths and mythic beings and to handle such spooky do's on their own, without the knowledge or observance of the authorities or citizens.

An intriguing episode that typically represents the mythic quality of the original three seasons, "Small Worlds" (1.5), introduces fairies into the series' canon. Two types of fey folk—both found within the hierarchy of Welsh mythology—star in this episode. More important are the ancient elementals. Jack refers to them as the "mara," using a term more common for Irish fairies, and explains that "nightmare" is derived from this term. The ancient, elemental fey are gray, winged creatures as tall as men; their long, thin faces perpetually snarl. They seek a Chosen One, a child, to join them, and they ruthlessly destroy anyone who gets in their way. They kill with rose petals or sudden storms; they can deceive "reality" by showing the Chosen One the way their forest looked millennia before. These ancient ones also can choose to appear as tiny winged fairies, looking a lot like the Tinkerbell-style lights portrayed in popular culture, and, indeed, sightings of "fairy lights" are part of Welsh myths. Several Welsh local legends revolve around fairy lights that lead travelers astray on foggy evenings, most never to be seen again (e.g., Deveraux 8, 16; Lloyd and Lloyd 293–294). Those long-missing humans who reappear do so in fairy processions (Lloyd and Lloyd 294). Whatever their appearance, *Torchwood* agrees with folklore that fairies travel at will throughout time; an old photograph of fairies, shown in close up in "Small Worlds," reveals the face of the latest Chosen One from the twenty-first century.

Along with *Torchwood*, other BBC Wales science fiction or fantasy television series deal with mythic elements, including but not limited to fairies and their Chosen Ones (or changelings, a concept common in Welsh myth, Jones 62–66). *Merlin*, for example, also features episodes about changelings, or human babies possessed by a fairy (e.g., "The Changeling," 3.6). The use of fairies in Welsh-produced science fiction or fantasy TV series is a typical plot device and usually portrays fairies as less than beautiful or helpful to humans. They have their own agendas, and they cannot be easily appeased by humans. In *Torchwood*, as in *Merlin*, the oldest, most experienced character — one who understands "magic" (i.e., what is unknown by most humans) or, more truthfully, knows of the existence and nature of fairies — understands how to deal with them. In *Torchwood*, the immortal Jack is the oldest and most experienced character, and he takes the role of sage (as the magician/healer Gaius does in *Merlin*). This story device, while common in many fantasy stories, seems to appear more frequently in U.K. series, especially those made in Wales.

An important character in *Torchwood*'s "Small Worlds," Estelle, is one of Jack's former flames. In wartime Britain, Jack and 17-year-old Estelle fall in love. Post-war immortal Jack, however, stays away from Estelle for decades. He returns to visit her only when he can pose as her former lover's son, although he doesn't talk about his "father." Estelle (whose name, meaning "star," indicates otherworldly potential) seems to accept Jack's explanation, but she tells Gwen that young Jack smiles and even walks just like his father. Perhaps Estelle buys into this fantasy because she, more than others, is comfortable with supernatural beings who transcend time. Not only does she seek out fairies, believing them benevolent, but she shares her photographs and experiences through public lectures.

Her photos resemble those reportedly convincing Sir Arthur Conan Doyle of fairy existence at the turn of the previous century. These photos turned out to be a hoax, as Gwen reminds the Torchwood team (and the audience). Jack further notes that he and Estelle have long been on opposite sides of the discussion about the true nature of fairies. Estelle's previous encounters have been positive, and her photos show dancing lights—very much like sightings of fairy lights in Welsh legends. Jack's encounters with fairies outside Cardiff (e.g., on a troop train in 1909) have been deadly and hardly magical. Instead they have been murderous, brutal, and fast—the fairies get rid of anyone who stands between them and a Chosen One.

Despite believing in the fantastic, Estelle approaches her study of fairies scientifically and methodically. Working like a journalist, recording her actions and observations before she takes photos, Estelle approaches her prey, who quickly turn predator in the opening scene. Giggling fairy lights flit around a stone circle in the midst of Roundstone Park. After Estelle snaps photos and turns away, the scene quickly changes. The playful music turns sinister; lightning-like flashes illuminate the circle; giggling deepens to guttural mutterings. The tall, gargoyle-like fairies glare at Estelle's retreating back. As Jack later tells Gwen, science is ineffective against the fairies; "normal" procedures can't be used against magical beings.

According to Jack, these fairies are "a touch of myth, a touch of the spirit world, a touch of reality, all jumbled together." Strangely enough, Jack uses a Christian metaphor to describe their activities as "all hell breaking loose," yet what he describes is far older than Christianity. Although other episodes involve supernatural beings from the Bible (e.g., Abaddon in "End of Days," 1.13), *Torchwood* does not use Christian symbols any more often than pagan ones. If anything, both generally mythic and specifically religious beings are plot devices to move along the story and illustrate Jack's perspective (in many ways an "alien" perspective), which conflicts with those of his team (the "real" humans). Jack firmly believes that nothing exists after death; in his many deaths he has glimpsed no happy afterlife, only an all-encompassing, frightening darkness. Suzie, returned from the dead, also reports only darkness, with others bumping around in the dark. For Jack, mixing metaphors is just a way of expressing to Gwen, who was reared in a predominantly Christian culture, the seriousness of the situation. His analysis of an alien in question—whether Abaddon or fairies—is more scientifically objective rather than spiritually informed.

Thus, when Jack sees evidence that the fairies have returned—a rose petal left as a calling card in the Hub—he immediately recalls that rose petals were used to kill his men in the troop train. As well, he finds the petal upon awakening from a nightmare about that attack. The link between Jack and otherworldly beings is strong; he receives messages through dreams and warrants a warning that the ancient elementals are back in town. His interpretation of this supernatural information, however, is not spiritual but merely pragmatic. Jack believes in myths, whether Christian or pagan, because their roots run deep in cultural traditions and took old in a seed of truth.

Ianto, too, has a tangential connection to the fairies' arrival. Working in the middle of the night, he tells the nightmare-awakened Jack that he has discovered strange weather patterns in the area. Fanfiction writers use this brief scene to suggest that Ianto knows more about the elemental creatures than he lets on, not too much of a stretch of fans' imagination given the previous episode, in which Ianto keeps secret from the rest of Torchwood his cybergirlfriend in the basement ("Cyberwoman," 1.4).

Fanfiction based on "Strange Worlds" often features Ianto either as a Chosen One now grown (but not transformed) or as a king of the fey folk. Fans perceive Ianto's "Welshness" as an integral part of his character, making fan authors' choice of Ianto as most likely to be leader of the fey another link between Welsh myth and its perceived place in *Torchwood*. Fan author Sparking_Off, for example, created an entire alternate universe (AU) in which Ianto is a human king of the fey folk. The first series within the fairies' universe reinforces the connection with "Small Words" with its title: "Come Away, O Human Child," a line from William Butler Yeats used at the end of the episode. Even years after the episode was first broadcast, Sparking_Off occasionally writes more in this AU, and by 2010 eleven stories have been written to further the adventures of fairy-king Ianto. Although other fanfiction authors play with this theme, Sparking_Off's series is one of the best written and developed.

Like the mythic Welsh fey, Ianto often seems exceptionally polite, almost courtly, a characteristic unusual for such a young man. He most often wears formal suits on the job, yet another aspect of "courtliness," and he playfully notes that "red is my color" ("Reset," 2.6). Books of Welsh folklore often describe fairies in similar terms, although Ianto is a much friendlier character (a trait emphasized in fanfiction) than fairies described in local legends. Malevolent fairies often dress in red (e.g., the "red caps" whose headwear is drenched in human blood, or the fairy queens wearing red capes; Silver 179). The Irish fairies, Fir Bolg, also dress in red (Silver 89), but other small or quiet supernatural beings going by a variety of names wear similar clothing. Like the Quiet Folk of Welsh lore, Ianto, as he explains to Jack, isn't much of a talker (*The Dead Line*), and he is unfailingly generous to Jack, yet another trait ascribed to this mythic people (Arrowsmith 43). In many ways, Welsh native Ianto seems a logical choice to be associated with Welsh lore. His canonical knowledge of strange weather patterns, his support of Jack even after he hands over a child to the fairies in "Small Worlds," or even his sensitivity to the supernatural Night Travelers in "Out of the Rain," make him a likely candidate to be linked with mythic beings in fans' minds and fiction.

Another link with Welsh mythology is made with season three's introduction of Ianto's sister, Rhiannon, her name that of a prominent woman in the *Mabinogi*, although the *Torchwood* character bears no resemblance to the legendary Rhiannon. Ianto's clothing choices, demeanor, acceptance of the supernatural and the difficult choices one must make within their presence, and even his sibling's Welsh name from mythology suggest that he is not only aware of

Welsh myths but, at least in fans' interpretation, could be a mythic creature himself.

The other Welsh character, Gwen, knows a lot about the Cottingley glass-plate photographs that so influenced Conan Doyle's belief in fairies. She tells the team that she once wrote an academic essay about the photographs. Gwen may never be linked with mythic beings, but her knowledge of them, in "Small Worlds" and allusion to them in "Children of Earth," highlights her Welsh heritage and common knowledge from her experience and formal education. Although Owen knows the strange folklore surrounding Roundstone Park, where Estelle sees the fairies, only Ianto and Gwen, in addition to Jack, seem to have a deeper initial understanding of fairy lore.

Estelle's house indicates her homegrown familiarity with folklore and magic. The décor is typical "old lady chic," complete with mantle of sepia-toned photos, including some of World War II-era Jack. However, the interior atypically seems protected from unseen outside forces. Gwen touches the wind chimes hanging just outside Estelle's door, a folk method of warding off fairies. Her garden boasts lush plants, not all of them flowering; perhaps Estelle cultivates herbs for healing arts or rituals. Her companion is a black-and-white cat, another "old lady" conceit that harkens to folklore about the familiars of those who dabble in witchcraft. Jack later comments to Gwen that Estelle "belongs in the countryside," yet another hint of her closer-than-typical connection with nature.

Estelle also practices candlelit rituals, and the green and red votives and candleholders she uses often symbolize the colors of god and goddess. She chooses white quartz, what she calls "the searching stone," as she asks to find the fairies again. (Many Wiccan or pagan websites note that Christmas colors of red and green were co-opted from pagan Yule rituals, and common lore among many pagans associates red and green with the goddess as mother figure. White quartz often is used in rituals to facilitate communication with otherworldly forces and to focus the seeker's intentions during the ritual, McCoy 100). After completing the ritual, Estelle immediately hears wings fluttering outsider her house, but this time two glittering eyes peer at her from the darkness. Before fairies can attack Estelle, they have to lure her from the protection of her home. The cat yowls when the fairies are near, leading Estelle outside to retrieve and protect her companion. Once outdoors, she is helpless against the fairies and is killed in a freak rainstorm. Her cat merely watches, indicating a stronger connection between the fairies and animals than between Estelle and her pet.

The reason for Estelle's death is unclear, except perhaps as a reminder to Jack that the fairies have powers well beyond his modern command of technology. Some ancient, Earth-bound beings can't be tamed or controlled, and Jack — by relinquishing the Chosen One — eventually pays them proper homage. A recurring theme throughout *Torchwood* is Jack's ability to do what is necessary, even if his choices may seem horrific to the more "human" members of his team or, indeed, the public at large. One of the earliest examples of Jack's difficult decisions, based on pragmatism and the greater good rather than consideration for a solitary child, takes place in "Small Worlds." Whereas Gwen's, or most modern citizens,' understanding of Welsh fairy lore may be romantic (as evidenced by Estelle earlier in the episode), this naïve romanticism is unsuitable for the reality of dealing with very real, not imaginary supernatural beings intent on having their way. Because Jack refuses to romanticize the fairies and instead sees them as yet another potential foe with the power to destroy humanity, his decisions come from a different knowledge and experiential base. Unlike Gwen, who sees Jack destroying a mother by handing over her only child to the fairies, Jack sees a bigger picture, in which the abduction of a Chosen One (or, in this case, her willingness to join the fairies) is a much better alternative than ongoing war with fairies who can manipulate the natural world to their advantage. Because Jack is more attuned to the mindset of these mythic beings (again illustrating that he is more of a mythic being — or "alien"— himself than anyone else on his team), he alone can make these decisions.

The Chosen One has roots in Celtic mythology, with its frequent tales of changelings and abducted children. In *Torchwood*'s story, however, Chosen One Jasmine simply chooses to go with the fairies, in part to save the world from destruction by angry elementals, in part because she simply wants to join her new friends. She is not abducted, and no substitute is given to the mother left behind. Nevertheless, the Chosen One still reminds viewers of mythic abduction stories in which beautiful children become the eternal companions of beings from another realm. Like the many variations among myths and legends across regions or nations, *Torchwood*'s tale of a Chosen One is simply a variation on a commonly explored myth, but it provides insights into the Welsh characters Ianto and Gwen and further provides evidence that Jack, even in these early episodes, is becoming perceived as an evolving mythic being.

The episode closes with a fairy chanting a refrain from William Butler Yeats's poem, "The Stolen Child" (Yeats 14):

> Come away, O human child!
> To the waters and the wild
> With a faery, hand in hand,
> For the world's more full of weeping than you can understand.

The poem's inclusion in *Torchwood* adds weight to a science fiction episode and establishes its theme clearly within Celtic mythology. Yeats's poem, written in 1886, refers to Irish fairies who coerce a child to come with them, just as the fairies in "Small Worlds" convince Jasmine to leave behind the 21st century human world. Whereas Yeats, and much of Victorian interest in fairies (again, as evidenced in "Small Worlds" with Gwen's reference to the Cottingley photographs of the early 1900s), romanticized fairy lore, *Torchwood* skews this romanticism with modern pragmatism.

Whereas the lure in Yeats's poem is seductive and rather benevolent, a call to return to the beauty of nature and the power of the natural world, *Torchwood* sees through this pleasant cultural veneer to remind viewers that myths, while based on grains of truth, often have been modified through the years to fit new cultural expectations. In a twenty-first century world more familiar with Disney fairies than violent elementals, or glossy, happy fairy tales rather than the stories told by the Brothers Grimm, the myths about fairies may have very little to do with their true origins. Similarly, a series like *Torchwood*, with one foot firmly in the mythic past, nevertheless is determined to be a modern science fiction series, one with a fifty-first century hero who knows better than twenty-first century humans the explanations for Cardiff's "unexplainable" occurrences. Jack, like Torchwood and *Torchwood*, often is blunt, pragmatic, and unromantic in his approach to the modern world. His and *Torchwood*'s approach to the fairies in "Small Worlds" is hardly Victorian.

In addition to television episodes, *Torchwood* references Celtic myths through its novels and official magazine comics. Very little is considered true canon in *Torchwood* or other BBC series, in part because of British license fees that citizens pay in order to access BBC programs on radio or television. Thus, *Torchwood* TV episodes or radio plays are canonical, but official publications, such as *Torchwood* magazine, or BBC-sanctioned novels based on its copyrighted characters and bearing the BBC logo on their spines can't be canon because audiences have to buy them — they are outside the episodic texts provided through television or radio broadcasts paid for by the license fee. Nevertheless, novels and *Torchwood* magazine are much more official than fanfiction or unlicensed merchandise and, as such, are considered much more authoritative than fan-based stories. The authors who write *Torchwood* novels frequently also write series episodes, for this or another BBC program. The comic "Selkie," first published in *Torchwood* magazine, gains further significance because it was written by Captain Jack himself — actor John Barrowman — and Carole E. Barrowman, two people who presumably understand Jack's character as well as anyone. Most *Torchwood* fans are familiar with these additional texts and use them to expand their understanding of the series (as well as to provide source material for fanfiction).

Trevor Baxendale's novel *Something in the Water* refers to a water hag, a mythic creature who lures men to their deaths underwater and then "impregnates" them with unnatural spawn. The corpses incubate the hag's "children" and create more hags to propagate the species. In Baxendale's novel, *Torchwood*'s Tosh accidentally unearths such an infested corpse from a local bog during an investigation of possible paranormal activity. A local expert tells her the legends of Sally Blackteeth, who "lurks in the ditches and drags the unsuspecting traveler down into the bogs" (38), and Black Annie, who dug a cave with her claws and "decorated it with the skins of the children she ate" (39). Both characters have what the expert calls "a bit of the bogie," meaning that they are shapeshifters.

When Gwen comments that the expert knows lots of creepy stories, he replies that he "knows all of them. And what's more they're all perfectly true" (40). Novelist Baxendale indicates the importance of local folklore and the assumption that legends have at least some basis in fact. Although Gwen and Tosh are skeptical early in the novel, they quickly learn that water hags are real aliens, following *Torchwood*'s premise that such weirdness is reality, no matter that most people choose to ignore the connection between myth and fact.

The story also involves the strange case of Saskia Harden, a young woman intent on having a baby yet suicidal enough to drown herself (turning up as a dead body) several times in the previous few months. Once again, Ianto discovers the link between strange data and a supernatural being; his analysis of hospital reports and unusual deaths helps uncover Saskia's whereabouts and true identity as a water hag.

Cardiff's location near rivers and seas proves ideal for the fast-multiplying hags. As in other myths of seafaring shapeshifters, the novel's water hag transforms herself from seaweed into a beautiful woman to tempt men. When Jack confronts the hag, she makes such a transformation to seduce him, but he resists. As she attempts to escape into the bay, Jack dives after her, but instead of being drowned — the hag's modus operandi — the immortal Jack is able to follow her through the Rift and back, allowing him to destroy her. The novel's sea hag follows in the tradition of Welsh mythology about undersea female creatures who lure men to their death. Seaweed turns into flowing tresses that trap sailors or fishermen long enough to drown them; such legends are common among coastal cultures. Some variations include the mother of *Beowulf*'s Grendel and the Celtic hag goddess, the Cailleach.[3]

This novel's hag, however, also follows in *Torchwood*'s tradition that aliens and other non-human creatures hide in plain sight. In one scene, the hag hides in the water of the Millennium Centre's fountain (perhaps even a passing reference to a version of the Arthurian tale, "The Lady of the Fountain," who was imprisoned within the stone fountain until freed by a knight, Hughes 9–30); passersby never realize she's there. Even Gwen, who knows the alien is close by, fails to notice until the hag taunts her. Only then does seasoned alien tracker Gwen see the alien standing right in front of her.

Like canon episodes, not all *Torchwood* novels incorporate mythical elements (or reveal that ancient mythic beings are really extraterrestrials). Nevertheless, Welsh mythology or folklore is one source of material that makes *Torchwood* novels different from those about other science fiction television series and furthers the connection between Jack's knowledge of and experience with mythic beings and the latter implication that, by the beginning of season four, Jack has become a mythic being himself. His long association with Wales and Cardiff, in particular, and his behind-the-scenes influence on citizens, whether by Retconning them so they forget what they have seen or by protecting them from apocalyptic horrors, makes him a continuing presence for much of two thousand years—certainly plenty of time for him not only to be aware of Celtic mythology but to become a part of its more recent myths.

Torchwood thus frequently builds its own mythology on specific Celtic themes and Welsh affinity for traditional tales of the supernatural interacting with everyday life, but it also illustrates how a character like Jack can become part of the mythology of his adopted homeland. In *Something in the Water*, Jack leads the Torchwood team into discovering the true nature of this mythic being and stopping her before she kills more humans. Only the immortal Jack can win in an underwater battle with this creature—it becomes a duel between two mythic beings.

Even *Torchwood* comics occasionally turn to Celtic mythology for a guest alien/monster. In 2009, *Torchwood* magazine published a special full-length comic made especially notable because the story came from Carole E. Barrowman and John (Jack Harkness) Barrowman and later was republished in a new series of sanctioned *Torchwood* comic books. Carole based the story on one of her earlier short fictions, and John suggested a way to involve his TV alter ego. Well-known artists Tommy Lee Edwards and Trevor Goring drew the story. The artists' attention to detail, especially Edwards's ability to make the art remarkably resemble TV's Captain Jack, make this text a "TV episode" in print. "Selkie"'s pedigree granted it plenty of publicity, and it became a well-read addition to the number of texts available to fans.

In this story, Jack works alone on a trip to assist Torchwood Glasgow. "Selkie" takes place on the Scottish coast, an area familiar to the Glasgow-born Barrowman siblings. Using a Scottish setting and Celtic legend as the basis for a Jack Harkness story unites *Torchwood* with a broader mythology as well as tying Jack to Barrowman's cultural heritage.

Like the water hag, the selkie is a type of sea monster who can lure the unwary to watery graves. Welsh folklore is full of references to similarly shaped beings, often called worms or dragons. A famous South Wales landmark, Worm's Head, is described as the body of a dragon turned to coastal land mass. During high tide, its body is inaccessible from the land, and only at low tide can the adventurous climb out to the dragon that is otherwise forever separate from humans, recalling the national symbol of Wales: a red dragon. Whether mythic beings exist on land, in the air, or in water, coastal Celtic communities share common depictions of long, slender, often shapeshifting monsters, whether dragons or worms that look more like animals, selkies that can take human or animal form (e.g., as seals with a skin they can shed when they take human form on land), or hags or mermaids that often appear first as humans before showing their true supernatural form. The Celtic legends of Dahut, who becomes a mermaid (MacKillop 300–301), or Hywel and the Mermaid (94–97) are connected to the themes presented in "Selkie." In the *Torchwood* story, the selkie fulfills the role of a female shapeshifter who can leave the sea to walk on land, a common thread among monstrous female characters going back to Grendel's mother. However, the selkie traditionally has more mystical qualities, and a human who finds a selkie's seal-like "skin" shed at the seashore when the creature shifts into human form can control (or kill) this mythic being.

In many ways, the traditional selkie is similar to the mermaid (prompting another tangential link to Cardiff's real Mermaid Quay, near the fictitious Hub), although it also bears similarities to other "worm" stories. *Torchwood*'s selkie, however, initially looks more like a sea serpent or a toothsome Loch Ness monster. Its form in later panels is decidedly female and more human. Instead of simply shedding her skin to walk on the land, this selkie likes to skin its victims.

Carole Barrowman adds another layer of meaning to the traditional Celtic myth by infusing the story with feminism; this female selkie avenges a fishing village's abused wives. The author's original story was part of a project in which she planned "re-imagining some of the traditional Celtic myths from a feminist perspective." With "Selkie," she combines two storytelling interests: gender issues (reflected in the selkie character) and morally compromised characters (represented by Jack Harkness). Barrowman (personal interview) finds "characters who are morally compromised or forced into the grey areas so much more interesting than traditional heroes" and is "also interested in gender differences and how they influence moral dilemmas when individuals confront them."

Although the selkie is a murderer, she chooses her victims carefully. The dead share a history of domestic violence against their partners. Hero Jack is the selkie's former savior; he initially saves her from a dying planet. By transporting the selkie to a new life, Jack inadvertently also provides the creature with a new, protective purpose, albeit one he could not have anticipated would turn deadly. Jack therefore must deal with the consequences of his previous heroic action. He must decide when to save life and when to take it.

Modernizing the selkie myth with moral dilemmas enhances its dramatic appeal. It also provides an added element for female readers, who might be *Torchwood* fans but not necessarily frequent readers of comics or hero stories. Although feminism isn't just for women, female *Torchwood* fans are more likely to be attracted to a feminism-infused plot. *Torchwood* heroes like Tosh and Gwen from the first two seasons' episodes or, again, Gwen and Lois Habiba from "Children of Earth" take just as active a role as men in saving the Earth. In fact, promotional photographs of season four's returning characters often show Gwen in the forefront and Jack in the background, indicating that Gwen's role in new episodes may take on greater significance. Just as *Torchwood*'s heroes often are women, so are its monsters (e.g., a half-converted Cyberwoman in "Cyberwoman," 1.4; mind-control villain Mary in "Greeks Bearing Gifts," 1.7; possessed terrorist Beth in "Sleeper," 2.2). "Selkie" continues this tradition with a strong female antagonist, but neither she nor Jack is completely to blame for the way they are. The selkie tries to protect other females from male abusers; she is a stranded alien with nowhere to go and, although she murders humans, she also is somewhat sympathetic. Jack, for all the dark decisions he makes in episodes as well as in novels or even comic book stories, also is a sympathetic character who is, for most of *Torchwood,* a stranded alien with nowhere to go. "Selkie" is true to the nature of *Torchwood* canon and mythology while forging a link between comics, more often targeted toward young male readers, and a different audience—female readers of any age.

"Selkie" helps ensure that *Torchwood* fans who may not be familiar with the selkie myth become aware of it. A village local tells Jack (and thus readers) that "folks here are weaned on that myth" and proceeds to explain it: "Story also says the selkie has the power to control the weather, shed its seal skin, and take human form whenever the island is in danger" (68). Although not everyone in the village may believe the myth, all are familiar with it. Again, this comment fits with *Torchwood*'s assumption that citizens in Celtic cultures are more likely to know such myths, whereas international readers may not be familiar with selkies, fairies, or water hags. Once again, Jack understands the true nature of a mythic being, and the story again becomes a battle between two mythic characters—with Jack as hero being the victor, even if a victory is bittersweet. In seeing the big picture and trying to protect the most people possible, Jack often sacrifices a single being, whether a human child or an adult alien.

In addition to the title selkie, the comic's opening panels allude to angels and fairies, which previously have been characters in *Doctor Who* (e.g., the angels in "Blink") and *Torchwood* (e.g., the fairies in "Small Worlds"). Adding another creature to the mythic pantheon found in these series' episodes gives more weight to a comic-book story. Jack's long, adventurous life fuels future myths, but his ability to investigate reports of mysterious deaths also relies on his knowledge of mythology. As long as Jack is the hero of a story, the immortal from another time and place is more likely to recognize aliens who may themselves be the source of human (specifically, Welsh, Scottish, or Irish) myths.

Torchwood is designed to be an "alien tracker" series, but its aliens often have been around long enough in the Cardiff area to have become the source of myths. Jack is a unique immortal in science fiction television in that he, too, is an alien (i.e., a human from another planet) who becomes so much a part of Cardiff's (or even pre–Cardiff's) history that legends may grow up around him, and he eventually is perceived by new characters as a mythic being himself.

Torchwood's lead character is an immortal shrouded in mystery, legend, and half-truths. Jack is as unknown—or unrevealed—as any creature from Welsh mythology. Team members occasionally find a photo (e.g., "Everything Changes," 1.1) or a bit of film ("From Out of the Rain," 2.10) that reveals part of Jack's past on Earth, but even his closest companions know little about him, a fact brought home during "Children of Earth." His past often is uncovered through reports of "sightings" or former colleagues who want to eliminate him because of his actions as an intergalactic Time Agent or a long-time Earth-bound Torchwood operative.

Jack has spent years either buried beneath Cardiff ("Exit Wounds," 2.13) or in Torchwood's vaults ("Fragments," 2.12); he has been imprisoned and tortured or sacrificed himself only to arise from the dead again and again (e.g., "Fragments," 2.12; "End of Days," 1.13; "Children of Earth," 3.2). In the most dire attempt to kill him permanently, government assassins plant a bomb in him, succeeding in destroying not only Jack's physical body but the entire Hub ("Children of Earth," 3.1). Jack's series of lives is the stuff of myth. That such a mythic being lives and works in modern Cardiff is another example of the permanence of Welsh mythology within current popular culture.

When Jack decides to leave Earth to go traveling once more among the stars, his departure dramatically takes place at night atop a hill ("Children of Earth," 3.5). This location is appropriate to the "death" of a mythic hero. Jack announces that it's time for a new life, effectively "killing" his Torchwood persona just before he ascends to a waiting spaceship. Whether Jack — or this character going by a new name — returns to Cardiff, the legend of Captain Jack Harkness undoubtedly will live in Welsh (televisionary) culture long into the future.

Even before "The New World" proscribes his status as mythic, Jack is the most "magical" being in *Torchwood*. In contrast to the very human Gwen, who Jack initially hires ("Everything Changes," 1.1) because she is compassionate and has a normal out-of-work life, Jack is far from typically human. He has become immortal through an accident with a time vortex (a backstory created and developed in *Doctor Who*), and even though he becomes a time traveler stranded on Earth in the 1800s, he lives through so much of Cardiff's history that he seems like a mythic part of the culture. References to Captain Jack Harkness go back decades, yet Jack gets away with fooling people from his past by claiming to be his father's son, for example.

Jack's "magic" goes beyond mere mortality. He contains too much life force — the reason he cannot remain dead. Thus, at a few points in the unevenly written first season, he apparently shares his life force with others who are near death, prolonging their lives. Most important, he apparently resurrects Ianto after a nasty encounter with an out-of-control Cyberwoman ("Cyberwoman," 1.4); he "awakens" Ianto with a kiss imbued with the essence of life. Although an episode two weeks earlier ("Day One,"" 1.2) shows Jack giving a woman possessed by an alien a similar life-affirming kiss, that episode portrays the kiss in a "magical" way — Jack and the woman bask in a golden glow for the duration of the kiss. No special effect accompanies Ianto's kiss, which made some viewers wonder if Ianto had been truly dead and brought back to life by Jack's kiss, although in later episodes Jack resorts to the Risen Mitten to revive a dead team member — or simply cannot bring back the dead (e.g., Tosh in "Exit Wounds," 2.13; Ianto in "Children of Earth," 3.4). Jack's immortality and any benefits from it are often incongruously illustrated throughout the series, but his encounters with life and death are unquestionably very different from mortals'—in terms of myth, he is a "magical being" because neither his immortality nor his superhuman gifts are understood by Jack or explained to the audience. They seem to be inexplicable or "magical."

Series creator Davies seems determined to move *Torchwood* away from a mythic Welsh past and into a cosmopolitan international setting full of modern political problems—such as global government conspiracies and terrorism—in which aliens or the supernatural are only a means of getting into a more modern plot. Although Davies insists that his home country Wales will remain one location for season four, the move to other scripted locations in North America and Europe broadens the scope of the story.

In many ways, "New World" is a new facet of television storytelling, in which an established TV series can become anything needed in the marketplace, despite its original premise or genre. In *Torchwood*'s case, a move from the ancient, mythic, and Welsh-based culture which framed the original two seasons and first part of the third is literally blown up in order that a new premise can extend the life of the series and take it, along with new characters, in an entirely new direction. Many fans loved the original premise because of its "Welshness," underground Hub, pet pteradon (a historic creature transplanted in time via the Rift that, in effect, becomes another mythic element in the original story—Ianto and Jack have a pet dinosaur as the Hub's "guard dog"), and other mysterious creatures based in Celtic mythology. These fans vowed never to watch "The New World." It seems that many fans of the original, Welsh culture-steeped series were happier in the Old World of Torchwood and continue to play with those themes through fan videos, fanfiction, and fan art.

The choice of Cardiff as a magnet for all sorts of alien and terrestrial spooky do's allows writers—BBC-sanctioned ones or fans—to incorporate mythology into science fiction plots. Welsh-born Russell T. Davies often seems gleeful about introducing Welsh characters and settings into television series viewed internationally, helping to put Wales on a larger popular culture map so that more audiences become aware of Welsh actors as well as cultural themes. This process makes *Torchwood* different from other science fiction series as well as makes international TV audiences aware of elements of Celtic mythology to which they might not otherwise be exposed. *Torchwood* may not be the most culturally accurate way to disseminate knowledge of Welsh myths or folklore, but it further integrates at least some Celtic mythology into popular culture and, more recently, vividly illustrates for viewers how myths are created.

Notes

1. In July 2009 I first visited the memorial at Cardiff Bay, noting during a return visit in October 2010 the document added by Mermaid Quay management. The inscription is quoted directly from that document.

2. One fanfiction writer theorizes in her story that Jack Harkness's two millennia buried under what would become Cardiff (a plot point introduced in "Exit Wounds" [2.13]) actually created the Rift as a result of all that immortal life force being contained below ground for so long. Other fanfiction provides a crossover with another BBC series, *Merlin*, in which the young wizard converses with the long-interred Jack Harkness in ancient Wales. Even such unofficial stories enhance fans' connection between *Torchwood* and Welsh mythology.

3. The origins of the Celtic goddess Cailleach is detailed in books such as d'Este and Rankine. This book explores the evolving myth of the crone or hag and her command of the elements, including water. As such, she is not a "water hag" but is one example of a mythic ancestor to the book's creature. One story involves an attack on Grettir by a troll who lives underwater. After unsuccessfully attacking the man and being unable to drag him to her watery cave, the wounded she-troll escapes to her lair (Leeming 125).

Works Cited

Arrowsmith, Nancy. *Field Guide to the Little People: A Curious Journey into the Hidden Realm of Elves, Faeries, Hobgoblins, and Not-So-Mythical Creatures.* Woodbury, MN: Llewellyn, 2009.
Barrowman, Carole E. Personal email interview. September 21, 2009.
Barrowman, Carole E., and Barrowman, John. "Selkie." *Torchwood Magazine*, 14 (April–May 2009): 61–75.
Baxendale, Trevor. *Something in the Water.* London: BBC Books, 2008.
Berriman, Ian. "The American Way." *SFX*, #199 (Sept. 2010), 52–55.
Davies, Sioned (Trans.). *The Mabinogion.* Oxford, England: Oxford University Press, 2008.
d'Este, Sorita, and David Rankine. *Visions of the Cailleach: Exploring the Myths, Legends, and Folklore of the Pre-eminent Celtic Hag Goddess.* London: Avalonia, 2009.
Devereaux, Paul. *Fairy Paths in Ireland and Wales: A Literature and Field Study of Cognised Landscapes in Two Celtic Countries.* International Consciousness Research Laboratories Report. Princeton, NJ: ICRL, 2004.
Heaney, Seamus (Ed.). *Beowulf: A New Verse Translation.* New York: Norton, 2000.
Hughes, Rhiannon (Ed.). *Legends of the Mist: A Magical Collection of Welsh Folk Tales and Legends.* London: New English Library, 1972.
Jones, Eirwen. *Folk Tales of Wales.* London: Thomas Nelson & Sons, 1947.
Leeming, David Adams. *Gods, Heroes, and Kings.* Oxford, England: Oxford University Press, 2001.
Lloyd, D. M., and Lloyd, E. M. (Eds.). *A Book of Wales.* London: Collins, 1953.
MacKillop, James. *Myths and Legends of the Celts.* New York: Penguin Books, 2005.
McCoy, Edain. *The Sabbats: A New Approach to Living the Old Ways.* St. Paul, MN: Llewellyn, 1999.
Merlin. "The Changeling." (3.6). Lucy Watkins, writer. Dave Moore, director. October 16, 2010.
"Mother." Pagan Dictionary. http://www.experiencefestival.com/a/MOTHER/id/188419
Silver, Carole G. *Strange and Secret Peoples: Fairies and Victorian Consciousness.* New York: Oxford University Press, 1999.
Stormsong, Rain. Wiccan Study—Color Symbolism for Sabbats. Herbal Musings. http://www.herbalmusings.com/colors-for-sabbats.htm
"Welsh Faeries." Mystical Mythology. http://www.bellaterreno.com/art/welsh/welsh fairies.aspx. Online.

Yeats, William Butler. *The Collected Poems of W. B. Yeats.* Ware, England: Wordsworth Editions Limited, 1994.

Torchwood Episodes

"Children of Earth, Day One.) (3.1). Russell T. Davies, writer. Dir. Euros Lyn. July 6, 2009.
"Children of Earth, Day Five.) (3.5). Russell T. Davies, writer. Dir. Euros Lyn. July 10, 2009.
"Countrycide." (1.6). Chris Chibnall, writer. Dir.Andy Goddard. November 19, 2006. BBC.
"Cyberwoman." (1.4). Chris Chibnall, writer. Dir. James Strong. November 5, 2006. BBC.
"Day One." (1.2). Russell T. Davies and Chris Chibnall, writers. Dir. Brian Kelly. October 22, 2006. BBC.
"The Dead Line." (Radio play). Phil Ford, writer. Dir. Kate McAll. July 3, 2009. BBC Radio Four.
"Dead Man Walking." (2.7). Matt Jones, writer. Dir. Andy Goddard. February 20, 2008. BBC.
"End of Days." (1.13). Chris Chibnall, writer. Ashley Way, director. January 1, 2007. BBC.
"Everything Changes." (1.1). Russell T. Davies, writer. Dir. Brian Kelly. October 22, 2006. BBC.
"Exit Wounds." (2.13). Chris Chibnall, writer. Dir. Ashley Way. April 4, 2008.
"Fragments." (2.12). Chris Chibnall, writer. Dir. Jonathan Fox Bassett. March 21, 2008. BBC.
"From Out of the Rain." (2.10). Peter J. Hammond, writer. Dir. Jonathan Fox Bassett. March 12, 2008. BBC.
"Greeks Bearing Gifts." (1.7). Russell T. Davies and Toby Whithouse, writers. Dir. Colin Teague. November 26, 2006. BBC.
"Kiss Kiss, Bang Bang." (2.1). Chris Chibnall, writer. Dir. Ashley Way. January 16, 2008. BBC.
"Reset." (2.6). J. C. Wilsher, writer. Dir. Ashley Way. February 13, 2008. BBC.
"Sleeper." (2.2). Russell T. Davies and James Moran, writers. Dir. Colin Teague. January 23, 2008. BBC.
"Small Worlds." (1.5). Peter J. Hammond, writer. Dir. Alice Troughton. November 12, 2006. BBC.
"They Keep Killing Suzie." (1.8). Paul Tomalin and Dan McCulloch, writers. Dir. James Strong. December 3, 2006. BBC.

Everyday Magic
Howl's Moving Castle *and Fantasy as Sociopolitical Commentary*

CAROLYNN E. WILCOX

Howl's Moving Castle, by British children's author Diana Wynne Jones, was first published in 1984. In this novel, Jones takes traditional fairy tale elements and adapts them to fit what appears to be, at first, a typical portal fantasy in which the characters can move from one world to another through a doorway. The story begins by introducing the reader to the situations of three sisters: Sophie, the oldest and the one doomed to failure should she seek her own fortune; Lettie, the beautiful one, who works in a bakery; and Martha, the talented one, who is apprenticed to a "honey witch," a witch who incorporates honey into all of her spells. The girls' father is dead, and their stepmother Fanny is largely absent. While Fanny is not wicked, she is only concerned with her own affairs. Sophie's casual acceptance of her "fate," combined with the "normal" treatment of such outlandish things as magic and seven-league boots sets the tone for the book. Jones clearly intends the reader to approach the land of Ingary as one would any other so-called normal setting, like London, England or Phoenix, Arizona. Magical elements and their consequences are handled so as to make them appear mundane (Mendlesohn 136). Within this framework of normalcy, Jones approaches social and political issues obliquely, using the microcosm of Sophie's relationships (including her inner life) to illustrate the power inherent in personal agency: the everyday magic — the only magic — capable of effecting change on any scale, great or small.

Jones's novel transforms several traditional role assignments found in the fairy tale. Consider the following formula: a pretty maiden falls into distress and is rescued, usually with the aid of a magic spell, an enchanted weapon, or a life-giving kiss, by a handsome prince who then marries her, and they live happily ever after. Traditional fairy stories often take place in a familiar location (like France, for some versions of Cinderella), or in a romanticized past in what was once the world of the reader, complete with symbols and imagery the reader recognizes. Charles Butler noted:

> This reliance on actual settings is far more than a matter of making use of images that happen to lie conveniently close to hand. John Rowe Townsend has observed that a local setting "gives the impression of authenticating the story" and therefore operates as a device through which to convince the reader that magical events are grounded in the real world [46].

This level of comfort allows the reader to confront the supernatural elements of the tale and assimilate them using the fairy tale formula. The "happily ever after" is anticipated, and magic is a necessary and spectacular element. The anticipation of formulaic outcomes is extended in the portal fantasy subgenre (sometimes referred to as a wainscot fantasy, where the fantasy world and the real world exist side-by-side with occasional overlaps, much like in the Harry Potter books).

In a portal fantasy, the real world of the reader coexists with the author's constructed world and is typically accessed through a door, a gateway, or other type of magic portal. C.S. Lewis's Pevensies enter Narnia through a wardrobe. J. K. Rowling's Harry Potter enters through various "hidden" gateways. Alice finds Wonderland by falling down a rabbit hole, and other heroes and heroines have accessed fantasy realms through fairy rings and standing stones. Time and other rules that govern the reader's reality may or may not be observed in the parallel world, and magic is almost always an accepted fact in the constructed world. In Ingary, where pretty damsels abound, distress roams the barren northern Wastes in the persons of both the Witch of the Waste and the Wizard Howl: the pretty maiden does fall into distress, and goes looking for a solution on her own, but along the way she also saves a prince, rescues two wizards, frees a fire demon, halts a war, breaks the curse she's under, and ends the tale by becoming engaged to the newly reformed Wizard Howl. Clearly, Jones has taken the fairy tale up a notch by modernizing the narrative with a self-sufficient female heroine. In addition to setting these fairy tale conventions on their heads, Jones inverts the portal fantasy construct by establishing Ingary as the primary world, much like an immersive fantasy, and links Ingary to modern-day Wales through a magic door that can open to more than one location, depending upon the setting of a color-coded dial. This magic door is central to the Wizard Howl's practice, allowing him to work in two different kingdoms and to return to his home world — the reader's world — of Wales. The inversion of fantasy world and real world forces the reader to accept wholesale the interpretations of the main character Sophie and to rely on the accuracy of her assessment of any given situation.

What Sophie accepts as normal, the reader must adopt as the status quo in Ingary. Jones reinforces Ingary's primacy by introducing the reader to the Wizard Howl's home world in a scene where Howl returns to Wales accompanied by Sophie, a technique which paints blue jeans and video games as strangely alien. Sophie's directness provides a matter-of-fact tone that anchors the reader in normalcy, even when faced with an animated, turnip-headed scarecrow or a castle that moves. This inversion of the subgenre obviates the need for a guide, as argued by Farah Mendlesohn in her book, *Diana Wynne Jones: Children's Literature and the Fantastic Tradition*: "in most portal-quest fantasies the comprehension of the protagonist goes unquestioned and is reinforced by the figure of the guide, who stories the world for us by dispensing knowledge and moral judgment as and when it is needed" (89).

One of the most fascinating aspects of *Howl's Moving Castle* is the character development of Sophie Hatter, whose surname is another nod to Carroll's Alice, and indirectly anticipates the fantastic. From the beginning of the novel, Sophie is resigned to a predetermined fate. While she is young, pretty enough to tempt the infamous heart-eating Howl, and talented enough to enchant the hats she makes just by talking to them, Sophie sees herself as insignificant and unimportant. Her personal happiness must give way to duty, according to the expectations that govern her role as the oldest. She is completely unaware of her own abilities to manipulate language to make things happen. At the time of the story in Ingary, the worst possible thing that could happen to a young girl is to fall victim to the Wizard Howl or to run afoul of the Witch of the Waste. Sophie does meet the Witch and is cursed by her because the Witch mistakes Sophie for her sister Lettie, who is training with Mrs. Fairfax to be a witch. The Witch believes Lettie is competing, both in the realm of witchcraft and for Wizard Howl's affections; consequently, the Witch's curse turns Sophie into an old crone, the stereotypical visage for a witch and the antithesis of everything desirable in a woman (18). Curiously enough, the curse converts Sophie's internal monologue into her external appearance: "Sophie felt as if the past months of sitting and sewing had turned her into an old woman or a semi-invalid." How Sophie views herself is an integral component of the spell, which is why later in the novel Howl can't remove it. In fact, Howl remarks to Sophie, "I had several goes at taking it off you when you weren't looking. But nothing seems to work ... I came to the conclusion that you liked being in disguise" (182–183). Thus, the whole fairy-tale convention of the curse is also turned inside out as the curse turns out to be the catalyst that forces Sophie to think and act for herself for the first time in her life, without regarding any familial obligations. She is free to think and act in ways she never would have attempted as her normal, younger self. She immediately decides that the best course of action is to seek out the dangerous Wizard Howl to see if he can help her lift the curse. In true oldest-child logic, she decides that since she was never beautiful and now is old to boot, her heart is safe from Howl. The magic of Ingary compels Sophie to accept agency and to live with the consequences of her actions. The curse frees Sophie from the self-imposed boundaries that govern her behavior.

Sophie's passive acceptance of the truism about the fate of the oldest robs her of her agency and blinds her to her true power for nearly the first half of the novel. Mendlesohn asserts, "Jones posits that power is a direct consequence of the acquisition of agency. Because agency is about the ability to make conscious choices ... agency cannot be solely acquired with the conferring of power" (21). Sophie's actions bear that out. As she finds she can make things happen just by talking objects into life, she becomes more intentional (and more successful) in her attempts to exercise power to effect change in the world around her. These attempts are encouraged and confirmed by other characters around her, who throughout the novel try to "convince Sophie Hatter that her position in life is determined only by her talent and effort, opposed by the energy that Sophie puts into convincing herself that she can only fail" (Mendlesohn 40). Ultimately, she triumphs over the Witch of the Waste's fire demon by ordering Sophie's stick to "'Beat Miss Angorian, but don't hurt anyone else'" (207). Her power meets her intention, successfully delaying the fire demon's escape so Howl can arrive to deal with it, and, in doing so, breaks the aging spell that was on her by taking a true step in personal agency.

Jones establishes language as the vehicle for power early in the novel. Sophie Hatter speaks to her hats, and the enchanted hats produce the scenario Sophie describes. For example, Sophie declares, "You will have to marry money" to a cream colored, rose-trimmed hat. Near the end of the novel, the reader discovers that Fanny kept that hat for herself and ended up married to a wealthy man and living in a mansion outside of Market Chipping (188). After Sophie's transformation and while working as Howl's elderly housekeeper, she wrecks his beauty products by muttering over them while tidying the bathroom and in a fit of pique, and she enchants Howl's favorite outfit merely by observing, "so you ate hearts, did you, suit?" (56). The other two magical figures introduced, Mrs. Fairfax and Mrs. Pentstemmon, both comment on Sophie's uncanny ability to "talk things into life" (117). In June, while preparing for the upcoming midsummer festivities, Sophie discovers how this new command of language brings her a profound sense of contentment as she experiments with her flower gardens (166).

This power for influencing reality with language, written or spoken, has been discussed at length by Deborah Kaplan in her chapter on "Diana Wynne Jones and the World-Shaping Power of Language." She posits "Jones's plots follow a similar trajectory to that of deconstructionist and post-structuralist theory, which concentrates on the power and danger of fluid meaning" (56). Furthermore, Kaplan suggests that this fluidity extends to the questions of "what is truth?" and "what is reality?" in *Howl*. Deconstructionists argue that signifiers (words) have no central or static definition (signified); instead, words create meaning through a web of association which approximate meaning and also encompass the opposite of the original signifier. This is best exemplified by Howl, a character who cherishes and nurtures his many aliases. In Market Chipping, he is the heart-eating Wizard Howl. In Portsmouth, he is Jenkins, a competent and friendly wizard, and in Kingsbridge, he is Pendragon, a rather high-brow magic practitioner. In the reader's Wales, he's Howell, the dead-beat PhD who'd rather carouse with his rugby mates than do any "real" work. By adopting various personae to evade personal responsibility, the Wizard Howl generated his own ambiguity; even he is no longer sure of who he really is or what he is actually capable of. This method of looking at language, developed by philosophers such as Claude Lévi-Strauss and Jacques Derrida, adds layer upon layer of complexity to words, producing an increase in ambiguity. Magic exists within this ambiguity, and this ability for reality to be flexible allows the world around Sophie to respond to her verbal observations as well as to her direct commands.

In addition to Sophie's (largely involuntary) power with words, Jones uses a poem by John Donne as a centrally organizing element. "Song: Go and Catch a Falling Star" is, within Howl's home world, used as an essentially harmless poem full of nonsense about falling stars, mandrake roots, and mermaids. In fact, it turns out to be a mislaid homework assignment belonging to Howell's Welsh nephew. In contrast, within Ingary, Donne's poem functions as a kind of winged curse, relentlessly dogging Howl's steps in spite of his creative attempts to weasel out of any responsibility (99). The lines not only provide both the reader and Sophie with clues to the true nature of the relationship between the fire demon Calcifer and Howl, but also provide the driving force behind the action in the novel, propelling the characters towards the final resolution. The first verse of "Song" is presented as a spell Howl's apprentice Michael is supposed to learn; unable to do so, he consults Sophie and, by trying to act out the first line of the poem, together they discover that Calcifer used to *be* a falling star. By the time Howl discovers that the Witch of the Waste's curse has found him, all but three of the aspects of the curse have come to pass. Each new element manifesting itself draws both the characters and the reader closer to the climax of the novel: the inevitable confrontation between the Witch of the Waste and Howl, together with their respective fire demons.

The implementation of the poem also acts to raise the level of ambiguity within the text itself. In Adrienne Gavin's article "Enigma's Variation," she examines how Jones utilizes elements of the mystery genre in other works to introduce a "slippery indeterminacy of meaning and solution; something enigmatic and shifting at their core, making it impossible to reach absolute conclusions" (211). *Howl* is similar to Jones's other novels as it has two central mysteries: the riddle-poem with multiple signifiers and the mystery of Howl's pact with Calcifer, which Sophie has to solve before Calcifer will break the spell she's under. But exploring issues of identity also raises ambiguity: Howl's reputation versus his actuality, Sophie's self-perception as a young woman versus her liberation/agency as an old crone, and the role of the "real" world within the fantasy wainscot. Gavin also suggests that some of these exemplary mysteries contain a higher level of "intertextual significance" (212). Donne's poem imbedded in the *Howl* text functions in this manner, as does the intrusion of the "real" Wales into the fantasy-scape of Ingary, even if it only appears in glimpses. It is interesting to note that the most potentially destructive forces in Ingary are both from the "real" world, forcing the reader to examine the implications of power in unready or (as in Howl's case) unwilling hands.

Wales is first introduced to the reader as the land of the "forbidden other." Sophie is curious about where the black paint setting on the magic door goes; however, without Howl, she can't penetrate the magic barriers he has erected to protect his family from the Witch of the Waste. For months, Sophie assumes Howl is using the black paint setting to duck his responsibilities to either the King in Portsmouth or the King in Kingsbridge. Eventually, Howl brings both Sophie and Michael with him to Wales to track down the origin of the poem/curse. The juxtaposition of comforting details like middle school boys who play video games and irate, belittling older sisters with sorcery and charms jars the reader, forcing him or her to re-attenuate his or her definition of reality. This happens again, when Michael reads aloud the first stanza of "Song": "Go and catch a falling star, / get with child a mandrake root / tell me where all past years are / and who cleft the devil's hoof" (1–4). The delight of recognition mingles with discomfort as worlds collide for the reader.

In addition to the readjustment the reader must make whenever he or she encounters a familiar Wales within the text, the reader also must come to grips with the fact that the two largest forces in Ingary for good and for evil originate in the "real" Wales. The Wizard Howl and Miss Angorian (the personification of the Witch of the Waste's fire demon) both have "ordinary" lives; in Wales, Howell plays doting uncle and the black sheep of his family while Miss Angorian poses as Howell's nephew's English teacher, as she works out the details of her plot to ensnare Howl for spurning the Witch of the Waste's romantic advances. Furthermore, Miss Angorian designs her curse to operate in either reality, making it the "ultimate" weapon against Howl, as it prevents his safe retreat to his home world. Howl's ability to traverse both the reader's world and Jones's constructed world reinforces the duality of his nature; by the climax of the novel, even Howl is uncertain if he can be counted among the "good" guys, or if he is, at best, self-interested. This self-interest, or perhaps enhanced self-preservation, is best examined in the context of Howl's actions (or non-actions) in the war in Ingary.

Howl's Moving Castle has several layers of social and/or political commentary. From the very beginning, it is clear to the reader that Sophie is unable to take charge of her own destiny, as contrasted with the behavior of her younger sisters Lettie and Martha. Placed in apprenticeships that do not suit either girl, Lettie and Martha use a purloined spell to trade places magically, allowing Lettie to study with Mrs. Fairfax, a local witch and Martha to apprentice at Cesari's, a bakery in town where she meets and falls in love with Michael, Howl's apprentice (12–13). Arguably more talented than either of her sisters, Sophie has internalized socially-accepted concepts of duty, and this abdication of personal agency is ultimately what gives the Witch of the Waste's curse its hold over her.

The Wizard Howl also has issues with social mores. Madame Suliman expects Howl to exercise his power in the service of the kingdom, and to act with a level of personal integrity that would exclude his compact with the fire demon Calcifer. Combined with the urgent entreaties of the king for Howl to locate the missing Prince Justin, and Howl's desperate need to evade the Witch of the Waste's curse that lays claim to Howl's heart, Howl's behavior becomes more and more reactive, creating finite boundaries within which he can operate. Fear and a lack of personal responsibility are what really steal Howl's freedom, not the circumstances that exist outside of himself. Interestingly enough, Howl's "real" life in Wales where he is known as Howell Jenkins is very similar to his life in Ingary. Howell Jenkins is a huge disappointment to his family, in the person of his very bitter sister Megan. Although Howell completed an advanced degree, the family clearly had expectations that he would do something other than lark about and play rugby with his mates. The similar characteristic — Howl and Howell's refusal to accept responsibility — reinforces the normalcy of the relationship between the portal world and the world of the reader. If familial expectations are the same, then perhaps other things are similar as well. In a way, the relational nature of the portal world to the reader's world also raises possibilities for magic to exist here as well.

More subtle are the political ramifications in Jones's novel. The main implication seems to be that the most random action has unforeseen, and potentially significant, consequences. For example, early on Sophie encounters a turnip-headed scarecrow and talks it into life. The scarecrow has an integral role to play in the resolution of the novel. Had she passed it by without speaking, Prince Justin may never have been located. Also, a number of other events would not have happened, or may have happened in a different sequence. While employing magic for the greater good is an implied civic duty, it is essential for each individual to develop strong agency in conjunction with that sense of duty; without agency, words are muted and action is impossible. The novel stops short of demanding that characters be proactive; Jones simply highlights the differences between characters who self-advocate, like Lettie and Martha, and those whose decisions to shirk social responsibilities ultimately restrict their choices. This social and political climate of Jones's portal fantasy attracted the attention of acclaimed filmmaker Hayao Miyazaki.

Hayao Miyazaki based his film on Jones's novel, as proclaimed in the opening credits of the 2004 release. However, it is clear from the first few moments of the animated feature-length movie that the novel and the film diverge. Miyazaki diverges from his source for a number of reasons. First and foremost, it is not unusual to see an anime film differ greatly from its source material; the idea is that each is its own art form and is viewed as a completely separate work of art. Secondly, according to Matt Kimmich:

[...] because of the different needs of the two mediums (i.e. novel and cinema) as well as the different cultural backgrounds of the novelist and director, changes to the narrative were inevitable ... due to these different equivalences, showing fidelity to the original text is a challenge as it is difficult to predict what will be accepted as equivalent by audiences [127].

As a result of Miyazaki's editorial changes in the narrative itself, the film has an entirely different look and feel from the story as written by Jones. In the novel, Jones's Ingary is full of stone cottages and weathered, rumpled hills, appearing in a reader's mind like a possible Wales, a Wales where King Arthur was real, and magic was an everyday occurrence. The setting for the film, on the surface, appears to be the same Ingary as found in the novel; however, "the world [Miyazaki's] film depicts is more readily impressive, and it is more historically and geographically specific than Jones's folk tale world. His Ingary is a steam- and electricity-powered place" (Kimmich 129). The viewer recognizes the practice of putting advertisements on the trolleys, and winces at the billowing pollution produced by numerous vehicles on land, sea, and air. The cities are tall and crowded, with narrow streets full of bustling people. These familiar images replace the objects that the reader identifies when Sophie journeys to the reader's Wales, and ultimately function in the same way, by creating a recognizable anchor to allow the viewer to establish connections with the fantasy world.

Other changes that are readily apparent include the depiction of the moving castle itself, as well as that of the main character, Sophie. Kimmach claims:

> Miyazaki converts Jones's depiction of a dark, sinister castle into "a rotund collage of chimneys, roofs, steam pipes, and other odd appendages, borne along on mechanized bird legs ... for all its mechanical elements, it seems strangely organic and alive, which is emphasized by its resemblance to a grotesque face of sorts, complete with eyes, mouth, teeth, and tongue" [128].

This vision isn't at all in keeping with the vision of Jones's castle in her novel, where the castle looks more like a collection of chimney pots, reflecting the personality of the fire demon who inhabits it; however, it does not detract from the overall story arc. The film does take the focus off the role of the fire demon, who fashions and maintains the castle together with his or her witch or wizard. In the book, Sophie is described as "a little gray mouse" with red-gold hair (10). In the film, she's a slender, brown haired, brown eyed girl—not beautiful or voluptuous, but still quite pretty. And these seemingly superficial changes are not trivial. In fact, each tiny detail reinforces the new interpretation of Jones's material Miyazaki brings, and underscores the political anti-war message the film carries.

In Miyazaki's treatment, the war plot becomes foregrounded, giving rise to the opportunity to compare the director's blatant anti-war stance on the war in Ingary to the growing unpopularity of the conflict in Iraq during 2004 and 2005. Kimmich argues that "the film's omission [of Donne's poem] and its addition of a war subplot largely foreign to the book seem like an intrusion of elements from Miyazaki's earlier films," (129) such as *Princess Mononoke* (1997). Everywhere in the early scenes of the film set in Sophie's home town of Market Chipping, soldiers parade, flags wave, airships patrol and patriotism is rampant. As the two respective kings call Howl into service on opposite sides of the war, Howl acts on his own to attack both sides, making his anti-war position clear in spite of a high personal cost. Employing magic for warfare dehumanizes and disfigures the practitioners, permanently transforming them into misshapen, soulless monsters. The longer Howl uses his magic to divert airships and bombing raids, the less human he becomes, transforming slowly into a large, black, feathered bird creature. While no overt comparisons are made in the film, it is easy to see that the film director intended the viewer to conclude that those with superior power who harness that power in service to an unjust cause imperil their own humanity.

Miyazaki is, of course, neither the first nor the last to incorporate personal experience or systems of belief in writing or on screen. Jones herself frequently incorporates autobiographical elements into her work; *Howl's Moving Castle* was no different. In an interview, Jones admitted to loosely basing the Hatter sisters on herself and her two sisters (Marcus 79–80). As for the incorporation of the war (which earned a brief two-line mention in the novel), one could argue that the war in Ingary rumbles in the background of Sophie's life much as mortar fire in World War II rumbled in the background of Jones's own childhood. The war was everywhere in 1940s England, and Jones stated that "[the war] left me with the feeling that the most appalling and peculiar things [were] liable to happen at any time" (Marcus 81). The war functions as a metaphor for instability and as a vehicle for abrupt, otherwise inexplicable change. However, for Jones, the war was simply not as pervasive as the magic of Ingary; for Miyazaki, the magic and the war were complexly intertwined.

The idea that practitioners of magic have a civic responsibility is also present in the film. Miyazaki links power with ethics very clearly in several scenes in the movie, where the novel uses mother figures such as Madame Suliman, Howl's teacher, to strongly admonish him on his ethical responsibilities. Howl reveals to Sophie that to graduate from the magic academy, he was forced to sign an oath requiring him to report to the palace whenever the king summoned him. In addition, Madame Suliman states that the kingdom cannot afford to tolerate renegade magical practitioners like the Witch of the Waste and Howl, both of whom formed questionable contracts with fire demons; the Witch's contract deadened her conscience and Howl's behavior indicated that his moral fiber may be decaying (Miyazaki). Miyazaki's Suliman takes the opportunity of her meeting with "Mrs. Pendragon" to try and corner Howl, threatening to strip him of his powers if he refuses to conform to her ethical standards.

The ethical practice of magic goes hand-in-hand with the concept of personal agency. After Howl throws a massive, slime-laden temper tantrum, he confesses to Sophie that he's on the run from Suliman and responsibility, from the Witch of the Waste and her disappointed hopes, and from anything else that scares him. Throughout the course of the movie, Howl's character develops a stronger moral imperative as his love for Sophie grows; this renewed sense of purpose gives Howl the courage to actively oppose the war and Suliman's henchmen who have orders to capture him. Unlike Jones's novel, the war, not the Witch of the Waste, is Howl's main antagonist in the film. Eliminating subplots containing the Witch of the Waste, Prince Justin, the Wizard Sullivan, Sophie's other sisters, and a mysterious, ensorcelled man-dog strips much of the complexity of Jones's original tale away. Instead of ruining the experience for readers of Jones's work, Miyazaki's film provides an entirely new experience, which carries a more strident, vocalized opposition to war, with characters calling the war "idiotic."

Sophie has a similar arc of character development in novel and film. Miyazaki handles the issue of Sophie's burgeoning agency brilliantly by allowing the curse to visually waver and wear thin whenever Sophie asserts herself or stands up to someone. This is especially true in scenes where Sophie is behaving the most selflessly and/or the most passionately, such as when Howl returns half dead from the war in his bird-man form (Miyazaki 2004). By the end of the film, when Sophie finally dissolves the contract between Howl and Calcifer, Sophie has transformed herself—returning to her correct age but with a head full of dazzling, silver hair. One might think that the selective emphasis of the film combined with the director's decision to omit intrinsic elements from the novel would create a negative or disappointing experience for a reader of Jones's novel upon viewing Miyazaki's work. However, that is not necessarily the case. In a way, Miyazaki's decision to bring the war in Ingary to the forefront of his film was a logical extension of the strong advocacy for ethical social and civic behavior found in the novel, and perhaps was a more appropriate choice for the reality his viewers inhabited, which is arguably different from the original audience of *Howl's Moving Castle* in the mid–1980s. Also, the visual trope Miyazaki employed to demonstrate the nature of the curse Sophie was under was sheer genius; the fluidity available through the anime medium enhanced an already sophisticated idea (the curse being subject to the character's personal agency) and made it visually elegant.

In spite of the film's many attractions, it is Jones's compelling characterization and unique treatment of the traditional portal fantasy that makes *Howl's Moving Castle* worth visiting again and again. Jones's presentation of a modified fairy tale set in a fantastic land that celebrates the acquisition of agency above that of magical powers draws readers of all ages. As powerful as this is for the reader, it isn't the main attraction. Jones's ability to transform the supernatural into the mundane works a kind of magic for the reader, allowing him or her to imagine or re-imagine the possibilities inherent in exercising agency within his or her own reality. By interweaving familiar images of her home in Wales, and recognizable poetry from any first year literature survey course, Jones establishes the idea that the boundaries of "ordinary" life are permeable. Diana Wynne Jones's and Miyazaki's crowning achievements include making this everyday magic accessible to all.

Works Cited

Butler, Charles. *Four British Fantasists: Place and Culture in the Children's Fantasies of Penelope Lively, Alan Garner, Diana Wynne Jones, and Susan Cooper*. Lanham: Children's Literature Association and Scarecrow Press, 2006.

Gavin, Adrienne E. "Enigma's Variation: the Puzzling Mysteries of Avi, Ellen Raskin, Diana Wynne Jones, and Chris Van Allsburg." *Mystery in Children's Literature: From the Rational to the Supernatural*. Palgrave: St. Martin's Press, 2001.

Jones, Diana Wynne. *Howl's Moving Castle*. New York: Greenwillow Books, 1986.

Kaplan, Deborah. "Diana Wynne Jones and the World-Shaping Power of Language." *Diana Wynne Jones: An Exciting and Exacting Wisdom*. Ed. Teya Rosenberg. New York: Peter Lang, 2002.

Kimmich, Matt. "Animating the Fantastic: Hayao Miyazaki's Adaptation of Diana Wynne Jones's *Howl's Moving Castle*." *Fantasy Fiction into Film*: Essays. Jefferson: McFarland, 2007.

Marcus, Leonard S., ed. "Diana Wynne Jones." *The Wand in the Word: Conversations with Writers of Fantasy*. Cambridge: Candlewick Press, 2006.

Mendlesohn, Farah. *Diana Wynne Jones: Children's Literature and the Fantastic Tradition*. New York: Routledge, 2005.

Miyazaki, Hayao, dir. *Howl's Moving Castle*. Vocal Perf. Jean Simmons, Christian Bale, Blythe Danner, Lauren Bacall, and Billy Crystal. Studio Ghibli and Walt Disney Entertainment, 2004. DVD.

Loosely Based
The Problems of Adaptation in Disney's The Black Cauldron

JEFF HICKS

In June of 1971 the Walt Disney Corporation bought the rights to Lloyd Alexander's five-part *Chronicles of Prydain* series with the hopes of turning the stories into a series of successful animated features (Sito 288). Inspired by the Welsh mythology contained within the *Mabinogi*, Alexander's five part series focused on the exploits of the young Assistant Pig-Keeper Taran and his desire to become a warrior of renown. Disney combined elements from the first two books in the series, *The Book of Three* and *The Black Cauldron,* to create an animated film that the studio thought would charm longtime fans of Disney fantasy and lure older viewers to the theaters. After lying dormant for several years and after a long ten-year production filled with cost over-runs and content changes, *The Black Cauldron*[1] was finally released in July of 1985. The end result, although not critically panned, was a financial failure so great that some at the time suggested that it would bankrupt the studio. The most expensive animated feature made as of its release in 1985, *The Black Cauldron* had over $45 million in actual production costs (Sito 292), but returned less than $22 million at the North American box office (IMDB, "The Black Cauldron").

Compare this story with the reception to Disney's 1963 film *The Sword in the Stone*: filmed with a modest budget, *The Sword in the Stone* was a financial as well as a critical success and went on to be the sixth highest grossing film of the year (IMDB, "The Sword In The Stone"). *The Sword in the Stone* too was adapted from a retelling of myth set within a child's world, but with T. H. White's novel[2] Disney was able to create a far more successful adaptation.

This chapter looks at the specific problems surrounding a successful translation of a literary interpretation of Welsh mythology to the big screen. It also looks at the ways in which Disney treated both Alexander's work and the tone of the original Welsh source material. Every film adapted from literature must necessarily lose some of its original content due to constraints of time, but the hope is that the visual aspects of a film might bring a new dimension to the written work, or even encourage the viewer to read the original material. The goal of most Hollywood adaptations is to retain the message and feel of the original work while increasing the exposure of its ideas. As an adaptation, Disney's *The Black Cauldron* fails to maintain the focus of the original work, even as it lacks the necessary plot cohesion to entertain, or even reach, a young audience.

Although Disney had acquired the rights to Alexander's Prydain novels in 1971 and mention of the film's development frequented trade publications throughout the seventies, the young animators on the Disney lot pushing for its production were forced by Disney management to wait until they had proven themselves on other features (Sito 288). By the time this group was given the go ahead the film had passed through numerous hands, each contributor further diluting the original work. The finished film lists nine separate writers including co-directors Ted Berman and Richard Rich, and producer Joe Hale. Throughout the process Hale tried to retain control of the film, and his vision was to create a fantasy epic that would lure fans of Alexander's work, as well as a larger share of the teenaged audience that Disney animated films failed to capture. Urged onward by the success of Ralph Bakshi's animated adaptation of *The Lord of the Rings* (1978), Hale was convinced that *The Black Cauldron* was the right vehicle to expand Disney's base, and that a certain amount of danger and violence was necessary to create the kind of film that a teenaged audience had come to expect.

While Disney had been making PG–rated live action films as early as 1979's *Tron*, *The Black Cauldron* was the first fully animated feature produced by Disney to receive anything stronger than a G rating. Indeed, *The Black Cauldron* remains one of the most violent animated films ever created by the studio. When Jeffrey Katzenberg became the new studio chairman in 1984, he was immediately alarmed by the overwhelming amount of violence in the film's early cut. Worried that a PG rated film would tarnish Disney's image, he ordered several scenes from *The Black Cauldron* to be cut due to concerns that their graphic nature would alienate children and family audiences (Stewart 70).[3] After seeing the original opening sequence, which featured a large dragon-like Gwythaint sinking his talons into a young boy and then flying away, even Roy Disney, who had previously been tacitly accepting about the use of violence in the film, had to admit that it needed re-editing (Stewart 68).

Among the scenes cut from the film were, a scene involving a "Cauldron Born" ghoul killing a person by slicing his neck and torso, a scene involving Taran wielding a magic sword and slaying his foes while he escapes the Horned King's castle, and a scene with Princess Eilonwy partially nude as fabric is ripped from her dress while she is hanging by her hands. Although removing these scenes prevented the film from receiving either a PG-13 or R rating, the editing process left the film with mismatched scenes and dropped music and dialogue cues. While Katzenberg took a hands-on approach to editing *The Black Cauldron*, at times actually cutting the film himself, he had little to no knowledge of animated film (Stewart 69, Masters 213). Unlike the feature films that he had produced in the past, animated film created no extra footage, and had no overlap between scenes. The cuts ordered by Katzenberg created strange gaps in the action, and did little to assist viewers in making the plot more intelligible. But this was just another symptom of Disney's underlying problem of allowing the film to rest in too many hands.

The lack of direction, along with a strong use of violence to attract new audiences, is evidenced by the trailer for the film.[4] The trailer stresses the darker aspects of the movie while saying little about the actual plot. Disney's marketing department chose to focus on the gruesome appearance of the villain of the film, the Horned King, featuring a slow pan of his skeletal face looming over a fire spewing cauldron. It is also clear that Disney wanted to market the film as a sword and sorcery fantasy as the trailer also features several shots of Taran raising his sword in battle, against numerous shadowy foes.

Although there is no mention of Prydain's link to Wales, or to the Welsh mythology in the film's introduction, the narrator lets the viewer know that there exists in Prydain a Black Cauldron, formed from the remains of a King "so cruel and so evil that even the Gods feared him," and that the cauldron had the power to "resurrect an army of deathless warriors, and with them, rule the world." The film then opens to focus on Dallben's small hut in the middle of a peaceful glade. Before the viewer even learns his name, Dallben lets it be known that there is "something wrong," and that the Horned King must be up to something.

Taran, a young boy of medium height and reddish-brown hair, is introduced to the viewer as a dreamer, staring wistfully from Dallben's window, and ignoring a burning pot on the stove. Broken from his stupor by Dallben, Taran expresses his desire to fight in a "war" that is left unexplained to the viewer. As in the novel, Taran is the Assistant Pig-Keeper of Hen Wen, but although Dallben mentions that the pig is special, Taran does not know her history. While washing Hen Wen in the yard, Taran begins to daydream and prances about the mud swinging a stick and challenging the farm animals, a goat standing in for the Horned King. After Hen Wen suddenly becomes agitated, Dallben then uses the pig to show him images of the Horned King searching for the Black Cauldron on the surface of the water in a large bowl. Dallben lets Taran know that the Horned King is searching for Hen Wen, so that he too might learn the location of the Cauldron, and that Taran must protect the pig and take her to a cottage at the edge of the forbidden forest.

Taran and Hen Wen make their way through the forest, but the boy soon falls prey to daydreams once again and Hen Wen runs off leaving Taran alone in a shadowed and gloomy section of the forest. Here Taran runs into Gurgi, a cross between a terrier and a gremlin, who immediately refers to Taran as "master" and basically serves as comic relief. Gurgi in tow, Taran finds Hen Wen, only to see her grabbed by one of the gwythaints and taken away. Taran watches the winged creatures take the pig to the Horned King's castle, now suddenly within view, and as he decides to rescue her, images of live-action storm clouds are superimposed over the animation, adding to the otherworldly feel of the scene. As with the transitions in previous scenes, the shift between a peaceful glade to a rock-covered wasteland is made far too quickly, detracting from any sense that Prydain might represent a real place, or that distance and location follow any kind of logic at all. Here the viewer sees additional evidence of the lack of coherent scene progression or continuity that plagues the entire film.

After making his way into the castle, Taran witnesses a hall filled with comical living warriors and a small, goblin-like creature named Creeper capering about the floor for scraps of food. The break between this scene, typical of Disney villain buffoonery, and the image of the Horned King is startling, and the appearance of his monstrous form seems jarring and out of place. It is almost as if *The Black Cauldron* is a combination of two completely different films: one a standard Disney adventure, and the other a darker, more violent fantasy. As the Horned King takes to his skull-lined throne, Hen Wen is led in bound by chains. After being captured by the King's soldiers, Taran must choose between forcing Hen Wen to reveal the location of the Cauldron, or watching the pig die. After being shown a pig-sized guillotine stained with blood, Taran finally decides to let the King have his way. But while the King is momentarily distracted Taran is able to free Hen Wen and deliver her to safety. Furious over the pig's escape, the Horned King throws Taran into the dungeon where he is left to wallow in self-pity.

Taran is eventually rescued by the Princess Eilonwy and as Taran and Eilonwy make their way through the secret underground passages of the castle, they stumble into the burial chamber of the castle's previous owner. Upon noticing a dusty sword held tight in the corpse's hands, Taran pries it loose and discovers that when removed from its scabbard it glows with a magical aura. As soon as Taran unsheathes his glowing sword his mood changes and he is lighthearted and jubilant as the sword moves of its own accord, slicing through his foes. Although it is understandable that Taran would be happy to be living out his fantasies, and this scene from the film does mirror the earlier scenes of Taran's daydreams, there is something a little too eager about Taran's stabbing and slicing here. The widening of Taran's eyes, his rapid breathing, and his almost manic actions create a disturbing undercurrent that is only heightened by his sword's ability to cut through stone as Taran lays waste to the entire castle. In *The Violence Mythos*, Barbara Whitmer suggests that myth often serves as a justification for violent acts and here Taran's overzealous performance with a real sword mirrors Whitmer's idea that "the discourse of the use of violence may be justified by appeal to myth rather than ideology as a justification for future violent behavior" (Whitmer 75). Both Taran and Disney use the mythological basis of the story to excuse Taran's joy found in the violence of swordplay even though there is little reason in the film to see him as a mythical figure.

Taran, Eilonwy, and Gurgi escape the Horned King, find — and then transport home — Hen Wen, and with the help of Doli, one of the "Fair Folk," learn the location of the Black Cauldron. Here the story takes another improbable turn. Rather than return to the safety of Dallben's grove where presumably there might be someone a little more qualified to retrieve the Cauldron, Taran decides to find it himself so that he might destroy it and thereby stop the Horned King's conquest. Again the viewer is reminded of those fighting the Horned King — and those heroes involved in the "war" are never mentioned. The viewer is left wondering just who inhabits the world of Prydain.

Taran and his band make their way to Morva where they find the Cauldron is guarded by three witches. The witches tell Taran that he must bargain for the Cauldron and Taran is forced to reluctantly give up his sword. The witches then let Taran know that the only way to stop the power of the Cauldron is to sacrifice the life of a living being. Before the group can decide what to do, the Horned King's men catch up with them and take them and the Cauldron back to his castle where they are forced to watch as the Horned King places the skeletal remains of a fallen soldier into the Cauldron, now dripping with blood. The corpse slowly returns to life as pale green smoke issues from the Cauldron, animating the other corpses around it.

While watching this scene the viewer can readily tell through the mismatched audio cues and the rough, obvious, visual changes that this was where Katzenberg did most of his editing. Although there remains footage of reanimated dead, the original footage was said to be much worse. The two minutes missing from this scene help to minimize the amount of violence witnessed by young viewers, but it also, presumably, lessens the meaning behind the animated dead and the necessity of stopping them. What could not be edited away is the demise of the Horned King. After Gurgi sacrifices himself to the Cauldron so that it might be stopped, the smoke from the Cauldron returns to it and the draw is so powerful that the Horned King is pulled inside. The viewer watches as the King's skin and flesh are stripped from his bones. The King's skeleton then explodes and the Cauldron pulls the castle, the soldiers, and the gwythaints down into the ground with it.

This scene contains some of the most gruesome images ever to be shown in a Disney animated film. Far more disturbing than the death of the fawn's mother in *Bambi* (1941), or the death of Simba's father in *The Lion King* (1994), the rending of the Horned King's flesh and the animation of skeletal corpses would seem to be far more typical of a movie receiving a PG-13 rating.[5] The main problem with Disney's use of violence in this film however, is that as an animated feature, the violence might be experienced by children as more intense than the violence of a live-action film.

In his work on animation, Paul Wells states that "in *literalizing* the tale in a *non-literal* image vocabulary, the deep-seated expressivity of the form connects much more viscerally with powerful emotions in the child, as well as in the adult" (Wells, "Thou Art Translated," 208).[6] With *The Black Cauldron*, the violence on screen is heightened by the unique effects of animation. Wells argues that by virtue of its ability to translate the feeling of violence more vividly than live-action, animation is able to have a greater impact on the mind of the viewer. Despite the manipulation of the earlier version of this film, Katzenberg and Hale present scenes whose effect on the viewer are not only negative, but are also so jarring that they actively work against the presentation of a cohesive narrative.

Still in shock over the death of Gurgi, Taran and his band escape and in typical Disney fashion the three witches of Morva appear and offer to give Taran one wish in exchange for the return of the Cauldron. When Taran is told he must choose between his sword and Gurgi, he chooses the life of his friend, but he, and more importantly the viewer, doesn't seem to learn anything from the choice. With Gurgi's resurrection there is more a feeling of equilibrium being maintained than of a lesson learned. And what exactly has Taran learned? The Horned King has been defeated, but not due to any particular effort on Taran's part. He has given away his sword, but there is no feeling here that he has learned that some things are more important than being a hero. In fact, it isn't apparent that Taran has learned anything at all. In the end, *The Black Cauldron* is little more than an exercise in fantasy.

As one can tell from the description of the film above, Disney's version of Alexander's work bears little resemblance to his actual novels. Instead the film becomes something of a greatest-hits package of action related scenes paired with just enough character introductions so that the viewer won't be too confused. Hale needed a frightening villain so he chose the Horned King; he needed a possible love interest so he kept Eilonwy. Add some soldiers, some action scenes, and a magical sword and you're done. The problem is that Alexander's work does not exactly fit the pattern of a typical sword-and-sorcery epic. The Chronicles of Prydain are about Taran's journey into manhood, his struggle to overcome his pride, and his search for identity. There are some places where the filmic Taran equals his written counterpart, such as when he is forced to swallow his pride and apologize to Eilonwy after they have a fight, but these moments are too infrequent and Taran remains an underdeveloped character.

As with the protagonists from many children's novels, from the earliest pages in *The Book of Three* Taran is given little physical description. This allows a wide variety of readers to see themselves in the place of the hero, and immerse themselves more readily into the world of the novel. The dialogue in the novel does a far better job than the film of filling out Taran's character.[7] We learn in the first two books of the series that Taran does not know who his parents are, or anything about his past. We see Taran's desire for an identity, a story, and a family in his insistence on becoming more than simply Assistant Pig-Keeper. Throughout the first two novels, Taran is given a number of possible role-models to learn from and to emulate who do not appear in the film. Coll, the blacksmith, shows Taran that even the most unlikely of people can be heroes; Prince Gwydion, war-leader of King Math, teaches him the difference between the warrior of his fantasies and the reality of battle; and Adaon, the bard, shows Taran that "there is greater honor in a field well plowed than in a field steeped in blood" (Alexander, *The Black Cauldron*, 27). Taran is also given a foil in the form of the overly proud and stubborn Prince Ellidyr so that he might know how not to behave. Without these characters Taran's own character remains undefined, his quest loses purpose, and unlike in previous Disney films, the audience learns little or nothing about their own ability to make their way through life. For example, in *The Fox and the Hound* (1981), the last Disney animated film released before *The Black Cauldron*, the viewers learn the damaging effects of prejudice and the meaning of true friendship.[8] One wonders what the viewer learns after watching *The Black Cauldron*.

Perhaps the difficulties involved with adapting Alexander's work for the big screen can best be explained by the words of George Bluestone, author of *Novels into Film*:

> What happens, therefore, when the filmist undertakes the adaptation of a novel, given the inevitable mutation, is that he does not convert the novel at all. What he adapts is a kind of paraphrase of the novel — the novel viewed as raw material. He looks not to the organic novel, whose language is inseparable from its theme, but to characters and incidents which have somehow detached themselves from language and, like the heroes of folk legends, have achieved a mythic life of their own [61–2].

Scholarship on text-to-film adaptations stresses the importance of preserving the characters from the text as closely as possible for viewers already familiar with the written work.[9] Animation allows for a film to not only maintain the aspects of the characters most familiar to the readers of the source text, but also to create a more vivid world within which they may exist. Wells, arguing that animation is particularly suited to translating the worlds found in children's literature, states that animation "engages with the *imagist* agenda within literary texts, stimulating not merely the resemblance of forms but propositional outcomes," (Wells 200), and defines the term "propositional images" as those images that one sees with the mind's eye. Wells and other scholars of animation believe that because of its ability to present mutable, fluid images on screen, animation is uniquely capable of recreating the "mental visualizations of images suggested by literary forms" (Wells 201).

The animation of *The Black Cauldron*, like *The Sword in the Stone* before it, should have been the perfect medium to translate Alexander's work, but what Hale and Disney failed to do with the film version of the novel was to imbibe the characters with a "life of their own." As James Griffith suggests of adaptations, "As with style, though, the real issue remains quality, not quantity.

If a film lacks certain events or characters, it becomes more or less a serious problem" (Griffith 67). Indeed, what is most lacking in the film is Taran himself. Alexander's novels, albeit light on physical description, present Taran as someone who the reader might be able to sympathize, or to identify, with. In the film, Taran is left incomplete; gone is the possibility offered by the books that Taran is a real boy.

In the novel, Taran is repeatedly called upon to make sacrifices. On several occasions he finds it necessary to overcome his anger and his pride in the name of the greater good. Several times Taran finds himself forced to restrain himself in the face of Ellidyr's overwhelming greed for fame, and in doing so Taran is able to choose a different path. This, in part, helps to define his character. *The Book of Three*, *The Black Cauldron*, and each of Alexander's successive three novels are about the journey Taran must make towards manhood, and about decisions he must make about the type of man he will become. Children's literature scholars such as A. Waller Hastings suggest that the simplification by Disney of the themes and ideas of children's literature in favor of a "Manichean world of moral absolutes" (85) is endemic to their animated films and part of an overall trend of simplifying American culture. In *The Black Cauldron*, Disney fails even to present a simplified version of a moral code, leaving Taran a character of simple experience.

While Alexander might not have seen all of the connections between Taran and figures from the *Mabinogi*, Donna R. White traces elements of his character to numerous characters from Four Branches including: Pwyll, Prince of Dyfed, whose "maturity and wisdom grows throughout the first branch"; Pryderi, Pwyll's son; and even Lleu Llaw Gyffes, whose relationship with Gwydion matches the paternal concern Dallben finds for Taran (103–4). The two themes linking each of these characters to Taran are the idea that each man or boy must overcome pride in order to learn humility, and that each character also must struggle to find his identity. The film lacks these connections, not only between Taran's lack of knowledge and the lessons learned by his Welsh counterparts, but also between the filmic Taran's lack of familial connection or concern and the paternal figures found for each of his Welsh cousins. Without having learned the lesson of humility, Disney's Taran—and the film itself—bears only surface resemblance to the Welsh legends that inspired Alexander to first create the character.

The Horned King is another instance where the lines between myth and fiction are blurred. Alexander bases his version of the Horned King on Gwyn the Hunter, or Gwyn ap Nudd, sometimes mentioned in the First Branch of the *Mabinogi* as the king of Annwn (Sullivan 62). Alexander separates Gwyn into two distinct entities: the Horned King, leader of Arawn's armies; and Arawn, king of Annwn and principle enemy of Gwydion and all of Prydain. In this way the Horned King stands as a parallel to Gwydion in his status as war leader. The Horned King of the Alexander's novel exists as a preliminary challenge that Gwydion must defeat without closing the door to a larger danger later. By failing to mention the existence of Arawn, or even Annwn, the movie leaves the Horned King's purpose vague and undefined. The viewer is never sure who the villain is fighting, or even who stands to oppose him. This detracts from his stance as a villain in the film and unlike in previous Disney films, the viewer is left wondering what relationship, if any, exists between the Horned King and Taran.

While Alexander is fairly faithful to the Second Branch of the *Mabinogi* with his use of the Black Cauldron in his second book of the series, the film misses the point (Sullivan 57). In the *Mabinogi* it is Efnisien, an otherwise self-centered and offensive character, who sacrifices himself so that the Cauldron might be destroyed. This character is matched by Ellidyr in Alexander's work. Both characters sacrifice themselves as part of a redemption, and both characters end their lives knowing that their sacrifice will make up for any wrongdoing in their past. This sacrifice represents what René Girard sees in *Violence and the Sacred* as the need for myth to establish a pattern of sacrifice divorced from the origin of its need, in order to obviate the violent conflict between two parties. Girard states that primitive religion and myth use sacrifice as a way of directing "violent impulses as a defensive force against those forms of violence that society regards as inadmissible" (20). Although it might sound reductive, Alexander uses the sacrifice of Ellidyr as a way of avoiding an eventual confrontation between him and Taran, and also as a way of avoiding any direct confrontation between Taran's band and Arawn's armies. While Alexander uses the legend of the Cauldron to remove the need for violent battle and to show Taran's growth as a character, Disney uses the destruction of the Cauldron only as temporary way of thwarting The Horned King. With the true nature of Ellidyr's sacrifice missing, the Cauldron becomes nothing more than a contrived plot device.

As the film veers from Alexander's work, and from the *Mabinogi*, it also veers from a purposeful use of violence. While the film version of *The Black Cauldron* doesn't shy away from scenes of violence and images of death, Alexander goes out of his way to avoid exposing his readers to the end of life. Throughout the first two novels of the Prydain series, Taran is purposefully kept out of battle and the suspense and drama in the work comes instead from a few key scenes where Taran realizes that he is not capable of standing up to Arawn's men. The few battle scenes that are described in the novels only help to underscore the tragedy of the loss of life — as when Adaon dies at the hands of one of Arawn's huntsmen — or to help show the dangers of growing up too soon.

Disney's *The Black Cauldron*, although a financial failure, is an important artifact for those seeking to study the ways in which Welsh mythology has been presented in popular culture, and for those seeking to study the ways in which the violence inherent in the myth has been dealt with by those wishing to present these stories to a mass audience. If the film is a failure of adaptation, it still serves as lesson for future animators, and as the study of film adaptation continues to expand its research of the capabilities animation brings to the genre, it becomes more important to understand the way that filmmakers choose to use the medium to bring text to life. Disney still owns the rights to Alexander's work and perhaps, in time, they will try again to bring the world of Prydain to life so that avid young readers might get to experience the thrill of seeing their heroes achieve a new level of reality.

Notes

1. *The Black Cauldron*. Dirs. Ted Berman and Richard Rich, Disney, 1985. All subsequent references are made to the DVD release of the film: *The Black Cauldron*, Dirs. Ted Berman and Richard Rich, 1985, DVD, Buena Vista Home Entertainment, 2000.
2. Disney's film is an adaptation of T. H. White's *The Once and Future King* (New York: G. P. Putnam's Sons, 1965).
3. Kim Masters also writes about Katzenberg's disastrous involvement with *The Black Cauldron* in *Keys to the Kingdom: The Rise of Michael Eisner and the Fall of Everybody Else* (New York: Harper Collins, 2001). 212–13.
4. The trailer referred to here was released as part of the special features of the DVD release of the film in 2000.
5. Although the PG-13 rating had been around for a single year, the purpose of the new rating was to protect children from a level of violence more appropriate for older audiences. In particular, these scenes are comparable to those from *Indiana Jones and the Temple of Doom* (1984) that helped convince the MPAA that the PG-13 rating was necessary. For a discussion of the MPAA's decision to create the PG-13 rating see: *A New Pot of Gold: Hollywood under the Electronic Rainbow, 1980–1989* (Berkeley: University of California Press, 2000)
6. See also Paul Wells, *Understanding Animation* (New York: Routledge, 1998).
7. See Taran's reflection at the end of *The Book of Three* for example, 185–6.
8. See Richard Corliss, "Cinema: The New Generation Comes of Age." *Time* July 1981.
9. See Bluestone, Griffith, and Jack Boozer, *Authorship in Film Adaptation* (Austin: University of Texas Press, 2008) 7–9.

Works Cited

Alexander, Lloyd. *The Black Cauldron*. 1965. New York: Henry Holt & Co., 1999.
_____. *The Book of Three*. 1964. New York: Henry Holt & Co., 1999.
The Black Cauldron. Dirs. Ted Berman and Richard Rich, 1985, DVD, Buena Vista Home Entertainment, 2000.
Bluestone, George. *Novels into Film*. Berkeley: University of California Press, 1957.
The Fox and the Hound. Dirs. Ted Berman, Richard Rich, and Art Stevens, 1981.
Girard, René. *Violence and the Sacred*. Baltimore: Johns Hopkins University Press, 1972.
Griffith, James. *Adaptations as Imitations: Films from Novels*. Newark: University of Delaware Press, 1997.
Hastings, A. Walter. "Moral Simplification in Disney's *The Little Mermaid*." *The Lion and the Unicorn* #17 (1993).

Masters, Kim. *Keys to the Kingdom: The Rise of Michael Eisner and the Fall of Everybody Else*. New York: Harper Collins, 2001.
Sito, Tom. *Drawing the Line: The Untold Story of the Animation Unions from Bosko to Bart Simpson*. Lexington: University Press of Kentucky, 2006.
Stewart, James B. *Disney War*. New York: Simon and Schuster, 2005.
Sullivan, C. W., III. *Welsh Celtic Myth in Modern Fantasy*. Westport, CT: Greenwood Press, 1989.
The Sword in the Stone. Dir. Wolfgang Reitherman, 1963, DVD, Buena Vista Home Entertainment, 2001.
White, Donna R. *A Century of Welsh Myth in Children's Literature*. Westport, CT: Greenwood Press, 1998.
White, T. H. *The Once and Future King*. New York: G. P. Putnam, 1965.
Whitmer, Barbara. *The Violence Mythos*. New York: State University of New York Press, 1997.
Wells, Paul. "'Thou Art Translated' Analysing Animated Adaptation," *Adaptations From Text to Screen, Screen to Text*. New York: Routledge, 1999.
_____. *Understanding Animation*. New York: Routledge, 1998.

We're Not in Cymru Anymore
What's Really Happening in the Online Mabinogi

CLAY KINCHEN SMITH

When we enter the world of the online game *Mabinogi*, we are like Dorothy when she enters the Land of Oz — amazed and bewildered by the discrepancies between our expectations and experiences with these worlds. Like Dorothy, we try to understand this new world in which we find ourselves — in this case a Korean MMORPG (Massively Multiplayer Online Role-Playing Game) named for the Welsh literary classic the *Mabinogi*, but presented as an anime-themed Ireland.[1] Nothing uniquely Welsh or relating to the *Mabinogi* greets us when we enter or explore this world. These discrepancies, we realize quickly, between our expectations (based on the game's title) and our experiences (based on actual gameplay) are significant. But what do they mean? Why are they here? Are they merely the products of misappropriation? The answers to these and similar questions come only through our understanding of this game's relation to its literary referent and to the larger issues that this and similar games elicit. The one thing that we do know is that we're not in Cymru anymore.

If we are not in Cymru, then where are we? Judging from the game's place names, we would have to say Ireland. In fact, the game defines the game world as "The World of Erinn" — a surprising identity since this game is named *Mabinogi*. A survey of places reveals that this game is replete with locations sporting Irish (or quasi–Irish) names.[2] The larger and more complete of the game's two continents is named Uladh (Ulster); it hosts several locations named for Irish place names. For example, the game locates Sen Mag Plateau in central Uladh; it further defines this plateau as the site of the battle between the Parthalon and Fomors, but then contextualizes that plain as an almost barren landscape with stunted grasslands struggling to recover and inhabited by numerous kinds of bears, mostly grizzlies (more on this aspect of inhabitants later). As those familiar with Irish geography and history can easily attest, these names are Irish, not Welsh: *Sen Mag* can be rendered *Shan Mag, Shan Maigh*, or *Sean Maigh, Uladh* is Ulster — all famous places of Ireland; the *Parthalon* and *Fomor* are two of the ancient, mythic peoples of Ireland. Similar sorts of appropriation of Irish identity occur throughout Uladh with such definitive Irish place names as *Emain Macha* and *Tir Chonaill*. The game even includes *Tir Na Nog*: instead of being the traditional paradise, it is overrun with savage animals and zombies — the very antithesis of *Tir Na Nog* and certainly not Annwn (which does not occur as a place name anywhere in the game). In such a landscape, we have Celtic and Gaelic (even proto–Celtic and proto–Gaelic) Irish people and place names, but no Welsh ones. Such misappropriation of Irish names under a Welsh title erases any connections between the game's world and that of the *Mabinogi*; moreover, it conflates the differences between Irish and Welsh cultures and languages. Cymru, in one shape or another, does not appear in this world.

If the landscape is predominately Irish, then shouldn't we also expect the people who inhabit this game world to be predominately Irish? Apparently so. While almost all non-player characters (or NPCs) have generic Celtic names, like Sion (Sean), Dougal, and Bebhinn, the game defines all its players and their player characters (PCs) as Milesians, the group who defeated the Tuatha Dé Danann in Irish legend. Although it does not require players to *celticize* their player names or character design (e.g., they can choose from a range of racial attributes and other design options), the game clearly defines them as Irish; in other words, players and their PCs are Irish by definition. Even the days of the week in this game have Irish — not Welsh — names. Consequently, players retain an Irish identity (despite their unique names and character designs) and (re)create in an Irish world (despite its nominal Welsh title).

As if such erasures of Welsh identity were not enough, the game invokes the Irish pantheon when creating its primary NPCs. Morrighan, Macha, Neamhain appear as goddesses with essentially their original functions. Lugh Lamhfhata is The Knight of Light, a legendary warrior who defeated the Fomors at the Battle of Mag Tuireadth. Cichol is the god of the Fomors (and the game's main antagonist). And Nuadha is a god who functions as the game's final boss while sporting his iconic silver arm. All of these NPCs retain their Irish names and, to varying degrees, their functions in Irish mythology. Neamhain appears as the Goddess of Light and Nuadha's spouse; Morrighan and Macha retain their original functions as the goddess of War and Vengeance and the Goddess of Destruction. In addition, supporting material like the game's official wiki defines these NPCs as Irish: "Morrighan is a Goddess of Erinn and is a friend of Nao. She is known as the 'Goddess of War and Vengeance' and is also referred to as 'The Goddess'" ("Morrighan"). In *Mabinogi*, Irish deities rule an Irish land and its Irish population. Noticeably absent are Welsh figures like Arawn, Branwen, and Ceridwen, or any of the members of the *Plant Dôn* or *Plant Llŷr*.

As if such absences were insufficient, the game represents the world of *Mabinogi* through an anime-themed design. Everywhere we look or go, we see generic, medieval figures indistinguishable from similar figures found in other online RPGs (role playing games) and even from other anime. This ubiquity is perhaps best illustrated by the NPCs' visual design. For example, the official *Mabinogi* website's video tutorials are hosted by two iconic *Mabinogi* NPCs, "Lorna, the adorable heroine, and Pan, her wisecracking pet sheep" as the official website's guide defines them (Guide).[3] These characters would easily fit into virtually any anime-themed media. We see the extent of such erasure in figure of Nao, the NPC goddess who shepherds players through their initial play and who has become the other iconic face for the game.

Similarly, the design for an icon like Morrighan is generic: while she sports black wings as an analog of her original divinity, such features are common throughout anime-themed media. The game's design combines anime and certain elements of a generic "Celtic" identity to create a hybrid anime–"Celtic" design for this world. Given that these characters are iconic for this game, we can see that this game resembles the *Mabinogi* only at some tangential level — a point underscored by the many *lolicon* images (a Japanese term describing eroticized images of young girls, or a "Lolita complex") like the one posted on the game's official wiki welcome page.

As these examples illustrate, the world in *Mabinogi* is not the world of the *Mabinogi*. This disjuncture is further emphasized by the absence of the text's iconic figures, like Pwyll, Manawydan, Rhiannon, Pryderi, Cigfa, Branwen, Gwydion, or Blodeuwedd. Similarly, the game contains no incidents from the *Mabinogi* like Goewin's rape and consequential cursing of Gwydion and Gilfaethwy, the mutilation of Matholwch's horses, or Bendigeidfran's beheading; it also contains no places from the *Mabinogi* or Welsh culture like Annwn or Dyfed. Absent as well are the games featured in the text like "Badger in the Bag."[4] Moreover, this world lacks even figures from other associated Welsh tales like Ceridwen or Taliesin and event like the shapeshifting duel between Gwion Bach and Ceridwen. In short, the game *Mabinogi* has none of the *Mabinogi* in it.[5]

At this point, we may very well ask ourselves: What is going on here? We have a game with a Welsh name, but nothing Welsh in it — an anime world featuring a generic "Celtic" cast and with no *Mabinogi* in it. As we have noted before, the disjuncture between the game's nominal and actual identities is disconcerting. However, it also points to a larger set of issues, a set that might help us reconcile (or at least understand) the disjuncture between our expectations based on the game's titular referent and our experiences with the game's Irish anime world.

If we turn for answers to scholarship on *Mabinogi* the game, we quickly realize that nothing substantial exists. We find nothing as sophisticated as examinations of the text's postcolonialism or its body politics and sexualities by scholars like Ingham, Kay, Millersdaughter, or Sheehan. What we do find are only a few academic articles that include the game as examples to illustrate their broad categorical examinations of game economics or game behaviors.[6] However, we can find a viable model in Umberto Eco's work on neomedievalism.

As Eco defines it, neomedievalism is an essential force in the plot fostering a "new feudalism," what he defines as the consumerism that seeks a corporate takeover of all economic systems. The neomedieval ultimately appropriates anything that will help sell its products and the ideology that accompanies them: for example, Eco argues that the sorts of mashups that we see in games like *Mabinogi, MapleStory*, and others are aspects of the same homogenization that produces what he ironically calls the "messed up" system written in "the Latin of the Gospel according to St. Luke Skywalker"— the blending of unrelated elements into a seamless (re)presentation (Eco 68, 61). As I say elsewhere, "This new feudalism would literally and figuratively remake the world into a transnational system of gated communities—fiefdoms overseen by new feudal 'lords' from their 'post modern neomedieval Manhattan new castles,' to use Eco's terms (62)" (Smith). Neomedievalism plays a key role in this remaking of the world because it provides a veneer concealing how online role playing games, for example, require players to operate within a production economy while they think they are escaping such an economy; in other words, such games redefine escape as exploitation.

Using Eco's model, we can begin to reconcile the game's apparent discrepancies like its Irish content, its Welsh name, and its anime design. The mashup that is *Mabinogi*-the-game represents precisely the sorts of misappropriation and consumerism that is neomedievalism. Starting with an issue like the names of the days used in this game, we begin to see how this game *and* its players and designers conflate Welsh and Irish identities into a pan–Celtism. Sources like Wikipedia, for example, provide a telling example of such conflation: "Weekday names used in-game reflect the Celtic mythology that the game evokes. In *Mabinogi*, actual days of the week represent seasons and are named for the traditional Welsh and Irish quarter days and cross-quarter days" ("Mabinogi (video game)"). However, a review of "the traditional Welsh and Irish quarter days and cross-quarter days" reveals that they are named differently in each language.[7] Such conflations erase the differences between Irish and Welsh language and culture and promote misperceptions like a pan–Celtic identity—despite the specificity of the game's Welsh title. Moreover, the authority carried by such official sources reflects and promotes misperceptions about the game (and consequently Celtic identities).

While conflation of Welsh and Irish names for days might seem minor, it indicates the larger issue of conflation and erasure determining much of the game's identity; it also indicates the larger misperceptions about such conflations and erasures evidenced by comments from sources like *Mabinogi* fans and reviewers. With one exception, all comments by fans define the game in terms similar to this quote: "Mabi's story, and many, many other aspects of the game, are references to pieces of Celtic mythology, namely from the 'Mabinogian,' [sic] the game's namesake and the four most well-known stories from Celtic mythology" (Funkymonkey654).[8] As such sources demonstrate, questions about the discrepancy between the game's title and its contents—and even its very identity—are subsumed by generalizations and conflations. Not surprisingly, media reviews of the game echo such misperceptions and usually in the same tone and with the similar language.[9] For example, IGN.com defines the game this way: "Mabinogi is a world that combines many elements of Celtic and Welsh mythology as the backdrop for a highly social play experience that emphasizes character skill development instead of linear class progressions" (Butts). One review succinctly reduces the game and any referents this way: "The universe revolves around Mabinogion, which is Celtic Mythology" (Forum). As with the comments by fans, only one review identifies the disjuncture between the game's nominal and actual identities: "Mabinogi brings a 3D world inspired from the Celtic and Welsh mythology—that's where the name comes from, the Mabinogi being a collection of prose stories from medieval Welsh manuscripts, although it seems that the game actually has little to do, in terms of gameplay, with Mabinogion itself" (Ciabai). Given the overwhelming conflation and erasure of such distinctions in the majority of reviews, we can see how a game with a Welsh name can have Irish content and an anime theme; in other words, we can see how the neomedieval works to deny specificity and identity and thereby promotes misperceptions about such factors.

Similar sorts of misperceptions are echoed by the game's official corporate sources. For example, a 2008 Nexon press release defines the game this way: "Dazzling 3-D graphics boast an art style based in Celtic and Welsh mythology, which also gives Mabinogi its name and foundation" (quoted in "Nexon America..."). In their published interviews, Nexon and devCat officials answer questions about the game's "Celtic" origins by promoting the game as a whole.[10] In short, almost none of the game's fans, reviewers, and designers seem interested in the distinctions between Welsh and Irish cultures or literatures or the discrepancies between the game's name and its contents. For them, the "Celtic" world is a world of homogeneity; as such comments indicate, the specifics of identity are insignificant and easily renegotiable in the world of the neomedieval.

Such comments also indicate that the appearance of the neomedieval world is equally insignificant and renegotiable. In large part, that explains why *Mabinogi* has an anime design. Comments by devCat executives confirm that the game's overall design was an intentional decision to acquire Asian market share. In a 2007 interview, for example, devCat senior developer Eun-seok Lee identifies *Mabinogi*'s "cartoon rendering" as part of the company's strategy to attract Asian "target markets," in contrast to the realistic rendering used to attract Western markets in *Mabinogi Heroes*, the latest reiteration of *Mabinogi* (Lunaria, "This is Game"). Moreover, devCat designer Young-hwa Kang attributes her artistic influences to Japanese anime and the perception that this style is "in" (Lunaria, "Speaking of Drawing"). Such comments also inform the underlying consumerism driving neomedievalism.

This last factor is tellingly illustrated by the way in which the game redesigns non-player characters to address perceived market share. Notably absent from most editions of the game are non-white NPCs. Prior to the 2008 release of its North American version, devCat altered and added a half dozen or so NPCs. For example, it changed the healer Manus into a black male and the storeowner Bebhinn into a non-white, though ethnically unspecified female character. The game retains these NPCs' basic anime-"Celtic" identities. The game's other NPCs of color include the human inhabitants of Cor, a village located in a jungle setting replete with a large number of African animals (e.g., zebras, elephants, and hippos). Cor's human inhabitants appear as stylized Native Americans and include Kousai (the village chieftain), Kusina (the village tailor), Tupai (the animal tamer), and Waboka (the village's warrior guardian). Neither the human inhabitants of Cor nor the NPCs of color have any analogs in the Welsh text of the *Mabinogi*. They do, however, have analogs in the market forces driving neomedievalism.

Similar factors determine the way in which the game fetishizes its female NPCs. Here they are as likely to appear in cheesecake poses and conventional costumes found in fetishized images of women (e.g. "good girl art").[11] For example, the game's iconic figure Nao appears in a series of revealing costumes. As these last images indicate, *lolicon*- and *moe*-based[12] images abound in this game.[13] For example, succubae appear in various colors of a standard cosplay[14] outfit complete with garters and high heels; moreover, they lose pieces of their clothing when attacked by a PC. Notably the game's sole incubus does not lose clothing when attacked. Even PCs create similarly themed characters.

As we have noted earlier, *Mabinogi* the game doesn't resemble much in the *Mabinogi*. As such examples illustrate, *Mabinogi* promotes sexism and exploitation as part of its strategy to capture market share. Once again, we see how consumerism drives neomedievalism. Such factors explain why the non-human inhabitants of *Mabinogi* run the gamut of possibility. Role playing games define elements that are not NPCs or PCs with the generic term *monsters*. Monsters function as potential sources of skill points and items: usually monsters increase the PC's stats and/or drop items when slain by the PC. In that sense, they serve as a primary means for the PC's advancement in the game. Like other RPGs, *Mabinogi* has its share of *monsters*. As with other aspects of the game, these monsters are not related to anything in the *Mabinogi*; instead, they represent a maximization of potential interest from players.

The range of monsters in *Mabinogi* illustrates how neomedieval this game is. Among this game's humanoid monsters, we can find Kitty Knights (humanoids with oversized cat heads), gargoyles, mummies, and zombies (including one made of snow). Among its nonhumanoid monsters, we can find glowing pot bellied spiders, grizzly bears (including red, blue, black, and white ones), bison (including one made of ice), not to mention giant ant lions, aardvarks, mongooses, armadillos, gnus, dingoes, and capybaras (in various shapes, sizes, and colors, as well as equipped with attributes like spiked backs for aardvarks and ram's horns for gnus). And foxes, from Fennec to red, overrun many of the game's locations.

As these examples illustrate, this game has appropriated animals from a wide range of continents and monsters from a range of cultures and time periods—all part of neomedievalism's reiterative process. So far ranging is this appropriation, that we can find a Wendigos (from Algonquian culture), Ifrits (from Islamic culture), Balrogs and Wargs (from J.R.R. Tolkien's works), Bandersnatches (from Lewis Carroll's work), and even grendels (yes, plural grendels, but none like the single one from the Anglo-Saxon poem *Beowulf*) in this game.

As this brief survey indicates, this world is replete with monsters of a staggering variety and number, but no monsters that appear in the original *Mabinogi*. As with the lack of distinction between Welsh and Irish identity that dominated the game's landscape, characters, and even the players, players and reviewers are not bothered by this lack of correlation or the fact that the game's monsters are so eclectic. Moreover, the multiple recurrences of monsters like grendels further illustrate the game's departure from the source material alluded to in the title and the monsters from their original identities; they also illustrate how the game subsumes identity as a function of the game's economy. In other words, these monsters have been stripped of their substance and thereby reduced to a mere surface used to sell the game.

We can see the extent of such erasure when we look at how the game modifies the monsters it draws from Irish mythology; the game repeatedly modifies that source material to fit within its storyline. For example, Morrighan and Nuadha are married. Neamhain appears not as an aspect of battle frenzy but as the Goddess of Light; moreover, she, Morrighan and Macha appear as separate goddesses. Other standards of Irish mythology undergo similar redefinitions in this game. Fomorians are reduced to goblinesque creatures usually functioning as monsters that attack and are meant to be attacked, although the named NPC Fomorians (e.g. Geno) are helpful to player characters.

Other monsters with Irish origins and names occur in the game, but in redefined forms. For example, Glas Ghaibhleann is a multi-armed boss of the Generation 1 dungeon, not the famous cow owned by Gaibhnen, the blacksmith of the Tuatha Dé Danann in Irish legend.[15] Bearing the appropriated name of an Irish demon destroyed by St. Patrick, Cromm-Cruaich appears as a fierce dragon who is the boss of the third Generation dungeon. The

Mabinogi designers redefined the Irish elements that they incorporated into this game to fit their conceptions of the game's most effective design. Morrighan's sister goddess Neamhain is conflated with their sister Badhbh Cath, as the official *Mabinogi* wiki explains: "Badhbh Catha Neamhain is the third Goddess; The Goddess of Light, the Irinid. ... In Irish Mythology, Neamhain and Badhbh Cath are generally considered separate but similar deities. Badhbh Cath is the Goddess who governs confusion on the battlefield, while Neamhain is the Goddess of frenzied warfare" ("Neamhain"). In the mash-up that is neomedievalism, anything can happen (and often does) in the name of selling the game.

And the name of the game is selling. As we have noted, consumerism defines much of this game as it does much of the neomedieval element in contemporary popular culture. We can see how determinant consumerism is in *Mabinogi* when we examine essential aspects like PC identity and activity, despite claims that this game differs from other online role-playing games.

The standard online RPG game has players level up (advance in the game) by completing quests (predefined missions which increase the players' skills and enable players to acquire new items) or undertaking individual play (usually through the accumulation of items, points, or other commodifiable elements or through the acquisition of new skills).[16] *Mabinogi*, as the reviews and the game itself argue, eschews this system to some degree by enabling character development through *alternative* means: everything from composing and performing musical and literary pieces to pursing activities like fishing. For example, comments by Nexon President and CEO John H. Chi illustrate this aspect of the game: "Playing Mabinogi is about more than just fighting and normal MMO fare. This is a chance for gamers to live a fantasy life in a place where communities build mutual beliefs of family, friendship and hard work." (Quoted in "Nexon's Mabinogi ..."). But players can "build" more than "mutual beliefs of family, friendship and hard work"; they can "build" or buy everything from costumes to castles.[17]

And they do. Consumerism permeates every aspect of this game, as it does with other neomedieval games. For example, it redefines the game's special events into orgies of literal and figurative consumption. Special events like the Mystical Turkey Event (held around Thanksgiving) and the Cookie Wand Event involve consuming designated items in order to acquire certain skill boosts and to have the chance to win large amounts of Nexon cash (for the top *consumers*).[18] Moreover, such events are regularly scheduled as means of promoting the game's economy (in-game through the acquisition and redistribution of wealth, and extra-game through peripheral sales).

The extent to which such a consumerist economy permeates the game can be seen by the way that it redefines the game's claims to alterity. As we noted earlier, the game promotes alternative means of character development like musical and literary composition. However, the game also allows, and even encourages, sales of such items: players can post such compositions for purchase by other players; in this way a composition becomes a commodity. Such transactions lead to extra-game legal issues.[19] These transactions also lead to instances of hacking into the game to steal more than $300,000 worth of in-game currency and exploiting the game's glitches in order to amass large quantities of the in-game currency (tellingly known as the Gold Dupe Glitch).[20] These transactions lead to other practices like using bots and gold farmers to gain unfair economic advantages. Moreover, they define game play from the moment that a player creates a character.

Using the game's Style Studio function, players design their characters; predictably such designs have nothing to do with the world of the *Mabinogi* and everything to do with the world of consumerism. For example, players can have their PCs sport a variety of hairstyles (everything from pageboys and Ivy League cuts to "emos") and wear footwear from Trudy Moroccan boots and Japanese sandals to duck boots and pirate captain boots; and such possibilities are only the beginning. Not only can players customize everything from what their player character is carrying (say, a blue rose or a ukulele) to that PC's eye color (even carmine?), players can design an Elvin or giant character with a range of such fashion possibilities. Moreover, through a variety of means players are actively encouraged by the game to create and recreate such products of consumption.

Shops form one of the game's most prominent means for promoting consumerism. As we noted earlier, game play centers around acquisition and transaction within the game's economy. Players frequent shops within the game world; however, they also frequent shops in the extra-game world. The homepage prominently features its shop and makes it easily accessible through options within the game play. The game brands its homepage shop with the overloaded title of "The Premium Shop"; this shop features a wide range of possible items—from pets to profiles. Similar sorts of promotion occur on the other *Mabinogi* sites where players can buy many of the same items and are solicited to do so using similar means and messages. The world of the neomedieval is the world of consumerism, regardless of language, server, or audience.[21]

In our final analysis, what can we say? We have seen that *Mabinogi* the game has nothing to do with *The Mabinogi*, despite its name. We have also seen that virtually every aspect of this game represents Eco's theory of neomedievalism. And we have seen that with very few exceptions, no one really sees the extent to which such economic forces manifest in neomedievalism surround us and redefine what is unique about Welsh culture and the *Mabinogi*. This state of affairs leaves us with some clear choices. Ultimately, we can either watch the "new castles" of Eco's "postmodern neomedieval Manhattan" continue to rise around us, replacing the unique worlds of the *Mabinogi* and other sources, or we can try to rescue those worlds from the homogenizing consumerism that is neomedievalism. Unlike Dorothy, we cannot simply click our heels and return home.

Notes

1. Resources to orient readers unfamiliar with the game are: The official North American and Oceania site (http://mabinogi.nexon.net/) and the game's official wiki (http://wiki.mabinogiworld.com/index.php?title=Wiki_Home).
2. For a brief survey of this continent, its place names, and other aspects of this continent, please see the entry on devCat's official MMO site for "Uladh."
3. The official North American website's Guide page is located at http://mabinogi.nexon.net/Guide/LornaPan.aspx.
4. *Mabinogi* lacks the sorts of game play that Spangenberg identifies as crucial to understanding the *Mabinogi*.
5. The single exception to this list of absences is the presence of the name of Pwyll and Rhiannon's son, Pryderi: it occurs as Nao's last name, Nao Mariota Pryderi, but never with any explanation as to its origin; moreover, she is never referred to by it. In other words, it is an empty signifier.
6. See articles by Yoon and by Oh and Ryu.
7. See sources like Mabinogi.Nexon.net's entry for "Weekday Bonuses" in its Strategy Guide.
8. Forums like the one entitled "Mabinogi Anime Based or Celtic Based Argument" seem to promise an informed debate about the game's identity, but feature a binary argument that reduces the game's origin to either anime or Celtic mythology. Only one post on the Mabinogiguru.com site questions the game's conflation of Celtic and Gaelic identity under a Welsh name; see the comment by "Orestes" (04/01/2008) for this counterargument.
9. Mabinogi.wikia.com argues that the game was "inspired by Celtic mythology. The Welsh word mabinogi is found in the original manuscripts of the Mabinogi" ("Mabinogi" on Mabinogi.wikia.com http://mabinogi.wikia.com/wiki/Mabinogi). Similar arguments can be found in many media reviews, for example "It's a beautiful Cell shaded MMORPG based of the Celtic Mythology Mabinogion." ... "This is a fantasy MMORPG based on the Celtic mythology, Mabinogion" (Sait) and "Mabinogi is a brand-new fantasy MMORPG game for 2010 featuring a manga look and the Celtic Mabinogion mythos" (Mooky Chick). Intriguingly, *Variety*'s review argues that "The name 'Mabinogi' is drawn from Celtic mythology, but don't expect anything particularly Irish. This is your typical fantasy world, with fairies and villagers all blandly drawn in simple cheery graphics that would make it easy to mistake for kiddie fare" (Chick).
10. When asked how the game reconciled its Celtic base with its anime design, Ray Cheon, Product Manager and Sr. Associate for Game Planning & Design team of Nexon America, replied that "Developing the perfect look and feel for a game is always challenging and Mabinogi hit the target. It has a serene and smooth feel to it but at the same time, there's no problem finding a dark and edgy look in the monsters and dungeons. Our developers and art team really did an awesome job" (Funk, "Q&A..."). When asked about the introduction Celtic content/basis for the game, similarly the interviewee replied that: "Iria is focused more on the introduction of Elves and Giants into the game. However, the previously paid content that held much of the inspired mythology is now available to all players for free!" (Funk, "Mabinogi ...")
11. While many of these female NPCs could be defined as either *lolicon* or *moe*, the game lacks any instances of *shotacon* or *henati*.
12. *Moe* is a complex term referring (primarily) to female characters in Japanese anime or manga. Literally signifying "budding" or "blossoming," *moe* frequently indicates a female character who inspires a protective response in a male who is attracted to this character. It involves many character types.

13. Similar sorts of fetishization recur in *Mabinogi Heroes*, the latest spin off of *Mabinogi*. *Mabinogi Heroes*, the latest development of the original Nexon game, features more conventional animation and game play. Just as with *Mabinogi*, this game has little to do with Welsh culture or the *Mabinogi*, and much more to do with profit. Similar costuming and posing of female characters occurs throughout this site.

14. A term that means "costume play" and has been described as "performance art" in which people enact identities derived primarily from popular fictions of many genres (especially Japanese), including graphic novels, video games, fantasy movies, anime, and manga. These are generally non-rehearsed and non-staged role-playing experiences.

15. For further details on this boss, see the entry "Glas Ghaibhleann" on the Wiki.mabinogiworld.com site. Glas Ghaibhleann is known as *Glas Gavelen* on servers outside the one for North America and Oceania.

16. Most MMORPGs require players to acquire items through capture (e.g. attacking a monster and collecting any items dropped by that monster), crafting (e.g., making an item or purchasing an item crafted by another player or NPC), or direct purchase of items through game-sponsored stores (either in game as part of the game's narrative or through some combination of extra-game shop where players can outfit themselves through purchase of items). The first two means of acquiring items involve game play and usually some form of in-game currency (or exchange mechanism); the last does not, but does require players to purchase items using credits purchased using extra-game currency (e.g., dollars or *won* converted to Nexon cash). In other words, players use a combat-craft-cash mechanism for acquiring items through the in-game economy.

17. Property may be owned and developed through one of the game's two guild castles. About every eight weeks, guilds may enter an auction at which they can bid for the right to own and develop one of the guild castles. Once the winning guild pays the bid price, it begins to build its castle and develop the land around it by building houses which it can rent to players. Construction follows a tight schedule predetermined by the game; failure to meet those construction deadlines can lead to loss of the castle and its being put back on the market. The guildmaster sets the prices for rent, passes to the castle, and other administrative fees; given the profitability of such fees, the guild currently owning a castle has a distinct equity advantage over other guilds when the next bidding time arrives. And arrive it does: the castle deteriorates over its contracted period; when it has deteriorated to a certain level, a castle goes up for auction.

18. As in *Maplestory*, another of Nexon's games, game play is retailored to coincide with certain events. For example, around Thanksgiving the Mystical Turkey Event occurs. During this limited time period, players can collect and consume mystical turkeys—objects dropped randomly by monsters and hit objects (e.g., posts, trees).

19. Yoon's discussion of property rights and items (particular illustrated by items in *Mabinogi*) is very accessible and useful for understanding this issue. Oh and Ryu's article provides a very detailed analysis of the different types of items and games economies found in online gaming.

20. For a summary of this famous hacking incident, see "Boy hacker scams 36 mil yen for virtual dress" at for a summary of the Gold Dupe Glitch, see the postings on the game's official wiki for news, "Wiki Home/WikiUpdatesOld."

21. We can see the consistency of the game's look across the range of its servers and editions with a quick survey of the game's homepages. Although each server has its own homepage of the game tailored for its perceived market, each edition of the game retains a consistent anime–Celtic design. For example, the images of Morrighan and Neamhain on the Korean and North American sites are identical; similarly, the images of Nao, Lorna, and Pan on the European and Mainland Chinese sites are also identical. In contrast, the Japanese homepage emphasizes the game's anime nature, while the European site emphasizes a more "realistic" look and feel.

Works Cited

AnjelusX. "Mabinogi ~ Bored with Life? Well Why Not Try a Fantasy." 13 February 2008. http://www.curse.com/articles/mabinogi-en-reviews/28191.aspx. Online.
"Boy hacker scams 36 mil yen for virtual dress." Pinktentacle.com. Online.
Butts, Steve. "Mabinogi: Nexon's free-to-play fantasy MMO blends Celtic mythology and karate chickens. Who are you to resist?" 6 March 2008. IGN.com. Online.
Chick, Tom. "Mabinogi." Variety. Apr. 17, 2008. http://www.variety.com. Online.
Ciabai, Calin. "Mabinogi Gets Some Spirit: Celtic and Welsh mythology-inspired MMO gets goodies." Softpedia.com. 31 July 2008. http://news.softpedia.com. Online.
Eco, Umberto. "Dreaming of the Middle Ages." *Travels in Hyperreality*. Trans. William Weaver. San Diego, New York, London: Harcourt Brace Jovanovich, 1986. 61–72.
_____. "Living in the Middle Ages." *Travels in Hyperreality*. Trans. William Weaver. San Diego, New York, London: Harcourt Brace Jovanovich, 1986. 73–86.
Forum. 23 May 2008. AnimeExpo.org. http://www.anime expo.org. Online.
Funk, John. "Mabinogi: Pioneers of Iria Q&A." Warcry.com. 9 March 2009. http://www.warcry.com/articles/view/interviews/5830-Mabinogi-Pioneers-of-Iria-Q-A. Online.
_____. "Q&A With Mabinogi Designer." Warcry.com. 26 June 2008. http://www.warcry.com/articles/view/interviews/4997-Q-A-With-Mabinogi-Designer. Online.
Funkymonkey654. "Mabinogi — Fun for most, but has it's [sic] shortcomings." Game faqs.com. 1 March 2010. http://www.gamefaqs.com. Online.
"Glas Ghaibhleann." Wiki.mabinogiworld.com. Online.
"Goblin." Wiki.mabinogiworld.com. Online.
"Guide." Mabinogi.nexon.net. http://Mabinogi.nexon.net/Guide/LornaPan.aspx. Online.
Ingham, Patricia. "Marking Time: Branwen, Daughter of Llyr and the Colonial Refrain." *The Postcolonial Middle Ages.* Jeffrey Jerome Cohen, ed. NY: St. Martins Press, 2000. 173–92.
Kay, Morgan. "Gendered Postcolonial Discourse in the Mabinogi." *Proceedings of the Harvard Celtic Colloquium.* Vols., XXIV, 2004 and XXV, 2005. 216–28. Cambridge and London: Harvard UP, 2009.
Kim, Eun Joo, et al. "The relationship between online game addiction and aggression, self-control and narcissistic personality traits." *European Psychiatry* 23.3 (2008): 212–218. *Academic Search Complete.* EBSCO. Web. 18 Jan. 2010.
"KR: 11/10/2007 — ThisIsGame Interview." MabinogiWorld.com. Online.
Lunaria. "Speaking of Drawing — An Interview." Mabinogiworld.com. 16 February 2008. http://mabinogiworld.comOnline.
_____. "This is Game Interview." 9 November 2007. Mabinogiworld.com. Online.
"Mabinogi." Mabinogi.wikia.com. http://mabinogi.wikia.com/wiki/Mabinogi. Online.
"Mabinogi Interview-Part 1." RPGVault.IGN.com. 30 April 2008. http://rpgvault.ign.com/articles/870/870281p1.html. Online.
"Mabinogi Anime Based or Celtic Based Argument." 25 December 2007. Forum. nexon.net. Online.
"Mabinogi: Heroes Bikini Girls Have Arrived!" News.mmosite.com. Online.
"Mabinogi: Heroes Unveils Sexy Screenshots for Cute Mage Evy." News.mmosite.com. http://news.mmosite.com. Online.
Mabinogi.Nexon.net's Strategy Guide. Mabinogi.nexon.com. Online
"Mabinogi: the best MMORPG yet, and it's free to play!" 9 March 2009. Suidoo.com. http://www.squidoo.com/mabinogi. Online.
"Mabinogi (video game)." Wikipedia.org. Online.
Millersdaughter, Katherine. "The Geopolitics of Incest: Sex, Gender and Violence in the Fourth Branch of the Mabinogi' *Exemplaria* 14. (October 2002) pp. 271–272.

Mooky Chick. "Mabinogi: MMORPG." Mookychick.co.uk. Online.
"Morrighan." Mabinogiworld.com. Online.
"Nao." Mabinogiworld.com. http://wiki.mabinogiworld.com. Online.
"Neamhain." Wiki.mabinogiworld.com. Online.
"Nexon America Delivering Open Beta for Wildly-Successful Fantasy Role-Playing Game, Mabinogi." 3 March 2008. MCVUK.com. Online.
"Nexon's Mabinogi Coming to the US." 19 January 2008. Kotaku.com. Online.
Oh, Gyuhwan, and Taiyoung Ryu. "Game Design on Item-selling Based Payment Model in Korean Online Games." Proceedings of DiGRA 2007: Situated Play. Tokyo: The University of Tokyo, September, 2007. 650–657.
Parker, Will. *The Four Branches of the Mabinogi: Celtic Myth and Medieval Reality*. Dublin: Bardic Press, 2007.
Sait. "Mabinogi Review: Enjoy the Life." Mmosite.com. 27 June 2007. Online.
Sheehan, Sarah. "Matrilineal Subjects: Ambiguity, Bodies, and Metamorphosis in the Fourth Branch of the *Mabinogi*." *Signs: Journal of Women in Culture and Society* 2009, vol. 34, no. 2. 319–42.
Smith, Clay Kinchen. "The Name of the Game: Misuses of Neomedievalism in Computerized Role Playing Games." *The Medieval in Motion: Neomedievalism in Film, Television and Digital Games*. Eds. Carol L. Robinson and Pamela Clements. (Forthcoming).
Spangenberg, Lisa Luise. *The Games Fairies Play: Otherworld Intruders in Medieval Literary Narratives*. UC, Los Angeles. Dissertation. 2008. Online.
"Uladh." http://wiki.mabinogiworld.com. Online.
"Wiki Home/WikiUpdatesOld." Wiki.Mabinogiworld.com. Onine.
Yoon, Ung-gi. "South Korea and indirect reliance on IP law: real money trading in MMORPG items." *Journal of Intellectual Property Law & Practice* 3(3): 2008. 174–179.
Zergwatch, Samhain. Samhain Zergwatch's. Review. March 31 2008. www.mmorpg.com. Online.

Temporality, Teleology and the *Mabinogi* in the Twenty-First Century

AUDREY L. BECKER

The medieval text that we call the *Mabinogi* challenges its modern readers. From the indeterminate meaning of the word "mabinogi," to its disorienting, serpentining narratives, these medieval Welsh prose stories have, according to Patrick Ford, "... been slighted more than most works of medieval literature in the matter of criticism." In the introduction to his 1977 translation, Ford continues by acknowledging, "... there are good reasons why they have been ignored."[1]

Here we are, just over thirty years after Ford's important translation,[2] and — fueled by a cultural revival in medieval fantasy literature — the *Mabinogi* is receiving some overdue recognition both from within academia and from outside the ivory tower. New editions have emerged, notably Sioned Davies's new translation which appeared in 2007, thirty years after Ford's; and selections from the *Mabinogi* are just beginning to be included in anthologies of British literature marketed in the United States.[3] We appear to be having a *Mabinogi* moment.

For that reason, it is particularly apt and resonant that in three creative adaptations of the *Mabinogi* from the years 2000 to 2009, the artistic refrain centers around palpable losses sustained in forgetting the *Mabinogi* and the fraught consequences resulting from endeavoring to remember the *Mabinogi*. The first adaptation of the past decade considered here is Derek Hayes's 2003 live-action/animated film *Otherworld* (released simultaneously in Welsh as *Y Mabinogi*); the second adaptation is a "point-and-click" gothic-tinged adventure video game from Arberth Studios entitled *Rhiannon: The Curse of the Four Branches* (2008); and the third, most recent, iteration of the *Mabinogi* is Owen Sheers's novella *White Ravens* (2009) which was published as part of Seren Books' series New Stories from the *Mabinogion*.[4]

Each of these adaptations—film, video game, novella—posits a teleological meaning in the *Mabinogi* by suggesting that the medieval text always already anticipates a modern present, temporally separate yet uncannily coexistent. In none of these texts is the connection to the medieval *Mabinogi* a case of simple time travel (not that time travel is ever truly simple). Rather, what resonates in all of these versions is that the *Mabinogi* reaches forward to modern Wales, affecting (directly and indirectly) Welsh men and women who themselves do not recognize (at least initially) their literary ancestry. The failure of recognition seems to be salient in these versions, indicating rupture and disconnectedness that call for repair. These atavistic adaptations insist upon a particularly Welsh eschatological experience located in the *Mabinogi*, an experience that characters and readers ultimately recognize as cathartic, transformative, and stabilizing.

What is more, these three appropriations articulate an implicit investment in locating a persistent meaning of the *Mabinogi*. The persistent meaning is, however, only part of the picture. The knotty intersections between twenty-first century appropriations and the medieval Welsh text shape the texts' meanings by offering particularly modern biases to the ways in which the *Mabinogi* can and should be read; and—as is characteristic of modernist and postmodernist adaptations—such projects are often fragmented. In each of these versions the trajectory is remarkably similar: characters move through a process by which they embody personae from the *Mabinogi*, share experiences with those personae, and internalize some aspect of meaning from the medieval Welsh world after they have pieced together at least *some* of the fragments available to them. The *Mabinogi*, these modern adaptations seem to say, resolves the sense of alienation, disconnectedness, and indifference that are characteristic of the modern world. As new meanings are sought from old texts, and as cultural memory is re-awakened and restored, the *Mabinogi* (or the glimpsed versions of the *Mabinogi* available within these modern adaptations) offers redemptive possibilities to characters who have the instincts to search for them.

Also notable is that these adaptations were created by Welsh production companies, artists, and authors. By asserting a specifically Welsh connection to the text of the *Mabinogi*, importantly, these Welsh adaptations stand in contradistinction to what is, undeniably, the most popular of the twenty-first century *Mabinogis*: an interactive online video game, developed by Korean-based Nexon/devCat studios which has now superceded the medieval *Mabinogi* in worldwide familiarity.[5] This game, a "Massive Multiplayer Online Role-Playing Game" (or MMORPG), allows players to assume identities of characters in the animated world. What the game doesn't do, however, is engage in any meaningful way with the actual text of the *Mabinogi*.[6] But Welsh filmmakers, game designers, and authors *have* engaged with the medieval *Mabinogi*, in each case demonstrating that the *Mabinogi* is more than relevant to the modern era: it is—in the worlds of these adaptations—indispensable, evocative, therapeutic, palliative, mystical, and potent.

Part of the potency in these three Welsh-originating versions comes from the forceful, over-determined association of modern characters with medieval characters; the creators pointedly give modern characters names which indicate their relationship to the ever-present medieval *Mabinogi* world. Rhiannon, Branwen, Bendigeidfran, and Lleu populate the modern settings, echoing and anticipating the meanings that the association generates. The telos is powerful in all of these three versions, dictating an interrelatedness while at the same time insisting upon an end-orientation of modern experience. Projecting backwards to the *Mabinogi* imbues the medieval narratives with unspecified mystical power, as if the text itself generated modern crises that it must continually participate in resolving.

Another correspondence between these versions is that the modern characters are in the midst of psychological or psycho-spiritual disturbances of some sort that motivate their actions and that bring them to a point in which they stumble upon the influence of the *Mabinogi*. Indeed, they seem to be always under the thrall of the medieval world although they do not recognize either their indebtedness to that world or the way in which their connectedness has programmed them for certain responses, experiences, entanglements, and vulnerabilities.

It could be said that Hayes's *Otherworld*, Arberth Studio's *Curse of the Four Branches*, and Owen Sheers's *White Ravens* each espouse a Jungian narrative by which the characters live and suffer in their *Mabinogi*-inflected worlds.[7] But it isn't that the creators are strict Jungians, rather they are suggestively Jungian — exploring the collective unconscious of the characters in ways that indicate the mystical, symbolic structures governing their human experience. Rhiannon, Branwen, Bendigeidfran, Lleu, and others become recognizable archetypes which induce modern characters to confront profound conflicts in their pursuits of self-discovery and transformation. This is not intended to suggest that the three versions are tonally similar. They are, in fact, tonally and generically distinct. But their overall projects coincide in ways which suggest a specifically Welsh zeitgeist.

In 2003, Cartwyn Cymru S4C productions released Derek Hayes's live-action and animated film based on the *Mabinogi*. From the time of its release, Hayes's film adaptation of the *Mabinogi* has not been available in North America: It is a Welsh film intended for Welsh audiences. Live-action sequences book-end the otherwise animated film. In the live-action frame, we are introduced to contemporary Welsh teenagers who embark upon an adventure and find themselves in the magical, animated Otherworld of Welsh folklore. The film makes a claim — often tacitly — to and for Welsh identity.[8] And, as it does so, this dual-language release remains fervently loyal to the source text. The fidelity of the animated core of the film stands in opposition to the creative manipulation of the source text in the frame. But value judgements based on claims about fidelity are often reductive. As Julie Sanders cautions:

> Intellectual or scholarly examinations [which think critically about what it means to adapt or appropriate] are not aimed at identifying "good" or "bad" adaptations. On what grounds, after all, could such a judgement be made? Fidelity to the original? ... [I]t is usually at the very point of infidelity that the most creative acts of adaptation and appropriation take place.... Adaptation studies are, then, not about making polarized value judgements, but about analyzing process, ideology, and methodology [19–20].

Although Hayes's adaptation retains—for the most part—the narrative structure (or lack thereof) of the original text and, in so doing, celebrates Welsh literature and Welsh identity, the film also raises questions about how that literature and identity is perceived by the characters within the film. Of the live-action frame, producer Naomi Jones commented, "... it is a device to simplify the story and make it more accessible."[9] But the frame does more than simplify the storylines or organize the text's complex, interwoven narrative elements. By introducing us to the animated Otherworld via the experience of the live-action frame, the film suggests that the medieval world can offer us of the twenty-first century an *ethical* template and a point of origin for modern identities.

How exactly the three Welsh teenagers are connected to this medieval Otherworld we never really know. But it appears that the frame in this film derives from something more than a pragmatic filmmaker's choice: the frame insists upon continuity from medieval to modern, suggesting that the literary Middle Ages—and specifically the Welsh Middle Ages—exerts a strong influence today. The three characters of the live-action frame, prompted by personal crises of various degrees, launch themselves into the Otherworld. There's young Rhiannon, who thinks that she is pregnant. There's Lleu who, on his eighteenth birthday, discovers that he's adopted. And there's Dan (short for Manawydan), nervous, well-meaning, but forgetful. These three meet on May Eve, the occasion of Lleu's birthday, to celebrate with him. But soon after they sail away from the coast on a hired boat, they notice a disturbance in the water. Encouraged by an in-the-know sailor, the three teens quickly don wet suits and dive in. As they descend, their human bodies transform into animated form; they shape-shift into their Otherworldly doubles and namesakes.

The transition between live-action and animation signals our entrance into the Otherworld. After this transformation, the three characters essentially watch the action that they are now a part of. They are bifurcated characters; spectators as well as spectacles—modern as well as medieval. At several times throughout the film, we watch them watching various episodes—and mostly this is when something violent, intense, and destabilizing is happening. Something else occurs in the transmogrification. The two-dimensional, hand-drawn Otherworld is flatter than the live-action modern age. But, in stark contrast with the drab, muted twenty-first century, Hayes's medieval Otherworld glows with a startling, rich saturation of color. This is a visual cue: the modern and the medieval are always somehow incompatible. The medieval appears to magnify the modern: the colors are deeper, the characters highly symbolic, their problems worse by many degrees.

In the film *Otherworld*, the merging identities of the modern and the medieval characters indicates a supernatural relationship. But it is also, importantly, a therapeutic one. We are being prompted to understand modern selfhood in context of the medieval world. This Rhiannon and *that* Rhiannon. This Lleu and *that* Lleu. The connections are intentionally over-stated. But in using *animation* to differentiate the Otherworld from the 'real' world, the film reminds us, too, about the radical 'otherness' of the Middle Ages.

"Animation,'" writes Paul Wells in his essay "'Thou Art Translated': Analysing Animated Adaptation," "is the most appropriate language by which to express the mental visualizations of images suggested by literary forms because its qualities are those which incorporate the hybridity, instability and mutability of the *perception* of textual allusion" (201). Elsewhere Wells argues that "Animation provides a particular model of adaptation in that in enunciating itself it foregrounds the concept of *translation, transmutation and transition* not merely as the vocabulary of the animated form but as the process of taking a literary text and making it a moving picture" (*Animation: Genres and Authorship* 64). Hayes's *Otherworld* is an apt case-in-point. Since so much within the medieval source text itself is about "hybridity, instability and mutability," the *Mabinogi* lends itself to animation.

Hayes makes what is essentially a "faithful" transposition or adaptation of the source text — the creativity more pronounced in the relationship between the frame and the animated core of the film. Most notably, the film's core retains the interlaced narrative of the Four Branches and works ambitiously through several of the core narrative lines in its hour and forty four minutes. Because of this fidelity to an already complicated text, the viewer needs to be somewhat familiar with the *Mabinogi* to understand the parallels between the modern teenagers and the medieval characters. Modern-Rhiannon's pregnancy scare, for example, links her to Medieval-Rhiannon who gives birth to a child only to have him snatched by an unidentified being from the Otherworld while she sleeps. Rhiannon's women servants, not wanting to be blamed for the child's disappearance, frame Rhiannon by killing

"Real" and animated Rhiannons glance at each other in Derek Hayes's 2003 film ***Otherworld***.

some puppies and covering her with their blood. When she awakens, the women claim that Rhiannon killed her own child and her punishment is to sit outside the gate of Arberth for seven years and to tell her story to all visitors who don't yet know it, performing the narrative of her own shame. All of this, apparently, is intricately connected with the mental anguish of the modern Rhiannon's anxiety about an unplanned pregnancy—though it is left for the viewers to make this connection.

This is one example of the film's attempts to make the *Mabinogi* more accessible. At the same time, the film embraces the serpentining narrative of the source material and doesn't ever unravel the twists and tangles of the many plots. Indeed, purists looking for fidelity from source text to film will appreciate Hayes's restraint in unweaving the complex narrative. Some critics, however, were less impressed. "What lets the production down," writes the BBC's Jamie Russell, "is the script's tendency to tie itself in knots."

In the diegesis of the film, the medieval world *mirrors* the modern world, and vice versa. As modern identities are projected onto those of the Welsh mythological figures they are, in turn, reflected back again. For example, each of the teenagers has at least one moment in the film where we see him or her gazing at the animated version of him or herself with a knowing look. (Medieval-Rhiannon, for example, picks up a plate at a wedding banquet, and sees Modern-Rhiannon looking intently back at her).

Throughout the film, we are aware that the experience of the Middle Ages is mediated by the gaze of the modern characters. At the outset, the characters view the past through the surface of the water and must descend to have this experience. They must take a literal plunge. It's a *katabasis* from which the teenagers return unscathed and therapeutically cleansed in some way as they apparently learn to value their choices. But what have they learned about themselves? About the Middle Ages? About Welshness? About violence? About guilt and shame? About self and identity? About the *Otherworld*?

Although they have had contact with stories that comprise, in Ioan Williams's words, the "central myths that had informed Welsh identity," modern-day Rhiannon, Lleu, and Dan are always somehow detached. Although the three teenagers have morphed into the characters from the *Mabinogi* in a manifest parallelism, they are always outside themselves watching—but we have little indication that they register their experiences, at least not very deeply. At the end of the film, there is only a brief dialogue in which the characters react to their Otherwoldy experience. "What happened in the water?" asks Dan. "I don't know," Rhiannon answers. "It's like a dream you can't quite remember," Dan continues. "But can't forget." Rhiannon concludes. In what may be an unintended echo of a famous moment in Shakespeare's *A Midsummer Night's Dream*, the characters emerge without full conscious recall of their enchanted, transformed selves. As Hermia reports in Shakespeare's comedy, "Methinks I see these things with parted eye / When every thing seems double" (4.1.186–

187). Demetrius seconds the experience "Are you sure / that we are awake? It seems to me / That yet we sleep, we dream" (189–190). The liminal post-dream phase signals re-entry for Hayes's characters as they puzzle out the hazy, visceral sensation of awaking from a deep sleep.

Viewers, too, attempt to puzzle out the various experiences of the live-action characters and their return from the animated versions of themselves. It's an elaborate set-up with little resolution. We don't know, for instance, whether any of these three teenagers have *read* the *Mabinogi*. Do they recognize that they have become their namesakes? Do they perceive themselves to be in a familiar text-world? Do they know the narrative storylines of the characters whose identities have subsumed them? If we compare to other Otherworlds, say, *The Wizard of Oz:* Dorothy at least marvels "I've a feeling we're not in Kansas anymore," acknowledging the strangeness of her experience over the rainbow. Lewis Carroll's Alice remarks of her own adventure, "Curiouser and curiouser!" In Hayes's vision, although the Welsh teens *voluntarily* plunge into the portal to the Otherworld, when they return, they are nonchalant about their experiences. While some critics of the film saw this as a flaw, it is arguably consistent with the source text in which characters have otherworldy encounters from which they too return nonplussed. Hayes's characters reveal an abiding and heuristic connection to their *Mabinogi* templates, though the connections are never explicitly articulated. Welsh identity, though unspoken, is ever-present.

The idea of the *Mabinogi* providing a template underscores another adaptation of the medieval text: a video-game entitled *Rhiannon: Curse of the Four Branches*. Created by Karen and Noel Bruton, and Richard Lee, the work features a crossing-over and, as in Hayes's film, it is a temporal crossing: "The game is set on the Celtic fringes of Britain; a place where myth and magic spill into reality, threatening the sanity of a teenage girl named Rhiannon Sullivan.... The story is the game ..." asserts the studio's web site, calling attention to the literary provenance of the main character's experience but at the same time offering players a new way of imagining the *Mabinogi* as something malevolent and forceful. Once again, recognizing the potency of the *Mabinogi* leads to a revelation and ultimately a conclusion (or a cure).

This adventure game, as in Hayes's film, posits a cultural amnesia of sorts—the player-character must reconstruct meaning from the *Mabinogi* in order to solve the various puzzles leading to the ultimate resolution of the mysterious events depicted in the game. In order to complete the game, the player must be able to piece together names and symbols from the Four Branches to essentially re-member the absent body of the character Rhiannon. In *Playing the Past: History and Nostalgia in Video Games,* editors Zach Whalen and Laurie N. Taylor write "as texts that are increasingly set in versions of reality, video games also offer experiences of remembering that may be either personal or cultural" (5). In *The Curse of the Four Branches*, the various cultural impulses dictate that the meaning (or the resonance) of the *Mabinogi* is attached to a range of contemporary experiences. And this is true in Arberth Studio's game in which remembering is a literal activity as the player gathers totemic and textual objects to reach different levels of game play—and thereby reconstruct several lost cultural and personal memories.

In a game replete with echoes, the player takes on the identity of gender-neutral Chris, house-sitting at Ty Pryderi. The Sullivan family has left the property to take their teenage daughter Rhiannon Sullivan for help. Rhiannon, it seems, has been haunted by ghostly voices. She has written a letter to her father in which she has specifically appealed for his help. Rhiannon has been reading the *Mabinogi* and has come to believe that the haunting of Ty Pryderi is connected to the medieval stories. Chris (the player) also discovers that Rhiannon Sullivan has been in contact with a historian who has traced a pattern in which this Rhiannon is curiously—menacingly—connected to the experience of another Rhiannon from the past: Rhiannon Wallace, a woman who had formerly lived in the house and mysteriously disappeared. Further along in the game, the player discovers that there has been an even earlier Rhiannon, Rhiannon Boswell, whose husband purchased the Ty Pryderi farm and discovered that there was a malignant presence and an apparent curse on anyone named Rhiannon. The player, too, hears faint voices calling "Rhiannon."

There are four Rhiannons in the game. The reduplication of Rhiannons suggests a postmodern hall-of-mirrors. Chris, looking for clues to solve the "curse," must listen to Stevie Nicks's popular Fleetwood Mac song "Rhiannon," adding another dimension to the Rhiannonicity of the video game. Nicks herself saw in Rhiannon a potent archetype of the goddess and the witch, but also recognized the contemporary resonance of the legend: "She is some sort of reality" Nicks is quoted as saying in a *Rolling Stone* article. "If I didn't know she was a mythological character, I would think maybe she lived down the street" (McLane 1979). The emphasis on the name Rhiannon prods at this notion of memory at the same time that it underscores the fragility of memory itself. The player may remember one Rhiannon, or two. But remembering all four Rhiannons, and the reverberations of Rhiannon in popular culture, is something of a meditative loop. In reading emails from the character Jon Southworth, the historian, the player "Chris" must translate Ogham script found in the world of the game. The translated script explains the curse: "I bind your soul upon death / to wander this land without memory." But whose memory is being invoked here? There's a syntactic ambiguity. Does the soul wander with no memory? Does the land itself have no memory? Or is there an elliptical other who will be without memory? The lack of precision in the curse itself is appealing: it's as if even the curse is clouded by the imperfection of memory.

In *Curse of the Four Branches* remembering becomes important as it leads to remembrance. The distinction in terminology here suggests that the priority or value is not placed on the cognitive moment of recall, but on the tangible memorializing of the past by connecting it to the present. This works on several levels: Chris (the player character) learns to remember Rhiannon. Chris's discoveries enable Jon Southworth (the non-player historian) to learn/remember that his own mother was Rhiannon Wallace. In an online interview, *Rhiannon* co-creator Noel Bruton was asked about the process of adaptation. The interviewer asks:

> A few classic adventure games have adapted elements from the Mabinogion myths, such as Al Lowe's *The Black Cauldron* and Roberta Williams' *King's Quest III: To Heir is Human* (with the magician named Gwydion). How well do you feel that such fairy tale adventure games capture the spirit of Celtic mythology? Why is your own adaptation of the Mabinogion modern instead?

Bruton responds: "we went for the almost-feasible with our story in 'Rhiannon.' We also wanted to give the player a recognizable frame of reference — the present day, with cars and Email and MP3 — and then blur it with the supernatural. There is a natural tension in taking the Everyday and poking it with the Inexplicable" (N. pag).

The "natural tension" in the encounter between the Everyday and the Inexplicable is yet another articulation of the Jungian elements working their way into these contemporary adaptations. The player of *Curse of the Four Branches* negotiates between the present and the past, looking for ways to resolve apparent malevolent energies through the process of interpretation. The house-sitter Chris is an outsider — a malleable identity with which the player merges for the duration of the game. This player-character resembles Carl Jung, whose elaborate dreams sparked many of his influential theories of the human mind:

> In one [dream Jung] discovered a seventeenth-century library in a previously unknown annexe to his house: and in the other some gates clanged shut behind him, trapping him in the same century. Patiently he began to assemble one of the largest collections of alchemical texts in existence, and it became clear to him that the alchemists had used a secret language which they expressed in arcane symbols. At first he understood little of what they signified, but as he worked along philological lines, compiling an elaborate lexicon of key phrases and cross-references [meaning was discovered] [Stevens 40].

In the game, Chris too discovers a hidden library (Malcolm's study) after being trapped in a house (Ty Pryderi) with doors shut behind him/her. Chris must patiently assemble a collection of texts (the texts used in the homeopathic — not alchemical — practice of Rhiannon's mother Jen). Furthermore, Chris must decode a "secret language ... expressed in arcane symbols" (the Ogham script) and compile a lexicon of key phrases, which ultimately communicate their meanings to the player. The player's successful interpretation of this dreamlike experience leads to the ending of the curse and the return of Rhiannon Sullivan.

But this depends upon playing the game well. The player must locate and organize the symbols — sword, claw, crown, and cradle — which draw the elements of the narrative together. Here, story and game are interwoven as narrative and ludic meanings are mingled in Arberth Studio's game. The game uses the text to provide clues, and is highly dependent on the textual material of the *Mabinogi* to frame the concerns of the player character and the mystery he/she pursues. It isn't a strict reading of the source material, but rather a suggestive one and players know that it is a *game*. Writes David Surman (162–3): "Conventionally speaking, written prose is not alterable, though we can choose not to read.... Regarding interactivity, videogames present a substantial change in the history of mechanical and electronic media experience. In videogames, play is the central activity through which meaning is produced." And yet in *Rhiannon: Curse of the Four Branches*, the game's meaning reveals itself to be connected to ideas of temporality, atemporality, and teleology. The game's diachronic elements guide players to suture the past and the present, aiming for some sense of narrative closure.

But even though, as Arberth's teasing phrase suggests, "the story is the game," is the game necessarily "the story"? Games, though they may be literary, are not literature; the rules of gaming are different from the rules of narrative.[10] As Steven E. Jones reminds us in *The Meaning of Video Games*, the early history of the scholarship on video games was marked by "an exaggerated debate" between story and game; narratology and ludology. He writes, "Ludologists deliberately placed video games in the larger family of games in general, cultural practices descended from go or chess rather than *Gilgamesh* or Chaucer" (4). In *The Curse of the Four Branches* the game merges with elements of the story; but it is not the story of the Four Branches. It is the story of discovering the story, thereby assuaging the pre-existing rupture from the story. If the past can haunt us, so the game seems to say, it can also exorcise itself. The text of the *Mabinogi* has become something else in this context: a guidebook for resolving modern anxieties about the power of history itself. The player might come out unscathed and triumphant; the player may "win" (sometimes by indulging in a few "cheats" along the way). But more important than the conclusive, affirming outcome, the story has created its own telos and that telos is reinforced by the very structure of the video game: the final resolution is already pre-determined by the Prime Movers who have set the game in motion. And part of that teleological imperative involves asserting the continuity of meaning in Welsh culture.

Indeed, the setting of the game and the name of the production company— Arberth Studios— serve to localize and re-enforce the cultural expression in this experience of the *Mabinogi*. Although played in English, its Welshness permeates the game-play.[11] In the Welsh-produced *Rhiannon: Curse of the Four Branches*, we recognize the distinctly Welsh elements—placenames, personal names, landscapes, and symbols. Saturated with expressions of Welsh identity and meaning, the game can only be concluded once identity and meaning have been examined, understood, and re-united.

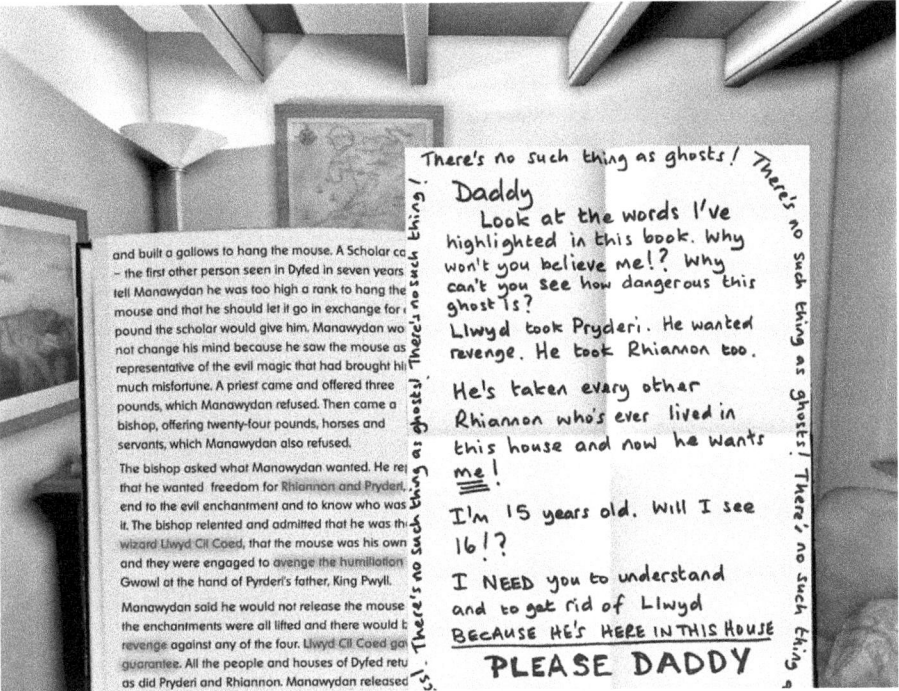

The text of the *Mabinogi* and Rhiannon Sullivan's diary in Arberth Studios' *Rhiannon: Curse of the Four Branches*.

Emphatic Welsh elements are also powerfully amplified in Owen Sheers's novella *White Ravens*, populated by characters with onomastic connections to the characters in the *Mabinogi*. As part of Seren Books' series New Stories from the *Mabinogion*, Sheers's novella promises a retelling of the Second Branch and foregrounds Welsh identity and identity formation. Rhiannon is here, too. So is Branwen, Bendigeidfran, and Efnisien: these are not only the identifiable characters from the Four Branches, they are the modern identities which have been shaped by and derived from these important Welsh stories. And, as the text seems to suggest, these modern identities are shaped by the collective or cultural unconscious. In Sheers's novel, as in *Otherworld* and *Curse of the Four Branches*, the experience of the *Mabinogi-Otherworld* leads characters to connect viscerally and powerfully with their namesakes. As one of the characters, Ben, insists: "These stories are with us for a reason you know" (95). It is in Sheers's novel that we find what may be the strongest expression of a connection between atemporality, teleology, and the text of the *Mabinogi*.

In *White Ravens*, the frame narrative introduces us to Rhian, a young woman in modern Wales who reluctantly colludes with her brother to poach and butcher livestock from other farmers after their own herd is destroyed to control the spread of hoof-and-mouth disease. Her brother initiates a lucrative plan to illicitly transport the ill-gotten meat to London suppliers. When her brother's complotter is unable to make one of their secretive drives to London, Rhian agrees to take the wheel for their nighttime run. She is therefore present during the butchery — which takes place in the back of the truck while it heads toward the city. It is a particularly grisly scene: "The stink of it hit me in a slow wave a rich, iron smell wafting out into the alley like a rotten memory of tougher times in the city" (44). It is crucial here that the London setting has brought Rhian "further and further away from Wales, home and my usual bearings" because Rhian's experience is traumatic, isolating, and alienating (40).

Ditching her brother, Rhian runs to a bench overlooking the Thames where, in the early morning hours she is chatted up by a friendly, elderly man. None of this seems very *Mabinogi*-like, of course. But the embedded narrative is where the references become more determined. The elderly man proposes to tell her a story. And, reluctant again, Rhian finally concedes. He begins a narrative that will comprise the bulk of Sheers's novel: the story of an Irish man named Matthew O'Connell and his experiences during and after World War II.

As the embedded narrative begins, traces of the *Mabinogi* are faint. But they grow stronger as the narrative continues until, gradually, the reader realizes how Sheers has suggestively overlaid the plots. Matthew O'Connell cannot help but be a figure of Matholoch. He *is* Matholoch in modern guise, ignorantly embodying the archetype of foreign interloper. As a wounded soldier, Matthew returns to civilian life, taking employment in a propaganda machine. He is sent on a perplexing mission: to collect six rare white ravens from a farm in Wales and return them to the Tower of London. Skeptical of the myth which asserts that in the absence of the ravens from the Tower "the monarchy and the kingdom of Britain would fall," Matthew takes the order sheet and accepts the mission.

It is at the farm that the links to the *Mabinogi* become clear: the farmer Ben (whose full name we later learn is Bendigeidfran) encourages Matthew's courtship of Branwen, Ben's sister. Their love grows quickly, but the joy of their impulsive marriage is overshadowed by the return of Branwen's other brother, who — himself a soldier — has been missing in action. His sudden return on the day of Matthew and Branwen's wedding drives him to a furious act as he mutilates the horse Matthew used to travel to the farm.

From this moment, the narrative follows fairly closely the Second Branch of the *Mabinogi*, "Branwen, Daughter of Llyr," and the story — as in the medieval narrative — explores the jealous passion of Efnisien; the heartsickness of Branwen as she fails to bring peace between the Irish and the Welsh; and the tragic economies of intermarriage and its consequent misunderstandings, losses, and betrayals. The narrative, too, intoned in a spare, colloquial delivery, achieves a double effect — evoking the unembellished style of the original medieval text while sounding fully contemporary. Here, for example, is how Sheers narrates the episode in which Efnisien (re-named Evan in Sheers's version) mutilates the horses owned by Matholoch: "It was the screams that woke them. After they'd heard the front door slam shut, bringing an end to the voices rising from below" (138). But in Sheers's novel, this episode — gripping, brutal, and agonizing — additionally conveys the post-traumatic effects of Evan's engagement in the violence of war. It's a violence that contaminates the love between Matthew and Branwen, and further indicts them in the suspicious, unwelcoming eyes of the community:

> A sober man during the war, Matthew had, since his return, increasingly been finding refuge from his family tensions in drink. On this occasion another argument with his father had sent him to the pub where a quick succession of whiskies [sic] loosened his tongue and seduced him into an indulgence of storytelling. Through the lens of those shot glasses he found a morbid delight in vividly evoking the scene for his enraptured listener; painting for him in gory detail Mullie's earless, lidless, lipless head, the great gashes torn along his sides and the flash of Evan's bayonet in the moonlight.
> It didn't take long for the story to spread [....] In the eyes of the village, as Evan's sister the shadow of his crime fell over Branwen too [152–153].[12]

While the characters experience each episode as if it is a natural and spontaneous occurrence, the reader familiar with the *Mabinogi* knows otherwise: the reader hears the unmistakable echoes. Sheers emphasizes this dramatically ironic layering throughout the novel. Matthew has a copy of the *Mabinogi* (given to him by Ben) but he curiously elects *not* to read it. He therefore doesn't learn until after he has played out his narrative fate that he has re-lived the experience of Matholoch; that the modern Branwen is an incarnation of the *Mabinogi*'s Branwen, and that, but for a heuristic insight, it might have been averted.

Matthew's refusal to confront the text of the *Mabinogi* in *White Ravens* initially resembles the teens' lack of explicit awareness of the *Mabinogi* in Hayes's *Otherworld*. But Sheers heightens the impact: Hayes's teens do not necessarily know that they embody the *Mabinogi* proto-selves; Sheers's Matthew actually has the book of the *Mabinogi* and he refuses to read it until it is too late, thus compounding the ironies. The reader knows that acceptance of the text and its pointed meaning could have spared him the tragedy. But it's an Oedipal drama in which Matthew's ignorance of the truth of his origins are disastrous; the *Mabinogi*, like the Greek Fates, must be fulfilled.

Sheers's adaptation, like *Curse of the Four Branches*, resounds with atavistic connections and teases out the characters' uncanny reduplication of Welsh mythological archetypes. One is tempted to call the effect in *White Ravens* that of Jungian synchronicity: the coincidences are startling. However, as it turns out in this novella, the apparent coincidences are nothing of the sort. The impression of synchronicity is revealed to be causally related events. There is, in the world of *White Ravens* an atemporal nexus that links the modern reality to medieval legend.

This collective memory evoked in Sheers's novel has a historical antecedent, as Philip Schwyzer details in *Literature, Nationalism, and Memory in Early Modern England and Wales*. Schwyzer points to sixteenth-century Welsh scholars Humphrey Llwyd and John Prise who "were ... among the first scholars in Europe to grasp that there was more to national history than books and artifacts. Emphasizing oral tradition and collective memory, they set out to rescue from the wreck of history a distinctively Welsh set of practices and attitudes which could be held safe from immolation on the one hand and appropriation on the other" (84–85). Our modern adaptors also aim to "rescue from the wreck of history" something distinctively Welsh, something not restricted by time. But, significantly, it is *by* appropriation that these distinctively Welsh meanings will be preserved.

The main characters in *Otherworld*, "Curse of the Four Branches," and *White Ravens* all mine meaning from the past in order to have any chance at a redemptive ending (which, not coincidentally, they are all able to achieve). At the end of *Otherworld*, Rhiannon has discovered that the pregnancy scare was a false alarm. At the end of *Curse of the Four Branches*, Chris has solved the mystery of the four Rhiannons and has enabled Rhiannon Sullivan to pursue her life uncontaminated by the curse. At the end of *White Ravens*, Rhian realizes that the old man telling her the story of Matthew is, of course, Matthew himself, now older and wiser. What is more, he is her grandfather who instructs her at the conclusion of the novella to "Go back to your brothers now. Help them. Be a bridge" (178).

Anthony Stevens explains that "... Jung [adopted] a teleological perspective, endorsed the freedom of the will, extended the developmental process beyond childhood to the whole span of life, proposed that illness is itself a form of growth, and saw religion as the fulfillment of a basic human need" (155). In all of these contemporary adaptations of the *Mabinogi* the ones who gain from encountering the archetypes of the medieval text are characters moving into maturity—shedding their past identities and transforming, through a confrontation with their inner selves, and resisting the confining determinants of modern culture.

Jung's "cultural role," according to Stevens, aimed to compensate for the detachment and "spiritual impoverish[ment]" of the western world. "The only remedy for our civilization's 'loss of soul' was a massive reinvestment in the inner life of the individual, so as to re-establish a personal connection with 'the mythic world in which we were once at home by right of birth'" (156). Derek Hayes, Karen and Noel Bruton, and Owen Sheers re-work the *Mabinogi* in service of re-establishing connections to a particular mythic world: a Welsh mythic world that continues to imbue the modern one with nuance, spirituality, and meaning drawn from nostalgia.

Schwyzer, following historian David Lowenthal, historicizes the concept of nostalgia: "'Nostalgia,' that name we now give to the yearning for the irrecoverable past, was not yet a word in 1549, but as many scholars have emphasized, it had a constant place in early modern thought.... The nostalgic image of the past incites longing precisely because it is *not* like life, but is rather *lifelike*" (73–74). Juliette Wood wrote in 1997: "Certainly there is a tendency to romanticize the past, to endow it with the desired identity of the present. This frequently expresses itself in back-projecting a view of modern Welsh national identity on earlier periods, in particular the Middle Ages" (94). In the case of Hayes, Bruton and Bruton, and Sheers the tendency is not so much to romanticize the past or to project backward. Rather, these adaptors of Welsh medieval source material suggest that the past informs the present; it is reciprocal and atemporal. It is a giving and a taking.

The *Mabinogi* continues to tie itself into intricate, winding knots. One could ask why there are so many new versions and adaptations in the first decade of the twenty-first century? What cultural impulses motivate the multiplication of *Mabinogi*s? And what accounts for the shared teleological emphases and the atemporality of these versions? These retellings are timely, yet out of time. It can be no coincidence that screenwriter, game designers, and novelist alike share similar preoccupations with the importance of the Welsh archetypes. The year 2000 brought with it a millennial discourse that has to date been insufficiently theorized. But we cannot overlook the effect of millennial thinking in these *Mabinogi* adaptations.

As these new works of film, video game, and novella look for meaning in medieval Welsh tales, they aim to connect to a past that seems increasingly relevant at the same moment that it seems ever more remote. Perhaps we feel the need to restore the old meanings, to embrace them, and to ask whether or not they still apply to our lives today. For this reason, all of these re-contextualized twenty-first century adaptations of the *Mabinogi* use a framing device; they are each, primarily, about atemporal interaction with something previously neglected or forgotten. In *Otherworld, Rhiannon: Curse of the Four Branches*, and *White Ravens* central characters suffer for not reading or heeding the stories of the *Mabinogi*. Surely, these modern re-workings seem to propose, it is time to open up the book and read it once again.

Notes

1. I had been teaching the *Mabinogi* in a survey course of early British literature for several years when I first became aware of a feature-length film based on the text. I hunted for a copy but was not able to acquire it. My paper began, really, as a self-serving means to get a copy of the film which I finally did with the help of the director, Derek Hayes; the producer, Naomi Jones (neither of whom had a copy) and two very obliging librarians at S4C.

2. In 2007, the University of California press released a deluxe 30 year edition of Ford's translation.

3. Broadview Press includes material from the First Branch, Longman includes Taliesin, but Norton doesn't include Welsh material.

4. Seren Books' New Stories from the *Mabinogion* has to date released four works: Russell Celyn Jones's *The Ninth Wave*, Gwyneth Lewis's *The Meat Tree*, and Niall Griffiths's *The Dreams of Max and Ronnie*. The series will ultimately include eleven re-workings of narratives from the *Mabinogion*.

5. This video game, popular throughout Asia, was released in North America in 2008. Judging by Google hits, the *Mabinogi* is now known less as a literary text and more as an MMORPG — a "Massive Multiplayer Online Role-Playing Game."

6. Clay Kinchen Smith's essay "We're Not in Cymru Anymore," in the present volume details the pan–Celticism and the perplexing erasure of Welsh specificity in the video game.

7. In 2009, Jung's long-secreted journal known as *The Red Book* was finally published. The text of the *Mabinogi* comes to us from two manuscripts, one of which is known as *The Red Book of Hergest*. Both of these Red Books derived their titles from the color of their binding. It's a suggestive correspondence, though perhaps does not rise to the level of being an example of synchronicity (Jung's formulation of extreme coincidence).

8. Similarly, *Mabinogi* the video game, *because* it is interactive, necessarily involves a "crossing over" as players create characters and take on roles in the Mabinogi landscapes. But the means by which gamers do this and the meanings generated by the crossings-over are fundamentally different than those represented in Hayes's film. The video game adopts the title *Mabinogi*, but Welshness is largely erased in the pseudo-medieval world of the game.

9. http://news.bbc.co.uk/1/low/wales/2492595.stm

10. Roger Ebert wrote on his popular blog: "I remain convinced that *in principle,* video games cannot be art. Perhaps it is foolish of me to say "never," because never, as Rick Wakeman informs us, is a long, long time. Let me just say that no video gamer now living will survive long enough to experience the medium as an art form." His words in defense of his position sparked a thoroughgoing controversy.

11. Contrast this with Nexon/devCAT's *Mabinogi*—a "massive multi-player online role playing game" or MMORPG — in which a videogame called *Mabinogi* has virtually nothing to do with the text of the *Mabinogi*. In the gameworld of Nexon's *Mabinogi*, the location of the fantasy realm is called "Erinn," or Ireland. What's more, a search for the word "Wales" in the game's comprehensive wikipedia entry turns up nothing. What would account for this apparent naive merging of Irish and Welsh? A September 2009 article entitled "The ties that bind Ireland, Korea" offers a possible explanation for this apparently de-politicized rendering of the Ireland/Wales locations in the game's world: "You may have heard some people refer to Korea as the Ireland of the East, in part because of the locals' affinity for downing adult beverages and bursting out into spontaneous song" states this article which appeared in an English language Korean paper. Answering the question "How Irish are the Koreans?"— the title of the Asia society luncheon, Eamonn McKee, Irish Ambassador to Korea, presented several parallels between Ireland and Korea, including how both experienced division at the hands of foreign powers. Apparently, the *Mabinogi* MMORPG has a cultural meaning of its own which involves projecting Korean identity onto the concept of Ireland superimposed with Welsh nomenclature.

12. In the afterward to *White Ravens*, Sheers describes how his own experience reading the horse mutilation episode in the Second Branch affected him: "Why should this passage, more than any other, have made such an indelible mark? I'm sure it's partly because of the quality of the writing — the mythic prose that describes the action so coolly while also hitting all the right triggers" (188).

Works Cited

Bruton, Noel. Interview. 30 Jan. 2009. Joseph Howse. 16 Oct. 2010. http://www.adventureclassicgaming.com. Online.
Cartmell, Deborah and Imelda Whelehan. *Adaptations: From Text to Screen, Screen to Text.* Routledge. 2006.
Davies, Hazel Walford. "Case Study: Refashioning a Myth, Performances of the Tale of Blodeuwedd." *The Cambridge History of British Theatre, Volume 3: Since 1895.* 273–287. Cambridge, England: Cambridge University Press, 2004.
Davies, Sioned. "'He Was the Best Teller of Tales in the World': Performing Medieval Welsh Narrative." *Performing Medieval Narrative.* 15–26. Cambridge, England: Brewer, 2005.
_____. *The Mabinogion.* Trans. Oxford: Oxford University Press, 2007.
Ebert, Roger. "Video Games Can Never Be Art." 16 April 2010. http://blogs.suntimes.com/ebert. 20 November 2010. Web
Ford, Patrick. *The Mabinogi.* Berkeley: University of California Press, 1977.
Lho, Jackie. "The Ties that Bind Ireland, Korea." *Korea JoongAng Daily.* 1 Sept. 2009. N. pag. Web. http://joongangdaily.joins.com. 10 Sept. 2010.
McLane, Daisann. "Five Not So Easy Pieces." *Rolling Stone.* 7 Feb. 1980: 36–40.
Russell, Jamie. Rev. of *Otherworld* (2003). bbc.co.uk. British Broadcasting Corporation. 17 June 2003. Web. 20 October 2007.
Sanders, Julie. *Adaptation and Appropriation: the New Critical Idiom.* London: Routledge, 2006.
Schwyzer, Philip. *Literature, Nationalism, and Memory in Early Modern England and Wales.* Cambridge Cambridge University Press, 2004.
Shakespeare, William. *A Midsummer Night's Dream.* The Norton Shakespeare. Ed. Steven Greenblatt, et. al. W. W. Norton, 2008.
Stevens, Anthony. *Jung: A Very Short Introduction.* Oxford: Oxford University Press, 2001.
Surman, David. "Style, Consistency and Plausibility in the *Fable* Gameworld." *Animated "Worlds."* 151–170. Eastleigh, United Kingdom: Libbey, 2006.
Vitz, Evelyn Birge, Nancy Freeman Regalado, Marilyn Lawrence, eds. *Performing Medieval Narrative.* Cambridge, England: Brewer, 2005.
Wells, Paul. *Animation: Genre and Authorship* London, England: Wallflower, 2002.
_____. "Literary Theory, Animation and the 'Subjective Correlative': Defining the Narrative 'World' in Brit-Lit Animation." *Animated "Worlds."* 79–94. Eastleigh, United Kingdom: Libbey, 2006.
_____. "'Thou Art Translated': Analysing Animated Adaptation." *Adaptations: From Text to Screen, Screen to Text.* 199–213. London, England: Routledge, 1999.
Williams, Ioan. "Towards National Identities: Welsh Theatres." *The Cambridge History of British Theatre, Volume 3: Since 1895.* 242–272. Cambridge, England: Cambridge University Press, 2004.
Wood, Juliette. "Perceptions of the Past in Welsh Folklore Studies." *Folklore* 108 (1997): 93–102.

Further Reading

This bibliography emphasizes publications after the year 2000, although several examples of essential reading published prior to that year are included. In some cases, we were compelled to list a publication in more than one category. We regret that we were only able to list English language sources: many excellent sources in Welsh have not been included in these selections.

Cultural Studies on Welsh Topics

Blandford, Steve. *Film, Drama and the Break-Up of Britain*. Bristol, England: Intellect, 2007. Print.

_____, ed. *Wales on Screen*. Bridgend, Wales: Seren Books, 2001.

Crampin, Martin. "Interpreting Welsh Medieval Narratives: Exploring Parallel Traditions and Historical Process through Contemporary Art." *Studi Celtici* 2004: 295–324.

Davies, Andrew. *'The Reputed Nation of Inspiration': Representations of Wales in Fiction from the Romantic Period*. Doctoral dissertation, Cardiff University, 2001.

Donahaye, Jasmine. "'By Whom Shall She Arise? For She Is Small': The *Wales*-Israel Tradition in the Edwardian Period." *'The Jew' in Late-Victorian and Edwardian Culture: Between the East End and East Africa*. Eds. Bar-Yosef, Eitan and Nadia Valman. Basingstoke, England: Palgrave Macmillan, 2009. 161–182.

Hurn, Samantha. "The 'Cardinauts' of the Western Coast of *Wales*: Exchanging and Exhibiting Horses in the Pursuit of Fame." *Journal of Material Culture* 13.3 (2008). 335–355.

_____. "Here Be Dragons? No, Big Cats! Predator Symbolism in Rural West Wales." *Anthropology Today*, 25.1 (2009). 6–11.

Jones, Elin Haf Gruffydd. "The Territory of Television: S4C and the Representation of the 'Whole of *Wales*.'" *Minority Language Media: Concepts, Critiques and Case Studies*. Eds. Cormack, Mike and Niamh Hourigan. Clevedon, England: Multilingual Matters, 2007. 188–211.

Morgan, Prys. "Keeping the Legends Alive." *Wales: The Imagined Nation: Studies in Cultural and National Identity*. Ed. Tony Curtis. Bridgend, Mid Glamorgan: 1986. 19–41.

Sims-Williams, Patrick (ed. and preface); Williams, Gruffydd Aled (ed. and preface). "Crossing Boundaries: Proceedings of the XXIIth International Congress of Celtic Studies." 24–30 August 2003, University of *Wales*, Aberystwyth/Croesi Ffiniau: Trafocion y XIIfed Gyngres Astudiaethau Celtaidd Ryngwladol 24–30 Awst 2003, Prifysgol Cymru, Aberystwyth. *Cambrian Medieval Celtic Studies* 53–54 (2007): 1–146.

Spradlin, Derrick. "'God Ne'er Brings to Pass Such Things for Nought': Empire and Prince Madoc of *Wales* in Eighteenth-Century America." *Early American Literature* 44.1 (2009): 39–70.

Stalmaszczyk, Piotr. *Celtic Studies in Poland in the 20th Century: A Bibliography*. Zeitschrift fur Celtische Philologie 54 (2004): 170–84.

Thomas, Alan R. "English in Wales." *English in Britain and Overseas: Origins and Development*, vol. 5 of *The Cambridge History of the English Language*. Ed. Robert Burchfield. Cambridge: Cambridge University Press, 1994. 94–147.

Williams, Colin H. "The Anglicisation of Wales," *English in Wales: Diversity, Conflict and Change*. Ed. Nikolas Coupland. Clevedon, PA: Multilingual Matters, 1990. 19–47.

Historical Studies

Borsay, Peter. "New Approaches to Social History. Myth, Memory, and Place: Monmouth and Bath 1750–1900." *Journal of Social History* 39.3 (2006): 867–889.

Fulton, Helen. "The *Mabinogi* and the Education of Princes in Medieval Wales." *Medieval Celtic Literature and Society*. Ed. Helen Fulton. Portland, OR: Four Courts P, 2005. 230–47.

Gibbard, Noel. *Fire on the Altar: A History and Evaluation of the 1904–05 Revival in Wales*. Bridgend, Wales: Bryntirion, 2005.

Gitre, Edward J. "The 1904–05 Welsh Revival: Modernization, Technologies, and Techniques of the Self." *Church History* 73.4 (2004): 792–827.

Textual and Onomastic Studies

Charles, Edwards, T.M. "The Date of the Four Branches of the Mabinogi." *The Mabinogi: A Book of Essays*. Ed. C.W. Sullivan III. New York: Garland Publishing, 1996. 19–58.

Daniel, Iestyn. "The Date, Origin, and Authorship of 'The *Mabinogion*' in the Light of Ymborth yr enaid." *Journal of Celtic Studies* 4 (2004): 117–52.

Hemming, Jessica. "Ancient Tradition or Authorial Invention? The 'Mythological' Names in the Four Branches." *Myth in Celtic Literatures*. Ed. Joseph Falaky Nagy. Dublin, Ireland: Four Courts, 2007. 83–104.

Postles, Dave, and Joel T. Rosenthal, eds. *Studies on the Personal Name in Later Medieval England and Wales*. Kalamazoo, MI: Western Michigan University, 2006.

Russell, Paul. "Texts in Contexts: Recent Work on the Medieval Welsh Prose Tales." *Cambrian Medieval Celtic Studies* 45 (2003): 59–72.

Literary Studies

Attebery, Brian. *The Fantasy Tradition in American Literature: From Irving to Le Guin*. Bloomington: Indiana University Press, 1980.

Hopkins, Lisa. "Welshness in Shakespeare's English Histories." *Shakespeare's History Plays: Performance, Translation and Adaptation in Britain and Abroad*. Eds. Ton Hoenselaars and Davis Kennedy. Cambridge, England: Cambridge UP, 2004. 60–74.

Keyes, Flo. *The Literature of Hope in the Middle Ages and Today: Connections in Medieval Romance, Modern Fantasy, and Science Fiction*. Jefferson: McFarland, 2006.

Mally, Willy, and Philip Schwyzer, eds. *Shakespeare and Wales: From the Marches to the Assembly*. Ashgate, 2010.

Meecham-Jones, Simon. "'Englyssh Gaufride' and British Chaucer?: Chaucerian Allusions to the Condition of *Wales* in the House of Fame." *Chaucer Review: A Journal of Medieval Studies and Literary Criticism* 44.1 (2009): 1–24.

Welsh Myth and Fantasy Studies

Attebery, Brian. *Strategies of Fantasy*. Bloomington: Indiana University Press, 1992.

Briggs, Elizabeth L. Pandolfo. "On the Inside Looking In: Contemporary Anglo-Welsh Fantasy." *Lion and the Unicorn: A Critical Journal of Children's Literature* 23.1, (1999): 67–78.

Butler, Charles. *Four British Fantasists: Place and Culture in the Children's Fantasies of Penelope*

Lively, Alan Garner, Diana Wynne Jones, and Susan Cooper. Lanham: Children's Literature Association and Scarecrow Press, 2006.
Clute, John, and John Grant, *The Fantasy Encyclopedia*. New York: St. Martin's, 1999.
Filmer-Davies, Kath. *Fantasy Fiction and Welsh Myth: Tales of Belonging*. New York: St. Martin's, 1996.
Fimi, Dimitra. "'Mad' Elves and 'Elusive Beauty': Some Celtic Strands of Tolkien's Mythology." *Folklore* 117.2 (2006): 156–70.
_____."Tolkien's '*Celtic*' Type of Legends': Merging Traditions." *Tolkien Studies: An Annual Scholarly Review* 4 (2007): 51–71.
Jacobs, Lesley. "Idealized Images of *Wales* in the Fiction of Edith Pargeter/Ellis Peters." Marshall, David W. (ed. and intro.). *Mass Market Medieval: Essays on the Middle Ages in Popular Culture*. Jefferson, NC: McFarland, 2007. 90–101.
Le Guin, Ursula. "Why Are Americans Afraid of Dragons?" *The Language of the Night: Essays on Fantasy and Science Fiction*. Rev. ed. New York: HarperCollins, 1993. 34–40.
Mendlesohn, Farah. *Rhetorics of Fantasy*. Middletown: Wesleyan University Press, 2008.
Pratchett, Terry. "Imaginary Worlds, Real Stories." (18th Katherine Briggs Memorial Lecture to the British Folklore Society, 1999). Reprinted in Terry Pratchett, *Once More (with footnotes)*, Framingham: NESFA Press, 2004. 239–251.
_____. "The Roots of Fantasy." Reprinted in Terry Pratchett, *Once More (with footnotes)*, Framingham: NESFA Press, 2004. 93–96.
Purkiss, Diane. "Women's Rewriting of Myths." *The Feminist Companion to Mythology*. Ed. Carolyne Larrington. London: Pandora Press, 1992. 441–457.
Spivak, Charlotte. *Merlin's Daughters: Contemporary Women Writers of Fantasy. Contributions to the Study of Science Fiction and Fantasy 23*. New York: Greenwood Press, 1987.
Sullivan, C. W., III. "Conscientious Use of Welsh Celtic Myth and Legend in Fantastic Fiction." *Celtic Cultural Studies* 4 (2006). www.celtic-cultural-studies.com. Online.
_____."Kenneth Morris: The Milestone in Welsh Celtic Fantasy Fiction." *Journal of the Fantastic in the Arts* 16.2 (2005): 142–51.
_____. "Lore of the Rings." *New Welsh Review: Wales's Literary Magazine in English* 56 (2002): 34–40.
_____. *Welsh Celtic Myth in Modern Fantasy*. Westport, CT: Greenwood Press, 1989.
Tolkien, J.R.R. "On Fairy-Stories." Reprinted in *The Tolkien Reader*. New York: Ballantine Books, 1966. 33–99.
White, Donna R. *A Century of Welsh Myth in Children's Literature*. Westport, CT: Greenwood Press, 1998.
Zahorski, Kenneth J., and Robert H. Boyer. "Evangeline Walton Ensley: Introduction: A Biographical/Critical Essay." *Lloyd Alexander, Evangeline Walton Ensley, Kenneth Morris: A Primary and Secondary Bibliography*. Eds. Kenneth J. Zahorski and Robert H. Boyer. Boston: G.K. Hall & Co, 1981. 113–138.

Welsh Folklore and Mythology Studies

Breeze, Andrew. "Some Critics of the Four Branches of the *Mabinogi*." *Constructing Nations, Reconstructing Myth: Essays in Honour of T. A. Shippey*. Eds. Andrew Wawn, Graham Johnson, and Walter John.. Turnhout, Belgium: Brepols, 2007. 155–66.
_____. "Welsh Tradition and the Baker's Daughter in *Hamlet*." *Notes and Queries* 49.2 (2002): 199–200.
Bromwich, Rachel. "The 'Mabinogion' and Lady Charlotte Guest (1812–1895)." *On Arthurian Women: Essays in Memory of Maureen Fries*. Eds. Bonnie Wheeler and Fiona Tolhurst. Dallas, TX: Scriptorium, 2001. 321–34.
Bromwich, Rachel, A. O. H. Jarman, and Brynley F. Roberts, eds. *The Arthur of the Welsh: The Arthurian Legend in Medieval Welsh Literature*. Cardiff: University of Wales Press, 2008.
Cartwright, Jane. "Virginity and Chastity Tests in Medieval Welsh Prose." *Medieval Virginities*.

Eds. Anke Bernau, Ruth Evans, and Sarah Salih. Toronto, ON: University of Toronto Press, 2003. 56–79.
Constantine, Mary-Ann. "Welsh Literary History and the Making of 'The Myvyrian Archaiology of Wales.'" *Editing the Nation's Memory: Textual Scholarship and Nation-Building in Nineteenth-Century Europe*. Eds. Dirk van Hulle and Joep Leerssen. Amsterdam, Netherlands: Rodopi, 2008. 109–128.
Davies, Hazel Walford. "Case Study: Refashioning a Myth, Performances of the Tale of Blodeuwedd." *The Cambridge History of British Theatre*, Volume 3: Since 1895. Ed. Baz Kershaw. Cambridge, England: Cambridge University Press, 2004. 273–87.
Davies, Sioned. "'He Was the Best Teller of Tales in the World': Performing Medieval Welsh Narrative." *Performing Medieval Narrative*. Eds. Evelyn Birge Vitz, Nancy Freeman Regalado, and Marilyn Lawrence. Cambridge, England: Brewer, 2005. 15–26.
d'Este, Sorita, and Rankine, David. *Visions of the Cailleach: Exploring the Myths, Legends, and Folklore of the Pre-eminent Celtic Hag Goddess*. London: Avalonia, 2009.
Edwards, Owain. "Welsh Saints' Lives as Legendary Propaganda." *Oral Tradition* 23.1 (2008): 148–158.
Ellis, Bill. *Lucifer Ascending: The Occult in Folklore and Popular Culture*. Lexington: UP of Kentucky, 2004.
Freeman, Mara. "The Wide-Spun Moment: Ecstasy and Madness in Celtic Tradition." *Parabola: Myth, Tradition, and the Search for Meaning* 23.2 (1998): 29–35.
Fulton, Helen. "The *Mabinogi* and the Education of Princes in Medieval Wales." *Medieval Celtic Literature and Society*. Ed. Helen Fulton. Portland, OR: Four Courts P, 2005. 230–47.
———. "Reflections on Rhiannon and the Horse Episodes in Pwyll." *Western Folklore* 57.1 (1998): 19–40.
Jarman, A. O. H. "The Merlin Legend and the Welsh Tradition of Prophecy." *Merlin: A Casebook*. Eds. Peter H. Goodrich and Raymond H. Thompson. New York, NY: Routledge, 2003. 105–30.
Loomis, Roger Sherman. *Celtic Myth and Arthurian Romance*. New York: Columbia UP, 1927.
Lupack, Alan. *The Oxford Guide to Arthurian Literature and Legend*. Oxford: Oxford UP, 2005.
Lyle, Emily. "Narrative Form and Structure of Myth. *Folklore: Electronic Journal of Folklore* 33 (2006): 59–69.
McKenna, Catherine. "Revising Math: Kingship in the Fourth Branch of the *Mabinogi*." *Cambrian Medieval Celtic Studies* 46 (2003): 95–117.
Meister, Peter (ed. and preface). *Arthurian Literature and Christianity: Notes from the Twentieth Century*. New York, NY: Garland, 1999.
Padel, O. J. "Geoffrey of Monmouth and the Development of the Merlin Legend." *Cambrian Medieval Celtic Studies* 51 (2006). 37–65.
Parker, Will. *The Four Branches of the Mabinogi: Celtic Myth and Medieval Reality*. Dublin: Bardic Press, 2007.
Rhys, John, *Celtic Folklore: Welsh and Manx*. Vol. 2. London: Wildwood House Ltd, 1980.
Sullivan, C. W., III. "Inheritance and Lordship in Math." *The Mabinogi: A Book of Essays*. Ed.C.W. Sullivan III. New York: Garland Publishing, 1996. 347–66.

Welsh Myth and Gender Studies

Aaron, Jane. *Nineteenth-Century Women's Writing in Wales: Nation, Gender and Identity*. Cardiff: University of Wales Press, 2007.
Bromwich, Rachel. "The 'Mabinogion' and Lady Charlotte Guest (1812–1895)." *On Arthurian Women: Essays in Memory of Maureen Fries*. Eds. Bonnie Wheeler and Fiona Tolhurst, eds. Dallas, TX: Scriptorium, 2001. 321–34.
Cartwright, Jane. "Virginity and Chastity Tests in Medieval Welsh Prose." *Medieval Virginities*. Eds. Anke Bernau, Ruth Evans, and Sarah Salih. Toronto, ON: University of Toronto Press, 2003. 56–79.

Kay, Morgan. "Gendered Postcolonial Discourse in the Mabinogi." *Proceedings of the Harvard Celtic Colloquium.* Vols., XXIV, 2004 and XXV, 2005. Cambridge and London: Harvard University Press, 2009. 216–28.
LeBlanc, John. "Return of the Goddess: Contemporary Music and Celtic Mythology in Alan Warner's Morvern Caller." *Revista Canaria de Estudios Ingleses* 41 (2000). 145–54.
Millersdaughter, Katherine. "The Geopolitics of Incest: Sex, Gender and Violence in the Fourth Branch of the *Mabinogi.*" *Exemplaria: A Journal of Theory in Medieval and Renaissance Studies* 14.2 (2002): 271–316.
Nugent, Christopher G. "Reading Riannon: The Problematics of Motherhood in Pwyll Pendeuic Dyuet." *Domestic Violence in Medieval Texts.* Eve Salisbury, Georgiana Donavin, and Merrall Llewelyn Price. Gainesville, FL: UP of Florida, 2002. 180–202.
Purkiss, Diane. "Women's Rewriting of Myths." *The Feminist Companion to Mythology.* Ed. Carolyne Larrington. London: Pandora Press, 1992. 441–457.
Prescott, Sarah. "The Cambrian Muse: Welsh Identity and Hanoverian Loyalty in the Poems of Jane Brereton (1685–1740)." *Eighteenth-Century Studies* 38.4 (2005): 587–603.
Sheehan, Sarah. "Matrilineal Subjects: Ambiguity, Bodies, and Metamorphosis in the Fourth Branch of the 'Mabinogi.'" *Signs* 34.2 (2009): 319–342.
Spivak, Charlotte. *Merlin's Daughters: Contemporary Women Writers of Fantasy. Contributions to the Study of Science Fiction and Fantasy 23.* New York: Greenwood Press, 1987.
Valente, Roberta L. "Gwydion and Aranrhod: Crossing the Borders of Gender in *Math.*" *The Mabinogi: A Book of Essays.* Ed. C.W. Sullivan III. New York: Garland Publishing, 1996. 331–45.

Wales and Medievalism

Cohen, Jeffrey Jerome. *Medieval Identity Machines.* Minneapolis: University of Minnesota Press, 2003.
_____. *Of Giants: Sex, Monsters, and the Middle Ages.* Minneapolis: University of Minnesota Press, 1999.
Davies, Wendy. *Wales in the Early Middle Ages.* Leicester, UK: Leicester UP, 1982.
Earl, Benjamin. "Places Don't Have to Be True to Be True: The Appropriation of King Arthur and the Cultural Value of Tourist Sites." *Mass Market Medieval: Essays on the Middle Ages in Popular Culture.* Ed. David W. Marshall. Jefferson, NC: McFarland, 2007. 102–12.
Eco, Umberto. "Dreaming of the Middle Ages." *Travels in Hyperreality.* Trans. William Weaver. San Diego, New York, London: Harcourt Brace Jovanovich, 1986. 61–72.
_____. "Living in the Middle Ages." *Travels in Hyperreality.* Trans. William Weaver. San Diego, New York, London: Harcourt Brace Jovanovich, 1986. 73–86.
Faletra, Michael. "Chivalric Identity at the Frontier: Marie's Welsh Lais." *Cygne: Journal of the International Marie de France Society* 4 (2006): 27–44.
Fradenburg, Louise. "So That We May Speak of Them: Enjoying the Middle Ages," *New Literary History* 28.2 (1997). 205–230.
Frantzen, Allen J. *Desire for Origins: New Language, Old English, and Teaching the Tradition.* New York: Rutgers University Press, 1990.
Ganim, John. *Medievalism and Orientalism: Three Essays on Literature, Architecture, and Cultural Identity.* New York: Palgrave Macmillan, 2005.
_____. "Presidential Address: Cosmopolitan Chaucer, or, The Uses of Local Culture." The New Chaucer Society 16th Biennial Congress, University of Wales, Swansea, Wales, UK. July 18–22, 2008.
Ingham, Patricia Clare. *Sovereign Fantasies: Arthurian Romance and the Making of Britain.* Philadelphia: University of Pennsylvania Press, 2001.
Knight, Stephen. *Arthurian Literature and Society.* New York: St. Martin's Press, 1983.
_____. *A Hundred Years of Fiction, Writing Wales in English Series.* Cardiff: University of Wales Press, 2004.

_____. *Merlin: Knowledge and Power Through the Ages.* Ithaca: Cornell UP, 2009.

_____. "Resemblance and Menace: A Post-Colonial Reading of *Peredur*," in *Canhwyll y Marchogion: cyd-destunoli* Peredur, ed. Sioned Davies and Peter Wynn Thomas (Caerdydd: Gwasg Prifysgol Cymru, 2000), 128–47.

Marshall, David W. Introduction. "The Medievalism of Popular Culture," in *Mass Market Medieval: Essays on the Middle Ages in Popular Culture*. Ed. David W. Marshall. Jefferson: McFarland, 2007. 1–12.

_____, ed. *Mass Market Medieval: Essays on the Middle Ages in Popular Culture*. Jefferson: McFarland, 2007.

Meecham-Jones, Simon. "'Englyssh Gaufride' and British Chaucer?: Chaucerian Allusions to the Condition of *Wales* in the House of Fame." *Chaucer Review: A Journal of Medieval Studies and Literary Criticism* 44.1 (2009): 1–24.

Millersdaughter, Katherine. "The Geopolitics of Incest: Sex, Gender and Violence in the Fourth Branch of the *Mabinogi*." *Exemplaria: A Journal of Theory in Medieval and Renaissance Studies* 14.2 (2002): 271–316.

Redknap, Mark. "Crossing Boundaries-Stylistic Diversity and External Contacts in Early Medieval *Wales* and the March: Reflections on Metalwork and Sculpture." *Cambrian Medieval Celtic Studies* 53–54 (2007): 23–86.

Sklar, Elizabeth S., and Hoffman, Donald L., eds. *King Arthur in Popular Culture*. Jefferson: McFarland, 2002.

Postcolonialism and Postmodernism in Welsh Studies

Cohen, Jeffrey Jerome. *The Postcolonial Middle Ages*. New York: Palgrave Macmillan, 2001.

Green, Diane. "Welsh Writing and Postcoloniality: The Strategic Use of the Blodeuwedd *Myth* in Emyr Humphreys's Novels." *Revista Alicantina de Estudios Ingleses* 16 (2003): 129–46.

Heng, Geraldine. *Empire of Magic: Medieval Romance and the Politics of Cultural Fantasy*. New York: Columbia University Press, 2003.

Ingham, Patricia. "Marking Time: Branwen, Daughter of Llyr and the Colonial Refrain." *The Postcolonial Middle Ages*. Ed. Jeffrey Jerome Cohen.. New York: Palgrave Macmillan, 2000. 173–92.

Kay, Morgan. "Gendered Postcolonial Discourse in the Mabinogi." Proceedings of the Harvard Celtic Colloquium. Vols., XXIV, 2004 and XXV, 2005. Cambridge and London: Harvard University Press, 2009. 216–28.

About the Contributors

Audrey L. Becker is an assistant professor in the English department at Marygrove College in Detroit. She received a Ph.D. from the University of Michigan. Recent publications include "De Do Do Dowland: Sting's Re-Voicing of Early English Ayres." She is working on a study of Renaissance entertainment in the modern era: *That's Ren-tertainment: Role-playing, Renaissance Festivals, and American Nostalgia for an Idealized British Past.*

Susana Brower received an M.A. in English from the University of California, Riverside. Her areas of interest include American literature from the 1850s to 1950s, fantasy and science fiction, and folklore. She has written on such topics as Sylvia Plath's relationship to nature, Tolkien's illustrations, and connections between the treatment of the "Other" in Christopher Columbus's writings and *Battlestar Galactica.*

Jonathan Evans received a Ph.D. in English literature at Cardiff University, his dissertation titled "People, Politics, and Print: A History of the English-Language Book in Industrial South Wales, 1536–1900." The son of a mining engineer and the grandson of a collier, his research interests continue to be in the literature produced by industry in Wales.

Jeff Hicks is a Ph.D. candidate at the University of California, Riverside, whose interests include American film and the U.S. studio system, cult and grindhouse films, and science fiction and fantasy. He has published reviews in *Science Fiction Studies* and *Science Fiction Film and Television.* He is currently researching the ways in which twentieth-century literature and film have responded to the explosion of urban populations.

Deborah Hooker is a teaching associate professor at North Carolina State University, where her areas of interest are women's and gender studies, fantasy, and ecocriticism. She has written on Margaret Atwood, Alice Walker, Keats, Tennyson, and Shakespeare.

Stephen Knight is Distinguished Research Professor in English Literature at Cardiff University, where he has been since 1994, having come from a Welsh-speaking family. He has written widely on the social meaning of myth, with books on King Arthur, Robin Hood, and most recently *Merlin: Knowledge and Power* (2009). He has also written essays and books about Welsh writing and, crime fiction.

Megan MacAlystre teaches children's literature and British literature at Clemson University. She has worked on *Harry Potter,* archeology, art history, film studies, American poetry, and Victorian literature. She explores the portrayal of bisexuality in popular media, the shifting concept of the taboo in *Harry Potter* fan fiction, and Pre–Raphaelite influences on Emily Dickinson and on horror films.

About the Contributors

Kristin Noone is a Ph.D. candidate at the University of California, Riverside, writing a dissertation on the links between medieval literature, fantasy fiction, and popular-culture medievalism. Her publications have covered Shakespeare in Terry Pratchett's *Discworld*, *Beowulf* on film, heroism and hybrid bodies in *The Wizard of Oz* and *Tin Man*, and ghouls in the television show *Supernatural*; her short fantasy fiction has appeared in *Marion Zimmer Bradley's Sword & Sorceress 23* and *Aoife's Kiss*.

Tyler D. Parry is a Ph.D. candidate at the University of South Carolina, researching the African diaspora in the Atlantic world. He is a research fellow at the Institute for African American Research at the university, expanding his research on marriage patterns and cultural constructs among common whites and enslaved people in early American society. He is interested in memory and the importance of oral history.

Lynnette R. Porter, Ph.D., teaches humanities and communication courses at Embry-Riddle Aeronautical University in Daytona Beach, Florida. She is the author of *Tarnished Heroes, Charming Villains and Modern Monsters* (McFarland 2010) and many articles on television and film. As a member of the Tolkien Society and Popular Culture Association, she often speaks at academic conferences and fan conventions.

Geoffrey Reiter is assistant professor of English at the Baptist College of Florida. He holds an M.A. in church history from Gordon-Conwell Theological Seminary and a Ph.D. in English from Baylor University, where he completed a dissertation on Arthur Machen. He has published essays on fantasy and weird fiction writers such as George MacDonald, Clark Ashton Smith, William Peter Blatty, and Peter S. Beagle.

Clay Kinchen Smith completed his Ph.D. in 2002 with a revisionist history of captivity narratives. His research and teaching interests range from popular culture to technical communication; his publications range from the rhetoric of race in *Peter Pan* to encyclopedia entries on world literature. He teaches full time at Santa Fe College and occasionally at the University of Florida.

C.W. Sullivan III is Distinguished Professor of Arts and Sciences at East Carolina University and a full member of the Welsh Academy. He is the author of *Welsh Celtic Myth in Modern Fantasy* (1989), editor of *The Mabinogi: A Book of Essays* (1996) and seven other books, and editor of the ejournal *Celtic Cultural Studies*. He is a past president of the International Association for the Fantastic in the Arts, and has written articles on mythology, folklore, fantasy, and science fiction.

Nicole A. Thomas is a Ph.D. student at Cardiff University, researching "The Unnatural Natural Woman: Evangeline Walton's Feminist Re-visioning of *The Mabinogi*." She received an M.A. in English literature from Cardiff in 2008, and an M.A. in poetics from New College of California in 2007. Her work encompasses twentieth century women's fiction, French feminist theory, and medieval folklore.

Carolynn E. Wilcox holds master's degrees in both curriculum and instruction (2003) and English literature (2009). She teaches English full time for Early College of Arvada and works as an adjunct for both Metropolitan State College and the University of Colorado–Denver's CU Succeed program.

Index

Aberystwyth 92, 95, 100
Adaptation: novel to film 166, 171–181
Age of the Saints 66
Alexander, Lloyd 13–15, 81, 171, 176–178; see also *The Black Cauldron*
Anglo-Welsh 92
animation 171–172, 176–177, 178, 195, 197–199
anime 166, 184, 186
antebellum, American South 108–125
anti-Celtic prejudice 16n.4, 78n.18
Aranrhod *see* Arianrhod
Arawn 20–21
Arberth Studios 195, 204
archaeology 13
Arianrhod 43, 45–49, 53–54, 56–57, 85, 86–87
Armstrong, Cora 108
Arnold, Matthew 9–11
Arthurian knights *see* knighthood
Arthurian literature 12, 37, 67, 94, 133–137, 141
arwyddfardd 96
Attebery, Brian 2, 45, 58
Azusa Street Mission 65

BBC 140–141, 146, 151
Bagnall, Norma 14
Ballantine Books 19
bard 27
Beckett, Samuel 13
Beer, Gillian 31
Bendigeidfran 30, 205–206
Beowulf 152, 188
besom brooms 113
Bhabha, Homi 104, 106
Bible 73
Biseniek, Dainis 14
The Black Cauldron (film): as financial failure 171; selection by Disney for adaptation 172; violence in 174–180
The Black Cauldron (novel) 176–180
Blake, William 12
Blodeuedd 27, 56, 85–86
Bond, Nancy 15–16
Borgstrom, Carl 12

Bourdieu, Pierre 81
Bradley, Marion Zimmer *see The Mists of Avalon*
Branwen 30, 33–40, 206
Bromwich, Rachel 9, 12
Brontë, Charlotte 93
broom ritual 109 *passim*
Brothers Grimm 151
Bruton, Noel and Karen 201
Burnett, Mark 82
Byron, Lord 10

Calumniated Wife 36
Camelot 38
Camelot (musical) 15
Cardiff 142–146
Carroll, Lewis 162, 188, 201
Cartwyn Cymru 197
Cauldron of Rebirth 22, 36, 172, 175
Ceiriog Valley 108
Celtic fringe 1–2, 201
A Celtic Miscellany 10
Celtic myths: linked to other cultures 12
Celtic saints 66–67
Celtic Studies 9–12
Chadwick, Nora 12
changelings 146
Chaucer, Geoffrey 81
childbirth 53
The Children of Llyr 22–23
children's literature 14
Chrétien de Troyes 68
Christianity 20, 32, 38, 86, 124, 147; in Welsh history 62 *passim*
Cinderella 91, 160
clasau 66
Cole, Harriet 100
colonization 92, 98–99, 103
color symbolism 149
comic books 155
commodification and exchange 81–82, 87
Communist party 43
Conan Doyle, Sir Arthur 146, 149
consumerism 88, 189
Cooper, Susan 13–14

221

cosplay 187, 192n.14
"Culhwch and Olwen" 1, 77n10, 133–138
Cymraeg 92–93, 100
Cymreig see Cymraeg
Cymru 182
cynghanedd 96

Dale, Heather 132–138
Daughter of Earth 43 passim
Davies, Sioned 7, 133, 195
Davies, Wendy 87
decadent novels 61
The Decameron 132
de Certeau, Michel 82 *passim*
Dee, John 96
Depression-era America 18, 19, 42–43, 58
de Troyes, Chrétien 68
devil 105n3, 112
Disney, Walt see Walt Disney
Doctor Who 140, 142
Donne, John 164
dragon 153
Dundes, Alan 111

Earthwitch 16
Easter 66
Ebert, Roger 210n.10
Eco, Umberto 185, 190
Efnisien 18, 20, 22–23, 179, 207
Elizabeth I 48
England 64–66, 92–93, 95, 98, 105
English hymns see hymns
englynion 96
Equiano, Olaudah 115–116
Erinn 182
Eve 86
Evnissien see Efnisien
Equiano, Olaudah 115

fairies 144–148
fairy tales 160–162
fan fiction 158n2
fan productions 131, 143, 148, 157
feminism 30–32, 34, 36, 154
Fielding, Henry 97
Filmer-Davies, Kath 14
first-contact romance 98
Fisher King 67, 73, 75
folk music 130–138
Ford, Patrick 195, 209n.2
Fraedenburg, Louise Aranye 4
Frantzen, Allen J. 4
Freud, Sigmund 34

Gaelic 114, 183
Galahad 74
Gandhi 132
Ganim, John 1
Garner, Alan 15–16
Geoffrey of Monmouth 19
gift economy 82, 87–88

Gilgamesh 204
Gilvaethwy 46
Girard, René 179
The Girl 43 *passim*
Glendower 94
Goewin 83–85
Goux, Jean-Joseph 54
graal (etymology) 73
grail 62 *passim*; see also graal
Great Depression see Depression-era America
The Great God Pan 78n.5
Greek and Roman myths 11, 15, 132, 207
Green, Danita Roundtree 110
Grendel 152
Griffiths, Niall 210n.4
Grimm, Jacob and Wilhelm 151
Guenever 37
Guest, Lady Charlotte 7–8, 45, 58n.3, 87n.1
gwerin 106n.13
Gwydion 16, 18, 25–26; 46, 56; and Arianrhod/Aranrhod 45, 48, 56–57, 86–87; and commodity culture 81–88; and paternity 53–54, 57; rehabilitation of 25–26

hagiology 62
Harward, Vernon J. 12
Havgan 21
Hayes, Derek 195 *passim*
Heng, Geraldine 7, 18
Henry, Patrick Leo 12
Henry VIII 97
Holy Grail see Grail
Honourable Society of Cymmrodorion 93
house concerts 131
Howl's Moving Castle (film) 166–170; see also Miyazaki, Hayao
Howl's Moving Castle (novel) 160–166
hymns 71–72

Idylls of the King 19
Ilar 75
Iltyd 74–75
incest 54
Indiana Jones and the Last Crusade 67
Ingary 6, 160–162
Ingham, Patricia Clare 2, 185
Internet 131
Ireland: association with Korea 210n11; in *The Children of Llyr* 23, 30, 33, 38; in *Mabinogi* (MMORPG) 182 *passim*
Irigaray, Luce 34
Irish gods and goddesses 183
The Island of the Mighty/The Virgin and the Swine 25–27, 43, 45–49
Ivanhoe 93

Jackson, Kenneth 10
Jewish character 102
Joan of Arc 132

Jones, Diana Wynne: adaptation by Miyazaki 166–170; autobiographical fantasy 168; personal agency theme 160, 162–166; portal fantasy 161
Jones, Inigo 106n.16
Jones, Naomi 198
Jones, Russell Celyn 210n.4
Jones, Sally Roberts 14
Jones, T. Gwynn 112
Jones, W. Rhys 108, 113
jumping the broom 108–125
Jung, Carl 203, 208, 210n.7

katabasis 200
Katzenberg, Jeffrey 172
Keats, John 10
Keyes, Flo 2
Kgatla people 110
Kiefer, Barbara 14
King Arthur 1; Grail legend 67–68; in *Le Morte D'Arthur* 37–38; in music 132–137
King James Bible 89n.8
knighthood 68, 135
Korea 182, 196, 210n.11

"The Lady of Shalott" 133
Launcelot 37, 133
Lawrence, Louise 16
Le Guin, Ursula 15, 20
Le Sueur, Meridel 43 *passim*
Lewis, C. S. 161
Lewis, Gwyneth 210n.4
life after death 144
Llantrisant 74
Lleu Llaw Gyffes 25–26, 56–57, 178, 197–198
lolicon 184
Loomis, Roger Sherman 12
The Lord of the Rings 19
Lovecraft, H. P. 69, 77
Lowenthal, David 208
ludology 204

Mabinogi: animals in 83; in anthologies of British literature 209; audiences of 31; branches of: First Branch 199, Second Branch 21, 30, 32, 34–35, 38, 179, 205–206, Third Branch 23–24, Fourth Branch 4, 16, 25, 81, 112; editions 7–8, 195; pre-Christian 32; versus *Mabinogion* 7–8
Mabinogi, characters in *see* Arianrhod; Branwen; Efnisien; Gwydion; Manawydan; Matholoch; Rhiannon; Pryderi; Pwyll
Mabinogi (online role-playing game) 182–192; design 186; neomedievalism in 185–190
Mabinogi Heroes (video game) 187
Mabon 136 *passim*
Mac Cana, Proinsias 32–34, 36
Machen, Arthur: "The Bowmen" 61–62; *The Great Return* 62, 69–74, 76–77; reputation of 61

magic, ethics of 168
Malory, Thomas 37
Manawydan 18, 23–25, 198
MapleStory (video game) 185
mara 145
marriage practices 31, 33, 49, 108–125
marwynad 96
Massive Multiplayer Online Role-Playing Game (MMORPG) 182, 189, 191, 196
Math son of Mathonwy 25, 56, 85
Matholoch 30, 38, 206
matriarchy 20
matrilineage 33, 43, 46, 104
medievalism 4, 197
memory 202
Merlin 10, 97
mermaids 153–154
A Midsummer Night's Dream 200–201
Miéville, China 42, 58
millennialism 209
The Mists of Avalon 15
Miyazaki, Hayao 166–169
moe 187, 191n.12
monsters 187
Monty Python and the Holy Grail 67
Morgan, Prys 2, 68
Morgan le Fey 133
Moses 102
music 130–139

Napoleon 93
Narnia 161
neomedievalism 185, 190
neo-pagan 124–125, 149
New Chaucer Society 1
New Welsh Review 15
Newstead, Helaine 12
Nexon/devCat 196, 210n11
Nicks, Stevie 202
non-player characters (NPCs) 183 *passim*
Norman Conquest 66
nostalgia 68, 208

Ogham script 202
Ogunleye, Tolagbe 110
Oliver Twist 102
Olmsted, Frederick Law 114
Olsen, Tillie 51–52, 55; *see also* Yonnondio
Olwen 78n.10; *see also* "Culhwch and Olwen"
oral history 120
Otherworld (film) 195–197–201
The Owl Service 16

pastiche 139n.2
Paton, Lucy Alan 12
Perceval 104
Pope Gregory the Great 66
Prichard, Thomas: and hybrid identity 91, 101, 103–105; personal life 93, 95; revisions and rewriting 102–103; *Twm Siôn Cati* (1828) 91–93, 98–105

The Prince of Annwn 21–22
Pryderi 83–85, 178; as place name 202
Puhvel, Martin 12
Purkiss, Diane 31–32
Pwyll 18, 20–22, 178

rating systems, film 172, 180n.5
reality television 83, 88
Rebecca Riots 95
Red Book of Hergest 20, 28, 45, 81, 210n.7
Renan, Ernest 10
Rhiannon 25, 148, 284, 199–200, 202
Rhiannon: The Curse of the Four Branches 195, 201–204
Rob Roy 99
Roberts, Evan 62 *passim*
Robin Hood 92–94, 102
Roman Empire 66
Romantic movement 9, 68
Roots (television series) 109–110
Round Table 133
Rowling, J. K. 30, 161

S4C 197
Saint David 73–74
Saint Patrick 188
Saint Teilo 74, 76
saints 73–75; lives 66
Sanders, Julie 197
sangraal *see* graal
sarhaed 37
Schultz, Albert 9
Schwyzer, Philip 208
Scott, Sir Walter 94; *see also Ivanhoe*
Scottish mythology 141
"Selkie" 151
Seren Books 195
Shakespeare, William 9, 112, 200
Sheers, Owen 195, 205–206, 210n.12
Skelton, John 97
slave narrative 116–117
slave trade 119
Smedley, Agnes 50–51, 55
sofraniaeth 104
The Song of Rhiannon 24–25
Southey, Robert 10
Star Trek 18
Stone, Lawrence 112
Sullivan, C. W. III 3–4, 14, 59, 111
Survivor 83 *passim*
The Sword in the Stone 171, 177
synchronicity 207

Teilo *see* Saint Teilo
Tenby 78n.7
Tennyson, Alfred 12, 19, 81, 133; *see also Idylls of the King*
Thomas, Dylan 13
Thompson, Derrick S. 32

The Three Impostors 78n.5
time travel 156, 196
Tir Na Nog 183
Tolkien, J.R.R. 14–15, 19, 45, 188
Tom Jones 97, 103
Torchwood: comics 153–155; fanfiction 148, 151, 157; Jack Harkness 155–157; mythical creatures 142; science-fiction tropes 140, 144, 155; spin-off novels 151–153; tourism 141, 143
translation 7–8, 27, 45, 97, 195
Travis, James 12
Tudor England 95
Twm Siôn Cati 91–110; sixteenth-century roots 96–97
The Types of Folklore 40

uchelwr 96, 100, 103

video games and cultural memory 196, 202
The Virgin and the Swine 14, 43, 45–49
virginity 46, 49, 112
vitae see saints, lives

wainscot fantasy 161
Wales as fantastic space 3, 131, 165
Walt Disney 171–181
Walton, Evangeline: feminism 30–41; the Great Depression 43; maternity 45–49; mythic space 18–19; narratology 39; novels 5, 14; representation of death 21; *see also The Children of Llyr; The Island of the Mighty/The Virgin and the Swine; The Prince of Annwn; The Song of Rhiannon*
Wells, Paul 176, 199
Welsh: accent 118; audiences 197; churches 65; immigration to the Americas 113–144; journals 94; language 7–8, 116; nationalism 3, 67
The Welsh Law of Women 34, 37
Welsh Minstrelsy 93
Welsh mythology: cosmopolitanism 1–2, 4; critical studies 2
The Welsh Revival 28n.1, 62 *passim*
Welsh themes in modern fantasy 10, 13–16
White, Donna 14–15, 178
White, T. H. 15, 171
White Book of Rhydderch 45, 81
Wicca 125, 149
Wikipedia 185
The Wizard of Oz 182, 201
women in myth 13, 31
wynebwerth 37

Y Mabinogi (film) 195
Yeats, William Butler 9–11, 13, 148, 150–151
Yonnondio 43 *passim*
Ysbaddaden 134–135

www.ingramcontent.com/pod-product-compliance
Ingram Content Group UK Ltd.
Pitfield, Milton Keynes, MK11 3LW, UK
UKHW041949140426
5217IPUK00014B/718